My Favorite Mistake

My Favorite Mistake

MARIAN KEYES

Doubleday Canada

Doubleday Canada and colophon are registered trademarks of
Penguin Random House Canada Limited

Library and Archives Canada Cataloguing in Publication data is available upon request.

Original trade paperback ISBN: 9780385675390
ebook ISBN: 9780385675406

This book is a work of fiction. Names, characters, places and incidents are products of
the author's imagination or are used fictitiously. Any resemblance to actual events or
locales or persons, living or dead, is entirely coincidental.

Cover: adapted from a design by Lee Motley // MJ
Cover illustration: Gemma Correll
Typesetting: Terra Page

Printed in Canada

Published by Doubleday Canada,
a division of Penguin Random House Canada Limited,
and distributed in the United States by Penguin Random House LLC

www.penguinrandomhouse.ca

10 9 8 7 6 5 4 3 2 1

Penguin
Random House
DOUBLEDAY CANADA

For Beth Nepomuceno,
with love and gratitude

His gaze moved over my face. "I'm trying to remember the last time we actually met . . ."

My heart almost seized up in my chest. Were we really going there?

He glanced away, then refocused, all bright-eyed candor. "Was it my engagement party to Elisabeth?"

That was the last time we'd occupied the same room. But we hadn't even spoken that night.

"So about eight years ago?" he said.

"About that." (It was eight years and four months.)

He was trying to set the tone for the next two or three days. We could neither ignore nor acknowledge our long and complicated history. But by presenting a sanitized version of events, he was laying out a surface we could walk on. It was as fragile as thin ice over a deep, dark lake but if we stayed light and careful, we could probably do it.

I

There's more to this story than the clickbait headlines, but yes, in simple terms, I had a dream life—then I took a flamethrower to it. In no particular order, I broke up with my long-term partner, bought a small loom, gave away all my stilettos, resigned from my fabulous-if-frightening job, got into a situation in the street with five teenage boys, received a medical diagnosis which didn't delight me, bought a slightly bigger loom and, after living in Manhattan for nearly twenty years, relocated back to Ireland.

The first sign that something was up came one Friday morning, in an apartment on the Upper West Side, eight months into the pandemic. Deep, discordant moans dragged me from the depths of sleep.

A quick look at my phone confirmed I was still entitled to a precious sixty-seven minutes of slumber and I flared with fury.

The first time I'd ever heard the atonal groans, I'd thought Angelo was in the next room playing a didgeridoo. But the noise came from a large group of *monks*. Not actually clustered in their orange robes in Angelo's living room, swinging their canisters of butter-tea, but on Zoom from Tibet. Having been prematurely woken by them most mornings for the last several weeks I felt as if I knew each one personally.

Effing lockdown.

Angelo Torres and I had been in each other's lives for over a decade. We loved each other, spent at least four nights a week together but had always kept our own places. Slightly irregular perhaps, but it worked.

Then along came Covid. Angelo and I had to choose between living together in a bubble or being separated indefinitely. We went for the bubble and we picked his place because it was bigger.

But being trapped together almost all day every day, in an apartment that seemed to shrink by the hour, was tougher than expected.

The monks were still giving it socks out there so I pawed for my earplugs. The most important thing was to *not think about work*. If even one thought got in, it would destroy any chance of getting back to sleep.

You'd never think from the nervy state of me, curled in a resentful knot in bed, that I had The Best Job In The World. But ask anyone. As a senior executive at "legendary" New York PR firm McArthur on the Park, which represented some of the most covetable cosmetic brands on the planet, I could have as much free product as I wanted.

This was to the utter amazement of all who had known me during my under-achieving teens and twenties. Especially my family, where I'd occupied the Failure slot for so long they considered making it a lifetime award.

(Admittedly, getting the job was a bizarre stroke of good fortune, nothing more. I wasn't—and I'm still not—a go-getter.)

In my crazy-happy early days, they could have paid me in blushers. But in fits and starts, I'd been given responsibility, respect and decent money.

. . . But I'd also accumulated anxiety. Lots of it.

It had always been a . . . let's call it a *lively* place to work: best suited to those with robust central nervous systems. Take your B vitamins, would be my advice. My life was polished and stressy: early-morning manicures, meetings with powerful neurotics, last-minute flights to Bologna.

Looked at objectively, cosmetics are never a matter of life and death, but when you work in that pressure-cooker world, you sort of *forget*. Until one day you find yourself more worried about bagging a five-star review for an eyebrow pencil than the state of the planet.

The big boss, Ariella McArthur, doled out extra responsibility—more fear—like it was a delicious treat. Throughout my thirties I'd been resilient enough to power through the terror. But more recently, whenever I "won" a new account, I had to swallow repeatedly and tamp down the urge to howl.

Another look at my phone told me I still had sixty-one minutes of sleepy time. Sternly, I reminded myself that my current set-up was absolute paradise compared to countless others'—a roof over my head, a steady income and enough lifting and firming serum to keep a small nation perky. I needed to *cop on* and be *positive* and *accept* these strange days, so I tried to hook on to the chanting sounds, lengthening and deepening my breath in time with them. Glorious, gorgeous sleep was once again creeping over me when the chime of a prayer bowl *vibrated* through the apartment, trembling the surface of my glass of water and sending a mascara trundling across the dressing table and bouncing onto the floor.

This was too much! I flung back the duvet, sat upright in bed and declared, "For God's sake!"

Moments later the bedroom door opened and there was Angelo, a leather gong in one hand. "Problem?" He was icily polite.

Yes, problem.

Oh, without a *doubt*, there was a problem, lots of them in fact. The monks were only the start of it. My body clock was badly out of sync with Angelo's: I got a buzz from exuberant late-night Peloton classes; Angelo went to bed at nine thirty. (*On Tibet time*, I used to say. Only in my own head but I suspected he knew.) He liked us to prepare an adventurous evening meal together; since lockdown had kicked off, I preferred to graze all day long on cheese, apples and protein bars. To combat my anxiety, he urged me to join him in daily mindfulness but I got better results from wine.

That Tuesday morning, Angelo and I glared at each other. Despite my fury, the truth presented itself in all its stark glory: after so many happy years (and one very *un*happy one), Angelo was driving me mad.

More alarming was his inability to hide his irritation with me. Angelo was a wonderful person who tried hard to practise patience towards his fellow man. That he could no longer keep his exasperation under control was a sign we were in big trouble.

We won't survive this.

I was scared stiff. Then exhilarated, relieved, sad, anxious, hopeful and confused all at once.

2

Maybe if my love for Angelo was all that had soured, my life in New York could have been salvaged.

The second warning sign, like the first, was just one short conversation. But it was the most recent of a tower of almost identical conversations, stacked one on top of the other. That particular Tuesday, it reached critical mass.

As soon as Angelo had stalked off with his gong, I'd reached for the landline to call Mum. In those terrible days, trapped in the US while my parents and four sisters were three thousand miles away in Ireland, I rang home every few hours.

My greatest terror was of my parents catching Covid, because from all the evidence, they were unlikely to survive. Daily, I wasted countless hours doom-scrolling. The dangers kept changing, becoming a different version of the same disaster. There was always something new to panic about: extra symptoms, different variants, allergies to the vaccine . . .

Often I'd wake in the middle of the night, so choked with fear I'd have to make a quick call to one of my sisters, usually Claire (the eldest and most controlling), asking, "Are they sanitizing their shopping properly?" Or, "Any idea when the vaccines might start?"

At that stage, thanks to various rules and bans, it had been eight months since I'd visited Ireland. The biggest impediment was having to quarantine for ten days on my return to the US; I couldn't get that long off work. But there had been recent intimations that this requirement would be dropped— so hopefully soon I could fly home for a much-needed visit.

I could not *wait* to get on that plane.

Which goes to show that life really is full of surprises! It wasn't so long since I'd hated planes, all airports, even the word "gate." Overhearing "Tray table" and "upright position" filled me with tearful fury. All because my job made me go to Switzerland every six weeks.

May I pause here to offer some unsolicited advice? If your job involves air travel, *never* complain about it. Oh, how expressions *curdled* when I bemoaned my lot. How angry everyone's response. "Boo fucking hoo, Anna! Flying business class to the land of crystal air and excellent time-keeping. You want me to play the world's smallest violin?"

"But my carbon footprint is horrifying and my circadian rhythms are shot."

"Carbon footprint? Circadian rhythms? Wow, Anna, is there nothing you don't have?"

"Listen to me." (Usually uttered through clenched teeth.) "I land in Zurich at six a.m. on a Monday morning, my body convinced it's midnight on Sunday—because back in the US, it *is*. I'm ferried straight into the Lucerne Bio HQ, where I work two thirteen-hour days, fly back to New York, directly to the office, staying late to catch up on my other accounts. I live on coffee, melatonin, adrenaline and unbearable guilt about the planet."

"That so?" (Often accompanied by a pugnacious jut of the chin.) "I live on lost dreams. My life story could be called *The Flights Not Taken*."

But having been grounded for eight months, my attitude had changed. As soon as the draconian restrictions were lifted, a magical plane would take me to Ireland, perhaps even in time for Christmas. I hit my parents' number and heard it ringing.

There was a click, then with a heavy sigh, Mum said, "What *now*?" She didn't have caller ID.

"I might not have been me," I said. "I could have been someone else."

"Who else would it be?"

"Well? Any news?"

"Since you rang six hours ago? Hold on, actually, I have—you're banned! You can't come into Ireland!"

"What have I done?"

"Not just you, you gomaloon, all 'persons from the US.' New rules from the government; that eejit was on the telly again. If you came, you'd have to quarantine for *two weeks* in a rotten oul' hotel and be charged a small fortune!"

"Mum." I felt absolutely sick to hear this. "Why are you so excited?"

"Because it's exciting."

". . . But it's *bad* exciting."

Suddenly gloomy, she said, "I'll take what I can get." Then, "Lookit, I've no symptoms, neither has your father, we'll do our best not to catch Covid before your next call. Talk cha!"

Desolate, I hung up. Mum was making light of something terrible, but it hit me like a train that I might never see her or Dad again. People died, I knew it for a fact.

That was when something began to turn, a retreat from the life I had and a circling back towards the place I'd come from. Why was I trapped in this city when, with the exception of Angelo, everyone I loved lived in a faraway place?

Even before the pandemic, a drift had begun from New York. My friend Nell fled to rural Kentucky, to a life with hens, chicken wire and barky dogs. Another friend, Maira, relocated to Nevada and my beloved colleague Teenie returned to her native Oregon. Without exception, they insisted they were happier. Obviously anyone brave enough to leave New York had to talk a good game, but I believed them.

That particular morning, as I frantically googled "Latest Covid Restrictions Ireland," and discovered that Mum hadn't been exaggerating, I vowed that once this ended—if it ever did—I was moving my life back home.

3

I'd delayed it as long as I could but it was time to start work. At my desk in the spare room, before I'd even clicked on my new emails, my heart rate increased.

"Honey?" Behind me, Angelo put a calming hand on my shoulder. "You need anything?"

Gratefully, I reached up to grasp his wrist. "Thank you. Can I—"

"The usual? Got it." He kissed the top of my head, grabbed a mask and left the apartment to buy a decaf latte and a muffin. I exhaled. He was an angel—the kindest, the most supportive man. My earlier burst of irritation shamed me. I could hardly complain about Angelo's spiritual capers; they made him the amazing person he was.

Proof—he'd gone down to the outside world to buy me hot, calming things even though he was busier than I was. He worked as an art dealer, a job title I automatically translated to "con man," at least before I knew him.

He'd come into my life via my sister Rachel, who moved in the same Personal Growth circles as him. (They'd first met at Finding Inner Peace While Your World Burns. Just leaving that there.)

Rachel, an addict in recovery, was on an open-ended quest for enlightenment. All Angelo had was a commitment to being "The best version of himself." To use my best friend Jacqui's phrase, he was a full-blown Feathery Stroker.

The concept of a Feathery Stroker dated back to the early aughts when Jacqui had spent a disappointing night with a man who'd done nothing but stroke her in a gentle "feathery" fashion. She'd have preferred to be flung about the bed, perhaps even to have an inexpensive item of clothing torn from her body.

Describing a drama-free, drippy man, the phrase was an instant hit. But as time passed, it widened to encompass men who noticed you'd had your hair cut, men who were good to their mothers, men who ordered a dessert that wasn't cheese and men who changed their sheets more than once a year. It was a damning diagnosis.

Time passed, though. Life happened, sensibilities softened and by the time I met Angelo, a Feathery Stroker was just the ticket—and he was *peak* Feathery Stroker.

Mind you, with his long hair, gaunt face, dark clothing and multiplicity of tats, he looked like trouble. But he was light-hearted, always interesting and gave me space.

And here was my favorite Feathery Stroker, back with my latte and muffin.

After the calming effects of hot milk and sugary carbs took effect, finally I opened the emails. For years, each day used to begin with me lunging for my iPad, diving head first into a pool of stress. Now I deferred anything daunting for as long as possible.

And it didn't get more daunting than this, the time around the launch of a new brand.

What happened was, over a year ago, my most important client, a heritage cosmetic brand (beloved by bony white ladies—I'll say no more) decided they wanted in on the lucrative BIPOC market. Although they had several diffusion lines, this was the first to cross color lines. The result, conjured up in a marketing meeting, was Yemoja, a fake "street" brand aimed at black women. All the formulations had been appropriated from actual street brands, then repackaged and presented.

The unfairness had made me deeply sad. Unfortunately I was paid to be manically enthusiastic, usually something I managed even if it was as fake as my eyelashes. This time it was almost impossible. The phrase *burnout* had been floating in my head for a while. But whenever I tried it on for size, a voice in my head yelled, "Poor Anna, oh, poor, *poor* Anna." I wasn't a nurse working in ER, I wasn't a shelf-stacker on a part-time contract, I had the best job, with unlimited access to liquid exfoliators.

When the pandemic first hit I felt certain that a nation under lockdown was hardly going to buy beauty products—which meant I'd be fired. While the US is not a great place to be without an income, I was calm. Even hopeful. Perhaps I could move to a farm and grow strawberries?

Except . . . sales of beauty products increased. It made no sense. None! We were trapped in our homes: who were we wearing it for? The only physical humans we clapped eyes on were the drivers dropping off our plentiful online orders. So . . . were they delivering cosmetics for us to wear to open the door to them, dropping off the boxes of beauty stuff?

. . . Had I stumbled on some essential truth about the self-perpetuating nature of capitalism? I meditated on it for a good four or five minutes, then felt as if my brain had tilted to one side and things were falling out.

Suddenly I had more work than ever but each day was a joyless grind of Zoom meetings where motivating my staff was impossible because of the strange pouch of skin which had appeared between my chin and the top of my neck. I looked like a pelican! When had this happened? And how come it didn't show up in mirrors or photos?

Even more demoralizing than the Pouch was knowing I should never have been in charge of Yemoja. Two of my colleagues, Kamilah and Monifa, were brilliant publicists and, unlike me, were African American. Before the project began, I pleaded with the grown-ups (Ariella and Franklin, both white) to reallocate the account.

Instead, they seconded Kamilah and Monifa to my team. Suddenly, two women who, like me, were Account Presidents became my juniors. Obviously it humiliated them but it was also some kind of weird slap down of me. *Knock it off, Anna, you and your woke bullshit.*

(Like many women, I had imposter syndrome. But not just the usual one, where I felt I didn't deserve my job. I also felt as if a cynical, money-mad person colonized my body for eleven hours a day, living a life the real me despised.)

Right away with Yemoja, there was just so much cultural nuance I missed. Without Kamilah and Monifa I'd have gone under. Quickly, they identified the foundation as the hero product. It was the obvious choice to launch the campaign.

Yesterday, samples had been couriered to four hundred hand-selected beauty influencers across the USA. Waiting for their verdict was always an anxious time. It was probably too soon yet to have heard anything, but you never knew.

As soon as I logged on, the enormous volume of new emails in my inbox indicated something was afoot. My heart pounding, my mouth dry, I powered up my cell; immediately it began beeping and binging with countless notifications and missed calls.

Fuck. Fuck, fuck, fuck.

Ariella had left a voice message, yelling at me to pick up my calls and, oh yeah, the samples of Yemoja foundation contained a skin-lightening agent— one of the vloggers had made the discovery and had put us on blast. A second voice message followed, in which Ariella yelled that it was in *all* of the samples.

Sitting at my desk, I almost vomited: makeup formulated specifically for black skin contained bleach.

Bleach doesn't just accidentally pour itself into bottles of foundation, this *had* to be sabotage. Maybe someone protesting the land grab the bony white company had made in an African-American marketplace? Who could blame them? But sorting that out was someone else's job. Mine was to protect the entire company—not just Yemoja but the bony one and their other diffusion lines—from the mother of all backlashes. Specifically a catastrophic drop in their share price.

Fixing the unfixable was what I did but, oh my God, the horror. I called an emergency Zoom meeting, my heart pounding in my ears, my breath coming in shallow sips.

Here was Ariella, big-haired and breathing fire. And Franklin, twitching away goodo, a nervous breakdown barely contained by a Dior suit. And three, four—no, *five*—senior staff from the client, including their CEO Mr Vogt. Whenever I saw the man, I heard the three violin shrieks from *Psycho*.

Everyone was freaking out and demanding to know my plan. I was adamant that our only option was sincere remorse.

"We personally speak to each influencer, doing everything to persuade them the company isn't racist."

Mr Vogt didn't like that. "Makes us look weak."

"How can we style this out? There's literal *bleach* in the product."

Everyone seemed startled by my belligerence including, I must admit, myself.

"We need a fund." I named a large sum of money. "Donations to African-American charities. The influencers get to choose."

"Ariella?" Mr Vogt asked. "You trust her?"

"Sure." But Ariella's shrug was an exercise in hedging her bets.

Vogt leant nearer his camera and narrowed his eyes. "Anna, if this doesn't work, it's on you. Hear this, the share price is down sixteen points, those shareholders are *pissed*. You have to fix it."

Briefly I considered the impact of a class action taken against me by the bony shareholders. I'd be bankrupted for a thousand lifetimes.

As everyone logged off, I had a moment of deep calm: *I can't do this anymore.* It wasn't the first time I'd thought it, but it was the first time I knew it was true.

4

At the end of that watershed day, I didn't just start boxing up my stuff and immediately book a flight to Ireland.

Instead, I took the odd step of ordering a miniature handheld loom and a weaving kit. No clue why. I wasn't remotely craft-y. All I knew was that I needed *something* to soothe my many anxieties: my beloved books had stopped working because my concentration was shot and I couldn't keep depending on my evening alcohol.

Then, in a bargain struck deep in my subconscious, I made myself forget the truths which had revealed themselves. My current circumstances were known quantities. Unhappy as they made me, I was more frightened of venturing into a vast unknown.

And there were plenty of distractions. Well, one big one really—work. Kamilah, Monifa and I were going all out, talking down influencers who were hurt and angry.

Our little crack squad emailed, Zoomed and phoned, apologizing over and over. Because our remorse was sincere, the influencers went easy on us. The formula returned to the lab and reappeared, this time without the color-lightening chemical. Then we launched it.

As expected, thousands upon thousands boycotted the product, but it wasn't a wipe-out. Then, quietly, it began to sell. Seven months later, the sales figures were exactly as predicted before the sabotage. To celebrate I bought myself a skein of wool.

Despite my job creating so much internal noise, clarity often broke through, reminding me I couldn't go on this way. Quickly I'd pick up my loom or open a bottle of wine or contemplate being a bankrupt and that was enough to knock all thoughts of radical life change from my head.

One thing keeping me anchored in my New York life was my bone-deep judgement for anyone who "walked away from it all." I wasn't a naturally ambitious person but living in Manhattan had infected me. A persuasive little voice would insist that burnout was just a made-up thing like the compulsion to eat coal. *You want to be a weak, lazy loser? One of those also-rans who earned lots of money but preferred to have a rest? We rest when we're dead, right! You there, Anna Walsh, yes you, you dedicated workhorse, you can buy anything you want right now! How about an air fryer! You never cook and you don't know what an air fryer actually does, but that's not important.*

Detaching from that mindset was hard work. But financially supporting myself when—if—I "walked away from it all" was a genuine worry. Beauty PR was the only real job I'd ever had. In my twenties I'd worked on car production lines, in canning factories, running bars on Greek islands. If it involved back-breaking work, no qualifications and lots of freedom, I'd done it. But those were not jobs for the less-young woman—which was what I was. This came as a shock every time I realized.

It took at least a year for the pendulum of my indecision to stop swinging. In the intervening time I crossed the line, back and forth, back and forth. I'd make peace with living in Manhattan forever. Then something odd would happen, like realizing the only time I felt calm was when I was weaving a small square of fabric. Or I'd get into an altercation with teenage boys in the street. (A one-off, but it was enough.) That incident prompted a visit to the doctor where perimenopause was finally diagnosed.

The subject had been tiptoed around in other visits—my irregular periods, ever-present anxiety, faint mustache and outbreaks of unbearable heat. My doctor and I had told each other it was all down to stress. *Adrenaline*, we said. It was as if she was too embarrassed to tell me I was aging and I was too frightened to admit it. But the results of the blood test were unequivocal: I was approaching menopause.

But menopause was for other women! Women like my sister Margaret, who'd been eagerly anticipating it since her thirty-fifth birthday. Not me, though. Not yet. I was only in my forties. Admittedly more than halfway through, but still too soon for perimenopause, surely? Actually no, as it transpired. I was right on time.

Wary of HRT, I began a regime of natural products. But after three months without any improvement, desperation made me submit to the hormones.

Things immediately got better. But thanks to the diagnosis itself, I felt like an aircraft which had started its final descent. Life seemed suddenly more *urgent*. I upgraded my loom for a slightly bigger one. I fantasized about living a gentle, Wi-Fi-free life where I ate home-grown carrots from self-made plates. Very late one night I rang Ireland to tell Dad I loved him. (Mum grabbed the phone from his hand and angrily told me that he was terrified.)

Then Angelo and I broke up.

After that Tuesday morning when I'd lost my temper over the prayer bowl, we'd talked, acknowledging we were under atypical stress. But at that stage, we weren't even a year into the pandemic. As the weeks, then months continued, Angelo seemed to be continually laundering the bed sheets—some sort of stress response. Him marching past me, his arms full of white cotton, giving off a low-grade rage, felt like a twice-daily event.

As for me, we were eating dinner one evening when a strange noise began—as if Angelo was engraving something on his plate. He was putting so much weight into it, I half expected ceramic splinters to spark into the air. *Why* did he have to carve so hard? It was only *cauliflower*. When had *this* started?

But a coldness in my gut told me he'd always done it; I just hadn't noticed before. And now that I had, I would never un-notice it again.

Occasional breaks in lockdown bought us some time, but by late spring of 2022, when I could return for good to my own apartment, we were beyond saving.

"Angelo?" One night, with no warning, I knew it was time.

"Yeah." He nodded. "Let's sit down."

Oh, okay. He *knew*.

Facing each other, he tucked a strand of my hair behind my ear and said, "Looks like we've come to the end of our rainbow."

"I'm sorry," I said.

"So am I. But it's the right thing."

Sad as I felt, it wasn't enough to change my mind. Briefly I wondered if all we needed was a short break. But we'd had breaks in the past—well, one in particular—and this was different. I still loved him, I still respected him, but I no longer wanted to attach my life to his.

I was now free to move back to Dublin, if it was really what I wanted.

Testing the waters, I emailed an Irish recruitment consultant who assured me that after bossing it for eighteen years in the toughest city on earth, I'd be concussed by a hail of job offers. As—just like me—her job was to be a professional liar, I was somewhat skeptical. Immediately I contacted another consultant who was less excited but still confident I'd land something decent. "They won't match your New York money," she warned. But that meant that they wouldn't match my New York stress either.

Doing full due diligence, I spoke to yet another, who simply couldn't believe I was walking away from beauty PR. "That's where you've the best chance of getting a job."

"I'll do anything but beauty," I said.

"The prison service is looking for a communications officer. On a quarter of your current salary. How does that sound?"

But the next consultant said that as a result of working at "legendary" McArthur on the Park for almost two decades, I could walk into any job in Irish PR.

It was impossible to know whom to believe, but even the most cautious of them seemed certain I'd get *something* if I wasn't too sniffy about salary.

The more positive consultants were keen to get me in front of potential employers right away, but I knew I wanted to live in Ireland for a while, boots on the ground, to get a sense of what was out there. The changes I was making were already huge so I might as well explore all possibilities.

It would mean a couple of months without an income. I was anxious but it could be done.

Then, on a warm night in May, getting ready for bed, I saw the butterfly. It was no big surprise to see a butterfly, it was almost summer—except butterflies tended to be daytime creatures.

What you need to know is that butterflies and I had history—details will come. Call me a credulous magical thinker who wasn't courageous enough to take full responsibility for my decisions but at many pinch points in my life, a butterfly had appeared; I'd always taken it as a "sign" that it was safe to proceed.

This particular one moved around my bedroom with . . . well, what looked to me like purpose. It sat on my wallet—telling me I'd be okay for money? Next it visited my keys—I'd have a place to live? Briefly it landed on my face, as if giving me a kiss, then flew out of the window. "Thank you," I called after it.

The visit gave me enough steel to give notice to Ariella, who insisted I work "every damn second" of my five months' notice period: it would be a tough time.

All the same, my exit plan was in place—time to start spreading the news.

After eighteen years of my parents and sisters *begging* me to come home to Dublin, they were finally about to get their wish.

They weren't going to like it.

5

Stunned into silence, six faces stared at me.

Claire was the first to find her voice. "Anna, you've gone insane."

A quick introduction to my sisters. Claire, the eldest, had an important job in the upper echelons of a global charity, wore covetable clothes, and talked a lot about sex *and* sexism. She budgeted for Botox the way other people budget for car insurance. (A necessity.) She was insanely generous and shared four adult children with her long-term partner, Adam. Most likely to say, "Aaah, what time is it? Nearly lunchtime? G'wan then, not *too* strong." (In fact, so was Adam. They were very well matched.)

"Completely insane," Helen insisted. "Who wants to live in Ireland? It's a shithole!"

"An absol*ute* shithole," Mum insisted.

Helen was the fifth Walsh sister, the only one younger than me. At first glance she seemed like a high-spirited teenager. Devoid of filter, her combative energy won her enemies wherever she went. She'd never fitted in and she'd never cared. Self-employed (because she'd kept getting sacked), she made a decent enough living as a private detective. She was in a long-term, opposites-attract relationship with a calm, quiet, ridiculously good-looking man called Artie, with whom she had a little girl, Regan.

"Anna? What about your job?" Margaret, the second eldest, was direct but never cruel. The polar opposite of Claire, she had zero interest in injectables and had long stopped covering her grays. Partial to slow-fashion clothing in shades called Woad and Black Cabbage, but when she made the effort, she—in Helen's immortal words—looked "like a social worker who's having an affair." (Even though she worked in the legal profession.)

"Will you be working remotely?" Margaret asked.

I braced myself. "I've handed in my notice—"

As expected, uproar ensued.

"I can't do that job any longer." I needed them to forgive me. "Not for any money. I'm broken."

"You need a rest and a reset," Claire said. "Spend a little time in this country where the restaurants are pathetic and a funeral counts as a day out, where you have non-existent public transport and zero privacy."

"Where there's no opera—" Margaret said.

"—thank Jayzus," Helen said.

"—or ballet—"

"—thank Jayzus again. I love Ireland."

"You're stressed," Claire said. "Everyone is stressed. Look at Rachel there, holding the lives of addicts in her hands!"

Rachel, the middle sister, was the Convert—a good-time girl who went to the bad then returned to the good. Wise and clean-living—except when it came to expensive trainers—she worked as an addiction therapist.

"I'm more sad than stressed," I said.

"But you've The Best Job In The World, tee emm!" Mum choked out. "I've lorded it over my sisters for years. Don't take this away from me."

"Sorry, Mum. In five months' time, I'll no longer work in beauty PR."

"No more free stuff?" Helen sounded faint. "But this is . . . *illegal*. Imma get an injunction."

"Instead of free skincare, you'll have *me* around all the time! That's so much better, right?"

Helen's sour look made me laugh.

Rachel clicked into therapist mode. "Anna, has something happened? To make you blow your life up like this?"

"Not any one particular thing. But the pandemic made me re-evaluate everything."

"Oh, the old 'pandemic re-evaluation.'" Claire was caustic. "It's not real, just horsewallop that people say to sound superior."

If Claire—the most zeitgeisty of us—hadn't had a pandemic re-evaluation, it didn't exist.

Even Rachel, who genuinely believed in personal growth, seemed unconvinced.

"It's real," I said. "I didn't get to see any of you for, at one stage, eleven *months*. It was horrible—"

"We didn't see you either," Mum said. "And you don't see us threatening to move to . . . to . . ." She turned to Helen. "Say some awful spot."

"Castellucio."

"Castellucio was beautiful!" Rachel said.

"If you like cutesy, *pretty* places," Helen said. "It made me itchy."

"She had to take antihistamines," Mum said.

"I was afraid you might die," I admitted.

"Who?" Mum looked around. "Helen? Margaret?"

"Well, anyone really. Covid was unpredictable. But I realized that you won't be around forever."

"Wh—*Me?* What do you mean I won't be around forever? You cheeky pup!"

"Or Dad."

"Him, yes, you've a point. He's frail."

"Am I?" Dad looked surprised. "Now you tell me."

Margaret, as ever, was about practicalities. "Honestly, Anna, I can't see Angelo Torres living in Ireland. He's so 'New York-y.'"

I took a breath. "Angelo won't be living in Ireland."

"You see." Mum was pleased and gloat-y. "Didn't I—" At the same time as everyone else, the subtext hit her. "What? Have you—"

"—broken up with Angelo? Yes."

Shock prevailed. "That's terrible!"

Gasping for breath, Mum beseeched the five of us. "Will I ever get you all boxed away? Ever? At this stage, I'll be on my deathbed, walking towards the pearly gates, the Man Above will have his arms out to welcome me and next thing one of you will pop in and tell me you're after marrying a tree." She buried her face in her hands.

"Cheating fucker," Helen hissed. "Like all men. His brains are in his flute—"

"He didn't cheat."

Claire focused on me with interest. "So it was *you?*"

"No one cheated."

"He was a clown," Helen declared. "With his"—she put on a goofy voice—"'spiritual way of life.' I'm sorry we ever called him the Sexy Guru, the cheating prick."

"He's a wonderful man," I snapped.

"Holy fuck," Helen said. "Are you, like, *mature* now? Is that the way all your break-ups will be? 'Going forward.' 'We'll always be friends' . . ."

"Angelo was just that type." Claire defended me. "There's no other way to break up with him. He was perfect."

In many ways, he was. Never controlling or manipulative, he received even the most outrageous suggestions calmly, instead of flying off the handle and yelling that this (whatever it was) was a load of bullshit (and he probably wouldn't have said bullshit; he rarely swore).

"Lockdown." I didn't want to go into all the details here. "Living together full-time didn't suit us."

"I hope you've given up on sex forever," Claire said. "Because the absolute *state* of any Irish man from twenty-two onwards. The baldness, the bellies, the boringness. Even *I* wouldn't touch them and you know what I'm like."

Courtesy of her testosterone gel, Claire said she thought about sex once every six seconds.

"At least in the US," she said, "You have lumberjack silver foxes, with pierced ears and pierced dicks. Men who make the *effort.*"

"They're more likely to have basements, though," Mum said. "Terrible things go on in them. In Ireland there's no basements. She's safer here."

"She's seventy-three," Helen said. "She can take care of herself."

"What age *are* you?" Mum asked me.

"Seventy-three," Helen repeated.

"Twenty-one," I said. "Well, that's what I feel today. But mid to late forties, if we're going by the calendar year."

"*If* you were to relocate to Ireland?" Margaret asked me. "*Where* would you live?"

"I *am* relocating to Ireland where eventually I'll buy a place. I'll need a temporary base for a while but I have two parents and four sisters, all with their own homes. I'll be spoiled for choice."

Claire's home fairly hopped with activity. So did Helen's, because in addition to Regan, her little girl, she had three stepchildren. Rachel's was also busy, mostly because she and her ex-husband Luke never stopped having sex (long story but they were very happy). Margaret, though, hers was peaceful. No sex there. Dead from the neck down, she often said, and delighted about it.

"You can't live with Helen." Mum was quick. "Regan is possessed by demons. You'd be in danger. Demons are drawn to good girls like you."

Regan was *not* possessed by demons but it made them so happy to say it, why deny them their pleasure?

"I see you're all looking at me," Claire said. "Because I've the biggest house. But I'm overrun with Gen Z offspring and their polyamorous capers. You'd be lucky to get a bed and even luckier if a selection of strangers didn't join you in the middle of the night, looking for shenanigans."

Of Claire and Adam's four children, only one, Francesca, identified as "polyamorous." But Claire never let the facts get in the way of a good story. It was the trait I liked best about her.

"Claire," Mum asked, her voice sing-song, "how do you know someone's polyamorous?"

"They tell you," Claire said and they both laughed. This seemed to be a well-practised routine.

"Mum?" I asked. "Would you give me a bed?"

Her mouth moved convulsively. She wouldn't meet my eyes. "No, Anna. For a short while, if you were stuck. I was always fond of you, you'd nearly be my favorite, after Helen. But you'd be making me eat out-of-date yogurts and giving me food poisoning. At this time of my life I don't want to be scolded. Or poisoned."

"Of course you can live with us." Dad was totally ignored.

"It's me who scolds you about the yogurts," Margaret said.

"There she goes again, trying to make out I've dementia so she can put me in a home."

"You mad old fool," Helen said. "*I'm* the one trying to put you in a home, not Margaret there, who is *good* and *decent*."

"You're welcome to move in with Luke and me," Rachel said.

"You won't get a wink of sleep there," Helen said. "The pair of them . . . Never not at it."

All my money was on Margaret—and like the reliable woman she was, she said, "My spare room is yours for as long as you need it."

God, she was the best.

"You'll love it there." Rachel became wistful. "Homemade cake in a tin. Wildflowers in a jam jar on your dressing table. Porridge made in an actual saucepan."

"No Netflix, though." This from Mum. "No *Virgin River*."

"Thank fuck for that." Helen, of course.

"I can pay for Netflix," I said.

"How?" Margaret asked. "If you don't mind me asking? Have you savings? Investments?"

A sore subject. After working like a machine all these years, I'd accumulated surprisingly little. "I'll get a job."

"WHAT!" Dad almost levitated. "You mean you've given in your notice without having another job to go to?"

"Get the defibrillator," Mum yelled. "He's having a stroke."

We hadn't a defibrillator and Dad wasn't having a stroke—but he *was* profoundly distressed. "That's the most IDIOTIC thing anyone has ever done."

"We were wrong to say you weren't a failure," Mum said. "You were just hiding out in the long grass these last eighteen years. You *deceived* us."

"I've spoken to lots of recruiters. I'll definitely get a job."

"Doing what?" Helen was suddenly breathless with hope. "Beauty PR? Right here in Dublin?"

"Not beauty. Something different."

"Pivoting." Claire was, once again, scornful. "You're just ticking boxes here, Anna. Reassessing your life because of the pandemic? Tick! Ending a long-term relationship? Tick! Pivoting? Tick!"

"What's pivoting?" Mum shifted anxiously. "It sounds like getting something pointy shoved up your bum-hole."

"What are you thinking of pivoting to?" Claire asked.

The six of them were one big cluster of suspicion.

"I haven't decided yet. But something gentler. Less stressful."

"No one gets paid six figures to do something gentle," Claire said.

"That's okay with me."

"Why would anyone give you a job doing not-beauty?" Helen asked. "You've no experience."

"I've a lot. Managing projects, staff, budgets, expectations . . . You name it, I've managed it."

"You've managed to break my heart." Mum, who had become a sullen lump, suddenly spoke up. "You can add that to your list."

"Will do. I need to leave for the airport now."

"Don't bother coming back," Mum said.

"Who's driving me?" I asked.

"None of us," Helen said.

Grand. I got out my phone to call a taxi, then went to wait in the hall. That had gone about as well as I'd expected.

6

Although I tended towards optimism, I'd expected that my re-entry into Irish life would be bumpy. But nothing could have prepared me for just how bruising it had been.

The long and the short of it was that no one should move jobs, countries and continents because they saw a butterfly.

In the five months since my return, I'd remained unemployed. I'd come close once or twice to landing a position, but I seemed to puzzle potential employers: I was too experienced—but not experienced enough in *Irish* PR. I'd been too senior for too long: they feared I'd never adapt to a job requiring more grunt work. High-end PR was all about personal relationships— and I knew nobody. I insisted over and over again that I was a quick learner, that I could gear up in no time, but they were all doubtful. And although none of them dared to say it, the main issue was that I was in my late forties.

This is a warning against being a person who tends towards optimism—I hadn't thought of myself as middle-aged, never mind old. You could blame my mindset on Manhattan where, once you hit forty, aging no longer happened. Or rather, an elaborate protocol was used to blur the evidence, including (but not limited to) Restylane, retinol, HIIT yoga, hair-Botox, edible collagen, low-carbing, no-carbing, intermittent fasting, B12 injections and wearing trainers and diamanté canes to black-tie galas. This seemed to work efficiently until maybe the age of ninety-two, when your hip broke unexpectedly while you were opening the fridge, then a conversation had to be had.

Because I'd done spin classes four times a week, had a high metabolism thanks to my stressful job and—also courtesy of my job—a face riddled with Botox, fillers and Profhilo, I told myself I could pass for a woman of thirty-seven. Admittedly, there were times when I made an involuntary grunting noise getting out of a low-slung chair but I still felt *very much in the game.*

All of a sudden, though, I was back living in Dublin, undeniably forty-eight. As insignificant as a speck of dust, with no partner, no children, no pets, no job, nothing to define me.

At other times in my past I'd felt I was staring into a yawning abyss but life had always started up again. This time, though, I'd peaked. From now on, it would be smaller, lesser versions of the glory I'd once had, decreasing and reducing, as I filled in the hours, trundling towards death.

"But what do you expect?" Mum said. "You're not much good at anything. It was only my prayers that got you that job with the makeup. Which you threw back in the Lord's face. He won't oblige you a second time."

Immediately I reverted to the age of sixteen when Mum and Dad had realized I was in my last year at school. Up till then I'd managed to stay beneath their radar, but suddenly they were all hand-wringing anxiety about "what would become of" me.

Almost from the day they'd been born, it had been decided that Claire and Margaret were their clever children. Rachel was a worry, Helen was the most powerful person in the family and I was the spacer.

The only subjects I liked were English and art. "They're fecking useless!" Dad declared. "What kind of a job will they get you? Maths, Anna, try harder with the maths."

But maths might as well have been Martian.

Surprising everyone, though, I displayed an aptitude for business studies and got an A plus in my Christmas exam. When my report card arrived, I found Mum and Dad in the kitchen, in a huddle.

"That can't be right," Dad was saying.

"Should we query it?" Mum asked.

"I'm good at it," I said.

"You are not." Mum was adamant. "You're for the birds. But, Anna, what are you going to do with your life?"

"I'll go to the Greek islands and work in a bar."

"You'll do no such thing!" Dad was mortified. "You need a post with a pension!"

Alerted by the ruckus, Helen had turned up. "What about being a person who tastes dog food? It's an actual job."

"Stop." I felt sick.

"Bus driver?" Again from Helen.

"You could be a human guinea pig?" Rachel had just come in.

"What's that?" Mum asked. "Dressing up in a furry costume, giving out leaflets about a golf sale?"

"It's a person who tests out drugs before they get approved."

"Has it a pension?" Dad demanded.

"I just want to be content," I said. "I don't need lots of money."

"Why not? You . . ." Mum searched for the right insult. "You hippie . . . communist!"

The truth was that all I really wanted was to be answerable to no one. But I'd since discovered that that sort of job didn't exist.

Anyway, I'd been regarded as "not the brightest" and I'd believed it. But out in the world, when I found things I was actually interested in, I discovered I wasn't such a thicko, after all.

But that still wasn't enough for anyone to employ me right now.

Over and over I asked myself: What have I *done*? I was frightened I'd never get a job again. But it was me who had created this situation and I had to own it. There were positives, of course—hanging out with Mum and Dad, my sisters, nieces and nephews was definitely nice. Except they all had busy lives and, now I was in Ireland indefinitely, my novelty had worn off. Living here was nothing like as much fun as a whirlwind five-day visit.

When I spoke to Angelo—we'd given each other lots of space after our break-up but we were far friendlier now—he urged me to "look for the lesson" in this. I didn't bother, it was a lot easier to nurse a passionate resentment against butterflies.

Not all was lost— I *could* return to New York. I'd rented out my apartment rather than sold it and Ariella had said if I returned within a year, I could have my job back. But now that I'd left that life, I couldn't believe I'd managed it for so long.

At least I had a place to live in Dublin. Margaret, as promised, had opened her home to me. Once the Netflix situation had been normalized, it was so comfortable there with her lovely husband Garv and their two sweet teenage children.

But was this it? Forever? Apart from my sisters, I had no real friends in Ireland. I didn't have a car, the Luas system was illogical and I couldn't get a doctor's appointment anywhere in Margaret's catchment area.

Which became important when my fancy New York HRT gels began running low. A nice old duffer called Dr Waterbury had been the Walsh family doctor for decades so I asked Mum to get me an appointment. But he'd retired.

"There's a couple of new lads there," she'd said. "Young. Useless. And not taking on any new patients. But Shannon O'malley is still the receptionist there." She'd been at school with Helen. "Because I like you, I'll ring and beg."

Somehow she bagged me a consultation with Dr Lowry Riordan. "Take Shannon O'malley a tin of Roses," she'd said. "And don't forget, you owe me a very big favor."

7

"I don't think we've met." With a flourish, Lowry Riordan indicated that I sit down.

He wore khaki chinos, hiking boots and a couple of layers of frayed T-shirts. Dr Waterbury had favored three-piece suits and, honestly, I preferred it.

"I lived in New York until October just gone."

"Great city." He sat, resting his left ankle on his right knee. "What can I do for you today?"

"I began taking HRT about fourteen months ago. I've the names of the hormones here." I got out my phone. "The brands will be different but you'll know the closest dupes to prescribe."

"Yeeeeaah." He displayed his lower teeth in a theatrical wince.

"So the progesterone was—"

"I'm gonna stop you there. In the Western world, we over-medicalize what is a perfectly natural part of a woman's life."

Wait now, *what*? He wasn't . . . no, he couldn't possibly be about to fob me off with black cohosh and yams? US doctors *adore* over-medicalizing things. Their prescription writing is inspired by Tolstoy, lengthy narratives full of twists and turns. Usually starting with something new that people were "seeing great results from." Followed by three other medicines to counteract the side effects from the new product. Then a couple more to counteract the side effects from the earlier side-effect-cancelling remedies.

"In league with big pharma" is a familiar accusation. To which I say, And what about it? In my clueless youth, overburdened with idealism, I might have agreed with Dr Lowry Riordan here, but that was before I'd hit perimenopause.

"Take a country like India," Lowry Riordan said. "A female population of six hundred million and only a tiny percentage take HRT. The rest just get on with it."

My brain was scrambling *hard*. It produced, "Lowry, I've been to India and I loved it. But fifteen percent of the population don't have running water either."

He set his mouth in a displeased line, then said, "There are cancer risks associated with HRT."

"It's low. And there's no history of breast cancer in my family. I check my breasts daily." Maybe not literally daily but I would if he'd give me a prescription. "Please. I've already tried natural remedies. They didn't help."

"In good conscience, I can't prescribe HRT."

In good conscience? What did that mean? "But you don't have to take it!" Then, more calmly, "You don't know what perimenopause feels like. It's really tough, in lots of different ways."

"I don't have Crohn's Disease either but I'm also qualified to treat that."

Into the ensuing silence, he said, "Research proves natural supplements work as well as . . . without any of the risks of breast cancer . . . best practice . . . serving women . . . blaaaaaaaaah . . ."

As I paid the bill I asked Shannon O'malley, "How retired is Dr Waterbury?"

"He's in a home with Alzheimer's."

"So? Working part-time?"

"Jesus Christ!" Claire raged. "If a man came in with an itchy bollock, he'd be prescribed painkillers, antihistamines and a hot girl in a porn-y nurse's costume to scratch it for him. But if a woman shows up with a sinus infection or a verruca, they get antidepressants. Except if they're actually depressed, then they're told to get a dog."

"I didn't want HRT," Margaret said, "because I just wanted it to be over— periods, mood changes . . . I didn't like that I'd no control over myself. Now that I'm through it, I feel safer. Neverthe*less*, Anna, you should be allowed as much HRT as you like."

"I'm planning on taking it till the day I die," Claire said. "Even when I'm lying in my coffin, could one of you rub on a pump of testosterone gel, it's *great* for hair growth. Also for the libido." She levelled a look at Margaret. "Talking about you, Mrs Dead from the Neck Down."

"I wasn't allowed HRT," Mum said. "Because it gave us breast cancer."

"Everyone? You mean your entire generation?"

"That's right, all of us. So they said."

Mum's menopause might not have been as obvious as other mothers' because she'd always been short-tempered. Yelling angrily was her—and my sisters'—preferred mode of communication. Conversations moved from innocent questions to shrieked denials in under a second. Even so, I remembered everyone laughing at Mum as she'd raged and wept. With my new knowledge my heart hurt for her.

"I'll *have* to get HRT," Helen said. "Otherwise I'll end up in a maximum-security prison. I can barely control my rage as it is. Once the—what's the calming hormone, Claire? Progesterone? Once it's gone, I won't be able to not kill people. I bet there's loads of women doing time for murder just because some mansplainy doctor wouldn't give them HRT. Miscarriages of justice. We should do a podcast about them!"

"Rachel?" Claire said. "What do you thi— Rachel!"

"Sorry!" Rachel had been smiling at nothing. "I seem to be okay. A few symptoms but I'm grand."

Of course she was. She and Luke had had a messy break-up over a decade ago. But since they'd got back together, a blanket of endorphins surrounded her, like her own micro-climate. A small thing like menopause wasn't going to leave a scratch.

"How come you get all the HRT you need?" I asked Claire.

"Because I see a consultant. If you have loads of cash you can see her too."

"I'll chip in for an appointment," Margaret said.

"We'll all club together," Rachel declared.

"I can pay." I'd been trying to budget, but I was still transitioning from earning plenty to earning nothing. These huge attitude shifts take *time*.

However, the first available slot was seven months hence. Reluctantly, Claire donated a month's supply of hormones but not before warning me that this was strictly a one-off.

I assured her of my gratitude, then silently addressed the universe. "Any chance something good could happen soon? I'd really appreciate it."

8

Eventually, the universe threw me a bone . . .

"Did I wake you?" Rachel sounded surprised. "It's gone eleven."

"Aaah. No, no, not at all," I lied, unconvincingly. "Awake for ages."

As I sat up, a slice of sharp March sunshine cut through the gap in the curtains, nearly blinding me.

"Sorry for ringing," Rachel said. "But would you be interested in some PR work? Urgent."

"Um, *sure.*" My mouth was dry. Hope, it's a terrible thing. "What is it?" My parched lips made popping sounds.

"Tell you when I see you. You'll get paid. *And* you'll reconnect with a blast from the past. So get up, get dressed, Brigit and I are on our way."

Still dazed, I sat on the edge of the bed, knocking a couple of books to the floor. Unsure of my next move, I could . . . brush my hair? Beg Margaret to bring me a latte?

I hung my head—then, aghast, thought, *Are those* my *feet?* Unrecognizably unkempt, their unvarnished state would have got me an angry-not-disappointed work warning a few short months ago.

A soft knock at the door announced Margaret. In her hand was a latte. For me.

"How did you know?" I was grateful but confused. I'd never had her down as a mind-reader: she was far too matter-of-fact. But now that she'd officially "menopaused," perhaps witchy skills were sprouting in her, along with—and these are Margaret's words, not mine—her "Elvis-in-Vegas style sideburns."

"Rachel texted. Said you needed caffeine." She moved into my bathroom, switching on the shower. "She told me to do this too. Get in. Wash your hair."

Meekly, I obeyed. There was a relief in being given orders.

*

Margaret was waiting, plate of toast in her hand, when I came out, wrapped in a towel. "Rachel's coming over?" she asked.

"And Brigit."

"How's Queenie?"

Brigit's thirteen-year-old had been in and out of hospital thanks to a series of inexplicable falls.

"On the mend," I said. "Finally. So Rachel said something about PR work, it must be for Brigit."

Margaret's smile was radiant. Nothing frightened her more than unemployment, even other people's. "It must be to do with her feathery-strokery retreat!"

Oh, I hoped so.

Brigit, like Rachel and me, had once lived in New York. Manhattan had suited Brigit: shiny, hungry people, designer sample sales and impossible-to-access parties. Irish men were not for her—until she met Colm, a man in constant motion, talking fast, laughing often, keen to hear your opinion on movies, design, art, politics, telling you about what he'd seen or read or eaten.

Together they became *that* couple—cool but never try-hard. After watching a documentary about the rock-hewn churches in Lalibela, they went straight out to a travel agent (different times) and bought flights to Ethiopia. They were the first people I knew whose home featured taxidermy. By the time a squirrel riding a penny-farthing had become a commonplace living-room fixture, they'd long moved on.

The first big surprise was that Colm was originally from a farm in the wild beauty of Connemara, where the nearest town, Maumtully (population 1,271), was a four-kilometer drive on bad roads. The second big surprise was that he persuaded Brigit to live there.

Even then—by leaving city life behind, a decade before it really caught on—they were ahead of the curve.

To house themselves and their—eventual—four children, they designed and built a home of glass and local stone, so beautiful that, on departure, their many visitors were often in a pink-cheeked fury, threatening to burn their own shithole of a place to cinders.

Brigit, always enterprising, converted an old shed into a charming Airbnb; it won an award. Then she repurposed an unused barn into a light-filled studio which hosted yoga weekends and artists' workshops. Its reputation spread so quickly that Brigit overhauled a second adjacent barn and linked the two. Next thing, one of the yoga bunnies wanted to get married there, so now the yoga/

painting devotees were in frantic competition with the wedding hopefuls over availability.

Then the pandemic arrived. Six short weeks into it, both of Colm's parents died. Colm inherited their adjoining farm, fifty scenic but otherwise useless acres. During the long, tedious hours of lockdown, he and Brigit began playing around with ideas for a high-end retreat, called Dolphin Cove.

Because they'd never believed it would become a reality, their imaginations went nuclear, conjuring up a next-level escape. Accommodation, deftly integrated into the landscape, would be in glass and stone cottages, similar to their own home. Views would be stunning, the interiors intuitive and the prices high.

Food would be fresh and simple. (Or exotic and complicated. I wasn't sure what their latest thinking was.) No gym or swimming pool because nature would provide: guests could immerse themselves in the bracing Atlantic and return ecstatic. Instead of a thirty-minute sprint on a treadmill, they and a wise guide would climb a local mountain, occasionally accompanied by hares, sheep, maybe even hailstones. Upon their return, they'd be wrapped in a khullu blanket, seated by the fire, given a hot whiskey and insist they'd never felt so joyous.

Massages and yoga were a given. Also on the menu were sound therapy, psychics-on-call, an adult-proportioned playground, "managed boredom," digital detox and star-gazing, alongside more hardcore wellness stuff, such as rebirthing and Ayahuasca ceremonies.

Their tag line was *Give us your body and we'll give you back your soul.* I wouldn't have minded six months there myself.

Somehow—probably because they knew all kinds of people—their lockdown hobby came to the attention of venture capitalists. Next thing you knew, Dolphin Cove got green-lit, a ton of investment money showed up and construction began.

Margaret said, "It would be great if you got some work."

"Doing what, though? They're still about a year out from opening, I thought."

"Eat your toast," Margaret said as I got dressed. "And tell me how you are today."

"I feel like a blank space," I said. "I'm not the person I was but I've no clue who I'm going to be."

"Ah, yeah." Margaret nodded. "I used to feel the same."

I perked up. "Tell me!" I *so* enjoyed our morbid little chats.

"For years I loved being a mother but when the kids became teenagers I realized they weren't going to be mine for much longer. The truth is they never belonged to me, but I forgot. Then I felt . . . like the hole in the doughnut."

"But you had Garv. And your job."

"I loved Garv, I still do, but even now I wonder if we'll be enough for each other when the kids leave? As for my job—I don't hate it but . . . So it was up to me to find a new purpose. And I didn't know where to start. All I knew was I didn't want to start any of the mad stuff women over fifty do."

"Like what?"

"Oh, you know. Going swimming in the sea in the nip with a hundred other menopausal women. That seems to be a thing. It's not so much that my body has gone to hell. It's the compulsory jolliness which would destroy me. Dancing around on the freezing sand, our nipples bouncing around our knees, yelling, 'We're old and saggy and we don't care'! While some mortified nineteen-year-old lad from the local paper takes our photo."

I could see her point.

"He'd make us run towards the sea so he could photo us from behind. A hundred old bums running towards the waves." She shuddered. "Or having an affair? Anna, no. The thing I realized is that everyone has times when we're forced to stop. To pause and take a look around, so we can see what we have, what we might want . . . It's a good thing."

"Were you always this wise?" (Walsh family shorthand had Margaret as "good with money" and "very practical.")

"You know, I *might* have been," she said. "But anytime I tried, everyone started yelling, 'Shut up and tell us about savings accounts.' Anyway! At the moment you're an empty glass but in time you'll fill up again. But make sure it's with the right stuff because we only get one go. People spend their lives in the service of others or afraid to take what they want. I spent years putting my children first and I forgot all about me."

"Honestly, Margaret, you're blowing me away here. You're really good at this!"

"Ah, I'm not." She seemed delighted. "Rachel's the enlightened one."

"Not in the last few years. Too busy floating around on a cloud of Luke Costello-scented hormones. She's impossible to get sense out of."

"Helen?"

"*Enlightened?* HAHAHAHAHA—"

"They're here," Holly called up the stairs. "Even Luke!"

33

"Don't look," Margaret yelled.

"I don't know how not to!"

Luke Costello was dark and devastating, his jeans worn just that smidgeon too tight. His shady secret—that he was essentially a nice, uncomplicated man—dialed down some of his crotch power. Nevertheless, being around him, trying not to stare at his region, could drain the life from the strongest person.

Holly, a very innocent eighteen-year-old, found it tougher than most.

9

Margaret and I hurried down the stairs to marvel at Brigit's radically short blonde hair. "I cut it myself, it's a mess."

"No, it's iconic!"

Her dropped-crotch leggings were "Sully's old GAA tracksuit bottoms." And her bouncy yellow clogs were "Made of sugarcane, I got them in Mumbai."

"You're amazing!" I declared. "As always."

Only then did I realize Brigit was atypically subdued.

"Can we sit?" Rachel seemed anxious to move this forward.

"Sure," Margaret said. "Go into the conservatory. Can I come too?"

In the conservatory, Holly, her gaze fixed on her own feet, served drinks and homemade lemon cake. "Ring for me if you need anything," she whispered, then withdrew discreetly. It felt like living in a home for distressed gentlefolk.

"Okay." Brigit's chin began to tremble. "My little girl, Queenie, you know she hasn't been well?"

"I thought she was getting better!"

"So did we. But on Wednesday she couldn't move her legs. Paralyzed. Turns out she has a tumor on her spinal cord. Cancer, I mean."

"Oh God, Brigit, I'm so sorry!" Queenie was a gorgeous kid: wild, charming, mad about animals. This was *horrible* news.

"At least we've a diagnosis now." Brigit's blunt delivery was at odds with the tears which flowed freely down her face. "Colm's been useless, though. Just fallen apart. Hasn't left home in weeks."

That didn't sound like Colm. The man I knew would talk to a literal stone.

"I'd kill him but I'm too busy," Brigit said. "I've been driving Queenie up and down from the hospital here in Dublin, but now they're keeping her in while they figure out what treatment has the best chance of . . . of." A bout of wild sobbing followed. When she could speak again, she said, "I'm not leaving her, not for one second. I'll sleep on the hospital floor if I have to."

"Oh, *Brigit*."

Brigit spoke again, her voice thick. "My mind hasn't been on anything but Queenie for the last ages. And there's no *way* I can think about work now. Anna, I've lived in M'town for fifteen years. Colm was born there. His family goes back generations. Our kids go to school there. The townspeople, they're our community, our friends. I thought everyone was fine with the plans for the retreat"—she fixed me with a look of despair—"I don't know what's gone wrong, but last night the builders had their work vandalized and machinery disabled."

"The investors have frozen funds," Luke said. "The builders have had to stop work, they're not allowed back until this is fixed. Brigit has to find someone to talk with the locals, find out their exact issues, so they can be made right."

No way was I kicking someone who was down but this should have been done before the work started.

"A PR person *was* sent." Luke had read my mind. "Few months ago. Apparently he was a patronizing arse in a suit who talked down to everyone. If there *were* concerns, no one told him."

"Anna." Brigit's tone was urgent. "If this falls apart, Colm and I are wiped out financially. We're utterly fucked. We need a nice PR person to fix this. You're nice, Anna, really nice."

My mouth was dry. I wanted to do this, not just because Brigit's pain had now become mine, but because I needed a job. However, the fear of failing was enormous. As was the thought of being run out of Maumtully, pelted with turnips.

"But I've never talked down an entire town."

"You're good with upset, angry people," Rachel said. "Look how you got that Yemoja shitshow under control. Different product, same job. People need to feel heard and respected."

"What's causing the upset?" Margaret asked.

"A quick look at Facebook has some people annoyed that high-net-worth individuals will be coming to the area but staying away from the town," Brigit said.

"And will they?"

"They won't be using the hotel or the B and Bs. But there's nothing stopping them going up and having a pint or buying an Aran sweater. Others think the place will be overrun with limos stealing their parking space outside the vape shop."

"Which is nonsense," Rachel said. "Because M'town already has plenty of famousers."

Maybe because of its astonishing beauty, the hinterland of Maumtully was home to a fair few creatives. One or two were bona fide celebrities, the director Ben Mendoza being the best known.

"But they pretend they're one of us," Brigit said. "Downplaying their huge success. Saying 'Jayzus' and 'Grand.' Never wearing coats. But . . ." She squirmed. "The tilers, joiners and decorators we've hired aren't local."

That was a rookie mistake.

"We're using local lads for the construction work but the interiors spec is too high. We need specialists."

"Another thing," Luke said. "Someone let it slip that the staff, like cleaners, drivers, chefs, will have to sign NDAs."

"What's wrong with that?"

"M'town thrives on gossip," Brigit said. "Swearing people to secrecy is an insult. Anna, what's your thoughts on telling the cops?"

"No. It would only escalate divisions."

Margaret sounded worried. "Sorry, but is *Anna* likely to be vandalized?"

Brigit shook her head. "Lenehan—you know, my eldest lad?—sent photos this morning. The damage is amateur hour. People are upset, they're not dangerous."

"If something else happens, maybe you should rethink going to the cops," I said. "But as of now . . ."

Brigit managed a small smile. "Agree. The investors let me have this one."

"Who *are* these investors? Which one is your point of contact?" Because they'd be my point of contact now.

"None. Communication is always through the broker." There was surprise, perhaps even disappointment, in Brigit's tone, as if I should know this. But I'd spent the last eighteen years flogging skincare. How was I meant to know the ins and outs of feathery-strokery venture capitalism?

"Okay," I asked. "So who's this broker?"

"What? Don't you . . . ? It's Joey." She seemed astonished. "*Joey* Joey."

Did she mean . . . "*Narky* Joey?"

"Joey Armstrong," Rachel clarified.

Helpfully, Luke said, "You know Joey."

Oh, I definitely knew Joey.

10

I'd have to forget about taking this job. Unless . . . "Will I have any dealings with Joey?"

"Any?" Brigit asked. "You'll have *all* the dealings with Joey. For the next however-long, I can only think about Queenie. Wait now. What am I missing? Is Joey a problem?"

I hesitated. *Why* did it have to be Joey?

"Oh, *right.*" Rachel had just remembered.

"Oh, *right,*" Luke echoed. "But that was *years* ago."

Brigit looked baffled. "What's thi—"

"Does Joey know about you hiring me?" I interrupted. "Because he might not be keen."

A hundred questions battled it out on her face; then she reached for her phone. "I'll text him."

"It'll be all good." Luke's voice was balm. "Everyone's more grown-up now."

After some moments of silence, I said, "So? How *is* he?"

"Divorced." Luke was terse.

Yes. I'd heard. It had been a surprise: Joey and Elisabeth had looked built to last. She was—of course—beautiful, in a slender, refined way. The one time I'd met her, she'd been friendly, almost funny.

Loaded, too. Well, her dad was. She represented everything Joey thought he'd always wanted and, in a bittersweet way, I'd felt happy for him.

They'd been based in some massive house in Dublin: Joey, Elisabeth and their three children. At least before things had veered off track.

Delicately, I asked Luke, "What went wrong? The . . . usual?"

Meaning Joey's world-famous wandering lad.

"No." Again there was something in Luke's tone. A defensiveness. "She . . . Look, it's not my story to tell."

I murmured, "Of course."

How *infuriating*. I'd hoped he'd spill the beans because the most Rachel ever gave me was "Joey's trying his best."

"But it's amicable," Luke said.

That made a change.

"Let's stay on track here." Luke was quick to shut this down.

Back to business. "Brigit, even if Joey gives me the go-ahead, you're sure you don't want someone from a big Dublin PR firm?"

"That would make things worse. If you can tell the townspeople you're my friend . . . ? That would be best. And you don't have to fix a single thing, Anna. Just get a list of every grievance M'town has."

"Is there any individual who might be the figurehead for this resentment?"

"I haven't a clue." The tears began again. "I thought everyone was happy about it. Tipper Mahon is the construction foreman but there's no way he'd damage his own gear."

"What about Vivian?" Rachel asked.

"Vivian Hogan-Bancroft," Brigit said. "'Queen' of M'town, self-elected, like. She's commander-in-chief of the festivals."

"Festivals?"

"The literary week every July," Brigit said. "I know nearly every town in Ireland has one but the Maum festival is a big deal. There's the traditional music hooley and the painting school in August, then every Whit weekend, there's—"

"—the Loaves and Fishes Feast!" Claire had gone one year. It coincided with me being on a visit home and coverage appearing on the six o'clock news. Mum and I had watched footage of barefoot thespians in straw hats and rolled-up linen trousers, upright and wobbling in wooden boats, scanning for fish, yelling directions to the locals, who were crouched beneath them, heaving oars back and forth.

On her return, Claire's appraisal was damning. Apparently when the sun set, the "catch" (heavily supplemented from the display fridge in Aldi, she claimed) was barbecued on the beach, eaten with bread from the artisanal bakery in Clifden. Tall torches formed a circle, within which a poet stood on a tractor tyre and read "fifteen thousand" of his poems, then a drunk man insulted another drunk man's novella. "Full of knobs cosplaying James Joyce" was her conclusion.

"Vivian's a massive dose," Brigit said, "but she's delighted with our plans, already angling for freebies for the festivals. And she's away—she 'winters' in Barbados—"

"*Such* a dose," Rachel said.

"Is there anyone I should talk to?" I asked. "Who might know who was upset about what?"

"The woman in the Aran sweater shop." Rachel was certain.

"Ferne O'dowd?" Brigit said. "Great call. She's on the committee of town traders, she knows everyone. You'll find her in the sweater shop on Main Street."

"Narrow it down," Luke said. "There are a *lot*."

"The one beside the post office. I mean between the post office and the Spar. Not the one between the post office and Eileen's Electricals." She looked at her phone. "What's keeping Joey? Usually he replies before you've even sent yours . . ."

Feck. This was going to fall apart before it ever started, wasn't it?

"Other good people to meet?" Brigit said thoughtfully. "Young Ziryan in the hardware store. Knows everyone and never stops talking. So, Anna, what's your plan?"

"I . . . ah." I flicked another look at Brigit's silent phone. What *was* my plan? Was there even any point if Joey was going to sack me? "I'll talk to people, like you said. Try to gauge the mood. Perhaps hold a public meeting where everyone gets their say." I was freewheeling wildly here. "Set up an email address where they can vent their spleen anonymously?"

"Sounds good. And you won't be too Manhattan-y? No stalking about in pointy Louboutins and pencil skirts? It's important you don't look corporate."

This was a relief. During lockdown I'd lost the ability to stand upright in any narrow heel, no matter how low. At five foot three, I was still fond of a heel, but now they had to be chunky. As for the pencil skirts, working from home had been their death knell. These days I was all about comfort.

"You can stay in the hotel in town," Brigit said. "Or in the Airbnb in ours, which is out of town. Your choice."

"Will there be Wi-Fi?" Because I'd heard terrible things.

"Of course!" Brigit said. "Often."

Oh. Kay.

"All your expenses will be covered. Now, let's talk your fee."

At least it was understood that this wasn't a freebie. But I hated talking money with friends. Or friends of my sisters. Or anyone, really. Yet another thing that the passage of time had let me down on.

It was infuriating: popular culture assured me that the older I got, the more unafraid I'd become. There were countless interviews with forty-something women boasting that the concerns of their twenties now seemed ridiculous. These fear-free creatures gave the impression that soon I'd be super-comfortable speaking any unpalatable truth ("drawling" it, probably); that I'd stop caring about fashion and start cultivating an odd look—perhaps wearing a poncho or a fedora. And instead of generating mocking laughter, I'd be considered a "character."

But none of those things happened and I still felt as if asking to be paid for the sweat of my brow was rude.

"Okay, how about a daily rate?" Brigit offered a sum of money that sounded generous.

"Too much! You have to get mates' rates. Any idea how long you'll want me for?"

"I don't know," Brigit said. "Look, go for a week. Stay till next Saturday."

"Grand." I was trying to hide my nerves. But a job was a job and surely I couldn't make things worse? "I won't waste your money. If I can't do any good, I'll tell you immediately."

"Don't tell me anything." She sounded exhausted. "Take it to Joseph. Yes, these days he likes to be called Joseph."

"He's been called worse in his time."

Brigit half smiled. "A lot worse. God, he was unbelievable."

Back in the day, his dick had made its way through almost every woman we knew—Brigit among them. Also my sister Helen, my ex-colleague Teenie, and he was the father of my ex-best-friend Jacqui's daughter, Trea.

Brigit focused on me. "Anna, I thought you hadn't but am I wrong? Have *you* had the pleasure?"

". . . Ah. No. *No.*"

"But he had a go," Luke reminded me.

Oh, *that*. "Just out of politeness, really." I recovered fast. "Doing the mannerly thing. So what's Joey's role in Maumtully? He's not . . . customer-facing, is he?"

Even Brigit managed a smile. In his younger days, Joey entered a room with a moment in the doorway so we could admire his sinewy height in low-slung black jeans, his fair hair slicing around an angular face, occasional slivers of green glinting from his sea-glass eyes. Using some fancy foot rotation to slam the door behind him, he'd grab an upright chair, twirl it so it faced backwards and slide onto it without injuring his nethers. Then he'd sit, watching the group in narrowed-eyed silence, a muscle jumping in his jaw.

In the days when people still smoked, he'd produce a pack of cigarettes from where it hugged his bicep in the rolled-up sleeve of his T-shirt, then hit the box in some magic fashion, making a cigarette jump right into his mouth. A long match would appear from thin air, which he'd light with an angry rasp against a brick wall or the sole of his boot.

He was skilled at silence. A great man for brooding. He also majored on long, brazen stares if there was a woman he liked the look of.

We were all used to his rudeness. Only when someone met him for the first time did their visible shock remind us how obnoxious he was.

"Joey's barely been to M'town," Brigit said. "Until Queenie—" She stopped. She had to take a moment before she continued. "Until Queenie got sick, Colm and I answered questions, gave information to the locals, did all the communications. So, no, he's not customer-facing. But he's the glue holding the whole deal together."

Wow. Who would have ever thought it?

Brigit put a hand on the top of her head. "I feel like I'm dreaming," she remarked. "My little girl has cancer. That can't be right." Then, changing tone, "Anna, can you pack your stuff and leave now? Every minute that's passing, I'm freaking out more."

Yes, but . . . "We still haven't gotten the okay from Joey."

"It'll be fine."

No. This wouldn't happen unless he agreed. "Maybe call him?"

"I'll do it." Luke picked up his phone. "Armstrong?" He began to leave the room. "You get Brigit's text? What do you think? No, about Anna." His voice faded away.

Then he was back. "All good." He slipped his phone into his pocket, his gaze skittering away from mine. "He can't get there until six tomorrow evening but he's looking forward to working with you. He says he's on the same number as always."

Fine. I just needed to unblock it and we'd be back in business.

II

I'd first met Joey Armstrong over twenty years ago, in Manhattan, when I was clinging on to my last few months in Arrested Development.

For most of my twenties, my boyfriend Shane and I had moved from country to country, doing unskilled, seasonal work. Four summers in a row, we ran a bar in Santorini. Another summer was spent on a yacht in the Aegean, me as hostess/cleaner/fixer and Shane somehow passing himself off as the chef and captain.

In the offseason, we taught English in Madrid, did several stints in a canning factory in Munich and spent one grueling winter in the car plant in Turin.

The work was always tough and the money meager. But we were happy and adaptable, absolute marvels at landing into a new job, in a new location and gearing up *fast*. Our real reward was freedom. Knowing that we could just throw everything we possessed into a rucksack and leave with an hour's notice was exhilarating.

But around the time I turned twenty-eight, I sensed that the life I loved was about to abandon me. The physical work was exhausting, starting afresh *again* was no longer fun and being perpetually penniless was starting to scare me.

I was only in the US because Mum and Dad had sprung for my plane fare. They'd lured Helen and me along because, although they wouldn't admit it, they'd become nervous travelers. Fear of undertipping was top of the list, but what if they hailed a cab going uptown when they wanted to go downtown? Or missed out on the 10 percent tourist discount at Macy's?

No one turns down a trip to New York but Helen and I were extra pleased because we'd get a good gawk at Rachel's boyfriend, Luke Costello, whose sexiness was the stuff of legend.

Luke was one of the Real Men, a gang of Irish lads in Manhattan, who appeared to have time-traveled from the early seventies. Their hair was long, their jeans *tight* and Eddie Van Halen was their god. (Well, one of them. They had a few.)

Before Rachel had slept with Luke, she and Brigit had sneered most cruelly at him and his pals. But all that came to an abrupt halt when Rachel fell in love.

Luke was dark, smoking hot—and unexpectedly obliging. Not every boyfriend would be game for doing the touristy stuff Mum and Dad enjoyed: a musical on Broadway the first night, dinner in a cheesy deli in Times Square on the second.

The third night was in a bar, packed with friends of Rachel and Luke. The Real Men were the star attraction.

"Christ on a cracker," Mum muttered at the onslaught of crotchtasticness. "I need to go to confession."

I, who had always admired those who swam against the tide, was charmed. The Real Men loved what they loved and made no apologies. Who could fail to applaud a man who rocked leather jeans with totally unnecessary lacing down the sides? (Johnno.) Or who showed up in public in a denim jacket worn over a naked chest? (Shake. Naked apart from the dense carpet of caramel-colored curls which festooned his pecs. Shake's superpower was his hair, I was told. More than once.)

And they were so nice. Gaz, kitted out in a Black Sabbath singlet, his hair back-combed into a candyfloss ball, was *sweet*. Johnno was very funny. Shake, who'd initially seemed dickishly over-confident, quickly dropped the preen-y façade and we began talking hair-dryers.

During a lively discussion on the merits of leave-in conditioners, I noted the arrival of another Real Man, as tall as Luke. Unlike Gaz and the rest, the new arrival spurned statement clothing. His black jeans, barely hanging on his hip bones, were cut low. The sleeves of his white T-shirt were rolled all the way up to reveal sinew-y arms, multiple tats snaking their way up and around taut biceps. His fair, shoulder-length hair hung in his eyes. And, oh my God, his *mouth*.

This new man scanned the crowd, his gaze passing over me. For an atom of time the smooth sweep of his search seemed to falter, but recovered so quickly I decided I'd imagined it. He kept searching until he'd located Luke and moved towards him. There was a brusque man-hug, then, their heads close together, an intimate conversation followed, with lots of nods and the occasional flash of a smile.

They were Light and Dark. Except that the dark one—Luke—had such cheerful energy. And the man with the light hair and light-colored eyes was *dark*.

Whoever he was, he and Luke were tight.

I must stop staring. "Rachel." Blindly I reached out a hand to touch her. "Who is he?"

She flicked a glance across the bar. "Oh. Joey. He's Luke's best frie—" Then, "Oh my God, NO, Anna."

"What?"

She was laughing. "No, no, no, no, no! Joey's awful. He's angry, he breaks hearts and enjoys it."

"I only asked who he was."

Her look was sympathetic.

"If he's that bad, why is Luke mates with him?" I asked.

"A complicated, man-loyalty thing. It's really only women that Joey is mean to. Listen to me, for a while everyone thinks they fancy him. Then they sleep with him." She paused. "Or spend five minutes in his presence. And that's it." She drew a finger across her throat. "Game over. His nickname is Narky Joey. To be honest, we pity him."

"But, Rachel, his—"

"—mouth. I know. That's what they all say. Hey!" She seemed concerned. "What about Shane?"

How to put it into words? "Shane and I? I think we've . . . outgrown each other?"

"That's very sad," she said. "But Joey is not the answer."

She was wrong. But we could agree to disagree. Even though Rachel didn't know that that was what we were doing because I just smiled and said, "Yep." No need for unnecessary discord.

I got myself another drink and moved about the room, acting oh-so-sociable. But even without seeing Joey and his slinky snake-hips, I could have told you their precise location at all times. Pretending to be fun (just in case he was looking), I'd moved away, circling the place, talking to everyone. Finally I let myself start my return journey, approaching him from behind. On the edge of a booth, half in, half out, his back was towards me.

Just as I reached him, as if he had sensed me coming, he swiveled his entire body, so that his thigh blocked my path. I looked at the long, lean muscles and wanted to claw his jeans off.

"Hey." He looked up from under his hair. "Who are you?"

"Anna. Rachel's sister." Then, going for brazen, "Who are you?"

His lips pressed together, he took a moment. God above, the sculpted beauty of that mouth. "Joey." One of his front teeth was slightly chipped. I was *helpless*.

From behind me came a shock invasion—Helen. She stuck her head over my shoulder. "What's going on here?"

"Fuck." Joey's blink was followed by a long, slow smile. "There's *two* of you?"

"Nope," Helen said. "Only one. And it's me."

That was it. All over. I'd witnessed this shift countless times. Helen and I were the same height, build, hair, just about everything. But our energies were unimaginably different. I was on the timid-to-normal part of the scale whereas Helen operated way up at the other end, between unpredictable to terrifying. Most men, especially risk-takers, were wild about her. Joey and she were made for each other. Briefly, at least.

I swallowed back my devastation and, unnoticed, slunk away.

Ten minutes later, Helen seized my arm. "Stay with Rachel and Luke tonight. I need the hotel room."

"Joey?" My mix of jealousy and despair was awful.

"Joey, indeed." Helen smacked her lips together. "Very. Fucking. Sexy. Christ, the *mouth* on him."

The next day, when I was permitted to return, I wanted to know everything—and nothing.

"Joey in the sack? Not bad." But she wouldn't go into detail. "Get ready. Rachel and Brigit are taking us for brunch."

Over eggs Benedict, it was no surprise that the discussion turned to Joey.

"He was okay." Helen sounded cagey. She focused on Brigit. "You slept with him a couple of times. How was it?"

"Oh my God, are you joking? It's all about him," Brigit said. "I don't know what I was thinking of. Well." She seemed to be speaking to herself. "I was very drunk. That was the first time. And the second time was the next morning and I was so hungover I was incapable of caring. What about you?"

"I made him beg." Helen smirked. "That was funny." After a long pause she admitted, "Then it went to shit. You're right, Brigit. As soon as he stuck it in, I could have been just anyone. He was going like a train for thirty seconds, then it was all over. Like *all* over."

Rachel frowned. "But didn't he take care of you?"

"Nope," Helen said.

"Me neither," Brigit echoed.

"Nothing?" Rachel was shocked. Which said a lot about what getting it on the regular from Luke Costello must be like.

"All I got from him was, 'Your panties are on the floor. See ya,'" Brigit said.

"My story? He whips himself out of me, gets rid of the condom and starts throwing his clothes on," Helen said. "Couldn't get out of the room fast enough. Swear to God, it was less than two minutes from initial penetration to the hotel door closing behind him."

"He's probably the most selfish man I've ever slept with," Brigit said.

"Same." From Helen. "And such a waste because his dick is huge."

"Is it, though?" Brigit was thoughtful. "It didn't just seem gigantic because he's so skinny?"

"Nah. Massive."

"He's not skinny," I heard myself say. "He's *lean*."

"Oh." Helen was wide-eyed as understanding, then a hint of guilt, appeared. "Something you'd like to tell us, Anna?"

"No. Just . . ."

". . . the facts are important." Helen was trying to make things right. "Anna's correct. Lean not skinny. That's Joey."

12

Mum had loaned me her twenty-five-year-old Fiat Multipla, a car model which had won Ugliest Car of the Nineties. But it did the job, getting me to the outskirts of Galway city in two and a half hours. Keeping me company was a disembodied woman with a cut-glass accent reading a Barbara Vine novel.

After Galway, the roads gradually narrowed and once I was through Oughterard, the landscape went full-on desolate. A thin line of black tarmac, with faded white road markings, twisted its way through rough grass and rocky, uneven ground.

On my right side, hills began to appear. Eventually, they became mountains, monsters of gray stone, appearing semi-covered with green moth-eaten blankets.

Above it all, a huge parchment sky soared. Suddenly only Sigur Rós would do: the expansive, poignant chords were perfect for this lonely grandeur.

Occasional bursts of silver light flashed from the land—small pools, I realized. Then a proper lake appeared, the water the same pale blue as huskies' eyes, so still that the nearby gray-green mountains were reflected perfectly in the surface.

A sudden longing to hire a camper van struck me. To just get in and drive forever with . . . my automatic thought was Angelo. For a split second I'd forgotten we were over.

It was a break-up like none other I'd had. When Shane and I had ended I'd been devastated. (I believe he lives in Thailand and has a pilot's licence now. Godspeed. I wish him nothing but the best.) The great love of my life, Aidan, was killed in a car accident; we'd only been married for ten months. It was years before I was halfway normal again. I'd sincerely thought that love was off the cards forever, but along came Angelo, and offered me exactly what I needed.

Now that was over, but he was okay and I was okay. So, I'd go off in my imaginary camper van with myself.

A black and white signpost appeared, the first evidence of civilization in ages: Maumtully was only twelve kilometers away. My stomach clenched. But I was able to do this. Yes, I was. I was an adult and a professional, I'd faced down worse.

At the final fork in the road before Maumtully, I veered off onto a finger of land which eventually led to the ocean. A quick detour to visit Colm was in order.

I bumped down a narrow track, until, without warning, a sharp turn revealed the most beautiful house in the world. Made from glass, blue slate, and stones in every color of gray from lead to silver, I had to swallow hard.

At the sound of my car, a lanky young man came into the yard: Brigit's eldest son, Lenehan.

"Anna?" His Adam's apple bobbed up and down. "How was your journey?" He was twenty but his freckled skin looked as soft as a peach.

"I'm so sorry about Queenie." I wanted to squeeze him.

"It's bad, all right. Thanks . . . Would you like a tea? No? Okay. Jump in the jeep there, I'll take you up to the site."

"I'll just say hi to Colm first."

"Oh. Ah. Sure . . . He's round the back."

My time in New York had overlapped with Colm's by a couple of years. Even though he was the nicest, most open person, I'd been in awe. He was one of those rare types who made things happen. He and his roommates Travis and Otto ran once-a-month club nights which felt like the best house parties ever, where the playlist was always an unsnobby delight, geared towards making people dance rather than showcasing the DJ's directional credentials. For four years in a row, it was on the Ten Best Clubs in New York.

The trio were always going to go on and do big things. Travis opened his first private members' club maybe fifteen years ago. Casa now had twelve outposts, spanning the globe from São Paulo to Sydney. Mumbai was the latest. Otto, a "lighting guru," choreographed light shows for stadium tours. Colm, working in IT, living in Connemara with his wife and four children seemed—at least on paper—like the underachiever. But look at him now, with his feathery-strokery retreat.

Despite the different directions they'd chosen, the three men still worked together. Colm did "consultancy" for Travis, where he, Brigit and their children visited his latest property and in return for a free holiday, gave their feedback. It was probably in Casa Mumbai that Brigit had got her yellow rubber clogs.

At the rear of the house, sitting on steps and staring at nothing, was Colm. He looked stunned to see me. "Anna . . ."

Shocked, I stopped. Even though I'd been warned, I'd still expected charming, chatty Colm, with his messy glamour.

This poor man was gray and defeated.

I hugged him. "I'm so sorry about Queenie."

"And I'm sorry I'm so fucking useless. Are you here because of the carry-on with the paint?"

"Yes. Lenehan and I, we'll head over to the site and . . ." There was nothing to be gained from lingering here, making small talk with a man who wasn't capable.

Colm nodded and resumed his sightless staring.

God love him. And poor Lenehan too—he was only twenty, this was a *lot*.

"Ree!" Lenehan called to a teenage boy, aged about fifteen, in the kitchen, staring at a screen. "Say hi to Anna."

Ree smiled. "Hi to Anna."

There was another brother, a year younger than Lenehan. "Sully? Is he around?"

"In Bolivia. 'Preserving wetlands.' That's the cover story anyway. More like partying his head off." Lenehan's smile trembled.

After a short, bumpy drive through a landscape which looked as if it had been ripped apart, then thrown carelessly back together, Lenehan spoke. "The damage in the cottages. It looks worse than it is."

He was trying to convince himself more than me. "A forklift was stolen. So were lots of pipes and timber. And they put sand in the tank of the digger."

"That's . . . bad, is it?"

"The engine will seize up if they try using it. It can be fixed but it'll be out of action for a while. Hold on." He was out of the jeep and squeaking open a five-bar gate. We rattled over a cattle grid.

"We're officially on site now," he said. "This is the old farm."

Surrounding us were a thousand different greens—scrub, moss and grass—punctuated by vivid clumps of wild daffodils.

"Is that the only gate?" I asked.

"Should we get more?" He was so anxious. "Or a padlock?"

"No, no, nothing like that, we're going to fix this. So that's the main building?" A large farmhouse was being given the glass-and-gray-stone treatment.

"Granny and Grandad's old house," Lenehan said. "Where they'll have the communal stuff like the yoga studio."

I jumped from the jeep into a yard that was half mud, half concrete. Stacks of blocks, bags of cement and coils of wire were scattered about.

"This is the broken digger." Lenehan indicated a tall orange machine, a can of Monster Energy still in the cup-holder. "Tipper Mahon, he's the foreman, he'll take it into Galway."

"Oh!" I'd just spotted the first cottage. Cleverly situated in some sort of sneaky hollow, it was almost invisible.

As my eyes adjusted, I noticed one more. Then another. A virtue had been made of the rocky, uneven ground, so each cottage had exceptional privacy. This set-up became more impressive the more I looked. Much bigger than I'd imagined. I loved how the original landscape had barely been disturbed: a lot of care had been taken.

"How many cottages are there?"

"Sixteen. Most of them sleep two, but at the far end there" —Lenehan pointed into the distance— "There's a two-bedroomed place, then one with three bedrooms. At the other end of the site we'll have the spa."

"It's much bigger than I'd expected."

"The retreat covers thirty acres. Then another twenty acres of no-man's-land for privacy. Fifty acres." To my uncomprehending face, he said, "Think of fifty football pitches."

Again, not my area: I'd zero interest in football. But it sounded big.

"We'll go over to that one." Lenehan led me to a cottage that was structurally complete; even the planks for the roof were in place.

As we crested a hillock, the sea suddenly appeared. "Oh, look!" Shallow green water, so clear the pale sand at the bottom was visible, bordered by a perfect sickle of pristine beach. If it had been ten degrees warmer we could have been in the Caribbean.

"Are there islands out there?" I exclaimed.

"Just rocks, really." But he smiled. "You can swim out to them."

"Is that . . . ?" Had I seen movement?

"Dolphins? Yeah. They're always here."

So there really were dolphins in Dolphin Cove? This place was *perfect*.

Up close, the cottage was just a concrete shell and roof beams. "So." Lenehan led me into one of the rooms. Abruptly I stopped, shocked rigid. Ropes of bright red slashed the floors and interior walls. It was only paint but it looked more like blood.

"There's no actual damage," Lenehan reminded me.

"Yes. Yep. Absolutely." I cleared my throat. "Did they do all the cottages?"

"Ah no. Only four," he said. "But we need to talk to them."

"Any idea who 'them' is?"

"No." He looked very young. "Not a clue."

"Don't worry. We'll sort it all out. I'll head into town now. Call me if you need, you know, anything."

"Sure." That Adam's apple again. I wanted to hug this poor boy until it hurt.

As we walked back to the jeep, a pickup truck came hurtling towards us, stopping with about an inch to spare. A man leapt from the cab, all sharp eyes and a bushy, black beard. "Tipper Mahon." He strode towards me. "Site foreman. You must be the woman down from Dublin."

"Anna Walsh."

"My brother, Hal." Tipper indicated a second man, a younger, skinnier version of himself.

Grinning widely, Hal loped forward, his energy somewhat untethered. The font of ancient wisdom which lived deep in my psyche cautioned strongly against ever getting drinks with this man. There would be some sort of "incident." Perhaps involving an electric scooter. Or a rabbit. Or stolen wetsuits.

But my inner seventeen-year-old who liked "spontaneous' and "mildly illegal" knew he'd be so much *fun*.

Tipper yanked his thumb at a third beardy man. "That's Declan Erskine."

Declan saluted me. Literally saluted.

"We're bringing Betsey into Galway," Tipper said.

"Betsey?"

"This brave lady here." Tipper patted the side of the orange digger (boasting a sticker with the legend "Diggers do it standing up").

"I'm sure this is hard for you all," I said. "You've done beautiful work and to have it vandalized . . ."

Tipper clenched his jaw and stared over my head. "A shock all right."

"Who do you think might have done it?"

Coughing out words, as if they were loose teeth, Tipper managed, "Some bad bastards."

"That's for sure." I watched Hal and Declan let down a ramp at the back of their truck, then attach ropes to the wounded digger. "But have you any idea who they actually are?"

"Not a one and I wish I did. I'm sorry for young Lenehan here and all the Kearneys. But it's hard on me and my crew too. No pay till it's all sorted."

Oh no, this was bad.

"We've wives and children," Declan said.

"In all honesty, I've neither," Hal called. "But there's other expenses. I'm hopeless with money . . ."

Right. This had to be my first suggestion to Joey. "Lads, I can't promise, but I'll do my best to make sure you're paid for the stoppage time."

The three men seemed extremely surprised. "Well, now . . . that's very decent. What did you say your name was, again? Anna? Anna Walsh? That's a name we'll remember."

"I can't promise," I repeated. "But I'll try."

13

Back on the main road, the route hugged the Atlantic, revealing a muscular expanse of green-gray water, stretching to a far-off horizon. Closer to shore, waves rose and crashed, then fizzed out, flinging swathes of white lace onto the pale sand. A few surfers were out there—hardy creatures. By which I mean lunatics. You wouldn't catch me at it, not at this time of year.

A sharp turn had me driving inland, to the town. I half expected jeering crowds to be lining the roads, armed with cans of red paint. But nothing to report.

Dominating Main Street was the Broderick, the town's only proper hotel. An institution, according to Brigit, it boasted a function room, a fifties-style diner and a bridal suite.

It was a good idea to be right in the thick of things. If I'd stayed in Brigit and Colm's Airbnb, I'd seem aligned with them, instead of being "a neutral presence." It also meant that if anyone needed to speak with me, I'd be right on the spot.

I pulled up outside the hotel, then discovered I was in an actual parking place. How about that for luck!

But that was because it was only March. Maumtully's permanent population was tiny but apparently, from Easter onwards, the tourists swelled the numbers to approximately eighteen million.

The reception desk at the Broderick was deserted. A small, silver-nickel dome sat on the mahogany counter but it was only for foreign tourists. If I "binged" it to summon the receptionist, as soon as they discovered I was Irish, I'd be flagged as entitled.

There was nobody around, so I continued to sneak looks at the bell. No. It was better to just wait it out. After a while a woman in a navy skirt suit zipped past, all business, carrying a tray of drinks. "I'll be with you in two ticks."

Within seconds, she was sliding behind the counter. "I'm Courtney Burke. How may I help?"

"Can I check in?" I asked. "My name's Anna Walsh."

Speedily she clicked, watching her screen, giving off highly efficient vibes, from the top of her short brown hair to the tips of her comfortable block heels. "There you are. Seven nights, is that right? No need for a credit card, all your expenses are covered by Mr Joseph Armstrong."

This was a relief. After Luke said the investor funds had been frozen, I'd been unsure about who was paying for what.

Courtney looked up and smiled. "You might as well order yourself a magnum of Moët, so." She whipped a key from a row of hooks and grabbed my suitcase. "Room Seventeen. Let's go."

"There's no need." I was embarrassed by another woman carrying my bag. I tried to wrest it from her but she was as strong as she was efficient. "And I can find my own way."

"I can promise you now you most certainly can't." She flashed another smile and we were off. Up a flight of stairs, down a short corridor, through a fire door, up a half-flight of stairs then along a hallway. The hotel was bigger than it looked from outside, going back, around and up for a long way.

"Minnie Driver slept in that room there." Courtney kept up a stream of chat. "When she was here for the Good Thinking Festival. So did that man who wrote that book. But not at the same time. Right, here's yours. It's just been redecorated, en suite and all."

She swung the door open to reveal a bland space boasting a double bed, a faded painting of a stag and a window offering a view of the bottle bins. The bathroom was a nice surprise: pretty tiling and a second window.

Courtney stepped in behind me and clicked a switch, illuminating a round mirror. "A magnifying makeup mirror. My idea. Trying to make the place more women-friendly. Although you'd swear I was asking for the Atlantic Ocean to be dyed pink." She shook her head. "Moving on, the minibar's complimentary." She rattled it open. "Because there's nothing in it except water and Sprite."

No complaints from me. I'd much prefer a basic minibar to the flavored lube and multi-packs of condoms you got in newly opened, black-lacquered hotels. I hated the assumptions implicit in those wares. Like, *Oh yeah, you're so cool, we're so cool, all of us groovy fuckers, having nonstop sex, hey, we get it.*

Because what if you didn't want to have sex? What if you and your partner hadn't even touched each other in two months? And if you were honest with yourself, it was more like five months. Or perhaps eleven or twelve.

Something on Courtney's person beeped. "I've to go. If you need anything, ring zero for reception. Although no one will be there." She flashed a smile. Then it was just me and the stag.

Too much had happened today and I was still catching up with myself. I'd woken in mild despair in suburban Dublin; five hours later, I was in an unfamiliar town in Connemara, having committed to a job that was daunting the daylights out of me. So far I'd kept ahead of the sheer unlikeliness of pulling it off, but now the full fear of failing hit me. This wasn't just professional, it was personal: I *cared* about Brigit, Colm, Queenie, all the Kearneys. I was powerless in the face of Queenie's terrifying diagnosis. The only way I could help was to try my best to tidy up this mess.

It was five twenty. Even though I might crash and burn spectacularly, I had to give this a go. So, I'd better find—who had Brigit said?—Ziryan in the hardware store and Ferne O'dowd in a knitwear shop.

My case overflowed with a smash-and-grab selection of "relatable." I threw on jeans, a hoodie and a pair of Converse which sported a small but much-appreciated platform sole. Next came tinted moisturizer, cream blush and pink-tinted gloss, then I gathered my hair up into a ponytail. Perky, I'm sorry to say, because the unpalatable truth is that the world is more likely to reward Attractive People. And I was somewhat at a disadvantage: a scar ran the length of my right cheek.

Over the years it had faded. It was only when I met someone new that I remembered, because they couldn't stop sneaking glances. In one big way it was actually useful—it distinguished me from Helen. We were both short and slight, pale-skinned and dark-haired; until I'd acquired the scar, there were times we'd actually been mistaken for each other. Helen, a person of singular frankness, made enemies with ease—which could lead to awkwardness. There was a time I was asked to leave a funeral because Helen had offended the widow some months previously; on another occasion a glass of Pimm's was yanked from my hand at a summer fundraiser because Helen had flirted madly with the yanker's husband at some other do.

Protesting that I wasn't Helen but an entire other person had never worked. But once my face was marked, well, all of that changed! So you could call it a positive. (Claire had once described me as an Instagram platitude made flesh. Which is a terrible thing to say. But we all have our ways of making the unbearable bearable and I'd prefer a positive spin than a negative.)

Into the mirror, I said, "I am nice. I am on your side. You can trust me." And I believed myself. I lacked the characteristic weapons-grade confidence of your average PR. Surprisingly this often worked in my favor because people forgot to be suspicious of me.

Reluctantly, I eschewed my beautiful, warm puffer coat in favor of an anonymous navy anorak I'd borrowed from Margaret and went downstairs.

14

Courtney was restocking bottles in the lounge, an expanse of sofas, armchairs and low stools.

"Which way is Ferne O'dowd's sweater shop?" I asked. "Or the hardware store?"

"You going down the town to talk to people?"

News traveled fast around here. "You know about the damage out at Kearney's Farm?"

"I do, yes." There was definitely sympathy in her. "What's the latest on Queenie?"

"You know she's been diagnosed with—"

"I do. I do. Terrible news. If you're talking to Brigit or Colm, tell them I was asking for them. Right, so. The hardware place is straight across the road. And Ferne is just up beyond the monument. Fine Irish Knits is the shop."

"Grand. Thanks."

Unexpectedly—because this was a solid town, not a flimsy seaside set-up—the air smelt like waves and water and childhood holidays.

In Hegarty's Hardware, the man in the blue work coat looked neither young nor talkative. It was unlikely this was Ziryan.

Nevertheless I smiled. "Lovely day."

Not-Ziryan watched me with curiosity. Obviously I didn't look like I was there to purchase a spanner.

"Would you be Ziryan?" I asked.

"I'm Ralph. Ziryan will be in on Monday."

That was too long away. I smiled even harder. "My name is Anna Walsh, I'm a friend of Brigit—"

"I don't want to get involved."

"I understand. Of course." But I kept talking. "Brigit and Colm know they've upset people. They'd like to make things right."

"Personally I've nothing against what they're doing up there."

"Good. Good."

"But they've gone about it all wrong. It's not Brigit's fault, she isn't from here. But Colm knows how things are done."

"Is there anything in particular . . . ?"

Ralph gave the far wall a hard considering stare, then swung his gaze back to me. "Look. The Skeretts have leased that three acres of Kearney land going back a good sixty or seventy years. All of a sudden the Yellow Meadow is to be fenced off and Aber Skerett's sheep will have no place to graze." For a man who hadn't wanted to get involved, my new friend had become quite chatty. "For 'privacy,' they're saying. Like any of Aber Skerett's twenty sheep would be ringing the papers."

I hadn't known about this. No wonder people were pissed off. ". . . Is there more?"

"They want to block the right of way to the beach."

Oh God, no. "This is news to me, Ralph. Could you fill me in?"

"There's been a shortcut on the Kearney land from the Galway road to Silver Strand as far back as I can remember, and I'm nearly seventy. But someone said they're blocking it off."

Delicately I asked, "Would you be able to tell me who that someone is?" In a rush, I added, "I won't say it came from you."

"I can't remember and I'm being straight with you. How's Queenie?"

"Do you know she was diagnos—"

"I do. That's desperate. I'm sorry for them all." After a pause he said, "Maybe you should talk to Ike Blakely."

"Who is he? Any idea where I might find him?"

"Often in McMunn's this time of a Saturday. Big fella. Beard. But once he hears you're in town asking questions, I'd say he'll make it his business to find you."

Well, that didn't sound alarming at all.

I wanted to know more about this Ike Blakely, but I couldn't bother Brigit or Colm, so I tried Lenehan.

"Ike Blakely?" I asked. "What's he like?"

"Just a guy. I don't *know* him. I think he's a tree surgeon. Maybe does stuff with the nature reserve? He's, ah . . . yeah, I don't really know."

I stifled my frustration. Lenehan was a child, basically 90 percent Adam's apple. It wasn't fair to press him. "Okay. Thanks. All fine."

Why didn't I just go straight to McMunn's, wherever that was?

Further along Main Street, it transpired, claiming to be a Lounge Bar and Purveyor of Spirits. I pushed the door open and, in the hazy amber light, everyone looked up. Mortified by the hush, I crossed the swirly carpet to the bar, holding on *hard* to my manufactured smile. A few solitary older gents were dotted around the room; they had the look of career drinkers. But a gang of younger men was clustered at a circular table. My arrival had interrupted a lively discussion, the ragged edges of it still hanging in the air. One of the men was half a head taller than the others. He and I locked eyes.

The barman's face was a picture of glee, as if anticipating drama. This was a worry. "What can I get you?" he asked.

I'd been planning to go with water. "A gin and tonic."

"What sort of gin?"

For a moment I almost engaged, then, in the nick of time, checked myself. "Anything. The cheaper the better."

"We've a homemade batch in a tin bath out the back."

This was probably a joke. "Lovely."

A man appeared at my side, the tall one, all biceps, bulk and beard. "Visiting for the weekend?"

I made an extra effort with my smile. "My name is Anna. Anna Walsh. I'm a friend of Brigit and Colm's."

He shook his head. "That didn't take long."

Had Not-Ziryan called ahead? ". . . Are you . . . Ike Blakely?"

"Yep."

"You've been expecting me?" My tone was friendly.

He just shrugged. "Small town. News travels fast."

It was hard to pin down his age. Late thirties? Something in his forties?

Just as confounding was his vibe. He didn't seem unfriendly. Not exactly friendly, either. Cagey was probably the best word.

He wore workman's trousers and some sort of utility shirt. His dark brown hair was cut very close to his head.

"So you know what happened out there last night?" I asked.

"I do, yeah."

A rap on the wooden counter heralded the arrival of my suspect gin and tonic. Ike Blakely was already reaching for it. "I've got this." The knuckles on his right hand were bruised and one of them was cut.

"No—"

He communicated some silent command to the barman, then told me, "I'm buying you a drink."

"Okay." I'd been told he was the person to talk to, so I might as well. "I'll get the next one."

He steered me to a corner table, equidistant between two of the dedicated solo artists.

"So?" he asked. "You're here—why?"

The deep crease between his brown eyes made him look as if he was frowning. Or worried, perhaps. He reminded me of a beleaguered teddy bear, one who had seen the worst of human nature.

"Brigit and Colm want to make things right," I said. "But Queenie is very sick, so I'm here on their behalf."

He nodded. "She's a great kid."

"You know her?"

"I do stuff with the school. Take them on biodiversity trips to the reserve in Derryclare." His eyes kept flickering towards the scar on my face.

"A bar fight in Guadalajara," I said.

He looked embarrassed. I wished he'd just asked me about it. If a person couldn't ignore it—and nobody could—a series of furtive glances created more awkwardness than a straightforward question.

"I'm in town to hear people's concerns."

"Look now. No one here objects to anyone making money. But removing ancient rights of way, demolishing a famine memorial—"

"Wait, *what*? I didn't know about that. God." I pressed my hand to my forehead. "There's been some breakdown in communication." Poor Brigit must have lost *all* interest. "Listen, is there any chance you could spare me your time and fill me in on the issues?"

"I'm no one's mouthpiece." He sounded angry. Or perhaps worried?

So why had Hardware Ralph sent me here? Just to get rid of me?

"Ask around if you want to know why people are upset. Then hold an open meeting. Have someone there to listen—you, if you're all that's available."

Oh now! There was no need for that.

"Hold it there, I'm not just Brigit's friend, I'm—" I stopped. The last thing I should do was boast about my New York glory years.

A public meeting was exactly what I'd promised Brigit when I'd been flinging panicky solutions around—but I'd forgotten. Brain fog, courtesy of my age-related hormone shortage. It frightened me every time it happened. Maybe I could see a doctor here in Maumtully?

First, though, I had to focus on the work. Where would I hold this meeting? And when? However, I'd rather nail my tongue to the table than ask this man. Instead, I'd sound out Courtney, if she was still on duty.

"A public meeting." I stood up. "Thanks. I'll do that. Before I go, what can I get you to drink?"

"You're leaving already?"

"I've a meeting to organize."

"Then you can get me back another time."

"Will do." My smile was as tight as a cat's bum.

"Aren't you going to ask if I know who did the damage?"

I stared down at him, the smug fucker. "Do you know?"

"Like I said, this is a small place." He lounged in his chair, his head tilted back, holding my gaze.

Most of the time, it astounded me that I was a woman in her late forties: I felt *decades* younger. But now and again, all the living I'd done let me know when I was being toyed with. Maybe Ike Blakely knew who'd vandalized Kearney's Farm. But he wasn't about to tell me.

Not yet, anyway.

I made for the door, feeling his eyes on me the whole time.

15

"Far as I know the parish hall's empty tomorrow night," Courtney said.

But tomorrow night seemed too soon. News spread quickly here, that was obvious, but was twenty-four hours enough time to let everyone know? More to the point, *I* wasn't ready. I'd got no real sense of the place yet. "Monday would be better."

"It's Zumba on Monday. Tuesday is Living Well with Dementia. AA on Wednesday. Thursday is usually free but we've the Paddy's Day stuff starting then."

"What about here? In the hotel? You've a function room?"

"And a meeting room." Courtney paused. "Not telling you how to do your job, but the function room would be too big. A get-together about Kearney's Farm, you'd be looking at fifty or sixty people. I've a lovely space for you. All geared up with microphones and a dais. We could do biscuits, tea and coffee. It's often booked for funerals of townspeople who weren't highly regarded."

I had no choice but to trust her. She seemed to know more about my business than I did and she certainly knew more about Maumtully.

"And the cost?"

"Don't worry about that," she said. "Mr Joseph Armstrong's credit card will cover it."

Something about the way she kept referring to Joey and his line of credit made me ask, "Have you met him?"

"I have." She smirked. "He's quite the go-boy."

Go-boy. I didn't know that phrase.

"Monday night it is," I said. "What time?"

"Seven thirty. So you'll want to get the word out?" She was ahead of me at every step. "Write something on your laptop and I'll put it on the socials. If you want, I'll print you out a bundle of flyers. You can distribute them before half-eleven mass tomorrow."

"Okay! Thanks."

In the deserted lounge, I had a toasted sandwich and another gin and tonic and tried to compose a notice, using phrases like: "Everyone welcome," "Refreshments provided," "No concern too small."

Terrified of coming across as patronizing, I agonized over the wording, typing, deleting, then staring motionless at the screen.

Courtney looked over my shoulder. "Don't make a meal of it. Just say it out straight and I'll stick it up on Facebook."

My phone rang—Mum. "Have you arrived?" she asked. "Is the hotel nice? I hear Narky Joey's paying for it. If we come down for the weekend, can we bunk in with you?"

"Who's 'we'?" I asked. Then, "*No*. I'm working. And I'm leaving Saturday."

"Myself and Helen. Maybe Regan. Your father, if you think there's space. And maybe Margaret. We're thinking of staying till Monday. They've a funfair and a ceili."

"Mum," I said. "I'm begging you. Please don't come." I hung up and rang Helen. "Do you know about Mum coming here for the weekend?"

"Yeah! Me, Mum, Dad, Regan, Artie and My Best Friend Bella Devlin."

Artie was Helen's partner and Bella Devlin was his twenty-year-old daughter with his ex-wife.

"Margaret, Garv, Holly and JJ are also in!"

"Helen, no. Absolutely not. I'm here to work." Frustration made me loud. "And you cannot bunk in with me, my room is *tiny*."

"Hardly tiny." Courtney just happened to be breezing past. "You got a free upgrade to a double deluxe. Remind me to show you a classic single, if it's tiny you want to see."

After a muffled shriek, Mum's voice was in my ear. "I heard all that, I'm here with Helen. So there's plenty of space for us in the room that Joey is paying for? But you'd deprive your impoverished mother of a weekend in the west?"

"You have more money than Jeff Bezos," I said. "Pay for your own mini-break. But please don't come."

As soon as I hung up, I signalled the barman for another drink, then looked up "go-boy." According to the Urban Dictionary, he was: "Generally, a swagged-out gentleman that gets all the bitches, has hella benjamins & wears the best clothes."

Benjamins were hundred-dollar bills. Right, so that was Joey these days.

Courtney was back, with a cardboard box, a roll of Sellotape and a pair of scissors. "Some will be too shy to say their worries out loud in the meeting, so we'll make a suggestion box and stick it on the counter out front."

"It's nearly nine o'clock," I realized. "Are you staying late just to help me out?"

"My shift ended at eight, but we might as well finish the job."

"Should I put my phone number on the flyer?" I was halfway through my latest drink and feeling increasingly cheerful.

"Do." Courtney was thoughtful. "If you want every man within a fifty-mile radius to bombard you with pictures of their mickey."

That made me laugh far, far too much. I decided I might be in love with Courtney. Or mildly drunk.

"Give them an email address. Like . . . Kearneysfarm@gmail.com?"

Yes! Hadn't I suggested the *very* same thing to Brigit? Courtney and I were clearly twin flames.

"But shouldn't it be dolphincove@gmail.com?"

"Hah! If you put Dolphin Cove no one would have a clue what you were on about. Stick with Kearney's Farm. Go on, add it to the flyer and I'll print out a hundred of them."

"Can I buy you a drink?"

"Shur, go on." She called up the underworked barman. "Glass of Merlot."

Because we were literally the only people there, it arrived almost immediately. "Good man, Emilien," she said. "Anna, this is Emilien. He's from Mauritius. God alone knows what he's doing in this fecking place."

"Lovely to meet you," I exclaimed, to the kind, *kind* man who'd been looking after me. "You remind me of my dad!"

With a sharp look, Courtney asked, "How many drinks have you had?"

"But much younger," I told Emilien, realizing he was barely thirty. "Sorry if I offended you."

"Ah, you're fine."

"Poor divil came one summer for the work," Courtney said. "Then fell in love with Aoife Gallowglass from out the Shore Road. They're married now, so he's stuck here."

"Yep. My life is ruined."

Courtney took a sip of her wine. "God, that's lovely." She focused on me. "Tell me to hump off and mind my own business and sorry for being personal but what happened to your face?"

You see, *this* was how it should be done. No suffocating build-up of unasked and unanswered questions.

"Car crash. It was a long time ago." Because she'd been so obliging, she deserved the full story. "I got off lightly. My husband died. Aidan. We'd been married less than a year."

Her shock seemed sincere. "That's a terrible thing. A terrible, terrible loss."

"It was sixteen years ago."

"My mother is dead nineteen years and I still miss her. Again, tell me to mind my own business but has it got easier for you?"

For a long time I couldn't have said that: losing Aidan had destroyed me. Looking back, it was clear that during the three or so years afterwards, I'd been off my rocker—dogged by guilt that I had survived and he had died. Torn between wanting to grab every bit of living available and feeling that I should have died too.

I'd been told that when enough healing had happened I'd be able to let Aidan go. Instead, I held him more tightly. So close that along the way he became part of me, absorbed into my cells.

A morning came when he wasn't my first thought when I woke up. His loss remained an ever-present noise, but slowly it dialed down until eventually the inconceivable happened and entire days passed without thinking about him.

Although it was still enormous, his death had stopped being the defining event of my life. Time had set me free.

"He's always with me." Momentarily I considered confiding in her about the butterfly, then stopped myself. "The memories don't hurt now. I just feel bad for him that his life was cut short."

I was also able to acknowledge that Aidan and I could have gone the way so many other couples had: ten, maybe twelve good years before things went off the rails.

He could have turned into your run-of-the-mill cheater. Or I could have. Perhaps we could have done a lockdown curdle, the way Angelo and I had? There were many ways our story could have played out, not all of them happy.

Courtney gestured to Emilien. "Another, good man." Then, to me, "And . . . ah, did you ever meet someone else? Was it as good?"

I'd thought the real me had died when Aidan had. That if I ever cared about another man, it would be a pale imitation of love, assembled from the broken bits of me that remained.

But I no longer thought I was living a consolation life: this was the one I'd always been meant to live.

"I met another man—Angelo—and we fell in love. We had our ups and downs but we were very happy." It was miraculous really. "But we broke up during lockdown."

Courtney nodded with sympathy. "Ah, shur. That's a shame." Then, "Before I forget, breakfast's between eight and ten. No room service, because it's the offseason. But you can come down in your PJs, take whatever you want and bring it back to the room. And stick a couple of bananas in your pocket for your lunch, no one minds. Tell me, is that your real hair or is it extensions?"

"Extensions?! How many drinks have *you* had? The *state* of my hair."

She leant back to inspect me. "It's lovely, you madwoman. Don't you mind it being long?"

It was only long because I'd been too depressed to get it cut. *Or* colored. The chestnut-colored gloss I favored was a distant memory.

Courtney said, "I used to have hair down to my waist. Well, not my *waist*. You hear that a lot: 'hair down to my waist.' It wasn't. But it was below my shoulder blades. The upkeep was like a second job. Day I got it all cut off was a great one." She smacked her lips together. "So you were out on the site earlier? Who was there?"

"Apart from the Kearneys, you mean? The foreman Tipper Mahon, his brother—was it Hal? And another man."

"Declan Erskine? Nice quiet fella. Couldn't say the same about poor Hal."

"He seemed a little . . . *lively*?"

"Wild out. Some unasked-for advice, Anna: if Hal invites you for a drink, and chances are he will, make an excuse. Before you know it you'll be dancing in your pelt in a thunderstorm above on the cliffs, swigging magnums of port." Her look was assessing. "Unless that's your idea of a good time, in which case, work away. There's no badness in Hal, not at all, he's just a bit . . . what was your word? Lively. Easily led. He should probably be on tablets, poor divil. Anyway, I heard you met Ike Blakely today."

"Who told you?"

"The barman in McMunn's? He's my dad."

Who? The gleeful one?

"I know. His nickname is Grinner McGee. He's not as delighted as he looks, that's just the way his face is, he has a condition. Poor Dad," Courtney said. "Anyway, what did you think of Ike?"

I shook my head. "I don't know what to make of him."

She clenched her jaw. "I know what I'd make of him, if I was given the chance."

That started me laughing again.

"He's a snack," she said.

"He's too big to be a snack, more like a four-course dinner."

"That works for me."

In the midst of our bonding laughter I wondered if she'd help me get an appointment?

"Is it illegal?" she asked. "Whatever it is you're going to ask me?"

". . . No. I just want—Any chance you could get me an appointment with a local doctor?"

"Is that all? I was afraid you wanted to break into Ben's mansion. The number of *Portal* obsessives who turn up here to pester him . . . The poor man. He makes a film, it wins an Oscar—to be honest, it was too convoluted for me, multiverses aren't my thing—"

· "I *adored* it. The multiverses aren't the point, it's a love story . . . Have you—"

"Met him? Bitch, I run this town."

I snort-laughed and Courtney grinned. "There's only one man in this town I fancy more than Ike Blakely and that's Ben Mendoza. Beautiful eyes and he comes across as normal. You'd never know all that stuff went on in his head. Tell me, what's wrong with your GP in Dublin?"

"I don't have one. I lived in New York until October. I've tried to register with a GP but they're all full. Thousands of them resigned after the pandemic."

"And what ails you?"

"The menopause."

Shocked, she inhaled sharply, then glanced around the lounge.

"It's okay," I said. "Nothing terrible happens if the word is said out loud. To be accurate, Courtney, it's the perimenopause that ails me but no one seems to know what that is. 'Menopause' gives the gist."

"It sure does. But you don't look like you're about to break every plate in the place."

"Because I'm on HRT. Well, I was, but it's nearly all gone, I've been on reduced rations for the past couple of months and the situation is defcon two. Any day now I won't be able to remember my own name. Is there a woman doctor in town?"

"Leave it with me. I'll see what I can do."

16

I fell into a deep sleep, only to be woken at some ungodly hour by cascades of bottles being thrown into the bin beneath my window. Oh, *please*. I grabbed my phone to see the time—twenty past twelve. I'd been asleep for a mere forty minutes.

Yanking back the curtain, the apologetic face of Emilien was looking up. "Sorry," he called. "I tried to do it quietly."

"Ah-haha." I faked an absence of fury, as etiquette insisted. "No bother at all. I was awake anyway . . ."

Now I really *was* awake. Long after the bottle-smashing ceased, I lay staring at nothing, unable to resist all my dark truths.

Relocating to Ireland had seemed like a great idea until I'd actually got here. Everyone else my age seemed anchored by proof of their time on this earth: long marriages; children, even grandchildren; homes with attic conversions; pension plans. They had good neighbors, a shared postman, a street WhatsApp group. They'd paid off their mortgages, could recommend bakers for special birthday cakes, and had the comfort of knowing their place in the world.

I'd spent my life terrified of being trapped; suddenly I saw the value in stopping and growing roots. It was too late now. I'd achieved nothing, accumulated nothing. As insubstantial as a wisp, I could blow away and land anywhere.

As the night ticked by, my head remained defiantly active—but I would not check the time! It was hard to know if this was menopausal insomnia or mid-life-crisis insomnia and perhaps, when the outcome was the same, it didn't matter. But too many of the symptoms that had plagued me before I'd started HRT were back—not just insomnia, but night sweats, brain fog and bouts of rage.

To soothe myself, I thought about how great life would be when Courtney came good with a sympathetic doctor and I was back on the meds again. Eventually I got back to sleep. It was probably no surprise I dreamed about Jacqui.

"A cailíní, this is Jacqui Staniforth," Sister Xavier said.

Twenty fourteen-year-olds presented blank faces to the super-tall newcomer.

"Who's this freak?" Hazel Dwyer said, loudly enough to generate covert sniggers.

My heart hurt for the new arrival. But she smiled, revealing a mouthful of retainers. "Hi."

As one body, my classmates recoiled. Confidence? No! New arrivals had to act painfully shy, blooming into their best self only under the warm attention of the class stars. Barging right in, already socialized, broke all the rules.

"Sit there." Sister Xavier pointed to the empty place beside poor Hilary Dole. Thanks to her port-wine birthmark, Hilary was invisible to the popular girls. Today I was beside Emilia Romano, who was also shunned because she "smells of chips."

As Jacqui passed my desk, she caught my gaze, cut her eyes to Hazel Dwyer, then flashed a gleeful grin which said, *Hazel Dwyer is a dope and so are her mean-girl mates.*

In that instant, my life changed. This new girl was fearless—and so *nice.* Look at her there, already talking with Hilary!

Although I wasn't lumped in with Hilary and Emilia, I existed on the fringes, very much a C-lister. Being inconspicuous was my superpower: if no one noticed me, no one could come for me. It helped that I was neither brainy nor hilariously stupid.

Low-level loneliness was my constant companion but I didn't want to belong with the bitches, who shrieked about clean-cut Jason Donovan or over-muscled David Hasselhoff. Beautiful, moody River Phoenix was my obsession. I kept that to myself though after Juliet Blaney said he looked like he never washed his hair; the last thing I wanted was drama—I got enough of that at home. A noisy household, my four sisters and Mum loved a good argument. Or a bad argument. Any kind of argument, really.

Wishing for an invisibility cloak, I hid away in books, music and movies, filling in time until I was old enough to escape—from school, home and Ireland.

But that September morning I sensed life was about to improve. Jacqui Staniforth was as tall as I was short, as friendly as I was quiet, but, one oddball calling to another, singing our silent weirdo song, we'd found kindred spirits.

Within days, we were spending every afternoon at my house, where we lay on my bed and discovered we felt the same about everything. We'd both read *Animal Farm* and *Brave New World* and loved Terence Trent D'Arby, Kate Bush and the Go-Betweens. *Beetlejuice* was her favorite movie but she also loved *Heathers* (my favorite) and her dream man was Christian Slater.

"There's nothing wrong with you," she told me. "It's those girls. They're so fucking narrow-minded." She looked around anxiously. "Is it okay to swear?"

"In this house? It's practically a rule."

"Seriously? Okay. Fuck, fuck, fuck, fuck, fuck."

Then we screamed with laughter.

"All they want is to get some crappy job, get married and be stuck here in Ireland forever, paying their mortgage on their crappy house."

"My worst nightmare," I said. "As soon as I can, I'm going to escape."

Over the weeks and months, Jacqui and I planned our perfect futures. Mine involved living on a houseboat in Amsterdam. "It's really cute. Everything is small but neat. There's a special place to stow everything. After that I want to live on a small Greek island. I'll sunbathe all day and work in a bar at night."

"Me too!" Jacqui said. "And I want a camper van—"

"—a VW one!" I gasped. "Light blue. Can I go halves?"

"Yes! Please! We'll hit the road. We meet these *hunks* in Italy, they'll fall in love with us, but we keep going—"

"No!"

"There'll be more boys. Tons of them!"

"Okay. We'll drive to Egypt. And Morocco. We'll have adventures, go to fancy weddings and stay in huge castles. Everyone will love us and give us bread and marzipan. Tell me about the boys we meet."

"My ones look like Christian Slater and yours are the image of River."

I shrieked with delight. "So we'll never fall out over a boy!"

"Never." Solemnly she said, "And everywhere we go we'll leave a trail of broken hearts."

"No babies, though." What I wanted from adult life was freedom to up and off from any stressy situation. You couldn't do that if you had children.

"No babies," Jacqui agreed. "Even though men will be *dueling* over us!"

In real life, though, we didn't fare so well. "We're nearly fifteen." Jacqui was *so* anxious. "We really should be getting some action."

The local boys' school offered a motley selection, of which only one or two were worthy of our love. I ate my heart out over a long-haired waif called Cuan Hartigan who never even looked in my direction while Jacqui decided she was mad about a hulking six-footer called Rozzer. From afar we stared, sighed and—after I'd found a well-thumbed copy of *30 Spells to Win Love* in the Oxfam shop—dabbled in witchcraft.

Our every free moment was spent cross-legged on my bedroom floor, casting spells left, right and center, even when it was impossible to locate the precise ingredients: a teaspoon of Schwartz dried herbs had to stand in for a bouquet of fresh rosemary; four drops of the Mazola oil Mum used to fry chips was substituted for the mysterious-sounding cinnamon oil.

We lit candles; burnt brown string even though the spell specified red yarn; made a vague stab at pointing a compass towards Rozzer's house, then Cuan's; wrote our wishes on pieces of paper and, with great reverence, tapped each other on the head with Mum's wooden spoon (as close as we could get to a wand), as we solemnly intoned "Alakazam."

Then, horrors! Word came down via—the cruelest cut!—Cuan Hartigan that Rozzer liked *me*.

Even though Rozzer couldn't have known that Jacqui fancied him, I was furious. "You're fabulous and I'd only come up to his knee. Maybe we pointed the compass in the wrong direction?"

"It's my fault because I'm horrific." Jacqui studied herself in her full-length mirror. "*Why* am I so tall?"

"You're beautiful. Like Geena Davis. *I'm* horrific. I look like I'm *eleven*. I'm invisible to Cuan Hartigan."

"He's a fool. You could be Winona Ryder's sister!"

We were each other's cheerleaders, even though we both suspected we were whistling in the dark.

Which was confirmed one day in the changing rooms after netball with Juliet Blaney bemoaning the size of her thighs. "How does Jacqui Staniforth do it? She eats loads but she's so thin. She could be a model."

"She could never be a model." Hazel Dwyer spoke with pompous authority. "She doesn't have the face for it."

"Yes, she does!" Loyalty made me reckless. "Once her teeth are fixed, she'll be gorgeous."

"She couldn't go down a catwalk," Hazel said. "Not with those knees!"

That provoked howls of laughter. The absolute bitches. There *was* something loose-looking about Jacqui's knees and elbows, as though the joints had been unscrewed slightly.

"She'll grow out of it," I said. "But will you grow out of being bitches?"

I marched away, shaking at my nerve. When word reached Jacqui of my steadfastness (from Stacy Ryan, pretending to be nice) she floated the idea of casting a "*slightly* evil" spell on them. But even though our success rate so far was zero, we decided—feeling very virtuous—not to harness our powers for bad.

After just four terms, Jacqui moved to England, because of her dad's job. Her parting gift was a deck of tarot cards, which I remained devoted to for well over a decade.

Naturally, after her departure, there came a flurry of taunts about having no friends. Then, surprisingly, I was left in peace.

Lonelier than I had been before, though. For about a year Jacqui and I rang each other whenever our parents were out, then lied through our teeth when the huge phone bills came in. But inevitably she made new friends and drifted away. They were lucky to have her, whoever they were.

During my responsibility-free twenties, I'd often drifted back to Ireland but returning forever when Shane and I broke up was a different story. Clearly, my life was over. But I had it all wrong. For starters, Jacqui was back in Dublin!

Like me, she'd avoided any kind of "career," but had fallen into a dream job as VIP concierge in a luxury hotel. Her brief was wide-ranging but vague. Sometimes she did mundane stuff, such as organizing late-night cosmetic dentistry. (You'd be amazed how often that was requested.) But frequently she had to socialize with the VIPs. Well, that's how it was described— "socializing"—but the real reason for her presence was to customize reality for them, ensuring that the ice was the correct coldness, the full moon wasn't too bright, etc.

"I haven't a single qualification," she told me. "I've no idea how this happened."

"Because you're amazing." I was still mad about her. "You're friendly, you're funny, you're effective. You're all the good things."

"So are you," she said. "What'll you do now?"

Well! Encouraged by Margaret's husband Garv, I went to college to do Public Relations. The moment I got my diploma, I was hired by a company which repped a cosmetic brand. Honesty compels me to admit that both the company and the brand were drab and sad—no wonder it had been so easy to get the job.

However, it gave me a sense of how great things *could* be—given the right circumstances. And the right location . . . New York was in my sights. My short visit there had made quite the impression but being with Mum, Dad and Helen meant my wings had been somewhat clipped. There was a lot—oh, an *awful* lot—I still wanted to do. "C'mon, Jacqui, let's move to New York."

"New York?" She thought about it for half a second. "Okay!"

17

When I woke, with a Jacqui hangover, I wasn't sure I could face a roomful of people tucking into rashers and sausages. In what unlikely circumstances did anyone think it would be a good idea to start their day with platefuls of fried meat?

(I understood I was in the minority on that.)

However, they'd have sugary, baked things down there—glazed Danishes, cranberry muffins, maybe even waffles . . . The older I got, the more irresponsible my diet. Why not? We're here for a good time, not a long time, et cetera, and why eat disappointing food just because it's healthy?

At "my age" I was meant to be eating lots of fish. But at "my age" I wasn't sure if I was old or not-old. The thing was, I was both of them, I was all the ages.

I wanted the freedom to hop from one to another, from seventy-seven to thirty-nine, from nineteen to forty-four, whenever the mood took me. I wanted a life where I could have a two-hour nap each afternoon, but where no one looked askance if sometimes I took a sexy man along with me. A place where I could complain bitterly about my arthritic knee, then rub on painkilling gel and embark on a brutal spin class. Where I could go out dancing (I *loved* dancing) or stay home alone, attempting to crochet a mouse. Where retinol, fish oils, statins and red lipstick were all part of my day. Where I was wise enough to know that someone's boyfriend was a tool but compassionate enough to say nothing unless my opinion was sought. Where I wore my niece's jeans and my mother's rain hat (I'd just had a blow-dry. It was like a hotel shower cap with ribbons. Portable and effective). Where I could go out for so much fun that I'd leave my phone in the taxi and during the subsequent forty-eight-hour hangover regret nothing.

Like every woman I'd spent my life being told nope, you're doing it wrong. Wrong, wrong, wrong. You're too serious, too short, too confident, too flat-chested, too ambitious, too repressed, too hard, too flirty, too fat, too thin,

too old, too hairy, too angry, too prissy, too messy, too stupid, too opinion-
ated, too lazy, too emotional, too . . .

Occasionally, though, I felt *this* is how to be me—at least for the moment,
because I might change my mind and be one of my many other versions.

Today I was the version who wanted to eat Danish pastries, so that's what
I would do. Courtney had said it was okay to go down in my pajamas, but
she'd had a couple of glasses of wine so I decided not to chance it. In the
breakfast room she was the first person I saw.

"Good woman, you're out of bed." She whipped past, laden with plates.
"I thought I'd have to come up and wake you." Moments later, she was back,
with a menu.

Troubled, I asked, "Are you the only person who works here?"

"I hate my husband and sons. I take as many shifts as I can."

This was a surprise; she really didn't give off husband-and-kids energy.

"It's been the slowest time of year, not much call for more than myself,
Emilien and her ladyship, who cleans the rooms. But it's all kicking off
this coming week with Paddy's Day. Take a look at the menu and I'll bring
you coffee."

"Tell me where to find it and I'll get it myself."

"Sit down, you lunatic. Brown or white toast? Would you like a scone?"

While I ate two slices of toast with Nutella, I texted Lenehan. There had
been no further damage, he said. Well, that was something. Relieved, I stole
a scone and a banana and returned to my room where I repeated the previous day's exercise with the tinted moisturizer, cream blush, lip balm and
perky ponytail. Then went out into the damp morning to pester the devout,
making their way to mass.

Everywhere were reminders that we were only a kilometer from the sea:
the salty air; seabirds screeching overhead; paint blistering on wood.

Setting my face into a fixed smile, I began thrusting flyers left, right
and center. "A public meeting about Kearney's Farm!" My voice was chirpy.
"Everyone welcome."

I'd been braced for some hostility—but people accepted my flyers and
expressed concern about Queenie.

These folk were warm, they *cared* . . . or were they just bored? It was a
fact that the demographic this morning heavily favored the elderly.

"I don't condone what happened with the digger," said a woman. "Putting
the sand in the tank."

But her brother disagreed. "They're going to bulldoze the Naughton house." He was upset rather than angry. "That entire family starved to death during the famine. It's wrong to wipe away every trace of them."

"Will you come to the meeting?" I said. "Have your say. We'll sort all of this out."

"Is it true?" The woman leant closer. "That they . . . did their business in one of the cottages?"

Did their . . . ? *What* business . . . ? I didn't even want to think about it.

"Moyna, stop it, you ghoul." Her brother pulled her towards the church.

I resumed my smiling. "A public meeting about Kearney's Farm," I said, again and again. "Tomorrow night. All welcome. Refreshments will be served."

One young fool, who wasn't even going to mass, just swaggering past the church, yelled, "Not in my name!" But skedaddled when he saw me coming to engage. Not a serious person, I decided.

Back in my room, I wrote a long report for Joey on everything I'd learned and done so far, ate my scone and banana, checked the email account for correspondence—nothing so far—and went down to seek out Ferne from Fine Irish Knits.

In the lobby, Courtney greeted me with, "Her ladyship had to leave. Another job to get to."

Who was her ladyship and why would I care?

"If you want your sheets changed, I can run up and do them."

Now I remembered: "Her ladyship" was the chambermaid.

"She knocked on your door, she said. You must have been asleep?"

I hadn't been. "Why is she 'her ladyship'?"

"Rose Tolliver. One of the 'gentry.'" Courtney gave at the knees in a tongue-in-cheek curtsey. "Lives in Tolliver Hall, the giant monstrosity far up on the cliffs. Hasn't a penny. Not the best cleaner in town, give me a Brazilian any day, but Kilcroney—that's our owner—is fond of her so she works whatever hours she likes."

"Thank you!" I had enjoyed this potted life story enormously. "No need for new sheets or anything. Okay, I'm off out."

Only to discover that Ferne's Fine Irish Knits was shut. A few doors down, Heather & Mist, another knitwear shop, was open. Several enchanted minutes were spent running gossamer-fine angora shawls and cardigans through my fingers—I'd actually *wear* these—before I remembered my brief was to find Ferne, not a knitwear shop. Besides, this high-end stuff was way out of my budget.

Back on Main Street, there wasn't a single passerby to pester, so I made my way down to the beach, planning to walk the length of it. But it was *long*—at least a couple of kilometers until it ran into the start of the cliffs— and Margaret's anorak was no match for the breeze. From a standing position, I admired it as quickly as possible, took several deep breaths of bracing ozone, then returned to the town, ducking into a narrow shop called Janette's Jumpers, covered in permanent stickers boasting a 30-percent-off sale. The clothes were fun, particularly the oversized boleros in Day-Glo colors. On a whim I bought one.

The salesperson greeted me warmly. "You're the woman down from Dublin? Anna Walsh, shur I know. It's awful news about Queenie. No, I'm not Janette, I'll let you into a little secret, Janette doesn't exist, I'm Valerie Leaver, you're very welcome to town, that's a beautiful little bolero, would you call it yellow chartreuse or blinding lime? Handy in a power cut, sez you. With the discount it's twenty-eight euro, we'll round it down to twenty-five seeing as I like the look of you, cash if you have it, no refunds, credit notes or exchange, I've no bags, can you get it in your pocket? I'm just closing up now, to spend quality time with my grandchildren, see you tomorrow night at the meeting, skin and hair will be flying!"

On that note, I found myself back on the street, with the uncomfortable sense that I'd been spiritually manhandled. As if a hit-and-run sprite had rummaged through the pockets of my psyche and frisked between my legs. But I owned a beautiful bolero. Perhaps "beautiful" wasn't the precise word and hard to know exactly when I'd wear it but with the discount, then the extra discount, it had almost been free.

I buried the thought that, in my new straitened circumstances, my attitude to money definitely needed work. Back in my room, I lay listening to Art of Noise, planning the following night's presentation. This community was wounded. People were pissed off or worried. My job was to coax their concerns from them.

I closed my eyes and imagined I'd lived here all my life; Maumtully was my home. But a big change was imminent, which threatened to upset several delicate balances in the town's social ecosystem. A right of way which had existed forever was suddenly to be fenced off. Now we'd have to go the long way round to reach the beach.

Or my neighbor's sheep were to be ousted from their fields. I was aggrieved on his behalf. Or anxious in case he began eyeing up *my* land?

Perhaps I was a carpenter. Jobs were never plentiful so the news of a big build on the Kearneys' land was very welcome—until I discovered none of the work was coming my way.

I needed to empathize, to sympathize, to listen and soothe. I opened my eyes to find a blue and white butterfly perched on the lamp. "Oh, hello!"

How did it get in? My window was cracked open: it *could* have shimmied through. Very early in the year for butterflies, though.

After Aidan's death, I'd read many bereaved folk insisting that the person they had lost visited in the form of a butterfly. Eventually it happened to me: I'd dreamed about Aidan, he'd told me to "look for the signs' and, when I woke, a butterfly was in our apartment, touching off objects which had mattered to us both. It had even dotted itself about my face, as if I was being kissed. I'd been 100 percent certain it was Aidan. The solace it gave me was immense.

Five or six times in the years since, invariably at a time of upheaval, a butterfly had shown up. Maybe they were around all the time but I only noticed when I was freaking out with worry?

It was so long since Aidan had died that I was no longer sure these visits were actually from him. I wondered if perhaps his spirit and my internal emotional radar had somehow merged? Either way, I always felt reassured that I'd be okay.

This unexpected blue and white visitor flitted around my room, idly inspecting my expensive foundation and the small pile of books I'd brought. Lightly, it touched my hand, before spending a moment on my eyebrow, then cheek.

I watched it float upwards to the open window, perch briefly on the sill, then disappear off into the world. Out loud, I said, "Thank you." Whether it was to Aidan or the universe or to the strongest part of myself, I was grateful.

A beep on my phone jolted me from my warm glow. A text from Joey. **I'm here. In the bar.**

18

My stomach plunged. It was more than eight years since Joey and I had crossed paths. The memory could still make me sweat.

I ducked into the bathroom to run cold water on my wrists to liven me up. Who splashes cold water on their *face* to achieve the same? That would only make your foundation streaky. Speaking of which, I did a speedy swoop across my face with one of the most expensive brands in the world. My stockpile wouldn't last forever but a meet with Joey Armstrong called for it.

The issue was that I didn't know if we were enemies or friends. Going by our last conversation, definitely enemies. But the last time we'd seen each other, although we hadn't spoken, we'd been civil. Hopefully now we could fake pleasantries, at least for a couple of days.

I reached for my hairbrush and pulled it through my hair. A sudden fierce urge descended, to race into the street and find an emergency colorist, who would wash in my beloved gloss, and give me a chic, sexy cut while they were at it.

Full of trepidation, I went down to the bar. And there was Joey, absorbed by his phone. I took a moment, just for a sneaky peek.

He was unrecognizable from the man I'd first met a literal lifetime ago. He'd always had presence but now he looked . . . like a man from Planet Prestige. One who'd be automatically led to the best table in a restaurant.

His clothing—some sort of relaxed suit—was pitch-perfect, the kind of get-up that could take him from a funeral to an orgy. As for his deceptively low-key black trainers? They had impeccable eco, street *and* high-fashion credentials.

He was wearing glasses! Since when?

But his hair hadn't changed—still a long way from short and the same browny-blond color it used to be. *He* must have a costly colorist? But his stubble matched the hair on his head. Maybe the costly colorist had something to do with that too?

His expression, fixed on whatever he was reading, seemed displeased. Nothing new there. Also familiar was the muscle jumping in his jaw.

. . . He'd spotted me. Startled, he whipped off his glasses and sprang to his feet. "Hey."

I was treated to a Joey Special—an unemotional assessment, his eyes flickering over me, trying to gauge my needs, wants, strengths and weaknesses.

"There he is," I said. Meaning, *The narky fucker I know of old.*

Holy mackerel, what had *possessed* me to agree to this?

"Anna Walsh." He paused. "It's so . . . weird to see you."

"Weird to see you too, Joey. Or I hear you like to be called Joseph now?"

"Call me whatever you like. Special privileges for old friends."

Old friends? So that was our cover story?

"Drink, Anna?" His accent still had its rough edges; he hadn't changed beyond all recognition.

I'd been planning to stay on the water. "Gin and tonic."

"Same," Joey said, then turned to the bar. "Emilien? Two—"

"—gin and tonics. I'll drop them down to you, Joseph."

"This table okay?" Joey asked me.

"Fine." I took a seat. "So, ah . . . any update on Queenie?"

He paled. "No. It's the worst. I feel so bad for them all."

"Me too."

An uncomfortable silence followed. Joey had never made small talk.

"So," he said. "Before we get down to business, I guess we should address the elephant in the room."

My heart clutched. He couldn't possibly mean . . .

"My marriage." He was somber. "Well, the end of it."

Oh, *that.* "It's a sad thing, Joey," I managed. "It must be tough. I'm very sorry."

Ten or fifteen years ago, the done thing would have been to joke, but these days, everything felt more fragile.

"And what's your story?" he asked. "Your relationship?"

Warily, I wondered if he was faking. Did he know it was over with Angelo? We had plenty of mutuals; it would have been easy to find out. But maybe he hadn't cared enough? At that thought, relief washed through me.

"Angelo and I, we, ah, broke up. About a year ago, officially. But a good while before that we were . . . you know?"

"Consciously uncoupling?" Joey scoffed. "He's a Conscious Uncoupler, if ever I met one."

"Stop!" Regretting having let my guard down, I said, "Angelo's a really good man and I'll always love him."

Joey stared. He'd been caught off guard and he didn't like it. "Sorry." Then, "I didn't mean . . . I'm a tool."

"Nice to know some things never change." I managed a shaky smile.

Breaking the tension, Emilien arrived with our drinks. "Bad news," he said. "Her ladyship will be in at seven thirty in the morning."

"Who?" Joey asked.

"The woman who does the rooms," I said. "Rose? Is that right?"

"If you want your room cleaned, be awake then." Emilien withdrew.

Cautiously, Joey and I clinked glasses.

"To?" I said. "Rescuing Brigit's retreat?"

"To rescuing Brigit's retreat."

"Okay, here's what I've done so far." I told him about the public meeting, the email address, meeting Ike Blakely, everything. "I've put it all in an email."

"I was just reading it there."

"Did you know about a right of way being fenced off? Or the famine house being demolished?"

He stared. "For fuck's sake. No wonder people are pissed."

"Brigit said that if it all falls apart, she and Colm are wiped out financially. Can you tell me why?"

"The investors can pull their money out now. They'd make almost no losses, not by their standards. But Brigit and Colm didn't have capital to invest, so their stake was their home and a two-hundred-year lease on the Kearney Farm. The consortium owns both now. If this collapses Brigit and Colm have no home and a farm of land they can't sell or lease to another party. They'd be left with nothing."

"The consortium wouldn't give it back? Just out of decency?"

He took another swig of his gin. We were getting through it fairly fast. "That's not how rich people stay rich, Anna."

"Joey, are *you* rich?"

"Nothing like that."

"What's the situation with the funds?" I asked. "Because the construction workers should be paid. It's not their fault the work has stopped."

He tensed, interested. "Convince me some more."

"They're just little guys in this mess, they've done nothing wrong. But they'll still have their usual outgoings. And their machinery needs to be fixed or replaced." Finally, I said, "And if you want to be cynical about it, it's good optics."

"I'll get an income stream sorted first thing, then call the foreman." He shifted to study me with renewed intensity. "You look *great*." It sounded like an accusation. "You've barely changed in all these years."

"Because I'm seventy percent Botox and twenty-two percent HRT. The rest is your bad eyesight. Put your glasses on."

"They're just for reading. I can see you perfectly." His gaze moved over my face. "I'm trying to remember the last time we actually met . . ."

My heart almost seized up in my chest. Were we really going there?

He glanced away, then refocused, all bright-eyed candor. "Was it my engagement party to Elisabeth?"

That was the last time we'd occupied the same room. But we hadn't even spoken that night.

"So about eight years ago?" he said.

"About that." (It was eight years and four months.)

He was trying to set the tone for the next two or three days. We could neither ignore nor acknowledge our long and complicated history. But by presenting a sanitized version of events, he was laying out a surface we could walk on. It was as fragile as thin ice over a deep, dark lake but if we stayed light and careful, we could probably do it.

"So . . . aaah." I sought a safe subject. "Tell me about your kids."

"Oh! Okay . . . As well as Trea, I've three sons, Max is seven, Isaac is six and Zeke is nearly five. They're great. D'you want to see a photo?"

"Um, *sure*." I really hadn't expected Proud Dad Joey to make an appearance.

"Here." A picture of three boys.

"Max there" —Joey tapped a finger— "the eldest. He's a mysterious one, always thinking about stuff."

Dark-haired and unsmiling, Max did look fairly serious.

"But Isaac?" A smile crept across Joey's face. "A right little brat."

I leaned closer. Isaac was grinning, blond and sly-eyed. He was the one who looked most like Joey.

"He's a riot." Joey couldn't disguise his pride. "Always pushing to see what he can get away with. A chancer."

"Wonder where he gets that from?"

"Wha— Oh, you mean *me*. But can't a man change?"

"Uh. Sure. And Zeke? What's he like?"

Looking at the curly-haired cherub, Joey sighed. "A beautiful little fella. Nothing but love. Another drink?"

I shook my head. "Not much of a drinker these days."

"Same!" He seemed pleased. "These days I run. You?"

"I had a Peloton in New York. But it was too expensive to ship here."

Details I hadn't immediately noticed were coming into focus. The Celtic warrior band was still inked on his left wrist, partially covered by a heavy metal-chained watch and a simple bracelet of silver spheres. No rings, but discreet symbols—Ogham letters?—were inked on the four fingers of his right hand.

"What brought you back to Ireland?" he asked. "Bit extreme. Giving it all up."

"I didn't want to grow old over there."

"Too late." He smiled *hard*.

"Haha. Anyway, *you* moved back here."

"Because I married a woman who wanted to live here and I did everything she told me."

Oh my God, I was just *dying* to know more. But I had to pretend I wasn't, at least for now. "D'you think you'll stay in Ireland or go back to New York?"

"What? *No*. I need to be near my boys. I live two minutes' walk from them. They matter more than anything."

"Wow . . ." His fervor was unexpected. "Fair play, Joey."

"Fair play?" His tone was sharp. "For what? Loving my children?"

"Sorry, I just meant . . ."

"You don't know me, Anna." He was matter-of-fact. "You haven't known me for a long time. Elisabeth and I made a commitment to parent our boys as if we were still together."

And he'd had the nerve to accuse me of being a Conscious Uncoupler!

"Well, aaah," I said. "Noice."

"*Noice?*"

"I don't know what to say," I said. "I praised you and you got cross."

"But you—" He stopped. All of a sudden, we were in danger. That hadn't taken long.

"Touchy subject." He cleared his throat. "Sorry."

"She's good, is she?" My tone was light. "Elisabeth?"

"What?" He sounded distracted. "Oh yeah. Great."

Frustratingly he said no more.

I'd met her only once. About five months after the most shameful act of my life, I received a stiff, cream card in the mail: an invitation in curlicued script to the engagement party of Elisabeth Boyd-Hamilton and Joseph Armstrong.

I went hot and cold with shock. After my feelings had settled, I did a deep online dive and discovered she was the daughter of a successful hotelier from Northern Ireland. Her Insta showed her skiing, horse-riding and attending charity balls. She seemed close to her mum and there was a disproportionately high number of pictures of her at afternoon tea in five-star hotels. Well, one must find ways to fill the days when one hasn't got a job, I thought to myself, shaken and sarky.

Hoping that I'd get to talk to Joey in person, I RSVP'd my acceptance. But at the party, he was in constant motion, dropping in on knots of people, smiling, receiving congratulations, sometimes laughing out loud—and always slipping away just as I arrived.

Elisabeth, however, made it her business to nab me. Impeccably polite, she was the last woman on earth I'd have matched Joey with. Probably a decade younger than him (actually, that part tracked), she had a pale oval face, pale slender limbs and an Hermès clutch in a meek shade of gray—although there was nothing meek about the woman herself. Undeniably likable, she had the cast-iron self-possession of someone who was born loaded.

"I met Joseph at a business dinner of my dad's." A story she'd obviously told eighty times already that evening, but was happy to do so again. "I said to him, 'Do something about that hair of yours and I might give you a chance.' The very next morning, at eight a.m., I got a photo. He'd had it cut short."

"Well. Yes. Lovely." I was shaking. "And how long ago was that?"

"Och, barely five months. It's been a whirlwind."

I could well believe it.

I remembered how, once again, I'd looked across the room at Joey. Facing in my direction, his eyes had slid over me as if I was blank air, then he'd smiled at Elisabeth.

Something was different about the smile—then I got it. He'd had crowns or veneers, some sort of fancy dentistry. The chipped tooth I'd found so sexy was now covered over. Made smooth and perfect.

Eleven weeks later, Joey and Elisabeth got married; a huge, three-day event in a stuffy five-star hotel in County Fermanagh.

I wasn't invited.

19

Back in my room, I was suddenly so tired I could barely brush my teeth. The anticipation of seeing Joey meant I'd been exhausted before we'd even met. Then, having to channel my best self was hard.

All credit, we'd both made big efforts tonight. The way Joey had referenced his engagement party—as if everything that night had been normal—had clamped a lid on the past.

But my eye needed to be on the ball for every single moment of the next few days. The smallest lapse in concentration could send me veering off the path.

He'd said he was leaving on Tuesday. Wednesday, at the latest. I. Could. *Do.* This.

Claire had texted, asking me to call her. Probably just for a check-in. If there had been a disaster, even the most minor, my phone would have caught fire. It would do me good to speak to someone who wasn't Joey.

"Claire. How's things?"

"Yanno, busy, like always. Tending to my gut biome, ob*sess*ing about The Row, doing a quiz to see if I'm autistic—"

"Claire, cop on!"

"Hey, I *could* be. Women are *woe*fully underdiagnosed. But yeah, I'm probably not. So? You okay down there in M'town? Met any male poets? No? Small mercies. Have you been to the Big Blue yet?"

"What's that?"

"A bar outside of town on the cliffs. Once you're inside, it's *the* most beautiful view you'll ever see. Any update on Queenie?"

"Not since yesterday."

"It's horrific. You wouldn't wish that news on your worst enemy—oh, Adam's here, I've to go. It's maintenance shag night."

"*Is it?*" Adam's voice asked, then he took the phone. "Anna, hey. How's

M'town? You're good? Okay, I'm gonna let you go now just in case that old romantic wasn't joking about the maintenance shag."

Gratefully, I climbed into bed and, within moments, was pulled into the undertow of a deep sleep—only to be woken at some unknowable hour. What had disturbed me? Right on cue, the noise of bottles crashing into the skip answered my question.

I checked the time. Ten past twelve. Oh please! This was too *early*!

Tonight I didn't bother going to the window. But Emilien must have seen the light from my phone because he called, quietly and apologetically, "Sorry, Anna."

"All good," I squeaked, even though I knew he couldn't hear me.

Seriously, though, in the morning I'd have to do something. Between the challenges of this job and spending time with Joey Armstrong, I needed my sleep. But if word got out that I'd asked to move room, the whole town would despise me. The day I'd arrived—was it really only yesterday?—maybe I should have hopped my hand up and down on the reception bell five or six times and accepted my fate as the entitled dose from Dublin.

Working with Joey Armstrong, though? How could this even be real? Would I ever have believed it, when I'd first moved to New York with Jacqui, all those years ago?

Rachel and Luke had let Jacqui and me crash in their tiny Alphabet City apartment until we found a place of our own.

One evening, early in our stay, Luke had said, "Scrabble night tonight. You in?" Unlikely though it sounded, the Real Men were big Scrabble fans. "Joey's on his way. Shake and Gaz are coming later."

When he was out of earshot, Jacqui groaned softly. "Luke. Costello. Oh. My. GOD! I am *sweating* with longing." She wiped her forehead with her hand. "Anna, look. I'm *drenched*."

I wasn't exactly a healthy temperature myself. Plenty had happened since the night Joey had discarded me for Helen, but he'd still starred in most of my fantasies. In the A-list version, he fell for me like a ton of bricks. (And because of the intensity of his love, had become amazing in bed.) In the B-list scenario, his raw sexiness had disappeared and I got to spurn him. But version B was no fun, so I rarely bothered.

I kept it all to myself though, because my humiliation still burned.

When Joey strolled into the apartment, his sea-glass eyes scanned my face, then he gave a brusque nod.

I mumbled, "Hi." Shite. B-list fantasy was a no-go; I still fancied him to death.

Moving on, Jacqui got a cursory full-body scan, then an abrupt dismissal, like an insect being tossed from his sleeve. As Joey went to the fridge for a beer Jacqui called, "Nice to meet you too."

Luke took Joey by the shoulders and said, "Come on, man, basic manners, would you? You remember Rachel's sister Anna? And this is Jacqui."

Joey gave another curt nod.

"Are you deaf too?" Jacqui asked, over-enunciating wildly. "Or just mute? Because I can do sign language."

After a tense pause, Joey said, "Let's see it."

Jacqui pointed at him. "You. Are. An." She turned and directed her index finger towards her bum. "Asshole." She grinned her irresistible grin.

He didn't even crack a smile, just stared, then got into a deep and meaningful talk with Luke. But I kept sneaking glances. During the intense chat, he absent-mindedly rubbed his stomach, shifting the cotton of his T-shirt. Suddenly there was a glimpse of tight abs, followed, for the briefest moment, by the sharp jut of one hipbone—the skin pale and perfect—which disappeared below the waistband of his low-cut black jeans.

I felt sick with want.

Later that night, when Jacqui and I were trying to sleep, I asked, into the darkness, "What do you think of Joey?"

"That fool!" Her derision was glorious. "The *rudeness*. Those men who think being mean is sexy? Like, fuck off! Get yourself a personality."

"Totally." Working hard at nonchalance. "Yeah."

In a few short weeks Joey became irrelevant as my life took off with a roar. Jacqui and I both got great jobs—Jacqui as a concierge in a luxury hotel, me blagging my way into McArthur on the Park.

It was such an exciting time—we were young! Ish! (Thirty was young, we kept telling each other.) We had boundless energy and we needed it.

Eventually, we found our Manhattan apartment, a crumbling single room, with the shower in the kitchenette. Humbled by countless other viewings, we considered ourselves unusually blessed.

And everywhere—everywhere!—were men. The quality was variable but the variety was enormous. Best of all, it was acceptable to simultaneously date as many as you liked.

"A *smorgasbord* of men," I said.

"A pick 'n' mix," Jacqui replied.

"A buffet! You see something, you don't recognize it but you try it as it's free and if you don't like it, you just go back up for something else."

Between our jobs and the Men Buffet, it was months before I met Joey again, when all I got was another curt nod, which seemed to be his trademark. The new, savvy me got it: Rachel was right. He was too sour. Sexy mouth or no sexy mouth, lean snake-hips or no lean snake-hips, if he couldn't be nice then I didn't want him.

But he must have had a sixth sense that I'd lost interest, because next thing he was standing beside me. "Hey, Anna." An appreciative up-and-down scan followed. "Looking gorgeous as always. How's tricks?"

"Um . . . tricks are excellent, Joey. You?"

"They suddenly just got a lot better." Slowly, he smiled.

My heart rate accelerated.

In hyper-aware silence, he fixed his stare on my mouth, before glancing at my eyes to check he had my attention, then back to my mouth.

My nipples hardened and my lips felt swollen. But I was indignant: he'd chosen Helen, subsequently ignored me and was now giving it full-on cheese. I walked away.

It became a regular thing, Joey subjecting me to a wordless, *intensely* sexy stare whenever we met. Which really wasn't often—my path crossed with that of the Real Men only every couple of months.

But he never made a lunge, or asked me out, like a normal person might.

Until one night I said, "Are you ever going to actually *do* something, Joey?"

That surprised him. He asked, his voice soft, "Is this an invitation, Anna?"

Resentment flared. He had so little respect for me.

"Just say yes," he said. "And I'm yours."

I took a breath. "All you ever do is play with me."

His inbreath was harsh. "Play with you? Jesus, Anna. You can't even imagine."

"The thing is, Joey, I'm a person, not a toy."

"What? No, wait—"

Dropping my eyes, I slid away from him, immediately bumping into Jacqui. "What the hell was going on there?" she demanded. "You two looked like . . . Anna, do you *like* him?"

"I am of sound mind, Jacqui. Of course I don't."

"Anna." She was doubtful. "Should I be worried about you?"

"Look. A long time ago when I was a much younger woman, I found him . . . rideable. If he was even ten percent less obnoxious maybe I'd do a one-night thing now. But he's awful. I deserve a much, *much* better man. So. Never going to happen."

Shortly afterwards, I met Aidan and everything changed. This—*he*—was different. He asked questions about me—so much rarer than you'd think—and remembered the details of my answers. After about four dates, he had strong likes and dislikes about all the people I worked with, even though he hadn't met any of them.

He didn't mess me around, he didn't play cruel games and, God, he was funny. His one-man version of *Zoolander* was pitch-perfect. When he was shaving he used to sing like a Smurf, making me literally cry with laughing.

He was so normal, it was almost suspect. He'd had a mundane middle-class upbringing in Boston, he worked in IT in a bank, he loved his parents and younger brother and had had the same best friend—Leon—since the age of five.

Because he so obviously had my back, I was afraid Jacqui would dismiss him as a Feathery Stroker, but after meeting him, she concluded he'd be "a hard dog to keep on the porch."

In other words, Aidan was just dangerous enough.

For the first time I saw the appeal of a regular life, where there was enough money for nice things. Where we could own a home, maybe a car. Possibly a dog. Unexpectedly, even the idea of having children wasn't terrifying.

I was almost disappointed in myself. But Aidan got it. "We don't have to move to the suburbs and get a station wagon. We can do it our way."

I'd burnt out on New York's mixed bag of men. The variety had once been fun but I'd grown weary of perverts, liars, screwballs and mad bastards. Looking for a decent guy in the five boroughs was like roaming through a wasteland, searching with your bare hands in mounds of smoking debris, while fighting off hordes of other desperate women.

Speaking of mad bastards, Jacqui was in love with a terrible man called Buzz. Like everyone she fell for, he'd started out perfect. On their second date he told her he would take her skiing in January (it was August at the time). In the space of a week he sent so many flowers, which rotted quickly in the summer heat, that our tiny apartment looked like an art installation. "A meditation on beauty and decay," I said. "We could sell tickets."

"If anyone could fit," Jacqui said.

Like all her boyfriends, Buzz curdled fast. He'd tell her to meet him in a restaurant and wouldn't turn up, then insist she'd got the night wrong. Within moments, though, he'd turn the conversation to Thanksgiving and hint heavily that she'd be spending it with his family.

He was a chronic gaslighter but this was back in the mid-aughts, when we didn't yet know the term. Words like love-bombers, narcissists, future-fakers and, yes, gaslighters were all ahead of us. (It didn't mean there were any fewer of them; we just didn't have the language.)

"Dump him," I begged her. "You deserve so much better. You. Are. Fabulous!"

Jacqui had really grown into her looks: long-limbed and smiley and, oh my God, her *clothes*. To be fair, she could wear anything. But the VIP guests in her care regularly gifted her with designer stuff. It was a part of her job to take them to stores like Barney's for after-hours sprees; with so much spendy adrenaline splashing about, the VIPs usually bought her something beautiful.

Meanwhile, quietly, steadily, Aidan and I were falling in love. We began to meet each other's friends, slowly exploring each other's lives. Eventually Aidan was introduced to Joey, who outdid himself with offhand froideur.

"That's the guy?" Aidan exclaimed, delighted. "The—what's the word, Anna?— 'Narky' one?"

This made everyone collapse. "Yep, that's Joey. He doesn't know how to be nice."

It was at Shake's house-warming when Joey finally made a move. Aidan wasn't there—maybe Joey thought we'd broken up? Or maybe he didn't care either way?

I'd been admiring the insides of Shake's new fridge, then turned to find Joey, a smile on his mouth and a glint in his eye. Softly, he said, "Hey."

"Hi, Joey." My tone was cheerful.

"I've been looking for you." Again with the soft voice.

"Well, here I am." I was even more cheery.

"Sooo." He moved closer and I let him walk me into a corner. There, he slid the palm of one hand high on the wall, bracing the muscles in his arm. His other hand, he placed beside my waist. "Anna," he said, "I'm crazy about you. This has gone on for too long. Come home with me tonight."

"No." I slipped out, under his arm.

"Your loss," he called after me.

"Not from what I've heard," I called over my shoulder.

"Hey." He caught up with me. "What do you mean?" He looked confused. Hurt, almost.

". . . Nothing, Joey. Forget it."

20

It was barely seven thirty when her ladyship rapped on my door and said, "Housekeeping." I was already washed, dressed, made-up and in an entertaining convo with my old pal Teenie, because it was still last night in Eugene, Oregon. "I've to go," I said. "Talk soon. Love you." Then at the door, "Coming!"

I admitted a woman who was mid-height and, even in leggings and a T-shirt, innately elegant. "My apologies for the early start," she said. Well-spoken too. She could have been an ambassador's wife down on her luck.

"No bother," I said, even though my night's sleep had been cut short by two hours.

An attractive woman, I observed, watching her set down a bucket bristling with cleaning accoutrements. Thick, auburn hair and gorgeous skin. She was easily forty but not a sunspot to be seen, however she'd managed it. I'd have bet everything I owned it wasn't courtesy of retinol, IPL or chemical peels. She had that refined, no-skincare vibe.

"I'm Anna Walsh."

"Pleasure," she purred. But didn't offer her own name. Which was her right. Of course.

Nevertheless, because almost everyone else here had zero boundaries, I'd expected more warmth.

Stealthily, I slunk downstairs, praying that Joey wasn't up yet. Emilien intercepted me creeping into the buffet. "The go-boy was already in. He's gone out looking for 'proper coffee.'"

I brightened, abandoning my furtive aspect. "In that case, Emilien, I'll take this table here. May I have two lattes and lots of toast and sorry for Joey being rude about your coffee."

"Not at all, no, it's swill. On purpose, like. Kilcroney, who owns this place, also owns Grinder, the coffee shop up the street."

"He sounds cutthroat."

"Putting it mildly, Anna. Putting it mildly. Sorry about the racket last night. Since Christmas, Courtney's been at Kilcroney to get the bins moved away from the rooms but he needs a permit or something."

"Not your fault, Emilien." My brave plan to change rooms had leached away in the cold light of day. I should eat something nice, then perhaps my courage would return. "Forget the toast, can I have pancakes?"

"No."

"Are you breakfast shaming me?"

"There's no pancakes."

"But . . ." And I had to check. "They're on the menu."

"No pancakes till June. They're a seasonal delicacy. Look." He shook his head. "The chef is a freak. But it's impossible to get staff. He has us over a barrel. No pancakes till June. Or omelettes. He says they're summer foods. Would you like a fry?"

I waited for the urge to puke to settle. "Ah no, I'm grand with the—" I gestured towards the stand of baked goods.

Happily ensconced with croissants and limitless containers of Nutella, I began planning my morning: Ziryan, then Ferne, then—Jesus, here was Joey! Crossing the room with great dynamism, looking like a high-powered lawyer in a slick TV drama. Literally suited and booted. Briefly, I flashed back in time to when Jacqui and I used to sing scathing songs about the same man's boots.

His iPad skated onto the table and he slid into the chair opposite me. "Okay if I join you?"

"Of course. Did you get your 'proper coffee'?"

"I did." Automatically he looked at Emilien. "Is he pissed off? But you might as well be drinking Oxo."

I laughed—and immediately had a moment: this was all so strange.

"You okay?" Joey's eyes narrowed.

"Just. It's wild, this."

He nodded. I could see it: he was finding this as difficult as I was. "Won't last for much longer. I've news. I made some calls. There are no plans to demolish the famine house. Or to interfere with the right of way to the beach."

"What? Seriously?"

"I've all the documentation, planning permission, architect's plans. I've sent them to you."

"I'll ask Courtney to post them on the local Facebook. Or maybe I'll join and post it myself. But wait now, Joey. Were they just rumors that got out of hand?"

"Looks that way."

Things couldn't be that easy, surely? "We still need to have this meeting. There's the shopkeepers' concerns. The pissed-off tilers, carpenters—"

"I know, I know. It's not over yet."

"What about the non-disclosure agreements the staff have to sign?"

Joey shook his head. "We don't have to cave on everything. We're bringing employment to an under-resourced area. We're not the bad guys."

"And Aber Skerett's sheep? Just another rumor?"

"No, that's real. Different though—it was a private agreement between the Skeretts and the Kearneys. Can you reach out to Mr Skerett? We'll offer to help find a new grazing spot."

"Joey?" My tone was urgent.

His eyes shot from his iPad to my face. "What?"

"Do you say 'reach out' automatically now? Or do you still feel embarrassed?"

To my relief, he smiled. "Said it there without even thinking." He hesitated, then admitted, "This situation . . . it's a lot."

"Brigit and Colm maybe losing their land and being penniless?"

"That too." A pause followed. "I hate failing." All humor gone, he added, "But you already know that."

"Cool coat," Ziryan called as I pushed open the door of the hardware shop. Then, as he got a better look, "Oh hey, you must be the woman down from Dublin that the whole town's talking about. Ziryan Barzani." He was smiley and adorable, with tufty brown hair and ginormous eyebrows.

"Is it Rick Owens?" he asked.

"What? Oh, my coat? . . . You know your stuff."

"May I?" He extended a hand to touch it. "It's so soft."

"It's like wearing marshmallows," I admitted.

It was far too noticeable for this mission: I should have left it in Dublin. But it was so comforting. "Brigit said you'd be a good person to talk to. About the damage."

"I haven't a clue who did it."

"Can I ask you about Ike Blakely?"

"Oh yeah. He's cool. Tree surgeon. All about the planet."

"He seems . . . angry?"

"Aw naw. More passionate, I'd say. He *cares*."

Cautiously, I asked, "Do you think—"

"No."

"But I didn't—"

"I know what you were going to ask—does Ike care so much that he'd try to stop a resort being built here? Not at all. He's a lover not a fighter."

"I saw him on Saturday. His knuckles were cut."

"So you think he was . . . what? Punching the walls over there?"

I realized how unlikely that was.

"He works with saws," Ziryan said. "And, like . . . *trees*. Tree trunks can be rough on the knuckles. You should really talk to Ferne and Rionna from the shopkeepers' committee, they'd have a good idea of the mood of the place."

I had another question. "Is there a hairdresser in town?"

"Course! What kind of backwater do you take us for!" But he was laughing. "Crowning Glory. Over the road. Karina and Gráinne. Gráinne cuts mine. But I hear Karina is better at the blow-drys."

"Who does color?"

"Both of them. And they do lamination, extensions, everything. Closed on a Monday though, in case you were thinking of—"

"Oh." For a moment, desperate for confidence for tonight's meeting, I'd thought I'd get my color done. "Ah well."

My phone rang—a local number. "Anna Walsh speaking."

"Dan Kilcroney from the hotel. Ferne O'dowd and Rionna Breen are here looking for you."

"Oh, ah, are they?" This was an excellent coincidence. "Thanks. I'll be there in two minutes."

I ended the call. "Dan Kilcroney," I told Ziryan. "The owner of the Broderick? What's he like?"

Was it too much to expect that my fashionable little friend could corroborate what Emilien had said, about Mr Kilcroney being *cutthroat*?

"A complicated man." Ziryan was thoughtful. "Hasn't always had it easy."

A seed of doubt took root. I'd a feeling Ziryan saw the best in everyone. In my personal life, it was a character trait I enjoyed but it was no good to me right now. I needed a jaundiced cynic. Helen would be ideal. Her private-investigating skills might also come in useful.

Perhaps I *should* let her—which meant all of them, because the Walshes traveled as a mob—come for the weekend?

Meditating on this thorny issue, I took my leave of Ziryan and narrowly avoided a collision with an officer of the law in the street outside.

"Watch where you're going!" he ordered. "Are you the woman down from Dublin?"

I turned. ". . . I am." Then, "Is that illegal?"

I thought he'd laugh. At least smile. But cozy-crime TV shows set in delightful villages had ruined me for real life.

I got a good hard stare, which lingered on my scar. "Don't get smart with me."

I turned away and mouthed *Don't get smart with me* silently but very sarcastically.

An "older" man stood behind the reception desk. This must be Dan Kilcroney. For a cutthroat with questionable business practices, I'd expected some roguish charm.

His immobile face reminded me of a shoe. Specifically a brogue, which was somewhat misshapen thanks to heavy usage. Sparse of hair and craggy of feature, he made me think of cut-price gangsters from fifties B-movies. Irish-American actors who looked as if they spent their spare time running, face-first, at brick walls.

"Dan Kilcroney?" I asked.

His eyes moved over me. The best version of myself would have called these eyes "shrewd." But Shadow Anna would have called them "cold," "calculating" or "conniving."

Into the silence I offered, "I'm Anna Walsh."

His inert aspect said, *The fuck would I care?*

Fury gushed, like oil from a lucky strike. "You called me literally two minutes ago." My tone was so polite it could have shattered. I was serving up supreme passive aggression because, although it had been a while, I was habitually overlooked. At least until people got to know me better.

Helen said it was because I had Resting Eejit Face. I preferred to think it was due to me being short and mild-mannered—at least until provoked, which I was now.

I hadn't always been an angry person, but once perimenopause was running the show, spontaneous eruptions of rage were likely. They'd calmed down once I'd started on HRT, but now there was almost none of it in my system I was dangerously close to blowing.

Your man's gaze began to roam anew. I knew exactly how he saw me—a nothingy woman, in bad need of a haircut, with an unsightly scar on her cheek. His eyes lingered scornfully on my extremely cool coat. It was clear he thought it was just a duvet with sleeves. It took everything in my power to not say, "Brogue-face, you know *fuck-all* about fashion. The only reason you think you're the clever one here is because you have no idea of the depths of your ignorance."

Biting the words out, I said, "Ferne and Rionna are here to see me?"

After a beat during which comprehension dawned and *Oh fuck* flashed in his eyes, he said, "... Yes. Of course. They're in the lounge. This way." He ushered me in exaggerated fashion, his arm outstretched, suddenly Mine Host par excellence.

Be kind, I reminded myself, *for everyone we meet is fighting a hard battle.*

Dan Kilcroney's disrespect, coming hot on the heels of the policeman's hostility, had pressed on old wounds; that's all that was going on. Plus, I was very tired. And deprived of the hormones. But it was infuriating to watch people assess my worth based on external signs of power, beauty and money. Especially because they thought *they* were clever operators. I longed to tell this arse how transparent he actually was.

Ferne was what my dad would have called "a fine woman"—tall, fragrant, bouffy. Rionna was small, dark, inquisitive. Together they were garrulous, likable and *delighted* about the proposed retreat.

"More celebrities coming to town," Ferne said. "Means more business for the local retailers."

"You know, between this new hotel and all of our festivals, we should rename ourselves Little Hollywood!" Rionna exclaimed. "Make a note! We'll table it for the next meeting."

All they cared about was "capturing sales" from Brigit's well-heeled guests. Their proposal basically involved bundling them into a car, then abandoning them on Main Street, M'town, for a couple of hours. Tactfully I ruled that out, so we discussed the resort having display cases featuring local pottery, knitwear, etc. If any of the guests expressed interest, they could be taken into town to the appropriate shops.

"Or we could pop out to them," Ferne said.

"It would be no trouble," Rionna said.

"None," Ferne agreed. "In fact, we could call once every couple of days—"

"—or every day," Rionna said.

"Every day is better," Ferne said. "We'll visit every day. So we're agreed!"

"The next step is, I'll go back to Brigit and the company and convey what we've covered this morning. What happens next is up to them."

"So? You're just . . . a message girl?"

"Absolutely not," I said. "I'm your advocate."

"Are you?" They exchanged a triumphant look and then stood up.

"Call up to me some time in Fine Irish Knits," Ferne said. "We'll look after you."

"And make sure you pop in to me in Luxury Irish Linens," Rionna echoed. "You'll be looked after there too."

In circumstances such as these, *We'll look after you* tends to mean *We'll give you a decent discount.*

I saw them out. After walking a short distance along the street, Ferne turned and gave me a wave. Then so did Rionna.

Enthusiastically I waved back and I was smiling, smiling, smiling, as I watched them make their way up Main Street.

Pair of chancers.

21

Dan Kilcroney was still behind the reception desk, engrossed in a screen. My throb of wounded fury was followed by a flare of courage, so noiselessly I moved to stand before him, like a creepy child in a horror movie.

It was a while before he felt my presence, then his face flashed white with terror. "Jesus!" With effort, he managed a smile. "Ms . . . ah Walsh. I didn't see you there. My apologies."

Apologize all you like, Arse-brain, I know your true nature. You could gift me the entire hotel as a show of remorse and I'd still know that you're an arse with the face of a brogue.

"How can I help?" he asked.

"I want to switch rooms."

There was a hiccup of time as he gave one of his calculating looks. "Is your current one not to your liking?"

"It's over the bottle bins." I withheld any apologies or further explanations. He had the facts.

How efficient things would be if I was always this blunt. Probably a full seven years of my life had been wasted constructing complaints in a manner which made the fucker-upper still like me. Same with over-apologetic, explanatory emails of refusal. It was definitely a woman thing. Meanwhile, men tap out a flat, "Can't do. Enjoy." And carry on about their business without worrying, *Was I too abrupt? Have I offended them?*

Much as I'd love that freedom, the only time I pulled it off was when an acute hormone shortage overrode my bone-deep social conditioning to "be nice."

Dan Kilcroney delivered a blank stare, then lifted a key from a hook and said, "There's a room. Come and take a look. If it suits you, we'll move your belongings over."

Up three flights of stairs we went, right to the top of the house. Brogue-face unlocked the door with a metal key and pushed it open. I was braced for something smaller and dingier than my current set-up but there was no bed at all, just two couches.

"The bedroom's through here."

It was a suite?

I followed him in. The bed was a four-poster. There was a dressing room, two fluffy robes and real-world-sized bottles of shower gel and shampoo.

On the wall was an actual painting, a cutesy domestic scene of children's wellingtons outside a door—quite a step-up from the stag.

Your man lifted a lace curtain. "You'll see it doesn't overlook anything. You won't be disturbed."

I needed to bite the bullet. "It's bigger than my current room. How much more does it cost? Because I'll have to okay it with Joey. I mean"—I laced my words with fake respect—"Mr Armstrong."

I bet he knew who *Mr Armstrong* was. I bet he would never subject *Mr Armstrong* to the same disparaging treatment I'd received.

"No extra charge," he said. "Does it suit you?"

"I'll miss the painting of the stag, but it'll do."

Back in the lounge, I decided to check the email account. Nothing had arrived when I'd checked earlier so it was a relief to see nine fresh arrivals.

To: Kearneysfarm@gmail.com
From: ProudIrishPatriot1916@hotmail.ie

My friend's partner wanted a job driving the visitors but they're only employing asylum seekers. Irish people needn't bother applying.

This was horrible. It was also nonsense.

To: Kearneysfarm@gmail.com
From: AnraiBridger@coola.org

What about the runoff from this hotel going straight into the seawater? Dolphins swim in that bay. There's diverse ecosystem along the shoreline and you'll kill it off. That's a terrible thing. All in the name of making money.

If this was true, it *had* to stop. I'd pass it to Joey and ask him to check it out.

To: Kearneysfarm@gmail.com
From: 123herewego@hotmail.com

Fuck off back to where you came from, you filthy slut

I swallowed hard. But I guess this was all part of being a woman. I moved on to read the next—and oh, hello! ProudIrishPatriot1916 was back with another missive.

To: Kearneysfarm@gmail.com
From: ProudIrishPatriot1916@hotmail.ie

The Kearneys are only a front. A Nigerian crime lord is the real owner.

Is that *so*, I thought. If he—and I was certain it was a he—had stuck to just one crank email, I might have taken it more seriously. But he'd lost any credibility now.

To: Kearneysfarm@gmail.com
From: MichaelMurphy8732@eircom.ie

What about my cattle? If there's going to be helicopters bringing in the rich people and they fly over my field, they'll upset my herd. I've 20 head and they're milkers.

Another one for Joey. There probably would be helicopters. But something could—*must*—be worked out.

To: Kearneysfarm@gmail.com
From: ConcernedCitizen@eircom.net

I'd fuck you if you had a bag on your head covering that face. What did you do to it? You ruined it.

Instinctively I lowered the lid of my laptop. Perhaps a break was in order. I focused on my breath, taking a long, slow inhale, holding it for four seconds, then exhaling on seven, waiting for my heart rate to return to normal.

Joey burst into the lounge, all business. Speedily he scanned the tables, until he found me. "There you are."

I made myself smile. "Here I am."

He hauled a low stool close to me. "One fewer job for you—I've checked the emails. Mostly baseless rumors, one about asylum seekers, another about runoff into the sea. I'll look after them."

"I've checked the emails too." Our eyes met.

Awkwardly he shifted. "I'll take them over."

"It's my job." I was embarrassed: I didn't want his pity.

"Some of them were . . . personal. Mean."

"I can handle it. And it's true. My face *is* scarred."

I watched him press his lips together. He'd never tell white lies to make a person feel better. "You'd barely notice it. Just some anonymous dick going for the easy target."

"I *know* I don't need a bag on my head for someone to fuck me." At the start of the sentence my tone was jokey but by the end I sounded sad. Maybe because I felt sad.

"Listen, I was thinking about Lenehan," Joey said. "Would it be good optics to have one of the Kearneys here tonight?"

"Joey. Lenehan's only a child."

Whenever I thought of his Adam's apple, of how he was trying to be the man of the house while his little sister had cancer, his mum was absent and his dad was laid low with depression, my heart caved in. "I don't want him here, listening to his family being trashed. We can't put him through it."

"I hadn't thought of it like that. You're absolutely right." He focused on me with evident respect. Then, "About the abusive emails, we could report them."

"Joey, *no*. It would be like reporting the rain for raining. Look, these emails are helpful. The sincere ones, we can deal with, no bother. The trolls like the racist IrishPatriot, we ignore for now. If things escalate, we'll take another look."

"Anna!" Here came Courtney, with a bunch of wilted flowers, wrapped in sad-looking cellophane. "You've an admirer. There's a note."

Intrigued, I unfolded the large sheet of printer paper. In blue biro was scribbled, "Thanks for sorting out the money. Very decent of you. Hal Mahon." Underneath he'd included his address and phone number.

"From Hal Mahon," I said. "How nice is that?"

"Who?" Joey asked. "And why's he sending you flowers?"

"One of Kearney's crew. The foreman's brother. Saying thanks for fixing their pay while the work is stopped."

"Technically, it was me who fixed it."

Immediately I passed the flowers to Joey.

"I was joking." He pushed them away. "You were meant to say, 'But it was my idea.' Anna! No 'bants'? You've changed."

That made me laugh.

Courtney said, "Kilcroney says I'm to help you move rooms."

"I can do it myself."

"D'you want to get me sacked? Come on. Let's get it over and done with."

Upstairs, as Courtney rattled my clothes off hangers, she said, "I'm sorry for giving you a noisy room. I let you down. I was too excited about the redecoration, especially the makeup mirror with the light. And the rooms out the front get the racket from the street. Although up on the third floor, you won't be troubled."

"Courtney, no. You're the best person in Maumtully, I won't hear a bad word about you. Listen, should I be saying 'Maumtully'? Or 'M'town'?"

"Whatever you like. Both work. Oh, wait, I've news. You're in at six thirty on Wednesday with Dr Olive. They offered Dr Drew but I said no, on account of him having a dick. Dr Muireann would be ideal but she's out the door with patients. Dr Olive is a woman but *young*." Said with disdain. "All over Gen Z issues—acne, social anxiety." She wiggled her fingers. "'It's good to talk.' But a prolapsed uterus? Grit your teeth and keep walking, Granny. What I'm saying is, she mightn't really 'get' menopause. So go in all guns blazing."

"I owe you big," I said.

"Let's see what you come out with before you start thanking me."

"But thank you for even trying. So. What's the story with Dan Kilcroney?"

"Why? Do you fancy him?"

At my evident horror, she collapsed into wheezy laughter. "You didn't take to him," she said. "Nothing new there. Ah look. He's a tough customer. But he does plenty for this town. Provides a lot of work."

"Hardly! Only you, Emilien and the mad chef are employed here."

"And her ladyship. Because we're offseason, I keep telling you. But big changes tomorrow, an influx of staff. And Dan owns other businesses— the coffee place and the Big Blue, that's the bar on the cliffs. Then there's the Banshee art gallery, Mike's Bikes. A right empire."

"Is there a Mrs Kilcroney?"

"I knew you fancied him! There was a wife, once upon a time, the lovely Olivia, but she left years back. Would you believe he's only forty-two? There's something about him, like he's always been fifty-seven, that he was born looking like that."

I could believe it. "So tell me about her ladyship."

"Rose? Nice enough but keeps her distance. Not a *penny*. Living in that massive old mansion on the cliff, up beyond the Big Blue. They say it's colder inside than out. She had a useless husband. A few years back he took up with a woman in Galway because, according to Vivian, he just wanted a hot bath. He enjoyed it so much he moved in."

"Is this her ladyship's only job?"

"Good God, no. She's an essential part of the festival mafia."

"Doing what?"

"You've met her—a good-looking, well-turned-out woman who can chat about Greek myths, Mozart, the Berbers . . . Fluent in five languages. She raises the tone. A *big* hit with the dusty old intellectuals. Catnip, is that the word? They all fall in love with her. Vivian throws her a few quid for the festival stuff. At the moment she's also the town taxi driver and she caters dinners in people's houses. As well as covering breakfast here whenever Steve quits."

"Steve is—"

"—our chef."

"The mad one?"

"The only one. Before the husband left, Rose and him tried one hare-brained scheme after another. Few years back they had a small zoo in the grounds but a child tripped on a hidden hoop in the overgrown croquet lawn and broke their arm. That put an end to that. Then they opened a few rooms for B and B but breached too many regulations. She'd sell that house in a heartbeat for next to nothing but it needs too much work. Only Zuckerberg or the like have the money to sort the place out."

"Maybe he'll come to one of the festivals and fall in love with it?"

"Maybe he will! She's resourceful, I'll tell you that. Don't let that perfect diction fool you. Rose is always looking for an angle—more power to her."

I found myself wondering, when all of this was over, if Courtney and I could be proper friends—my automatic thought whenever I met a woman I liked.

I was still trying to replace Jacqui. As with any loss, I'd learned to live with it. And, of course, other relationships had worked hard to camouflage the lack: Angelo had done a lot of the heavy lifting; I'd become closer to Teenie and Jennifer from work and because I had four sisters, I had oodles of overfamiliar interaction with other women.

But nobody ever measured up to Jacqui: sunny, supportive and hilarious, she'd been a one-off. We'd been so close our connection was almost psychic and even now I missed her. Well, the way we'd once been.

She made regular appearances in my dreams, nearly always the same scenario: to our delight, we bumped into each other. All the awkwardness was gone and we were instantly friends again.

22

By four thirty, everything was set for the meeting. My speech was written on my phone and I'd tested the mic. Fifty chairs were arranged in neat rows and Courtney was stacking cups and saucers on a table at the back of the room.

"Looks good." Joey had strolled in.

"All hail the go-boy," Courtney said, her tone damning, then left to get the biscuits.

Suddenly I saw Joey through Courtney's eyes and was overcome with dismay. His beautiful suit was *not* perfect for all events, certainly not tonight's. "Joey, have you a change of clothes? You look too corporate. And your hair's too . . . How is it so shiny?"

"How would I know? Good genes?"

"Joey, we're trying to build goodwill here—the last PR person alienated the entire town. Your look isn't friendly. See me." I stretched my arms wide to demonstrate my jeans and hoodie, then twisted left and right.

"*So* cute." It was clear he was annoyed.

"Shut it, Joey. My vibe is what you need. Come on, there's a gent's draper down near Ferne's."

He frowned. "You really mean this." Then, brightening, "A gent's draper? That sounds funny."

"It'll have to do."

But it was closed. "Oh no!"

"It's Monday." A nosy local woman had spotted my distress. "Micah never opens on a Monday."

Always with an eye on winning hearts and minds, I said, "Micah is entitled to a day off."

As soon as the woman was gone, I focused on Joey. "Have you *any*thing in the hotel? Jeans? Joggers?"

"No. And no."

"So what do you sleep in? You're hardly a pajamas man?"

His stare was deadpan. "That's right, Anna, I'm not."

"What about your running stuff?"

"Nope. I packed in a hurry."

What time did the shops close in Galway? I googled Dunnes in Eyre Square: it was open until seven.

"Joey, get in your car, drive fast but not recklessly to Dunnes in Galway. Buy jeans, joggers and a couple of cheap T-shirts."

"Okay. But you're coming along."

"You don't need me! What age are you? Eight?"

"Let's go." He was already halfway back to the hotel. "This was your idea."

"Okay, but only because I don't trust you to get the right stuff."

His four-wheel drive was parked on the street, behind Mum's Multipla. With a sidelong smirk, he said, "Sweet ride. Yours? Dublin plates, got to be."

"Hey! Don't car-shame me."

We took off in his jeep.

"You want music?" he asked.

"Depends." Shouty rawk was not my vibe.

"You choose."

I put on Saint Etienne. "Is this okay?"

Joey's head moved.

"Was that you nodding? Or a bump in the road?"

"I was nodding. It's a great album."

What? I didn't think he'd even have heard of them.

"I emailed the people complaining about the Nigerian crime lords and dolphins being poisoned," he said. "Nothing back from—what's he calling himself? ProudIrishPatriot. And there won't be, he's just a troll. The dolphin man is real. He can't remember who told him about the runoff going into the sea, but that it's 'common knowledge.'"

"How, though? Is someone going around spreading malicious rumors?"

"Or is it just conjecture? You know how it goes. One person says, 'What if there's a leak in Kearney's plumbing? And the water goes into the sea'? Next thing, dolphins are being wiped out."

"Maybe."

In about an hour, we were in the center of Galway, heading for the Eyre Square car park where Dunnes was located. As soon as we were parked, Joey tried to steer us to the street exit.

"Where are you going?" I asked.

"Brown Thomas."

"No! Nothing expensive. Dunnes is this way."

In the shop, surveying racks of clothes, I stopped at men's jeans. "What waist size are you?"

"Maybe thirty? It depends on the brand . . ."

I plucked a few different pairs of size thirty-twos and thrust them at him. "The changing room's over there. I'll get some joggers and tops while you're trying them on. Be quick."

He came out of the changing room in a pair of jeans and his suit shirt. He plucked at the waistband. "They're a bit . . . Should I go a size smaller?"

"Badly fitting is good. It's relatable."

"Oh, *Anna*. Once upon a time, you were so sweet." He nodded at the bundle of clothes in my arms. "What have you there?"

"T-shirts. Couple of hoodies."

"Let's give them a go." He was already unbuttoning his shirt, revealing a smooth chest and tight abs.

"Joey, do you *mind*?"

"Nothing you haven't seen before."

My blood turned to ice.

"Oh, right." He clicked his fingers. "I forgot."

His stare was brazen. Inside, I shrank. He hadn't forgotten. And I wasn't forgiven.

But we had a job to do; there was no room for anything else. Forcing cheeriness, I said, "I'm thinking about the other customers." I gestured around Dunnes. "You're not in Selfridges now."

"That's for *sure*. You know that in some high-end shops the changing rooms are as big as an apartment. Your girl can go in with you, there's a mirror, sometimes a chair and if you were so inclined you could . . ." He was being obnoxious to punish me.

"Stop. Just stop." His chest and stomach were still on full view, generating stares from other shoppers. I thrust the stack of tops at him. "Get back in there. Pick out two T-shirts and one hoodie. Quickly."

His mouth tight, he did as I asked.

Our walk back to the car park was in silence. As we drove, the sound of the radio masked the tension but my heart was pounding. I needed this job, I needed the money, but maybe addressing this was more important.

Joey spoke. "Should be back in good time." His tone was bland. "Okay with you if I do a quick FaceTime with my boys when we get in?"

"Of course." I cleared my throat. "Lovely."

"Thanks."

"Not at all." Tentatively, I asked, "You talk to them every day?"

"At least twice. I don't want to miss anything. This morning Zeke explained a satsuma to me. 'It's like an orange. Only smaller.'"

"Haha," I managed. "Cute."

"Yeah." He smiled.

. . . Were we in the clear? Perhaps.

That had been horrible.

23

In the function room, although it was only ten past seven, a healthy number of townsfolk were already drinking tea and eating biscuits. They greeted me eagerly.

"We're looking forward to a bit of argy-bargy," Moyna said.

It would certainly be a sure-fire way to identify "rogue elements." But to my disappointment, it looked like the mass crowd from the previous day had been transplanted whole. Obviously, sabotage could lurk in the hearts of the most harmless-looking pensioners, but I·sensed that the flingers of red paint had not yet arrived.

Was it too much to hope that a band of anti-capitalism brigands burst into the room chanting and waving placards? That would have made it all so much easier.

Another seven or eight pensioners flooded in, fluttering and calling greetings to their pals. Apparently they'd come "in the van" and were "making a night of it."

They crowded around the tea station, making startled noises at the availability of coffee. "At this hour!"

I embedded myself in their midst. One of them thanked me for "The night out," which triggered an outbreak of gratitude. But happy as I was to liven up a quiet Monday evening in March for these blameless souls, anxiety had me in its grip.

When Courtney came to replenish the custard creams, I grabbed her. "No one's coming."

"Calm down," she said. "The real players will arrive ten minutes late. Ah, here's the go-boy." She studied Joey. "Wearing, if I'm not mistaken, brand-new ultra-stretch straight-cut jeans from Dunnes Stores. My eyes, as they say."

"Anna's idea," Joey said. "To make me relatable."

"That's one word."

Suspiciously he watched her. "How are you so knowledgeable about men's jeans?"

"My useless other half has the same pair. I heard you were sniffing around Micah's earlier. Be glad he was closed. If he'd been open, you'd look—and I know you'll find this hard to credit—even worse than you do now."

Half-heartedly, Joey punched the air. "Winning, as my six-year-old says."

"Joey," I asked, "can you be my assistant while I'm up on the dais? Could you take contacts? Set up meetings?"

"Yeah. Grand."

Ziryan came in, then Ralph and Ferne. Who looked like an item. They all waved and descended on the refreshments.

"I'd better open another crate of biscuits," Courtney said. "Now that Ralph McIntyre has arriv—" She stiffened. "What the hell's *he* doing here?"

I followed her gaze. In the doorway stood a guard, the same one I'd had words with earlier, in full uniform and cap, his navy vest festooned with walkie-talkies and spiral cables. As he surveyed the room, Courtney whipped over and engaged him in low, jerky conversation.

I wanted to keep the law out of this. Assuming an attitude of calm authority, I approached your man. "Officer, we met earlier. I'm Anna Walsh, 'the woman down from Dublin.' Ahaha."

"Sergeant Burke."

With a glare in his direction, Courtney left us.

"What's going on here?" Sergeant Burke asked, doing a bit of swiveling and swaggering.

"I'm sure you're fully aware." My smile was pleasant. "A small amount of damage took place on private property. The proprietors want to listen to any concerns which may have triggered the . . . ah . . . vandalism."

"You can't go taking the law into your own hands."

"Of course not. We want to build bridges. But your presence here might deter the . . . aaah . . . mischief-makers from coming in tonight."

"You want me to leave?"

"I'd be grateful."

Suddenly Courtney was back. "Get out," she said to him. "*Now.*"

Astonishingly, instead of him arresting her for insubordination, they locked eyes. Impossible to tell who would prevail. Then Sergeant Burke turned on his heel and stalked away.

"Thank yo—" I began. But Courtney was distracted afresh as a gang of lads tumbled in. Wait now, one of them was the little feck who'd yelled "Not in my name" outside the church yesterday.

Tonight he was with four others, all bristling with unchanneled energy. I actually had some sympathy: they were teenage boys trying to endure the boredom of a small town, with precious few fast cars to steal and the spotty Wi-Fi interrupting their prepper playacting.

They descended on the refreshments and made loud fun of the urn of tea. Then they began throwing custard creams at each other, upsetting the elderly mass-goers. I had to do something.

Once again Courtney was ahead of me. She'd taken a firm hold of the main lad's wrist and was leading him towards the exit. "Ow." His voice was a whispered howl. "Let fucking *go*."

With a sharp summons from Courtney, the rest were also dispatched. Was there *nothing* this woman couldn't do?

Joey had been following the drama with quiet alarm. "It's nearly twenty to eight. Should we start?"

"Right." *Pray for me.*

That was when Ike Blakely and his merry band of tree surgeons arrived. Some of his crew sat down but Ike lounged against the back wall, his eyes on me. More people, all of them men, flooded in, in groups of two and three, in dark, functional clothing—overalls, cargo pants—Tipper Mahon and his brother Hal among them. These latecomers had none of the levity of the earlier arrivals. Courtney had, once again, been right.

Slipping my mic over my ears, I stood on the steps of the dais. "If we could all take a seat," I said, smiling as if I were the most confident person alive, "we'll get going."

"*You're* doing the talk?" one of the pensioners asked, with naked disbelief. "I thought you were just a girleen giving out flyers. What about—?" Her head whipped round to Joey, who was at the door. "—him?"

Just because he was a man. Joey might have done okay—he had a *good* voice, deep and just working-class enough. And he had presence. But he was never not on guard. What was needed here was friendliness, openness—and *I* could deliver it.

Perched on the dais, beaming fit to burst, I waited while my audience sat down, stood up, removed their coats, coughed, tinkled their spoon inside their cup, stage-whispered *Pass me another biscuit*, coughed again, stood up once more and slurped their tea.

About twenty men, most sporting beards, were still clustered in small, defiant knots near the door. "Plenty of chairs going." I gestured at the empty seats dotted about the room. Nobody budged.

"Okay! You'd prefer to stand . . ." and glower. Each to their own. I asked the universe for the right words and began. "Thank you all for coming here this evening."

At this point a woman came in. Definitely not one of the pensioners, she was maybe in her early forties. She carried a bursting briefcase, wore a crumpled skirt suit and had hair like an off-center wig: obviously the result of an overambitious home blow-dry.

Despite her dishevelment, she seemed both busy and capable—and well known to tonight's crowd, judging by all the discreet waving and mouthing *hello* that was taking place.

I carried on with my spiel. "My name is Anna Walsh, I'm a friend of Brigit's and I'm here because Brigit and Colm can't be." I outlined Queenie's condition and shocked gasps echoed around the room even though the entire town already knew every detail. Every word I said, every gesture I made, I was aware of Ike Blakely's focus, watching my performance with a quarter-smile.

"The proposed retreat on Kearney's Farm will bring employment and opportunities to this community, but change, even the positive type, is always disruptive," I said. "I can imagine that many people here tonight have worries, concerns and questions. If there's anything at all on your mind, I'd be grateful if you let me know. That way it can be addressed and fixed."

A sea of *extremely silent* faces presented themselves. Every mouth from here to Ballinasloe clamped itself shut.

Quickly I said, "If you're not comfortable saying it out here tonight, I don't blame you." I made myself laugh. "I'm *dying* of nerves up here!"

A healthy amount of sympathetic laughter followed this. Even one or two of the Beardy Glarers at the back cracked a smile. Automatically I took a look at Ike. Nope. Nothing.

Ms Lopsided Wig stepped forward. "Olivia French, proud to represent the people of Connemara Central on the Galway county council." Lovely confident delivery. You just had to admire her. "There's been talk you intend to only employ outsiders once the place opens."

. . . Hold on, was *she* IrishPatriot? Not a chance, I quickly realized. Why would she level anonymous accusations when she was confident enough to air her thoughts in a roomful of people?

"The plan is and always was to employ local people."

"We heard about some yoga teacher coming from Nepal?"

"There will be times when a specialist in a certain discipline will visit, whether it's a yoga teacher or a . . ." What else had Rachel told me about Brigit's ambitions? Past-life regression? Ayahuasca ceremonies? *Very* bad idea to mention them, I sensed. In this febrile atmosphere, it wouldn't take much for rumors of Satanism to start. Suddenly the word "herbalist" was in my mouth. Saved by my brain! ". . . or yes, a herbalist! But only if there were no locals to fill that unique position."

"The main reason planning permission was granted was to bring employment to the area."

"Which is exactly what we intend to do." I was very firm. "I guarantee it."

A warm wave of approval for Olivia French moved through the room. Holy mackerel, *politicians*. Taking credit for solving a problem which had literally never existed.

"I'm already aware of several of your concerns," I said. "I've good news." I told them the truth about the proposed demolition of the famine memorial, the interruption to the right of way, the danger to dolphins, etc. This caused an outbreak of chatter.

"Has anyone else a question?"

A shout came from the thick of the men at the back, almost certainly from Hal Mahon. "When are you coming for a drink with me?"

Dear *God*. But I had to laugh lightly and behave as if I could be amenable. Pressing on I said, "If I don't know the answer to your concern, I'll pass it to the most appropriate person. And I'll keep you informed every step of the way."

"Okay, I'll go." It was one of the chair refuseniks. He gestured to the three men with him. "We're tilers, between us we've thirty-five years' experience. Half the kitchens in town have been tiled by us. But that wasn't good enough for the powers that be, below."

"Thank you," I exclaimed. "I was hoping to get to speak with you. Could we have a more detailed chat perhaps tomorrow? Would you mind giving your details to my assistant, Joseph." I pointed at Joey, tilted against the door frame, his arms folded.

I could literally *hear* the surprise in the room. An almost inaudible squeak. Honestly! But fair play, Joey was reaching for his phone.

Several more questions followed, every single one from disgruntled workmen. Joey gathered their details.

Eventually it began to peter out so I resumed my exhausting beaming. "Thank you all for your time. If you've still got concerns please email me or leave something in the suggestion box at reception. I'll be here until Saturday, if you'd like to speak in person. Your identity can be kept anonymous, if you'd be more comfortable with that."

I descended from the dais to applause. Even some of the glaring men were clapping while continuing to glare. Through a sea of departing elderlies, Joey made his way up the aisle.

"I take it all back." He actually laughed. "You're still sweet." He seemed delighted. "You were great up there. Really great."

"Well . . . *good.*" I was happy too. Happy that it had gone well, happy to be worthy of Brigit's trust, happy that Joey was pleased.

Oh Lord! Hal Mahon was shouldering his way towards me. What if he'd been serious about us going for a drink? But hang on! Yet another man was swimming against the tide of pensioners: Ike Blakely, all bulk and attitude. In no time Hal was outpaced. He gave me a "Shucks, some guys have all the luck" eye-roll and conceded victory to Ike.

Who greeted me with, "You owe me a drink. When you finish up here I'll be in McMunn's."

I didn't like him giving me orders, but this might be useful. "Okay. Another fifteen minutes or so."

Appearing shocked, Joey had followed the exchange. The moment Ike was gone, he asked, "Who's the goon?"

"Ike Blakely. I told you about him."

"You're not actually going?"

"Of course I am. He might tell me something."

"But we have this under control."

"Steady, Joey. We don't know that at all."

"Have you your phone?"

"It's upstairs, in my drawer, turned off." Then, "Who do you think I am, Joey? My mum? Of course I've my phone."

"Grand." His tone was flat. "I'll call you in an hour."

"I'm a grown woman," I said. "*Don't* call me."

He took a moment. "Let me know when you're back."

"I might not come back." Then I got a grip. I was hardly going to spend the night with Ike Blakely. "I'm joking, you eejit. I'll let you know."

24

McMunn's was, just like the last time, low-lit and low on customers.

Ike Blakely was alone, standing at the bar and facing the door. Our eyes met and he actually frowned.

"What can I get you to drink?" I asked.

"Pint. What are *you* having?"

"Water."

"Have a drink with me. A proper drink." A hint of a smile softened his expression. "Go on. You've come to meet me. Commit to it."

I hesitated. "This whole business is so stressful that I'll have cirrhosis if I'm here for much longer. Oh, okay." I looked at Courtney's dad who, just like last time, was grinning enthusiastically, the poor man. "A pint, some very cheap gin and tonic, thanks. And whatever you're having yourself."

We found a table.

"You did a good job tonight," Ike said. "Calmed a lot of people down."

My nod was brusque. I was pleased but I'd set my hair on fire before showing it.

"But are any of them the ones who did the damage?" he asked.

"I guess time will tell."

"Don't you want to know who it was?"

"Obviously I'd love to." This was exasperating. "But if you're going to tell me, then do it. I've had a long day." I drank half my poteen and tonic in one go.

"Maybe," he said, "The people who did it aren't the ones who stand to benefit."

"So you're saying someone was paid to do it?"

"Me? I'm not saying anything."

Oh, come *on*. "Stop hinting, Ike, please. If you—"

"Have you ever been to Sky Head? Cliff top. About ten kilometers down the road. Bit of a climb but amazing views. You'd like it."

"How do you know what I'd like?" All of his cloak-and-dagger shtick was driving me mad.

"Come out there with me some afternoon."

"I'm not on holiday, I'm here to work."

"Which is why you should come with—Wait now! Did you think I meant a date?"

"Ah—" God, this was embarrassing. "I misunderst—"

"I'm sorry." He was suddenly contrite. "That sounded—"

"Nope, fine. It's all good—"

"Not that I'd mind, like—"

"—you're safe." *Not that I'd mind, like!* Could he sound anymore half-hearted? "It's a long time since I found a narky man a challenge."

"Narky? Me?" Confusion crossed his face.

Yeah, they can dish it out, these narky fuckers, but they can't take it.

Then he nodded. "Fair. I guess I can be. Sorry, Anna, I made a mess of that."

"You're grand. Thanks for . . ." Was there actually anything to thank him for? No. I stood up and tipped the last of my suspect gin into my mouth.

"Anna?" In a hurry, he was getting to his feet.

But I was gone.

In these heady menopausal days I had nothing like the patience I'd once had, particularly for undeserving men. My irritation with Ike was reminiscent of the disagreement I'd had with a cluster of youths in Manhattan, which had resulted in my menopause diagnosis.

I'd been walking home from the subway when, up ahead, was a crowd of young men, five or six of them. Aged? Well, how would I know? Sixteen? Twenty? A *selfish* age, judging by their loud laughter and confident occupation of the sidewalk. Shoving, skittering, basically *taking up space*.

Space I needed to pass through.

But these young men couldn't actually see forty-six-year-old women. When they focused on the spot I inhabited, they went temporarily blind.

It was hard to pinpoint when exactly my invisibility had begun. Had it been an overnight phenomenon or more of a gradual slide? Either way, it didn't matter. Because I wasn't having it.

I was getting closer and they weren't doing any preliminary rearranging of themselves, in order to let me pass. Just carrying on, *taking up all the fucking room*.

I had lived countless lives. I had survived more loss and gain than their foolish young heads could ever imagine. I had loved and been loved; I'd been courageous and tough, tender and resourceful. I no longer had the bouncy skin they were accustomed to in their women but I aspired to be kind. I was wise and immensely capable, skilled at listening to boring stories about people's drives to funerals and angry when I needed to be. Which was now.

Because I was almost upon them.

It was clear that they were not going to move.

But I was not about to stop.

I wondered what usually happened. Mrs Invisible stepped out into the road, risking life and limb? Or she hugged the wall, wriggling apologetically past them?

Well, today they were in for a surprise. The unstoppable force of an angry middle-aged woman would triumph over the immovable mountain of idiotic young men.

I barged into the throng, using my shoulders and elbows up top but underneath, maintaining the same steady pace. "Hey!" I heard. "Ow! What! You can't just—"

Oh, but I can, I thought, I very much *can*.

Joey's door opened immediately. Music was playing quietly. "Come in." He stood to one side.

"No, Joey. Too tired."

"Sorry to do this to you now but you've seven meetings tomorrow," he said. "With pissed-off tilers, joiners and decorators. Basically the whole of tonight's back wall."

My spirits plummeted, but this was what I was paid for. "I need you to get me everything on the spec for the cottages. The tiles, wallpaper, paint, wood. The planned effects, visuals, costs—" The sound of swelling strings distracted me. "—everything you can think of. As fast as possible."

"And what? You'll stay awake all night working? The first meeting's at eight thirty."

I winced. "For the last few months, I've been getting out of bed at lunchtime. If at all."

"You should be more like me, I'm up at six every day, even when I've nothing to do." He laughed. "Although that's never." That was Joey all right: he didn't do relaxation well.

Once again his music reached me and I had to ask, "What's that you're playing in there?"

"Oh." He hesitated. "Beethoven." Then, "Third Symphony."

I was surprised. Wrong-footed, even. The Real Men had had a very particular, very limited musical palate. "Wouldn't have had you down for a classical man."

Another hesitation. "Music was always my thing. I guess my horizons have expanded."

All of a sudden, his sophisticated musical taste seemed emblematic. "Joey. Look at you." A mix of pride and sadness brought a lump to my throat. "Remember when we first met? No, I'm sure you don't but you've achieved so much."

"You mean a failed marriage and—"

"Don't." Now I was blinking away actual tears. "Please don't."

Confused, he opened the door wider. "Look, just come in, would you?"

I shook my head. "Night, night. Sleep tight. Send me that info."

". . . All right then. Wait! Did the big bloke say anything useful?"

"Aaah. He hinted that he knew who had done the damage. He implied it had been on someone else's orders. But he wouldn't confirm anything."

"Time-wasting bullshit! He's just stringing you along because he's not man enough to ask you out."

"It's really not that."

"Ha! You should have seen the way he was watching you doing your talk tonight."

"That so?"

"Yeah. Like he wanted to eat you."

"Send me on that info, Joey."

"Anna. I need to say something."

"Oh God, *what?*"

"That email today? The mean one? They're wrong, Anna. Your face is very sweet."

25

Less than a year after we'd got married, Aidan and I were in a car accident, which killed him. He was thirty-five, no age at all.

The shock of his sudden death shifted me off my axis into a world where everything and everyone was alien.

Compared to Aidan's, my own physical injuries were small—a dislocated knee, a broken arm, an injured face. The emotional injuries, though, were huge: I simply couldn't grasp my reality. There had to be a parallel universe where the crash hadn't happened and he was still alive; I just needed to find a way into it.

Because if he really was dead, I knew how much he'd hate it. The thought of him being all alone, in a strange place, broke me over and over.

Even worse was the disconnection I felt from everyone I'd once loved. An unimaginable distance separated us, as if I was being beamed in from another dimension, millions of light years away.

I could attempt sociability but an hour was all I could manage before panic threatened to consume me.

It was head-spinning how quickly the world expected me to behave normally. Not to mention those with no experience of bereavement, who told me, "It'll be a while before you're back to your old self." Then expected my old self anyway. There was no chance of that, though—the guilt that Aidan had died and I'd survived made me feel I deserved nothing.

Except for those fractured moments when it seemed I owed it to Aidan to grab every second of life and wring it dry.

All around me, while everyone lived their regular lives and had their regular dramas, I'd started a covert other existence, consulting psychics and attending a Spiritualist Church in the hope of finding Aidan. Results were poor: I got swindled by a fake medium and the only "spirit" who made contact was dead Granny Maguire. In real life, I'd been terrified of her; for

"The laugh" (hers, I should clarify) she set her two greyhounds on me whenever I visited. She wasn't any more likable in death.

Meanwhile, the world kept turning. Five months after Aidan died, it was my birthday, my thirty-third. Rachel insisted that "lovely people who love you" would take me for dinner. I warned her I was in no way capable but, undeterred, she rounded up, among others, Teenie and Jennifer from work, Aidan's friends Leon and Dana, the inner circle of Real Men and, of course, Jacqui.

The night was such a disaster it was almost funny.

In the glitzy, buzzy restaurant, I saw nothing but death. While the "lovely people who loved me" worked their socks off to create a mood of celebration, I delivered long, slurred monologues on mortality. "You're going to die," I kept saying. "And it might not be in fifty years' time. You could be like Aidan and go like . . . that!" Every time I said it, I tried to click my fingers but was so drunk that it was just a disappointing flub.

As soon as was mannerly, each person ran away from me to the nearest source of limitless alcohol, where they drank with dark desperation. I can still see poor Gaz, sitting at the bar, pounding tumbler after tumbler of Jack Daniel's, casting occasional terrified glances in my direction. He refused to return to the table, even when the candlelit cake emerged from the kitchen.

In the midst of the gloom, Joey began singing a mean song about Jacqui to the tune of "Uptown Girl." "Wannabe Girl, she only hangs out with the rich and famous . . ." My nerves were so frayed that I had to ask him to stop.

Then, as if through a wall of thick glass, I understood that Joey fancied Jacqui! When did this start?

Did *she* fancy him? Without much curiosity, I focused properly. She was ignoring him and his sarky song, but that meant nothing, she'd never had any time for him. Tonight, in a pink satin camisole, super-glittery sandals and a tiny denim skirt exposing yards of tanned leg, she looked shiny and sexy.

Unsmiling but rapt, Joey was fixed on her, his eyes flickering as if a series of calculations was going on in his head. How best to get her into bed, I guessed. Not that he had a chance. Or perhaps he did?

It was wild to think that I'd ever fancied him. Not just because he was such hard work, but because it was unimaginable I'd ever wanted anyone but Aidan.

The night lurched on, and by the end I'd unsettled everyone to the point of crazed despair. Outside the restaurant the Real Men began howling at the moon, yelling about playing Scrabble until the sun came up. Off everyone went, clinging to each other, willing to do anything to avoid being alone. I'd broken them all.

The next morning, my actual birthday, my hangover was as crippling as my loneliness. Aidan's absence was even more pronounced than usual. "I wish you were here," I told the empty space in my bed, my apartment, my soul. "I miss you so so much."

A breathless email had arrived from Mum, offering cursory birthday wishes. ("I am remembering this time thirty-three years ago. Another girl, we said.") Then she asked if it was true that during last night's game of Scrabble, Joey had taken one of Jacqui's tiles and put it in his jocks, so that she had to rummage around to retrieve it.

I hadn't a clue. But I had to admit it tracked: courtship, Joey Armstrong style.

I rang Rachel, who confirmed that Joey had been "outrageous," doing nonstop meaningful staring at Jacqui and putting words like "hot" and "sex" on the board. Then he'd grabbed Jacqui's J tile (worth a not inconsiderable eight points), slid it into his underpants and announced that if she wanted it back, she'd have to get it herself. Undaunted, she rolled up her sleeve, dived in, rummaged until she'd located it, gave it a good wash and went on to win the game.

"Does Jacqui fancy Joey?" I asked Rachel.

"Anna . . ." Her voice was a little what-the-fuck? "She's *your* friend."

The unvarnished truth was that Rachel and Jacqui weren't wild about each other. They were so very different. Rachel was all "The unexamined life isn't worth living." Whereas Jacqui balked at any introspection.

Somehow the talk of last night's goings-on had breached the thick cladding of my emotions: I was curious. So I rang Jacqui. Who was at home, in bed, alone. She admitted that she'd taken her time as she'd rummaged for her Scrabble tile, but that she had no interest in Joey.

But a few weeks later, that all changed. The starter's whistle blew and she and Joey spent three days in bed. Unlike Brigit, Helen and Teenie, Jacqui—although she spared me the nitty-gritty—had nothing but praise for his performance. Then again, as the person who'd invented Feathery Strokers, her greatest compliment was: "Now *he* looks like a man who'd pile-drive you into a headboard."

Perhaps Joey gave good pile-driving? Or perhaps this time was different? Perhaps Joey was in love?

Because he certainly behaved that way. He and Jacqui went out, in public, as a couple, his arm slung casually but possessively over her shoulder. They made a good-looking pair.

Next thing, Jacqui was pregnant. It had actually happened sometime during their inaugural three-day love bender. As soon as she told him, Joey cashed in his chips: he was out.

Even I, who found it hard to feel anything except my own grief, was appalled. This had been Joey's chance to do the right thing and, as always, he'd blown it.

Over the nine months, Jacqui's mood swung from devastation to fury, but seasoned with a good sprinkling of I'm A Survivor, I'm Gonna Make It. Somehow I was co-opted as her birthing partner. It was the last thing I wanted but the will to resist just wasn't there. I was still struggling to get to the end of each day, still trying—and failing—to reach Aidan by supernatural means, still fighting off the pain from my injuries.

The first anniversary of Aidan's death came and went. I'd hoped for *some* sort of sign from him. But nothing. However, a couple of days later, I woke up feeling . . . different. No longer in physical pain. Something had shifted; perhaps a tiny amount of light had entered?

The old wives' tale about waiting a year and a day after a death made sense. I'd had to live through all of my Aidan milestones—his birthday, mine, our wedding anniversary, everything—without him, before I could know in my heart as well as my head that he wasn't coming back.

About two months later, Jacqui went into labour. We'd actually had a great day, Jacqui and I. Waiting for her contractions to be close enough together for the hospital to accept her, we wandered arm-in-arm through her neighborhood, singing songs about what an arse Joey was. In ever-decreasing intervals, we'd pause for her to writhe with agony as another contraction seized her, then we'd recommence our singing.

During one of her contractions, she ended up lying on the sidewalk. Quickly, two policemen appeared, one of whom—Handsome Karl—was known to Jacqui. She gave him her number.

Finally the hospital admitted her. First she wasn't dilated enough to have an epidural, then suddenly she was too far along. Then, with perfect, dramatic timing, just as Trea's head began to appear, Joey rushed into the cubicle and announced that he loved Jacqui.

26

My phone rang at 7.30 a.m. Joey. "Did I wake you?"

"No." I'd been up since 5 a.m., reading through the reams of information he'd emailed.

"Can I sit in on today's meetings?" Quickly, he said, "I know you can do this without me. But they're the types who feel better if another man is there. Please, Anna."

"Oooh. *That* sounded nice." Abruptly I shut up. Too reminiscent of the past. "Thank you. Perhaps that would be helpful."

". . . Grand. But you're just humoring these clowns?"

"Joey, *no*. The whole issue is that they were written off without being given their say. If they're able to do the work, we pass their details to the Project Manager."

"They won't be up to it."

"We don't know that. But if they're not, *they* need to see it. It's no good us telling them."

"Can I wear my suit?"

"*No*. And I do the talking. All of it."

". . . Have you music on there? The Cure?"

"To put me in a good mood. So which crew is first?"

"Tilers. Peadar Brady, the man from last night who's tiled every kitchen in Ireland four times over."

"Joey, lose the attitude or stay away."

After a pause, then a sigh, he said, "See you downstairs at eight thirty."

"Eight twenty. We need to be there before them." Then, "Are you busy? Could you bring me up a couple of Danishes?"

"Uh. Sure. Gimme a few minutes."

I dived into the bathroom. If I moved fast I'd have my hair washed before he got up here. Naturally, I'd barely rinsed my conditioner when the knocking began and I had to drag a towel around myself.

"Five Danishes—I got a selection." There was a tray in his hands. "Orange juice, yogurt with red jam in the bottom and a large pot of Oxo." There was even a slender vase containing a daffodil.

"Put it down anywhere." I was looking for a hair-dryer.

"This is a great song."

It was "Feeling Good," but the Michael Bublé version. I braced myself for snarkiness. "Yes, I know, Frank Sinatra's . . . *dog* . . . did a better version. But this is the one I love."

Joey seemed hurt. "The Bublé is class, puts on a great show . . . Wait, this is a *suite*? How d'you swing that?"

"My first room was over the bottle bin. I complained."

"You did? Not the Anna Walsh I know." He slanted me a sly smile. "Bet you were *lovely* about it, though."

"I actually wasn't. I intensely dislike Brogue-face Kilcroney."

". . . Brogue-face . . . ?" Suddenly Joey was laughing so hard he was almost unable to speak.

I'd unearthed a hair-dryer. *Thank God.*

". . . A brogue." Joey was shaking with hilarity. "It's *exactly* what he looks like."

"I've to get dressed. Out! Thanks for the food." I pointed at the door.

Wiping away tears, he collected himself. "There's a load of new people working here today. Well, two. One of them tried to stop me bringing this up to you. This is what happens, Anna, when you won't let me wear my suit."

"Leave, please."

Peadar Brady arrived with three other men. I welcomed them into the lounge and asked, "What'll you have to drink?"

"Tea?" Peadar consulted the others. "Yep, tea."

"Nothing stronger?" Good manners dictated that I ask.

"Cripes, no!" There was some nervous joking about accidentally gluing themselves to the floor, then we all sat.

"May I start," I said, "by apologizing that you weren't consulted before the work was allocated. The oversight occurred because the developers are planning to use Sundarata, a mosaic tile company based in Bali. They went with tilers who work exclusively for Sundarata, because they had more experience with those specific products."

"But . . . tiling is tiling."

"Absolutely! So let me show you some pictures. Unlike most mosaics, these tiles aren't just painted glass but pigmented right the way through." I clicked on several images where the little squares looked more like gemstones. I sighed and I meant it: "They're so beautiful."

"What they are," Peadar Brady observed, "is very small."

"Tiny," I agreed. "Very fiddly. But they need to be that small for mosaic art."

"What's that now?"

"All sixteen cottages will have unique bathrooms, with customized mosaic art." I clicked to the next photo, a wall which looked like a tropical jungle. "This is just a display but gives a sense of what the developers want." Dreamily, I said, "Hard to believe that something so detailed is done with tiles."

Peadar frowned.

"The imagery must reflect the local landscape, so the guest feels the outside is brought inside. Do you get me?" I checked that Peadar was still following. "But your brief is wide—you can do marine scenes, mountains, flowers, whatever you like, so long as they're of the natural world. And obviously each must be unique."

"Wait now," Peadar said. "Just so I'm clear—who's to do the marine scenes and that? You mean you'd be expecting *us* to design them?"

"Well . . . yes."

The four of them exchanged looks. "That'd be some load of work," one of the men said.

I nodded in full agreement. "It's a big project. Challenging."

"We'd need more lads," Peadar said.

Beside me, Joey tensed.

"And a design team," I said.

After a pause Peadar said, "You'd be looking at a hefty bottom line."

"How hefty?" I asked.

"Hefty."

There was actual heat coming from Joey, he was so anxious.

". . . Would you like Joey and me to give you some space?" I asked. "So you can do your calculations?"

". . . Ah. No. Look, we'll leave you to it and we'll do the sums back at the ranch." They were quick to get up.

I thanked them for coming. "Call if I can be of further help."

"Look. Anna, is it?" Peadar pulled me aside. His tone was hushed. "The job would be too big. We're only a small set-up. Even if we took on more lads, we've no experience in the fiddly work. I'll be straight with you. We were riled because we weren't even asked to tender but now we know the whole story, we understand."

"You should have been given all the facts from the beginning," I said. "I really am sorry that you weren't."

"That's appreciated." Surprising me with a smile, he said, "Good luck to ye. It'll be a great thing for the townland. Bye now." Abruptly he departed.

"Jesus." Joey made a show of mopping his brow. "I thought they were going to style it out."

"Joey, they couldn't. This gives me no pleasure, but they wouldn't have the cash flow to buy product in advance from Sundarata. Have you *seen* their prices? They're insane."

Joey's smile went all the way to his eyes. "I can't decide if you're an evil genius or . . . just a genius? But are we going to enact this pantomime in every meeting today? Can't we just tell them that they're not up to the task? You're too nice."

"Being nice is my literal job. The only reason I was hired."

"And you're brilliant at it. Those poor men. They fell right into your trap and they still think you're lovely."

"Yeah. Resting Eejit Face strikes again. Helen says that's my default expression."

"You don't look like an eejit."

"You're grand, Joey." I glanced at my phone. "Twenty minutes till the next lot. I'm going to 'reach out' to Aber Skerett. You check the email account, see if there's anything new."

"I'm across it," he called after me.

"Be *more* across it," I called back. "—Ah, hello! Is that Mr Skerett?"

After a quick conversation, I was back to Joey. "Aber Skerett will be in town tonight. He's bringing his mother to Living Well with Dementia so he'll pop in here while they're singing their songs."

"What songs?"

"How do I know? That's all he said, that he'd call in here 'while they're singing their songs.'"

"Oh, right!" Joey said. "It's a dementia thing. Before my dad died, he was totally loo-la but still recognized 'songs from his yoot.'"

I caught my breath—Joey had referenced his dad. Should I say something? "Joey—"

"Next crowd is here." He was staring out of the window. "Decorators, this time. Quick, do your sweet face and delightful voice."

I hissed, "They're my regular face and—Hiii! I'm Anna Walsh, thank you for coming."

". . . And don't hesitate to call," I did my final handshake of the day. "If I can be of further help."

I remained standing, watching the seventh and last of the crews leave the Broderick. As soon as they'd disappeared, exhaustion hit.

Beside me, I heard Joey say, "I'm fucked. Being nice is a killer."

"You weren't nice," I said. "You were just quiet."

"By saying nothing I was being nice. Bunch of operators."

"No! How could they know the work was beyond them if they weren't told? Now they've been treated as contenders and the disrespect has been erased."

Five of the seven crews told me there and then that the project would be too much for them. The other two said they'd call when they'd done their figures. Just about all of them expressed approval for the project, wished us luck, laughingly asked for a job for their wife, suggested that a cut-price rate be available for local residents, and so on. It was a good day's work.

"Are you back off to Dublin now?" I asked Joey.

"We're not finished yet. Aber Skerett will be here in a couple of hours. And there's a few more loose ends to tidy up."

"I've got this. You don't need to babysit me."

"I know you've got this. *That's* obvious. But it's been a day and I'm not in the mood for a long drive. What actual day *is* it? Tuesday? Okay, unless there's some disaster, the construction boys can go back to work Thursday morning and we can both go home."

The thought gave me a pang. "I've—mostly—enjoyed myself here. It's restored a lot of my confidence. Thanks for giving me the chance."

"Well, it was Brigit's idea. But a good one."

"I'm sure you had your doubts." To put it mildly.

"Ah, no . . ." Then he gathered himself and smiled, too brightly. "You've been great."

"Tell me, Joey, do you enjoy your job?"

"I do." He became thoughtful. "The start of a project, when everything is coming together. The excitement, the hope. I love it."

"But isn't it all so uncertain?"

"Oh God, yeah. Red tape. Investors getting a better offer. A million things could go wrong, sometimes they do, then the whole thing is derailed."

"*Oh no!*" I muttered.

He laughed. "It's usually around then I decide I'm throwing in the towel. But there's ups and downs in everything and over time you learn to be philosophical. The only part that really hurts is getting an idea, then discovering someone's got in just ahead of me. Or if I can't pull together the finance, but another broker does." He shook his head. "Hate that. Listen, I'm gonna call my kids, have a quick shower, then can we get some dinner before Aber Skerett arrives?"

"That's an idea. Why don't we go to the 'fifties-style diner'?"

"Because it's closed. Until June. We could go out." He indicated the metropolis of M'town beyond the window.

"But what if it takes ages and Aber Skerett arrives and we're not back and—no, Joey. We stay focused until the job is done. It'll have to be here."

My phone beeped. I took a quick look and smiled. It was from Angelo. **Hey. Facebook memories tells me it's four years since we were in Belo Horizonte. Heart full of gratitude for my time with you. Hope today is a good one. Sending all the love xxxx**

"Angelo," I said, to Joey's questioning face.

"You're still . . . close?"

"We text. Talk sometimes. We were lucky, we got out while we still liked each other."

Joey seemed stymied. Then he said, "He was so different from Aidan."

"I guess . . . that was the whole point."

27

When I returned, the lounge was empty. Moments later, Joey arrived, looking excited.

"You won't believe it," he said. "Courtney. Guess who she's married to."

I had no clue. "Ike Blakely?"

"You're obsessed with him! And you're ruining my great story."

I tutted. "Narky Joey."

He looked hurt. "I'm not so narky anymore."

"I've noticed."

"Have you?" He brightened. "Okay! Courtney is married . . . to the cop! Last night's officer of the law!"

I was dumbfounded. "You. Are. *Joking* me! How d'you know?"

"First chance to talk to her all day." He nodded towards reception. "I asked why he'd shown up last night. Just to piss her off, she said."

I shook my head. "Other people's marriages. *Baffling* . . ." I realized this could also apply to Joey, so I trailed off.

Too quickly, he turned and called towards the bar. "What's good, Emilien?"

"Nothing. Especially not the stew."

"The other night I had a toasted sandwich," I said. "Served with crimped crisps. Delicious."

"You had me at crimped crisps. Two toasted cheese and ham sandwiches with fries, Emilien." Then to me, "And to drink?"

"For people who don't drink a lot, Joey, we're . . . drinking a lot."

"Because I don't have my running stuff with me. Got to burn off the stress some way."

Surprisingly, there was a wine list. I gave it to Joey, who furtively slid on his reading glasses. "Don't laugh," he muttered.

"Who's laughing? You look like a man who can see."

"I look like my granddad."

"Give me a proper look."

Sheepishly, he lifted his head.

The tortoiseshell frames brought out the green in his eyes. "Bet *they* didn't come from Specsavers. They suit you. You're giving, like, 'hip business dude.'"

He scoffed at this.

"Seriously," I said. "If I didn't know you I'd think you looked hot. And cross."

"How come you don't need glasses?"

"Because I got my eyes lasered. But . . ." I wiggled my fingers at him. "I'm getting arthritis in my hands. Happy to show you my swollen knuckles next time I get a flare-up."

"Now there's an offer." He almost smiled.

"Lots of other parts of me are also kaput. My bone density is a shadow of its former self and I won't even start with my bladder. Getting old isn't ideal, Joey, but it's better than the alternative."

"Right! Thanks." Much happier now that he had examples of my oldness, he returned to the wine list. "There's a red Primitivo from Puglia. Dry, full-bodied. Or a Portuguese Grenache that's more fruity. Half-bottle do us?"

"Fine. And you choose."

"What? You don't care?"

"I *really* don't care. In New York, food and wine . . . the whole breathless drama is too much. Obviously I don't enjoy being hungry because I'm not, like, a *freak*. But I'd be okay to live on toast and Nutella forever."

"You still don't cook?"

That surprised me. "You've a good memory."

Cooking bored me senseless. By contrast, Angelo would return from the farmers market, bursting with plans because he'd found bunches of borage or Vietnamese coriander. Pre-pandemic I could muster enthusiasm for the multi-flavored extravaganza he served. (I'd eat slowly and announce each new spice as I identified it. "Is it . . . cumin? It is!") During the pandemic, not so much.

But I wouldn't say this to Joey; I still had lots of loyalty to Angelo.

"What *do* you like?" Joey seemed interested. "Yoga? All the girls love yoga."

"This one doesn't. And I know I'm not a girl, you don't have to tell me."

"I wasn't going to. *Touchy*."

"*Me?*" We exchanged a knowing smile.

Emilien appeared at Joey's shoulder. Joey tapped at something on the wine list and then continued asking questions. "Animals? Pets?"

"No."

"Anna." He looked concerned.

Tentatively, I said, "I liked making things with my hands. During the pandemic I took up—please don't laugh—weaving."

"Oh yeah. Crafting. Elisabeth does felting."

"But I lost all interest in my loom, Joey. Like, overnight. It was the last thing to go. I'd officially fallen out of love with every part of my life."

"Not just Angelo?"

"Seriously, Joey, everything. For so long I took pride in my job, then . . . all of a sudden, I felt heartsick. Weary. The end was fast and it was total. I even stopped loving New York."

". . . And just like that . . ." Joey murmured, which made me laugh.

"I don't know what I like because right now I don't know who I am."

I was treated to a silent assessment. "You're buffering."

"Yes!" I liked that concept. "Downloading the new me."

"You'll fall in love with your life again. Give it time. You might even decide to go back."

"To New York? I can't imagine it . . . But I haven't sold my apartment yet. Just wasn't quite ready, you know? Ariella says she'll give me a job if I'm back in under a year. But I'm too old to do stuff I hate, unless there's no other choice."

Emilien arrived with the wine. "I'd to go down to the cellar. I say 'cellar'—I mean the shed out the back."

"Whatcha get in the end?" I asked Joey.

"The Primitivo from Puglia."

"So you're a wine expert now?"

"Just a blagger. A good actor. Well, you know that. But I learned how to fake it in Elisabeth's world."

"Tell me about her." Pushing myself to be brave, I asked, "Why did you marry her?" Because maybe the timing had just been a big coincidence. "Obviously you loved her, but tell me the rest."

He became still and I thought I'd blown it. But when he spoke, it was with quiet sincerity. "I liked her. She liked me. More importantly, her father approved. She was so bossy . . ." He rolled his eyes and smiled. "She's from a world with rules. *Deadly* serious about them. About a week after we first, ah . . . she gave me a list of behavior she wouldn't put up with. This might sound . . . whatever, but I felt safe: I couldn't take risks or fuck things up just a little, the way I always did, because this time if I got caught, it would be game over. She scared me away from my own worst impulses."

His honesty was astonishing. I reflected that the reasons most people fall in love never crop up in Hallmark movies.

"She gave me the outline of a respectable, upstanding man, told me to fit into it or fuck off. Although she never swore."

"But you broke her rules?"

"You mean, did I fuck around? No, Anna." After a pause he said, "We got married for the wrong reasons. She wanted a bad boy who wasn't actually bad. Once she'd got me, she didn't want me any longer. I disappointed her."

"And what did you want?"

"I guess, a relationship where I wasn't hiding stuff. Or . . . where I didn't do things that contradicted the promises I'd made. I wanted to live honest and clean." He hesitated. "And I was looking for someone to take away my . . . loneliness is the closest word. I thought there was enough good stuff for it to work." He shook his head. "But we have our three boys. There isn't a day that passes that they don't make me feel like the luckiest man alive."

"Of course."

"Sometimes I'd see us from the outside." He sounded as if he was talking to himself. "Elisabeth and me, with our three beautiful children, with nice clothes and haircuts, maybe getting a business-class flight to somewhere sunny. It was a real stretch to believe that this was my life. The younger me would be so wowed. Then I'd stop looking at the outside and start looking inside. And I still felt . . ." He'd been staring at the table, now he looked at me. "Alone."

The ensuing silence ached.

"I hate saying this but maybe a year in, I sensed that once again, I'd done the wrong thing. I was too broken, disconnected, whatever the word is, to be vulnerable with her. But we bought a house, we had Max, we bought a holiday home, we had Isaac. I kept myself so busy that I didn't have to think about my inadequacies. Elisabeth deserved so much more than I was ever able to give her. I did the lot: couples counseling, then individual therapy. And I still couldn't make it work. So that's the story of my failed marriage."

I sought the right words. "Joey, your marriage didn't fail. It worked until it didn't. It was meant to last as long as it did."

"Ah, don't, Anna. Luke is always saying that too. But it failed. *I* failed."

"You can't say tha—"

"Anna, it's true. Not because I deliberately broke it, which made a change. But because—Elisabeth said it—I wasn't able for emotional intimacy. I didn't even know what she meant. I'm still fairly clueless but I think it's because the things I'm telling you now, I should have been telling her. Like the way I often feel hollow. How shut off I am."

"You're not shut off, though. You love your kids."

Courtney's voice cut in. "There they are, over in the corner guzzling wine and eating chips like they're in the Algarve. Anna! Aber's here to see you."

Startled, I jumped to attention. The Aber Skerett of my imagination was a huge half-man, half-sheep, whose wild hair was actually fleece, patterned with blue and red paint. His fictional overcoat was secured at the waist by a thick length of blue twine, tufts of fleece burst up through his collar and his trousers looked suspiciously like sheep's legs.

But crossing the lounge was a slight man, shaven-headed and kempt, wearing jeans and a nondescript jacket. *This* was Aber Skerett?

He turned out to be *lovely*—soft-voiced and reasonable. He told us there was another field that might suit his sheep. It would be a change in the routine, of course. But change can be a good thing, he suggested. In fact the other field was closer to his home. Since his mother's dementia had accelerated he liked to check in on her several times a day.

Joey and I offered to cover the first year's rent but he said there was no need.

"In that case," I said, "let us ply you with alcohol."

"I've to drive home," he said. "I'll stick to tea."

"Ice cream, then," I offered. "There's three flavors: vanilla, chocolate and strawberry. You get a scoop of each."

"Well, ah . . ."

"Excellent! That's agreed. Emilien, two bowls of ice cream—"

"Three," Joey said.

"You like ice cream?"

"I love it."

"Three, it is."

We got on so well that Aber forgot the time. It was after nine when he jumped up and said, "I'd better get back to pick up Mum."

"I'll walk you out," Joey said.

Moments later, all excited, Joey was back. "There's a woman at reception!"

28

"Ah." My tone was grave. "The Joey of old. I should have been expecting you."

"I'm not the Joey of old."

". . . Sorry."

"I think it's your woman, Vivian. The festival one!" His eyes were sparkling. "I don't know why, there's just something about her."

"You've gone native!" I was touched. "Thrilled to bits because a new person is in town."

"She's out front talking to Courtney. Come on, let's check it out."

Having also gone native, I was already on my way . . .

. . . only to discover a *young* woman. Well, probably in her thirties.

Due to her involvement in the festivals, I'd expected a seventy-something lady, serving up old-fashioned glamour. An intimidating, bejeweled creature with throat-catching perfume and rigid hair. Back in the day, when attending charity events was part of my job, those society queens had been an occupational hazard. With their performatively gracious "witticisms' and overly-languid speech patterns, they'd been hard work.

This woman's black vinyl jeans were collapsing on her. Her long legs ended at scuffed, pointy-toed boots and her unkempt hair was shortish, wavy and black as pitch.

"Vivian is back!" Courtney cried, flushed with excitement.

From ink-dark eyes, Vivian gave Joey and me an imperious stare. Her intimidating energy was no way diminished by the flecks of mascara scattered halfway down her face.

"Hi, hello, hey . . ." Joey and I mumbled, suddenly shy.

Vivian raised eyebrows at Courtney, who rattled off, "That's Anna from Dublin, Brigit's friend. And that's Joseph Armstrong."

"Of course!" As if a switch had been clicked, Vivian was *super*-friendly.

"You're the one with the sleeping bag coat," she said to me. Then to Joey, "And you're the go-boy with all the money."

She laughed and I admired her teeth, which were white and even. Nevertheless she looked a teeny, tiny bit *grimy*, as if she'd been sleeping in her clothes for a few days. Her neck, for example, could have done with a wash. And so, perhaps, could her hair.

"How long have you been gone?" Joey asked.

"Six months, nearly. And the first thing I'm gonna do is smoke a giant blunt and lie on the beach in the dark, talking shite." She directed her gaze at Joey. "Anyone like to join me?"

Wait a minute, now, this was meant to be a polite conversation, not a sexually charged . . . whatever it actually was.

"Kidding!" Vivian declared. "I've been traveling for twenty-one hours. I need a shower but my hot water and heating are MIA."

Perhaps this explained the hint of filth?

This time she included me as well as Joey. "I live over on Puffin Road, on the way out to the cliff. But I go to Barbados for the winter because even when my heating works, that house is Baltic. Every spring when I get home, I'm amazed the tide hasn't taken it.

"Courtney." Her smile was suddenly dazzling. "Any chance I could have a shower in one of the rooms? Or should I clear it with Dan?"

"Feck Dan! I'm the acting manager here," Courtney said. "Not that my pay packet knows." She reached behind her for a key. "I'd give you the bridal suite only Dan gave it to Anna here."

Everyone was astonished. Including me. "That's the *bridal* suite?"

"You think those fluffy robes are given to everyone?" Courtney asked. "And those beautiful cardboard slippers?"

"Look, anything will do," Vivian said. "You know me, Courts."

"You might as well stay the night, if your heating is broken too."

Vivian's white, even teeth made another appearance. "You're an angel," she told Courtney. She was grateful, but I would have said not terribly *surprised* at Courtney's gesture. I sensed that Vivian Hogan-Bancroft was used to generosity from many quarters.

"Ike said he'd come over to fix the heating *et al*," Vivian said. "But who knows when that will be. He's a busy man."

"All those trees to surgeon-ize." Courtney was in a reverie. "Yip. Aaaall. Those. Lucky. Treeees."

After Vivian's departure Courtney raised a finger to her lips. She appeared to be counting in her head. After about twenty seconds, she relaxed, leant closer to us and said, "Right! That was Vivian Hogan-Bancroft. She's our local . . . what would I call her?"

"Queen?" That had been Brigit's word.

"'Queen' will do. Loved by all. If you get my drift. Free spirit." She winked and repeated, "Free spirit, if you get my drift. Loved by all. Or should I say 'loved by many'? So her father is Jesper Bancroft. Of Quarter Bond."

"G'wan," Joey said in a tone which was "not impressed but polite enough to pretend he was."

Quarter Bond was a British prog-rock group from back in the mists of time. Five men. I knew more about them than perhaps the average person because, for a short spell in the nineties, Helen had been fixated. Their lyrics were quoted and mocked and a popular game in the Walsh household was Pick the Most Grotesque Quarter Bond Bloke.

"He lives in Barbados," Courtney said. "Owns a recording studio there. Her mother is Isidra Hogan."

Now I was impressed: Isidra Hogan was a badass. She'd started modelling at fourteen, married Jesper when she was twenty, did a stint as a rock wife, had three children, left Jesper, became a lawyer, then a politician. Now she was a big cheese in the European Parliament—looking lined but still *very* sexy—where she issued astute sound bites that made Brexiteers foam at the mouth. (Isidra is often cited as an exemplar of "aging gracefully" by judgy 22-year-old girls, who think aging is a choice and Botox an abomination. I mean, we'd all age gracefully if we had Isidra's bone structure.)

"And," Courtney continued, "her half-brother is Tayto McGuffin. The far-right melt? As you can imagine, because of her famous family, Vivian's met everyone in the world. But even if she'd grown up under a rock, she'd still charm the birds from the trees and persuade them here. She's a godsend. The big festivals are always trying to poach her but she's loyal to us."

"Wow," I said. "Well. So? I hear you're married to the copper?"

"God. Don't remind me."

"Is that how you're so good at 'policing' crowds?" I stopped. "That was a pun, you two. 'Police.'"

Joey and Courtney laughed heavily.

"The way you got rid of those teenage fuckers last night!" I said.

"Two of those teenage fuckers are my sons. Yeah." Courtney rolled her eyes. "The main lad? He's Winnie, my eldest. And Hannibal, my youngest, was there as well. Not their real names, but I haven't the energy to explain. Now you can see why I'd rather be here working day and night, than at home with that shower."

"Absolutely. Courts, tell us why you hate your husband."

She brightened. "God, he's awful. Power-mad. Money-mad. Sex-mad. Lazy as fuck. No sense of humor. Wants *everything* but thinks it should just be given to him, won't do the work. Hates anything good happening to anyone. Delighted at another's misfortune. I was nineteen when I met him and he was a tyrant even then, giving me orders, talking the big talk, then giving me the silent treatment because someone else had pissed him off, ya know? Because I was nineteen, I was mad about him. He had hair in them days. Next thing I'm pregnant, next *next* thing we're getting married—I know, pure lunacy—my mother's dying wish was that I'd jilt him at the altar. Like the silly girl I was I thought we'd be okay. We weren't, we're not but we can't afford to get divorced. Some advice for you, Anna, never marry a man you plan to change. Nicolas Burke hasn't changed one iota in the last twenty years. Except got worse, I suppose."

29

As I got ready for bed, I was wondering what it must have been like for Courtney—getting pregnant so young, by such a terrible man. This set off a train of idle thoughts, which eventually landed on Jacqui's life after she'd had Trea. In those early years she'd been in a state of almost constant rage.

I found myself thinking of one random night, when Trea was a year and a bit. I was just leaving my office when Jacqui rang.

"Babes. Emergency." She sounded tearful. "That asshole said he'd watch his own kid tonight—Father of the Fucking Year—but he's not here, not answering his phone, and I've to work—"

"On my way."

Outside, I grabbed a cab and was with Jacqui and Trea in ten minutes. (Trea had started life as "Treakil" but Jacqui and Joey had hammered out a compromise and she was now known as Trea.)

This—me deputizing for Joey at the last minute—was becoming a regular thing. In addition, I usually did one or two scheduled babysitting sessions with Trea every week.

Not that I was complaining. Now that I'd finally stopped using psychics to try to contact Aidan I had almost no life. Every second Friday, I caught the train to Boston, spent a grueling weekend with Aidan's family, then, hollowed out from fake-cheeriness, got the train home on Sunday.

The only other thing going on was my job. It was often stressful and always exhausting but it was a literal painkiller. The break I got from thinking about Aidan gave me enough endurance to live through the non-work hours.

I let myself into Jacqui's apartment—and there she was, full-on Glamazon, Trea in her arms.

"Wow." I inspected Jacqui's short fuchsia dress and long, long legs. "You are so *sexy*."

"Thank you for this." Jacqui passed Trea to me. "She's been off-form all day. A slight temperature, the thermometer is on the shelf, call me if—"

"Go," I said.

Jacqui cooed at Trea. "Sorry for leaving you with Anna again. But your daddy is an asshole. Yes, sweetie." Her eyes sparkled. "Not just any asshole. But the world's worst."

"Jacqui, please." If Trea didn't understand yet, she would soon. And Joey might be unreliable, but he was still her dad.

In a flash, Jacqui's mood changed. "I hate him, Anna. He's banging Scarlett."

"Who?"

"You know Nell's sister, Madilyn? Her friend."

I didn't know her. "But you're with Handsome Karl . . ."

"That's just to make him jealous."

Poor Handsome Karl, he deserved better.

"He could have any woman in this entire city," Jacqui said. "And he has to pick a mate! Well, a mate's sister's mate. Anyway, thanks for bailing me out again. I honestly don't know how I'd cope without you."

"You won't have to." We'd been here before and there was nothing new to say.

Briefly, I wondered how she'd be managing if Aidan hadn't died and I still had a life of my own. "Go to work," I said. "It'll all be okay."

Because maybe it would.

But it was so messy. On the night Trea was born, when Joey had arrived, declaring his love, it seemed we were all set for a happy ending. Quickly, though, it became clear it was a false alarm. The word "love" was never mentioned again. When Jacqui plucked up the courage to ask, he'd muttered something about "The heat of the moment."

And that was that.

He wasn't a total deadbeat: financially he behaved like an adult, paying generous rent and maintenance. Trea spent every second weekend with him. But, increasingly, he couldn't be depended on to show up on the evenings he was supposed to. Jacqui worked unpredictable hours; she needed someone reliable. "And," as she said, over and over, "she's his daughter, he should *want* to be with her!"

All credit to Jacqui, she'd made efforts to move on. Handsome Karl seemed like a great guy and was good with Trea. (It was a tragedy that a man was garlanded with praise just because he was cool about his girlfriend's child with another man, but there we are.)

"Go on," I said. "Off to work. Who is it tonight?"

"Darlene Ryker-Scott." An actress who was as famed for her extracurricular high jinks as her extraordinary talent. "It'll be a late one."

"No problem." I'd been sleeping on the divan in Trea's room so regularly, we'd formalized things. There were enough of my clothes and stuff in the apartment to see me through a few days.

With a swish of her pale, shiny hair and a puff of some powerful perfume, Jacqui was gone, leaving me and Trea watching each other warily.

"Mama?" Trea's voice flirted with breaking. She was a tearful little thing at the best of times.

"She'll be back soon!" *Don't cry. Please don't cry. For the love of all that's holy, please don't cry.*

Being in sole charge of Trea gave me anxiety. It wasn't my fault—until now I'd had no experience with babies. (Helen was three years younger than me, but my memory had her arriving fully formed and terrifying.)

"So, Bubba, let's find this thermometer!" I'd assumed my confident nanny voice. "Then we'll make your bottle and off to beddy-byes."

Another whimper came from Trea. She had an uncanny ability to pick up on moods.

Considering my lifelong fear of responsibility, the universe must have been having a good laugh for itself, that I'd ended up as almost a second parent to this little girl.

Before Aidan, I hadn't even wanted a pet. The idea of a dog, with their daily needs—every *single* day—brought on the panic.

The truth was, even owning a plant was too much. People thought that was a joke, but having a thing squatting in my apartment needing once-a-week watering ate away at my peace of mind. As soon as I'd watered the wretched thing, I had perhaps ten minutes of relief before realizing it would need to happen again in less than seven days. The regularity of the obligation was what freaked me out.

That changed when I met Aidan. We hadn't gone into great detail but children had been part of our plan. My terror was dialed all the way down because Aidan would be there.

None of it came to pass though, and when Aidan died, my desire for kids went with him. And seriously, the most broody person on earth might reconsider their longing when they witnessed Jacqui and Trea's chaos.

Being a single working mother looked brutally hard—even considering that Jacqui's situation was a lot better than many. Financially, she was fine. And while Joey had become unreliable in terms of childcare, he *did* show sometimes.

Then there was me. I was glad to help. It made me feel less disconnected. But if I wasn't ten minutes away, ready to jump into the breach at a moment's notice, life would be a lot harder for Jacqui.

I took Trea's temperature—slightly above normal. *Shite.* Immediately I was afraid she might die. An ever-present fear dogged me that people could die without warning.

"Cool down, good girl," I said, while I made her bedtime bottle. In the starry, blue-lit nursery, I read her a story, then put on the plinky-plonky lullaby carousel. "Time to go to sleep," I whispered.

I lay on the divan beside her cot and shut my eyes. I never slept well here, waking countless times in the night just to check Trea was still breathing. But for once I actually began to drift off. Letting go into delicious ease was rare and gorgeous . . . The buzzer blared, jolting all my nerves with adrenaline.

I swear to God, if this had woken Trea and I spent the rest of the night trying to get her back to sleep . . .

To my huge surprise, it was Joey at the door. In he came, wearing—of all things—a *suit*. He looked like . . . a businessman.

"Anna, hey. I'm watching Trea tonight?"

"Don't you have a key?" I spoke in a furious whisper. "You could have woken her. And you're an hour late."

"Sorry. I've stuff going on."

"I can only imagine." I bit the words out.

"I was working." His tone was surprised. "Is Trea okay? Jacqui said she was off-form."

He made to go into Trea's room and I blocked him. "Don't wake her. Her temperature is slightly up. Keep an eye on it. Here's the thermometer."

He examined it from a couple of angles, as if he'd never seen one before. "Thanks for bailing me out."

"Again," I said.

"Whoa." He recoiled. "Okay, 'again.' Sorry for messing up your evening. I've got it from here."

I turned to gather my stuff.

"She hates me, right?"

"Who, Jacqui? Or Trea?"

He went pale. "Trea hates me?"

"She's thirteen months old, Joey. How would I know if she hates you?"

"And Jacqui?"

Of course she did, but . . . "Ask her yourself."

"Okay. Sure. Sorry." He hesitated. "Anna? Do you hate me?"

I was too tired to spare his feelings. "You make it difficult to like you."

"Tell me what I can do differently."

"Why are you asking me?" Then quickly, because I wanted to leave, "Why did you sleep with Scarlett?"

"What does it matter to you who I sleep with?"

"Not me. Jacqui."

". . . But . . . she's with Handsome Karl."

"You could have found someone she didn't know." I stopped. "Or maybe you couldn't? Maybe you've slept with literally every woman in this city."

He rolled his eyes.

"You've slept with one of my sisters."

A small moment pulsed between us; then, chastened, he nodded.

"My work colleague, Teenie. Rachel's best friend, Brigit. You've slept with my best friend. And these are only the ones I know about. You could have slept with *all* of my sisters—"

"I haven't—"

"—*and* my mum—"

"Anna, for Christ's sa—"

"I'm almost the only woman I know that you haven't slept with!"

"You sound . . ." Briefly, he seemed pleased. ". . . pissed off. But I was always putting the moves on you. You weren't interested."

Anger rose in me. He was so flippant. "Everything's just a game, isn't it?"

"No. I was being serious there. I *was* always putting the moves on you."

"You ignored me—and Jacqui—for like the first six months we lived here. You literally wouldn't even say hello to us."

"Because Luke warned me off. Didn't want me bothering another of Rachel's sisters, but—"

He wanted to keep talking bullshit. Listening to his own lies and wasting my time. Then a wail sounded from Trea's room.

"Is that . . . ?" He frowned.

"Yes, Joey, your child needs you."

In the blue-lit bedroom, Joey lifted Trea from her cot, and held her against his shoulder. "Sssh, sssh, sssh," he said. "Daddy's here, it's all okay. Are you hungry, my little Trea?"

"She's just had her bottle."

"Does your diaper need to be changed?"

When Trea—naturally—didn't reply, he slid a sheepish look at me.

"Your guess is as good as mine." It was an effort to remain steely in the face of Trea's distress but this was for everyone's good.

He smiled. "I was just chancing my arm." He lay Trea on the changing mat and was snapping open the poppers on her onesie. "It's okay, little girl. Gonna get you a nice, clean diaper."

"I need to show you how the thermometer works."

"Anna. I *know* how it works."

Give the man a medal. "Keep an eye on her temperature. Oh, and Jacqui will be late. You'll probably have to stay the night." I pointed at the divan. "So change the sheets. Then change them again in the morning. Because I'll probably be the next person sleeping in it."

"We share a bed." He sounded entertained. "You and me."

I gave him a death stare.

"Sorry." He spoke quickly. "Did it again. Trying to be funny and just being dumb. Anyway, I do change the sheets."

But I'd caught hints of his musky male smell from the pillow. It always unsettled me.

"I do," he repeated. "Maybe I'm just very . . ."

"Maybe you are."

He laughed.

As I descended in the elevator I wondered if I'd put Trea in danger, leaving her in the care of that dummy. But Joey had to step up. Women were always cutting him slack and making allowances. I wasn't going to be yet another of them.

30

Wednesday morning and all was quiet at Kearney's Farm, Lenehan said, when I rang for our daily check-in.

"Great," I said. "And you're okay?"

"All good," he said.

"Well, if you need anything, you know where I am."

I hung up. I should be feeling relieved. Uplifted, even. Except . . . I didn't entirely trust the peace. Surely it couldn't be this easy?

My concern was that over the last four days I'd met a lot of people here and none of them, I'd sensed, had done the damage.

On the way down to breakfast I bumped into Joey, who looked dishevelled. "I'm going up to Micah's," he said. "I need clean clothes."

"You're *buying* stuff? You flash piece. Just wash them in your sink. Or . . ." I gave him a look. "You could get Vivian to do it."

"Hah! Jealous, are you? But you've got the goon hot for you." In a quick change of tone, he said, "When I'm back from Micah's, can we have a catch-up? See you in the lounge?"

In the breakfast room, two waiters I'd never seen before were darting about, carrying plates of food. This place was gearing up for a busy weekend. Right on cue, my phone rang. Mum.

"Here's our final offer," she said. "Just myself and Helen. No one else. Not a single other person."

"Just two of you."

"Just two of us. And Margaret."

"Just two of you? And Margaret? That's three, Mum."

"You're entitled to your opinion."

"What about Rachel?"

"No men are allowed and she won't come without Luke, she might have to last half an hour without him 'going down' on her. It's a disgrace that a woman of my age has to know such things."

"Mum, if you're really coming, you can't stay in my room. Book an Airbnb."

"I will *not* stay in one of them, there's too many rules. Locked drawers that could contain anything—severed heads, dead babies. And all the cleaning you have to do! I want room service and nice towels and people I can complain to."

"So pay for a hotel room. You have enough money."

"I do, I suppose."

In the lounge, as I waited for Joey, I checked the email account. More rumors. More racism. Two offers of sex.

The new rumors unsettled me, especially one insisting that the current build was only the first phase of the Kearney project. According to Hunter20246@gmail.com, a four-story edifice was in the pipeline and the Kearneys had the "planning permission people in their pocket."

Almost every rumor so far had turned out to be nonsense. The worrying thing was that they just kept coming. The feeling—that we'd placated people who'd never really been angry—arrived again.

And here came Joey, no longer wearing the hoodie I'd made him buy in Dunnes, but a soft, cable-knit *geansaí* in a dark blue.

"How was Micah's?" I asked.

"It was . . . like a time capsule. I was really only looking for the basics—socks and the rest. Lotta nylon up there. *Lotta* nylon. Scooby Doo jocks." He laughed. "I'd flashbacks to when I was six."

"But your new sweater is beautiful."

"Yeah!" He shoved up the sleeves and flexed his inked forearms, briefly revealing some words on his right arm. "I feel, yeah . . . *manly*, like I could go out and catch a boatload of haddock. It's not from Micah's but another shop. Some woman called Ferne? *So* friendly. Gave me twenty percent off."

I bet she did.

"Sit down." Curiosity got the better of me. "What's that ink say?"

He held up the tender inside of his right arm, so I could read it. It said, "I am not afraid to walk this world alone."

"Not true." There was self-mockery in his smile. "But when I got it done, I wished I was."

"Tell me about that?" I nodded at a colorful floral piece.

"The roses? For my granny—she was good to me. A great gardener. She died when I was nine, I was *heart*broken." He held up the inside of his left arm, displaying a column of four tiny hearts. "One for each of my kids. The Celtic warrior band?" He looked a little embarrassed. "Young, Irish, defiant, living overseas: it was a rite of passage. Luke has one too."

"And this?" An intriguing blue and black circle sat higher up, close to his elbow. "Oh, it's a *wave*." One perfect wave, curling over onto itself. "What inspired that?"

"My uncle Dinny. Mum's brother. Spent his life at sea. Working on cargo ships. I wanted to be him."

"It's absolutely beautiful. Right! There's new rumors we need to address."

Immediately he got out his phone, then slid on his glasses.

"Hot," I said. "And cross."

He actually grinned, then set about dismissing the emails. "This, about the planning permission, is absolute bullshit. So is the one about housing refugees. So is . . . Anna, they're all bullshit. Except for the offers you've been made. Up to you what you do with them. AubergineDick sounds promising."

"Right! I thought that too. I'll give him a shout."

"Seriously, though, these assholes should have the law on them."

"Joey. Stop. All women have to put up with this shit."

"Doesn't make it all right."

"We're not going to talk about it. So I'll put the info about the planning permission, et cetera, up on the various Facebooks."

"Face*books*? Plural? How many?"

"Loads. Well, five or six. You know how it is: Maumtully Chats; Maumtully Neighbors; Maumtully Potholes . . ."

"Strictly a WhatsApp man here. I'm in about fifty groups." Then, "Although I never look at any of them. Wheelie bins and stuff. So now we need to visit the site and talk through a new timeline with Tipper Mahon. The construction work can start again tomorrow. By close of business today, you and I can head back to Dublin. Job done."

"I was thinking I might stay a little longer."

"No need. You'll be paid for the full week."

"I've a feeling this isn't over yet."

"It's over." He was definite.

"Well, you're the boss. But there's a second reason I want to stay."

"To put the moves on Ike Blakely?" Sternly, but obviously joking, he said, "You're just out of a long thing with Torres, you shouldn't rush straight into a new relationship. You do know that?"

"Thank you, Agony Aunt Joey. No, it's Mum and Helen, you know, my sister?"

"Uh-uh." He colored slightly.

"They want to come for the weekend. Mum says there's a funfair."

"There actually is. I just saw them unloading bumper cars from a lorry."

"But I'll pay for my room from tonight."

"Nope. We'll call it a consultancy expense. You're good until, well, when do you want to leave? Monday? Tuesday? Monday it is. So, you're still very close, you and your sisters? Who else? Who are your ride-or-dies?"

This was still a surprisingly sore subject. "Everything got very . . ." I sought the correct word. ". . . *streamlined* because of the pandemic. So many people left New York. And now I'm here, having to construct an entire life from the ground up, after living in another country for eighteen years. So ride-or-dies? Nobody."

Embarrassed color edged his cheekbones. "I'm sorry," he muttered. "You still miss her?"

It was complicated. Who knew what she was like now. But . . . "I've never met anyone as suited to me as her. Maybe she's changed a lot and we wouldn't vibe now, but the way we were? Oh God, yes." My voice became wistful. "She was this amazing ally, always in my corner. And so positive, such fun. But because it had always been so easy with her and me, I hadn't a clue what to do when things got ugly." I stopped, then blurted, "I still dream about her."

"Anna." Joey sounded appalled.

"You see a lot of her?"

"Only because of Trea. I mean, we get along okay. Jacqui and Elisabeth, though?" His face went *Yikes.* "You couldn't get more different. You know she's—"

"—married? I do." Although I was blocked on Facebook and her Insta was private, Jacqui and I still had a handful of mutuals.

"Griff's his name. He's sound. They've a little boy, Ollie, he's nine. My three are mad about him. She lives in Banagher in Offaly. Do you know she works in 'the most expensive hotel in Ireland'?"

"No." I'd known she was still in hotels. But . . . "Do you mean Arcadia?" Fuzzy details were coming to me, probably from the magazine on the plane.

"That's the place. An upgraded Victorian mansion where you cosplay lord of the manor for a night, then fork out over a month's salary for the privilege."

"Everyone has dinner together at one long table? Kippers for breakfast? Shooting parties? Did Claire stay there . . . ? If it's the place I'm thinking of, it was 'death by upholstery.'"

Joey groaned. "But, Anna, it's so impressive. The old house was an absolute shambles—then two years and fifty million euro later, it's a world-class super-hotel. That was one of the projects I missed out on, by less than six months. Still hurts."

"I can't see Jacqui fitting in in a place like that."

"She says the guests are no trouble. None of the stress of New York."

"And she likes that? I get it. These days I prefer a quieter life too."

"Right . . . Totally." He looked mortified. "And she never . . . ?"

Forgave me? Spoke to me again? "No."

A new staff member, a young woman, looking excessively glam for eleven in the morning—lips, lashes, the lot—swished her way to our table.

Haughtily, she asked, "Are you Anna?"

I nodded, enjoying her attitude.

"And you"—she switched her disdainful stare to Joey—"must be the go-boy?"

"I must be." Joey seemed as entertained as I was. "And you're Teagan?"

She recoiled. "How do *you* know?"

"We met yesterday morning. You tried to stop me taking a tray up to Anna."

"Because, yeah, we don't do room service."

"But you weren't doing it. I was."

"Semantics." Teagan flicked her ponytail. "So, I've a message for the pair of you. From Vivian. There's a sesh tonight in the Spanish. A welcome-home thing. You're to come, she says. It's an order, she says."

Seriously? Vivian was hilarious. "What time?"

Teagan couldn't have been less interested. "Eight? Nine? I don't know. You can ask"—unwarranted contempt was applied to her next word— "*Courtney* when she's in."

A message was pushing its way up from my subconscious. "Are you . . . ? In some way . . . ? Related to Courtney?"

The girl shut her eyes, leant on the table and hissed, "Madre de Dios!"

"That's a yes?" Joey said.

"She's my mom," she almost wailed. "How did you know?"

"Your competence." Joey actually sounded sincere.

"Not because I look like her?"

She shouldn't have said that. Because as soon as I studied her face, I saw that yes, Courtney was in there. There was nothing wrong with Courtney but who wants to look like their mum?

With a flounce, Teagan was gone. Using her fist to bang open the swinging door behind the bar, she disappeared. Soon afterwards, a faint shriek reached us.

"Oh dear," Joey murmured. After a suitably respectful pause had elapsed, he said, "Should we go to Vivian's thing?"

"It would do no harm. Hearts and minds, Joseph, hearts and minds."

"Okay. But I need to leave early tomorrow morning. My boys are off to Fuerteventura for the long weekend. I want to see them before they go."

"Why aren't you going?" I was confused. "I thought you and Elisabeth got on great?"

"We do. Within reason. But . . ."

I held my breath.

". . . she's met someone else."

"Oh, Joey."

"Ah, yanno, he's grand. Wesley's his name. Solid man. Much more suited to her than I ever was. He's been gradually introduced into the boys' lives. This is their first holiday, the five of them."

"But what about you and Elisabeth parenting as if you were still together?"

"This is how we have to do it." He looked bleak. "Life moves on. She was always going to meet someone else. She's built for coupledom. That's the challenge, isn't it? Still presenting a united front to the boys even though she's got another partner. Husband, actually. He'll be her husband as soon as possible. I know her."

Tentatively, I placed my hand on his. Instantly, goosebumps puckered his forearm.

I moved back as if scalded.

"Jesus." He slid me a shamefaced look. "I'm not used to sympathy."

Not for the first time with Joey, I thought my heart would cave in.

"I don't mind Elisabeth meeting someone. But I'm afraid my boys will love him more than they love me."

"Oh God. Joey—"

"No." He held up his hand. "No platitudes."

"You love them so much. You're devoted to them and they know that. You're their dad and no matter who Elisabeth meets, they'll always love you the most."

31

It was a long day. We walked the entire site with Tipper, visiting every cottage, assessing what still needed to be done. Now that the work was about to recommence, Tipper was a changed man, garrulous and full of "hilarious" anecdotes. I'd never realized that pretending to be entertained could be such hard work.

The only time the joviality paused was at the mention of his digger. "Poor oul' Betsey is still in the hospital. She'll be laid up for a while. We'll hire a replacement. Funds will be needed."

"Send me the invoice," Joey said.

Afterwards, Joey and I dropped in on Lenehan. Just a short chat, I'd thought, to break the "good" news about the threat to the farm having gone away. (I still wasn't convinced.) But when we found him in the kitchen, Colm was also there. Without a word, he threw his arms around Joey. They stood for a long time, in a tight hug, Joey circling his palm on Colm's back.

Colm eventually pulled away and we all sat.

"Tea?" Lenehan offered. "Coffee?"

"Whatever's easiest. What's the news?" Joey's elbows were on his knees as he stretched close to Colm.

"She's having every scan known to modern medicine," Colm managed. "They're still deciding if they'll try to remove the tumor or go the chemo route."

"Surgery is risky?"

"Like you wouldn't believe. Everyone has an opinion but no one really knows. Our little girl will be slightly paralyzed or a lot paralyzed or not paralyzed at all, depending on who you ask."

I felt faint.

"What about chemo?" Joey asked.

"It'd be very hard on the little chicken. Make her very sick in the short term. Putting her through that . . ."

This was *awful*.

"There'd be long-term issues, like infertility. And after all that, it might not work."

"Man." Joey grasped Colm's hand. "That's the worst."

"I should trust the medics to decide on the right approach. But what if they disagree? Which one do you go for? What if you don't trust any of them?"

This poor man, the entire family, what a horrible set of choices they were facing.

On the drive back to town, I felt very low but Joey looked actually ill.

"You okay?" I asked.

"Queenie's a great kid. The thought that she might be paralyzed. Or worse. I mean, *God*." A pause followed, while his gaze remained fixed on the road. "And I know this sounds selfish but—"

"—you're thinking about your own kids. That's natural, Joey."

He sighed. "Soon as you're a parent, the world is altered forever." Briefly, his focus was off the road and on me, offering warm complicity. In a millionth of a second, I watched realization dawn, followed by alarm, then he was back to staring *hard* at the road.

Silently I watched the landscape flash by, the sea to my left, stony fields to my right and beyond the furthest edge of town, the steep climb of the cliffs, leading up to Sky Head. What had Ike wanted to show me up there? As soon as I had that thought, a building appeared: a flat-roofed structure, set close to the cliff edge. The views from it must be amazing, especially at sunset. But from down here it was a wound on the landscape.

I hadn't noticed it when I'd first arrived. "That must be the Big Blue."

Joey took a glance. "Yeah. It's . . . Wow, what an eyesore. How'd Kilcroney get planning permission? This country. The hoops *we* had to jump through to get the permit to build. 'Protecting the view' so it's only when you're right on the actual land you can see the cottages. And if you're out on a boat you can't see them at all."

"But that's good. I think they've got better at preserving nature in the last few years." I noticed something. "Further up the cliff, there's . . . a wood?" I trained my eyes on a large cluster of tall evergreens, erupting with outlandish unlikeliness from the wind-scoured plain of the cliff top.

As we got nearer, the tips of three, no *four*, gray-stoned turrets appeared above the highest trees. "It's a house! Hey, that must be her ladyship's freezing old mansion!"

Joey chanced a glance. "Rose's? Yeah, guess it is."

"Rose?"

"... Isn't that her name?"

Yes, but ... I'd thought "her ladyship" was her name. "Joey! Eyes on the road, please!"

"Sorry. It's more beautiful here than I'd realized," he confessed. "Luke and Rachel brought me along to Brigit's and Colm's one weekend. I was blown away by the potential in Kearney's Farm, their own cove, the mountains to the south. Then I was looking at infrastructure, bylaws, staffing ... and somehow I never focused on the cliffs to the north. They're spectacular."

"There you go. Another selling point."

It was almost six thirty by the time we reached the hotel. Joey asked, "You want to get dinner before Vivian's thing?"

"I've a doctor's appointment now."

"Why? What's wrong?"

"Nothing. I'm on the hunt for HRT."

"In that case ..." He raised his eyebrows. "Good luck? We'll have toasted sandwiches when you're back?"

Dr Olive was as young as Courtney had warned but she was friendly. "Come in. Sit down. How can I help?"

I outlined my circumstances. "Can you prescribe me HRT? Please."

"One moment now. What are your symptoms?"

Oh, come on! *Insomnia, amnesia, bleak thoughts, weight gain, a needy bladder...* "Rage."

Suddenly energized, Olive said, "Anger issues? Because anger has many caus—"

"Anxiety," I rattled off at speed, because I sensed a recommendation for therapy was imminent. "Night sweats, fuzzy thinking, cravings for carbs, hairy arms." I paused for breath. "But the hair on my head is thinner. How unfair is that?"

"Hair-thinning can be a sign of long Covid. Have you had your—"

"—bloods done? Yes. Flying colors, thank you."

"How recently?"

"Last week." This was a lie but I could not afford to get side-tracked. "I'm definitely perimenopausal. I've had almost no HRT for the past few weeks and the symptoms are back." *Particularly the rage.*

"Menopause is not an illness. HRT is not a medicine."

"So why do I have to see a doctor to get it?" Then, "Please." I was almost begging. "When I began it about twenty months ago, it transformed me."

Marveling, she asked, "You really think it makes that much of a difference?"

One random afternoon, young woman, with no warning whatsoever, you'll feel as if you've just been set on fire. Yes, on literal fire. For seven hours on a Tuesday in April, even under threat of torture, you'll be unable to remember Florence Pugh's name. You will awaken, some night, in the early hours, to the horrible sensation that you've wet the bed. And when you realize that the drenched sheets are courtesy of sweat, not urine, you won't feel any less upset.

I could have said all of that and so much more but I went for, "It made my life worth living again."

Shaking her head with performative disbelief, Dr Olive began clattering at her keyboard. "I've sent a script to Gannon's, the chemist by the monument. One month's supply."

I thanked her graciously and almost danced my way to Gannon's. Where they had no testosterone—it would have to be ordered from Limerick. Neither had they any progesterone tablets, although they'd be in the day after tomorrow. However, they furnished me with estrogen patches. Back in my room, I slapped one on. Immediately—psychosomatic? Perhaps not?—I began to feel less anxious, less irritable, less exhausted. Then I skipped down the stairs to meet Joey for our toasted-sandwich stomach-liner.

But was this what my life would be from now on? Moving from town to town around Ireland, trying to get an emergency appointment in a local surgery, where I'd throw myself on the mercy of a doctor in the hope of getting a handful of HRT here and there? It was no way to live.

32

"I'm not staying long at this thing," Joey said outside the door of the Spanish. "I need to be on the road first thing tomorrow."

"Okay, Boomer." But I was having doubts myself: it sounded *wild* in there.

Once inside, the noise was deafening and the mood riotous. Everyone seemed to be already drunk.

Joey fought his way to the bar, then we hovered uneasily in a corner, drinking too quickly and watching the revellers.

I became aware that he was shifting and twisting his body. "Joey?" I asked. "You okay? Are your Scooby Doo jocks too tight?"

He actually laughed. "I should have bought the Scooby Doo pair. The ones I'm wearing are like what old guys wear to bed in Westerns. The smallest pair were huge, they've twisted themselves around my—"

Quickly I said, "We should mingle. We're not here to enjoy ourselves. Hearts and minds, Joey. Never forget."

"No need. Job is done."

"Ten minutes," I said. "Go and talk to people. *Nicely*. Meet me back here and we can leave."

I dived into the throng, encountering several of Monday's Beardy Glarers. Different story tonight, everyone much friendlier. Each of them shouted, "Can I buy you a drink?" In reply, I yelled, "I'm fine for now." And kept moving.

Although it wasn't something to be proud of, I was looking for Ike. Finally, he appeared and smoldered down at me with unfriendly intensity.

"Anna, hey. I buy you a drink?"

"I've got one."

"Never hurts to have a new one lined up."

This was the most conversation I'd ever had from him.

"I hear you're shipping out tomorrow?"

"Only Joey," I yelled up at him. "I'm staying."

"And there was me planning on breaking another digger just to keep you in town."

He wasn't smiling. Perhaps he didn't know how? But he'd never been so chatty.

Focusing on the front of his plaid shirt, I found myself thinking about unbuttoning it. I could only blame the HRT. Ike was carrying slightly more weight than a judgy doctor might like but it added to his appeal. I'd lie him on his back, I decided. Straddle him. Smooth the palms of my hands over his hairy stomach then move lower, unbuckling his . . . was there a belt? Oh yes, there *was*—my mouth literally watered—then a woman in a glittery bomber jacket tumbled against my shoulder. "Sorry," she yelled, bumping me from my reverie. Surprised by how far I'd drifted, I met Ike's eyes. His expression was interesting. Extremely so.

He never made any effort to be pleasant. He kept dangling tantalizing information before me, then whipping it away. But I still fancied him. At any age, that was tragic. At mine, even more so. I was disappointed in myself.

"Bye." I moved away.

"Anna, wait!"

Joey was still in the same quiet corner, looking as if he hadn't budged.

"Did you mingl—"

"Nope." Then he grinned.

"Bad Joey."

"The worst. Finish your drink and let's get out of here. Hey! While you were at the doctor's I found Rose's property on Google Earth. Much bigger than you'd think. We're talking nine or ten hectares."

After several seconds had elapsed I ventured to ask, "Joey? Is a hectare bigger or smaller than an acre?"

That entertained him. "Bigger. More than twice the size. The house itself would be listed. Well, probably—"

"Heyyyyyy!" Vivian had found us. "You came."

"Too scared not to." Joey wasn't even trying to be funny.

Vivian tilted her head and suddenly I saw Joey the way she might: the jut of his hip bones; the sly green eyes; the *mouth*. This estrogen patch had a lot to answer for.

"Soooo." Vivian was giving it lots of flirty fizz. "I hear you're leaving tomorrow."

"Yep. But Anna's staying."

She treated me to an approving look. "We're gonna hang out." Then renewed her focus on him. "When will you be back?"

"No plans. Except for the launch of the retreat, whenever that is."

"I'll miss you. We've only just started getting to know each other."

Should I step away and leave them to it?

"Nothing much to know about me," Joey said.

"No," Vivian said. "No, no, no! You're wrong." Her tone wheedling, she said, "I really think you should come home with me tonight."

I flinched. *Bad manners, Vivian! Acting like I'm invisible!*

. . . But something was off. "Who, exactly" —Joey's tone was curious— "are you asking?"

Hold on, *what?*

Vivian displayed her teeth. "Both of you."

Startled, I turned to Joey. Our eyes met; thoughts flew between us like arrows. *What the hell . . . ? This is wild! What do you think? Are you going to . . . ?*

A thrill of curiosity flamed my body—I could almost feel my naked skin against his—followed immediately by a hot lick of jealousy at sharing him with Vivian. Quick on the heels of that came sanity. Joey Armstrong and I knew faaar too much about each other.

"That's quite an offer," Joey said, "and I can't speak for Anna, but I've an early start in the morning . . ."

Vivian was supremely unbothered. With a cheeky grin, she said, "If you change your mind . . ." Her focus shifted to me. "Anna?"

Surprised that she was still interested without Joey as part of the package, it took a moment. "Vivian." I was apologetic. "I think I'm straight."

"No one is straight." Her dark eyes twinkled.

"Of course. Right. It's a spectrum. I'm sorry, I forgot, I'm a Gen X, not a Millennial . . ."

"It's cool." She was finding this entertaining. "Relax. All good."

She put her hand on Joey's cheek. "Drive safe, Sexy Man." Then disappeared back into the throng.

In the emptiness left by her departure I cleared my throat and addressed Joey's earlobe. "I think I'm ready to leave."

"Me too."

As we pushed our way to the door, Vivian was head-to-head with Ike. He looked up when I passed. I could read it in his eyes: he knew what had just happened and he thought I was a square.

In the most lowering of silences Joey and I walked back to the Broderick. Once inside I muttered, "I need a drink."

Joey led the way into the lounge. Only after I'd swallowed a few large mouthfuls of gin could I speak. "I should be flattered. Life in the old dog, and all that."

Joey maintained sympathetic eye contact.

"I feel like such a, a *boring*..."

"So why didn't you go home with her?"

"Because I . . . Joey, I didn't fancy her. She's really not my type."

"Why's that now?"

"Sheee... didn't have enough testosterone? I guess I like men." I slapped my hand to my forehead and groaned. "Did you see the look Ike Blakely gave me when we were leaving?"

"Who cares what he thinks? Narky fucker."

Narky fucker. Two words which had been used about Joey more times than I'd had hot dinners. How the world turns.

"Joey? I'm sorry," I chose my words carefully. "If I got in the way there."

"You didn't."

"What I mean is, you could have got rid of me."

"I know what you meant."

"So why didn't *you* go home with her?"

"I don't do that anymore."

"Casual hookups?"

He considered the question. "None of it. Casual, serious. None."

"*No* sex? What? Ever?"

Wordlessly, his gaze holding mine, he moved his head very definitely from side to side.

"Why?"

"I hurt too many people in the past. If I could apologize to everyone of them, I would." He swallowed. "And it was when I felt my worst about myself. Not during it, but straight after. Always."

From what I knew of him, it made sense. "A long time ago," he said, "You said something."

I was tense. During our tangled history, we'd each said plenty. Which corrosively honest truth was it?

". . . That I didn't have to hate everyone who loved me." He looked somber. "It took years before I understood but you were right. I didn't hate them but I hated myself so much that it was hard to . . . respect them."

"Joey . . . can I ask—?"

"Elisabeth." He cut across me. "That's what you want to know? The last person I slept with?"

"No . . ." I'd wondered when he and Elisabeth had formally broken up.

"Yeah, Elisabeth. About, I don't know, two years ago. No, closer to three."

"Do you miss it?"

"Sometimes. But I don't miss the emotional hangovers."

"How do you know the words 'emotional hangovers'?"

"Because I went for counseling. I told you. Elisabeth made me."

"She sounds . . . impressive."

"She is." He smiled. "Very 'action driven.' She thinks every problem has a solution. When she realized I was unfixable she was . . . confused, I guess. Then she was out."

"When was that?"

"Christmas before last."

"Tell me to stop if I've gone too far but have you sworn off 'relations' for good?"

He shrugged. "No . . . But it would be different. Done right. Slow. Taking time to get to know the person. Holding back until I'm sure I deserve them, that I won't hurt them. We'll see." He yawned. "Time for bed."

I side-eyed him and we both smiled.

"It's been that sort of day," I said. "The Day of Innuendo." I got to my feet. This was goodbye. "Thank you for giving me the job."

"You've been great," he said. "Thank *you*."

"So. See you." I shrugged. "Sometime."

"Ah, *Anna*. We'll both be at the launch party? Won't we? So, see you then."

Uncertainly, we stood and watched each other. Then we were both stepping forward into probably our first wholehearted hug. Our ribs bumped and all four of our feet jostled for the same spot on the floor. In an effort to stay upright, I slid my arms around Joey's neck. His forearms tightened across my back until my nose was pressed against his collarbone.

"I can't breathe." I pulled away. "Oh my God, most awkward hug ever."

"Your fault. You're really short." But he was smiling with his eyes. "Short and sweet."

"And you're long. Long and complicated." I laid my hand on his cheek and said, "Drive safe, Sexy Man."

33

In bed, with the light off, my thoughts wouldn't stop. Angelo and I hadn't had sex for a long time before we'd broken up. After we had "set each other free" (his phrase, but please don't judge him, he's the best) I knew that, sexually, I didn't want to shut up shop.

Perhaps it was a post-pandemic response, perhaps it was my libido-boosting testosterone gel, perhaps it was because the world had become a dumpster fire, but my age felt irrelevant and living to the full felt necessary.

The three or four months when I'd been closing down my life in New York felt like a gift of time untethered from consequence.

Online was the only way I knew how to meet men. Straight away, business was brisk, just like my early days in the city, when Jacqui and I had been swamped with men—almost none of them viable.

Back then I'd wanted to find The One; this time round I just wanted fun. Even so, I had to sift through liars, adulterers, grifters and men who wouldn't date anyone over twenty-five, before I had a brief connection with "a younger man." Although, at forty-one and forlorn about his divorce, he seemed older than me.

Then I really did meet a younger man. He claimed to be thirty-two but when we met for coffee, I suspected he'd inflated the number by ten years. He mumbled that he was "down to fuck"—and straight away I was out. I hadn't expected love sonnets but there had to be *some* romance.

After that, I expanded my age limits up to sixty, because I hoped that the "less young" would be better at human connection.

And so it had proved. Robert was sixty-ish. A blue-eyed biker, he was interesting and full of questions and compliments. He also took longer over his hair than I took over mine, was deliberately vague about how he made his living and the longest he'd ever lived in one place (Montreal) had been three years. Only a masochist would fall in love with him. We had five amazing dates. When I texted, hoping for a sixth, he didn't reply. I endured a nervy forty-eight hours before having to accept that that was that. Because I wasn't a sociopath, I was desolate for a couple of weeks. Then, still in the spirit of grabbing life by the lapels, I bounced back.

Everything this evening, starting with Vivian's proposition, had churned up too many feelings. Eventually, I clicked the light on again and rummaged in my underwear bag, until my hand closed around my wand. I'd thrown it in at the last minute when I was packing and, oh my God, I was grateful.

I hadn't felt like this in a while; as my access to HRT had dwindled away, so had any interest in sex.

There was an ethical site, to which I had an annual subscription, for women-friendly porn. There was so much in life to feel guilty about and at least I wasn't giving Pornhub any traffic. But tonight none of the videos were right. The men were over-muscled, the squealing noises from the women were embarrassingly fake and all of them looked too young. Was a hot older guy too much to ask for?

Squeezing my eyes shut, I thought about Ike Blakely, imagining him standing over me, flinging his tool belt to the floor, then slowly unzipping his work jeans. Pulling them down, wrapping his big hand around a thick erection . . . *This* was definitely having the right effect.

Thinking about his hands on my hips as I lowered myself onto him. Him growling words of lust, thrusting upwards, grabbing me, speeding up . . .

The sound of my own gasps surprised me. After a burst of fireworks, my whole being was flooded with relaxed joy. That was *gorgeous*.

34

My dreams were inspired by a jumble of New York memories. Like the time Margaret came to visit, claiming she needed to buy "discounted boots in Woodbury Commons."

Two Martini Sours later, the real reason emerged.

"You should buy an apartment," she said. "It's what we all think. This is a great time to get a mortgage. Interest rates are blah-dee-blah . . ." I watched her mouth moving; the occasional word fell out—"property prices," "financial crash"—but couldn't find a landing place in me.

"You could just about do it financially," she insisted. "All you spend money on is rent, airfares to Ireland and trains to Boston to see Aidan's family. Look, Anna, losing Aidan is one of the worst things anyone will have to live through. But your life isn't over."

It was, though. I was still walking around feeling as if a thick pane of glass separated me from the world.

"Is it this apartment?" My home with Aidan. "Do you feel if you leave, you'll be abandoning him?"

"No." Aidan was everywhere but nowhere. "I don't think I'll renew the lease here when it's next up—"

"—so you need to buy a place!"

"I could just move in with Jacqui and Trea. I'm there a lot anyway." More and more so, as Joey's flakiness had worsened.

"That might change."

"How would it change? Look, if I was going to buy a place, I'd do it with Jacqui. For me, her and Trea—"

"Don't do that!" She looked worried. "You're not always going to feel the way you do now. You won't want to box yourself in . . ." She checked herself. "You'll still see Jacqui all the time. But buy a place by yourself."

She promptly signed me up with every realtor in Manhattan so I was bombarded with emails and calls inviting me to view my "dream home."

I'd have ignored them all, except that Margaret rang with regular motivational speeches, along the lines of: Future Anna will thank Current Anna if she buys her a beautiful apartment.

Over the hubbub of noisy, fashionable New York arty types, I heard, "Hey, Anna."

I turned. "Hey!" It was Rachel's friend, Angelo. Who had sort of become my friend too, over the previous few years.

We hugged. "Congratulations." I was unsure of the etiquette when a person had organized an art expo to showcase their clients. "Great turnout. Really beautiful pieces."

With his tattoos, dark clothes and gaunt face, Angelo looked like trouble and torment. But he was compassionate, optimistic and fun.

Sexy too, I was beginning to understand. In the two and a half years since Aidan, I'd been entirely numb, but I could see how others reacted. At first glance, they were all, *Not a chance.* Two seconds later, they'd go, *Waaaait a minute.* And before you knew it, they'd be full-on, *Right! I get it! Hot in an ugly-beautiful way!*

Today's exhibition was in an ungentrified but safe part of the Lower East Side, in which the rich guests could savor a sneaky thrill at their own edginess.

"Seen any pieces that speak to you?" he asked.

"Um. Actually, *yes.* A painting, but made of glass? Under the sea?"

"Parsla Koskinen. Let's go take a look."

We slipped through skinny women and boomy-voiced men, carefully skirting the central exhibit, a huge bull made entirely of cutlery.

Angelo stopped before a large colorful rectangle. "This?"

The piece was patterned with tendrils of glass in a hundred vivid greens, like seaweed in bright blue water. The skill with which they'd been woven in and out of each other made it seem as if they were swaying. Rising towards the surface, balls of clear glass were layered on the seaweed—water bubbles. A line of gritty gold—sand, obviously—lay at the base of the piece.

"I could look at it forever," I said. "Go on, break my heart and tell me the price."

He said a number and while it was a lot, it wasn't entirely ridiculous.

. . . But I needed all my money to buy an apartment, didn't I? I'd never before acknowledged it as a reality.

Dolefully I shook my head. "I'm wondering how hard life would be with just one kidney? Then again, this would be a literal heirloom. Something for my grandkids to fight over." I stopped. "I don't know why I even said that. There won't be grandkids. Because there won't be kids."

". . . Maybe I'm overstepping boundaries but can I ask why?"

I couldn't help smiling. He was charming and lovely, a total Mr Sensitive. Tone-perfect always.

"Please don't judge." But he was the least judgy person I'd ever met. "Since as far as I can remember, I never wanted to be trapped. Especially with people I'm afraid of. It's my idea of hell."

"Uh-uh."

"I love my sisters. Like, I *really* love them. But they're huge personalities. I'm not like them. Growing up, there was a lot of yelling . . . I couldn't deal—"

"Why can't we all just get along?" he interjected.

I laughed. "That's genuinely how I feel."

"Me too. I wasn't trying to be funny."

It was *so nice* being with a person who got it. "What if my kids were like my family? Because if they were my kids, I couldn't just run away."

"Yep." He was solemn.

"The only time kids seemed possible was with Aidan. But without him . . ." I shrugged. "What about you?"

"Lots of reasons. Already too many of us on the planet. But I totally get the family thing. Mine was messy."

I knew some details: his mom was an addict and his dad a sporadic presence. His first fifteen years were chaos.

"They weren't bad people but they did damage. I got out. Got better. Today, it's all good, but it takes work. So yeah, I'm scared that having kids would mean the return of anarchy. If that makes me selfish, then I'm selfish."

"You're honest and . . . and you've found a way to live life with your stuff. That's good."

"Thank you, Anna."

"For nothing. Just telling you the truth."

Silence fell between us. It went on a little too long. One of us needed to speak.

"So!" Angelo cleared his throat. "Here's the thing. Parsla's having a solo show in ten days. There are three more pieces like this, but smaller. Meaning they cost less. The dealer's this really cool guy, he could be persuaded to skip his commission."

I had to check. "The dealer is you?"

He flashed a smile. "Just come to the opening. See if you like anything."

"Will you be there?" It was a stupid question: of course he'd be there. But it wasn't what I'd meant.

Some small shift had taken place deep down in me. I felt dizzy. Then hot with guilt.

My phone rang. Jacqui. My heart slid into my boots.

Something has to change here. The thought shocked me.

"He's in an actual fucking bar, I could hear it." Jacqui was in tears. "Says he doesn't know when he'll get here."

I swallowed back my feelings. "On my way."

First I had to make a call. "Angelo? So sorry but I have to bail tonight."

After a moment's silence, he asked, "Watching Trea? Hey, don't worry. If any of Parsla's seascapes don't sell, I'll message you."

I was barely in the door when Jacqui flung herself into my arms. "He's a dick. He's ruined my life."

"Shush!" I was terrified Trea would hear. Only sixteen months old, but I sensed she understood plenty.

"I get it." I spoke quietly. Jacqui's life used to be fun and carefree. Now she was always tired and always angry. "Oh, hi, sweetie." Trea had toddled in, kitted out in a sparkly fairy costume. "Don't you look delicious!"

"Flammable shite," Jacqui said. "Courtesy of her useless dad. Thinking he can just buy her love. If only I never had to see him. The constant disappointment, not just for me, but for . . ." She flicked her eyes at Trea.

Trea stared back.

"Jacqui." I decided to take a risk. "I don't think Joey's going to change. He's not going to become the man you want him to be."

"Yeah." She bent to kiss Trea. "Be good for Anna. Your dad might be here later. But he might not. I'm sorry, baby." Her voice wobbled. "He's a flake."

"Jacqui . . ."

"Sorry. I know." She wiped away tears. Poor Jacqui was going insane from this. I'd suggested she see her doctor but she insisted that nothing was wrong with *her*, the only person who needed to change was Joey.

"*Any*way." She sniffed. "Gotta go. Table's booked for eight o'clock."

Wait. *What?* "Which celeb is it tonight?"

"Not work. Karl."

She was going on a *date*. Meanwhile I'd canceled something I'd wanted to do, in order to mind her little girl?

But how could I feel resentful when I'd assured her again and again she could depend on me?

Off she went. I'd coaxed Trea into her little white wooden bed when I thought I heard the front door. I went out to check and there was Joey.

"Anna, I know." He spoke quickly. "I'm late. But three days ago, I told Jacqui I couldn't commit to the time she wanted tonight."

Stonily, I looked at him.

"She set me up to fail. Not for the first time."

He was beyond contempt. Messing us all around and maligning Jacqui.

"She asleep?" He cast glances at Trea's bedroom. "Can I check on her? Then can you and I talk?"

About what? But he was gone. I didn't know if this was just a flying visit so I had to wait.

Judging by his murmured cadences, he was reading a story. After a while the plinky-plonky lullaby started, then he came out and softly closed the door.

He sighed. "So cute when she's asleep."

"You wanted to talk?"

"Yeah. I'm sorry for doing this to you yet again. You having to bail me out."

"You were in a bar when she called."

"A restaurant, actually. Because I was working. Trying to pull this thing together so I can buy Jacqui her own apartment."

I had only the vaguest idea of what his job was—something on the lower rungs in finance. "What 'thing' were you trying to pull together?"

"A business deal. Didn't Jacqui tell you? No?" He clenched his jaw, then sighed. "I can explain. If you want? Simplest terms, there are rich guys in this city with money to invest. I've a knack for seeing struggling businesses with potential. I do my research, run numbers on potential outcomes, then go to the money men with a proposal. If they invest their cash into something that becomes a success, I get a cut."

"Is somebody backing you?"

"Just me."

"So . . . where do you meet these rich men?"

His tone was weary. "That's the hard part. Even harder is persuading them you're not a grifter who'll lose their investment. But if you get one of them to trust you, it gives you a foot in the door. If you make them a profit, even better.

"I know that whenever Jacqui rings, it sounds like I'm in a bar or restaurant. Because often I am. Trying to make these guys trust me. And yeah, it's always guys."

It was exactly what I did in my job: convince people that I was for real. But, there was one big difference between his job and mine: I had a company credit card. "*You're* the one paying for the wine and dinner, without knowing if anything will come of it?"

"Yeah." He looked gray with exhaustion. "She tells me I'm the world's worst dad. But I'm working my butt off for Trea. Maybe you don't know but I pay the rent for this place." He indicated Jacqui's beautiful apartment. "And I'm in a shitty one-bed, sharing with Gaz." Quickly he said, "Not complaining. Just saying I'm not a terrible dad.

"Anna." He paused. "I hate admitting this now but I didn't want a kid. I knew nothing about them, all I had was one older brother, so when I got Jacqui pregnant I freaked out. But now Trea's in the world, I love her. Like, I love her so *much* and I want her to have everything."

I believed he loved her. The previous weekend, I'd met them both at a picnic with Rachel, Luke and various Real Men. It was obvious that they were mad about each other. But equally clear was that Joey's version of responsible parenthood was "To provide."

"Jacqui just wants you to spend more time with Trea," I said.

"Yeah, but—I can't do both. Not right now. This thing I'm doing, it's not nine to five. My first really big deal is maybe about to happen. Three different investors are buying an ex-cargo liner to convert to a luxury cruiser. But all this last-minute legalese has blown up and I'm running around putting out fires, shit-scared it'll all fall apart."

"Where did you learn how to do this?" I wouldn't have known where to start. "Did you go to school?"

"Nah." His laugh was tight. "I come from a family of entrepreneurs."

"What sort of business?"

"They can turn their hand to pretty much everything. So, Anna, I'm here now. You can go." With an attempt at humor, he said, "You and me, it's like we're trapped in one of those movies." He waved his hand. "Groundhog night. Me saying, again and again, 'Sorry for ruining your evening but I'm here now.'"

It was probably too late to get to the gallery to see Angelo. "Joey, you look really tired. Why don't you go home and get some sleep?"

"No. I'm good. Thanks again. See ya next time."

A few weeks later, I woke one morning at Jacqui's and found Joey in the kitchen, suited-up, smelling fresh and making coffee. It was very early, barely 6 a.m., and for a confused moment, I thought he'd just arrived.

"Anna, hey." He smiled, giving off the energy of a man about to embark on a day of successful wheeler-dealing. Then I stumbled into the truth: last night Joey had come home with Jacqui.

No need to ask where he'd slept.

Perhaps this was the start of their reunion? A vision appeared, of a future where Joey, Jacqui and Trea were a happy, cohabitating family—followed by a head rush of relief which kept me in great form for the rest of the day.

35

Dan Kilcroney was in the lobby, watching a man hoist an overpacked explosion of orchids, birds of paradise and countless other flowers onto the reception desk.

"Ms Walsh?" Kilcroney called.

Over-politely I turned towards him. *Arse-brain?*

"These are for you." He pointed at the vast bouquet.

The other man stepped forward and touched his chest. "Farrelly the Flowers. I don't shake hands, nothing personal. Even Ben Mendoza himself just gets a wave and he won an Oscar. You're Anna Walsh? Well, these are for you. From Mr Joseph Armstrong. Will I read out the card?"

"No! I mean, thanks, no need, I can read it myself."

"I'll save you the bother. 'Sweet-face,' he says." Farrelly the Flowers looked up. "A little nickname, is it? 'Sweet-face. I'm forever grateful. Narky Joey.' Another little nickname, is it? Then there's three Xs. He was very specific. Three, he said. Uppercase, he said."

". . . Thank you."

"The call came in at eight thirty-seven this morning. He was lucky to get me, I could have been below in Galway at the flower market. All business, he told me to put the entire shop into the bouquet. Money no object. I took him at his word and the Amex card worked—it's been like my own personal Valentine's Day. I'm thinking of putting a picture up on the website and calling it the Money No Object Arrangement."

My heart felt full: this was lovely. Not just the flowers themselves—at least they would be when Courtney helped decant them into several vases—but without addressing anything directly, Joey had erased a lot of the shame I'd been carrying.

"But"—Farrelly was still talking—"if anyone in the town dies between now and Tuesday, we're fucked. Not a cut flower left in Connemara. Apart from lilies. The go-boy was very insistent—no lilies."

"No lilies?" My voice was choked.

"He said they upset you. Have I it right? Otherwise I can go below and get you a few. On me."

"No need."

"They *do* upset you?" He stepped closer.

Seriously, the nosiness of Irish people! All right then, he'd asked for it. "My husband died suddenly. Killed in a car crash. The smell of lilies brings back the funeral."

That should make him sorry he'd asked. But it only made him worse. "Desperate stuff." He stepped closer. "Recent?"

"Sixteen years ago."

"So you got married when you were three?"

He was trying to be nice, so I let him get away with it.

Out in the town, festivities were in the air. Shop windows were decorated with giant, metallic shamrocks. The traffic in Main Street was diverted because men on ladders were hanging green bunting between opposite sides of the road. Dozens of crowd-control barriers were stacked against the wall of Carr's cars. For Saturday's parade, I suppose.

After the stresses and anxieties of the preceding few days, I was bone-tired, but in a pleasant way. Until Mum and Helen came tomorrow, I could just float aimlessly, maybe stroll down to the beach or revisit Heather & Mist.

Every few meters, someone greeted me. "Anna! Still here?" "Well done on Kearney's Farm. They're back at work this morning." "You're a great girl, Anna, you'll go far."

But every paradise has its snake. Blocking my path was Courtney's husband, giving me a baleful stare. "Sergeant Burke!" I raised my hand in greeting. "Lovely morning."

"Are you still here?"

I shook my head. "I went home yesterday. What you're seeing is a hologram."

Another man would have laughed. All he gave was a tight-lipped stare.

I carried on, sticking my head into the parish hall, the location for several events over the weekend. Right now, it looked dusty and uninspiring but presumably there were plans for a major glow-up.

In the clearing up at the monument a stage was under construction. For "The concert on Saturday night" said a Beardy Glarer, who behaved as if he knew me well. Had we met at the public meeting? Last night in the Spanish? Had we—heaven forbid!—had a sit-down on Tuesday and I'd already forgotten him?

Remembering names and faces had once been my party piece. But alas, no longer. Perhaps it was because, at forty-eight, I'd met too many people and there was simply no more room in my memory. Or it could be down to a dearth of HRT. Maybe when the progesterone arrived tomorrow in Gannon's, I'd be back in business?

"Anna, is it?" A woman with long, red-blonde balayage hair had popped out from a shop. I recognized her glittery bomber jacket from last night. She was cool, pretty and aged . . . forty-three, I decided. "I'm Karina." She nodded her stylish head at the building she'd emerged from. "Hairdresser. Come in and see myself or Gráinne any time. We'll *look after you*." Those words again.

Maybe I would! "You do color, I hear? What do you think?" I indicated my drab hair.

Her lips were pursed assessingly. "I'm thinking strawberry brown money piece."

"I don't know any of those words but I still like the sound of them."

She actually laughed. "Hairdresser jargon. Or how about glossy mocha, with color melt? I'll show you photos. We're slammed this weekend but come in—"

"I leave on Monday."

"Arra. That's a pity now. If you're ever back, the offer still stands. Thanks for sorting out the business below. Very nice to meet you."

"Very nice to meet you *too*, Karina."

The idea of new hair was exciting. When I got back to Dublin, I'd—
"Anna!" It was Vivian, with another person, on the far side of the street. "Wait." She jogged over and caught me up in a big, swingy hug. I'd been worried she'd hold a grudge for last night's rejection. Then again, she wasn't a man.

"Thanks for coming last night. Did the go-boy really leave? Oh, hey . . ." She gestured at her companion, who had crossed the road in more leisurely fashion. "Meet my friend Ben."

Her "friend Ben" was Ben Mendoza, the Oscar-winning director. He had the compact, neat look of Stanley Tucci. Soulful eyes. A shaved head. Expressive hands.

"Hi." I managed a hopefully normal-seeming smile.

Ben Mendoza was far from my first celebrity; in my old job they'd been an occupational hazard. They weren't all monsters but the only way to discern their true nature was to behave as if they worked in a preschool or a bookies. *Never* lunge and blurt that you loved their movie/album/whatever. If they were basically sound, they'd want to connect on a human level. But if praise was their thing, all the lauding in the universe wouldn't be enough.

Vivian indicated me. "This is Anna Walsh. The woman who saved Kearney's Farm."

"Wait, now—" None of that was certain.

"I've heard," Ben Mendoza said. "Good to meet you. Colm and Brigit are the best. In town for much longer?"

"Until Monday."

He and Vivian exchanged a glance.

"I'm having a welcome-home dinner for Vivian tonight," he said. "You must come."

"Well, ah, thank you . . ."

"I'll text you details," Vivian said.

Did she have my number? Oh, what the hell, she was Vivian Hogan-Bancroft, someone would give it to her. All my plans suddenly abandoned, I hurried back to the hotel, looking for Courtney. She was on the desk, flanked by a receptionist I didn't know.

"Courts!" I said. "I need you!"

"I've just had your mum on the phone," Courtney said.

"Who?" Oh, *her*. "Any chance of a chat? Quick one."

"Lyudmila?" Courtney spoke to her colleague.

"Go," the woman said. "I'll shout if there is a guest."

36

"Ordinary-looking, yes, I grant you," I babbled at Courtney. "But immensely . . . what's the word? Likable?"

"Okay." Courtney seemed . . . not interested?

But, high from meeting Ben Mendoza, I was unstoppable. "Hard to know if he 'seems likable' simply because he's so talented. Talented folk so often get a pass. Or if he actually is sound? . . . Courtney." A weird feeling had come over me. "I feel dizzy."

"Wouldja *stop*. You lived in Manhattan where the streets are lined with celebrities! In 2003 even *I*—Courtney Nobody Burke—cut ahead of Mandy Patinkin in a coffee shop. Oh, what? You thought I'd never left M'town?"

Too late, I saw she was pissed off. ". . . Courts? What's up?"

"I've lived in this town for thirty-nine years and I've never been over Ben Mendoza's threshold. You're here five effing minutes and you're in like Flynn."

These chastening facts snuffed out all gaiety. "Oh my God, Courtney, that's horribly unfair. I'm so sorry." A watery rearrangement of my emotions was under way, bringing me to the edge of tears.

Courtney's stare was nonplussed. "Are you okay?"

"Just really sad about how badly you've been treated. The world is a cruel place." Registering her evident unease, I said, "I'm fine. Still light-headed, though. Any chance of a Sprite—for the sugar? And chocolate?"

"Emilien!" Courtney got his attention, yelled my requirements, then said to me, "Have you PMT?"

"*Me?* I haven't had a period in, cripes, nearly two years—"

"Now I hate you even more."

"Please don't hate me, Courtney. It's only because of the HRT."

"Ah, how could I hate you? This is the most fun I've had in the last twenty years. But . . . How's your menopause? Didn't Dr Olive give you the stuff? You should be on the mend."

"I started the estrogen last night. But they'd no progesterone. Maybe I'm out of balance? Oh, thanks, Emilien." A glass of Sprite was placed on the table, as well as a big bag of Minstrels.

"There is a guest!" Lyudmila was in the doorway, looking harried.

"I've to go," Courtney said. "Why don't you have a lie-down? You've had a busy few days."

A lie-down would be bliss. Upstairs, I discovered that Courtney had decanted Joey's flowers into several vases, which were dotted around the room. Again, I welled up at Courtney's goodness, how little she was appreciated, how she wanted to see Ben Mendoza's house and had never been invited.

Sliding under the duvet, I surrendered to the tears, the first time since I'd left New York, grieving the self I'd left behind, the people who were no longer in my life, the person I'd been at fifteen, at twenty-nine, at thirty-seven. Mourning all the hopes I'd once had for myself—and where I was now.

Which was nowhere. Life's waiting room. It happened to all of us, probably several times, finding ourselves alone, at a deserted crossroads. Thinking, Seriously? I'm back here *again*?

The tears were tailing off until I thought of Joey. At different points in the past twenty years I'd fancied him, found him laughable, despised him and reluctantly respected him. But for a while I'd loved him. Keeping a lid on it all over the past few days had been exhausting; it was no wonder I was letting loose now.

Merciful sleep overtook me. I woke a couple of hours later, still tired but much more cheerful—the healing properties of a good cry. Right now, this no-man's-land was my life. The advice I'd give another person in my place was: Grow where you're planted.

Lunch was a purloined scone and an equally purloined banana. Emilien had said that room service was temporarily reinstated until Tuesday but only a fool would believe him.

Right then! Time to go down to the beach for some bracing-ness. But the window was spattered with raindrops. Promptly my plans were abandoned. There was a vital difference between being *braced* and being *drenched*.

This was my chance to watch some shite on Netflix. Although, with the Wi-Fi being the way it was . . . So, savoring the chance to do things at a leisurely pace, I washed my hair and tried to put order on my dreadful feet—Ben Mendoza was pretending to be regular folks but it was *mannerly* to make an effort. Life in the old dog yet.

While I was at it, I did some internet prying into Mr Mendoza. Born in Minneapolis forty-six years ago, showed an early interest in film, made his first feature . . . yes, yesyesyesgettothegoodstuff . . . aha! Married fourteen years ago to a woman called Hannah Black—and divorced six years later. No children. That was sad. Although they were still "best buds" according to several interviews . . . Aaaany chance of seeing said woman? Oho! Photos! Looking fun, smiley, gorgeous but no swollen, starlet lips or fakery in the chest area. Good for her! It's got to be hard resisting that stuff when you're in Hollywood. Buried in the small print was the fact that Ben was five years younger than her—this made me like them both more. She was a physiotherapist, they'd met when Ben did something to his hamstring. Seriously, how wholesome was *that* meet-cute. Here was Hannah, with her parents. Her mother looked *great*, good genes—or perhaps she'd had Hannah at sixteen? When I found myself embarking on a quest to discover the mother's date of birth, I made myself stop.

Emerging from the Mendoza rabbit hole, I realized I missed Joey. After all my worry, things had gone okay. Except . . . I still hadn't apologized to him. But I couldn't have, not while we were trying to manage the work situation here. It could have derailed everything.

Joey had known me during several incarnations. I was privy to information about him that almost no other person was. But our unique connection was bound up in pain. Better to park it in the past where it couldn't hurt us.

Even though my job here had ended, I took a quick look at the email account. Nine new messages. My old friend AubergineDick was back with another tempting offer. As was ProudIrishPatriot1916.

To: Kearneysfarm@gmail.com
From: ProudIrishPatriot1916@hotmail.ie

Next time we'll burn the houses won't be just paint

Was this a genuine threat? Or just a keyboard warrior entertaining himself? Should I tell Joey? Or perhaps talk to Helen? She knew people who could trace IP addresses—although it was costly and illegal.

Pause it for the moment, I decided. It might be nothing.

The other seven people had "heard" Kearney's Farm would generate so much rubbish that a landfill site was planned for the waste ground behind the school.

I wondered what their source was. As one of the seven was Aber Skerett, I gave him a call.

"Anna." Oh, he had *such* a gentle voice.

"Aber. Thanks for your email. There's no truth to the rumor. But can I ask where you heard about this landfill business?"

"Local Hero posted on Facebook—"

"Who now? Local Hero? Who's that?"

"I don't know his name, if that's what you mean. He posts a fair bit about Kearney's Farm, though. I think he might be a journalist."

"Where does he post? Maumtully Conservation? Mau—"

"Maum Notice Board. Maum Chats too."

"Thanks!" I was itching to embark on a search for this Local Hero but good manners dictated that I engage in chat about me, Aber, his mother, my mother, the plans for the weekend, etc. To be fair, it was no hardship.

Then I began scrolling through literal miles of Facebook stuff about second-hand wedding dresses, badly parked cars—and there we were! Local Hero posting about landfill. The photo was of a masked superhero, so no chance of identifying him visually. He claimed his information was "solid and verified." Further back I went and came across a post from yesterday claiming that Aldi was doing four bottles of rosé for the price of three but stock was limited. On Monday, he'd posted a story about the dolphins being poisoned by the runoff from Kearney's Farm. Again, he claimed his info was "solid and verified." Obviously, his info was complete bullshit and—my phone rang. An unidentified Irish mobile. "Hello?"

"This is Ike. Blakely? Got your number from Courtney."

Instantly, Local Hero was forgotten and last night's sexy fantasy was front and center in my mind.

Clearing my throat with effort, I said, "What can I do you for, Ike?"

"Sky Head? Cliff top. About ten kilometers out the road. I mentioned it to you before. You in the mood for a climb?"

"No." Then, "But I'm never in the mood for a climb."

"A drive, then?"

My back hurt and despite my snooze, I still felt exhausted. "Not today."

"I hear you're invited to Ben's tonight."

All of a sudden, my fatigue lifted. I felt reckless and alive. "You're going?"

"Yep. You want a lift?"

"Yes."

Right. Tonight, I was going to sleep with him.

37

Ben Mendoza's home was a couple of kilometers outside town. In the half-light of dusk, I bounced around in Ike's truck as we belted along the coast.

He'd been late to pick me up. But while I'd been hovering at the hotel door, Lyudmila had called from the desk, "Lorry overturn on Galway road. Traffic slow. Ike is late."

"How do you know?"

"My partner, Yakiv, he work with Ike."

"Does everyone know—?"

"That you go for date with Ike? Yes."

So it was a date and not just a lift? Well, *lovely*.

Some minutes later, Lyudmila said, "Is here now. I know sound of truck."

Right on cue, Ike came striding into the lobby of the Broderick. "A holdup on the Galway road," he stated. "I'm usually reliable."

"All grand!" My mood was upbeat. "I've no plans to marry you."

The urge to grab life and wring out every last drop had me, once again, in its grip.

"You look . . ." Ike studied me. ". . . good."

If only I'd known, while I'd been flinging things into a case in Margaret's spare bedroom, that I'd be hooking up with a big, growly tree surgeon before the week was out! I'd have packed a dress, better underwear and proper lipstick. Instead, I'd had to make do with eyeliner and a clean T-shirt.

In the truck, I asked, "You're friends with Ben?"

"Kind of. More friends with Vivian."

"I've a question. Do you know who Local Hero actually is? Posts on Facebook."

"Local Hero? Tuesday morning, 'Russian subs are off the coast of Connemara,' Tuesday afternoon, 'Prices slashed on Galia melons'? Yeah? No idea. But he's got it in for Kearney's Farm."

He certainly did. In January, out of nowhere, Local Hero had begun popping up on four local Facebooks, averaging two or three negative posts a week about Kearney's Farm and one or two about local bargains. Despite their claims of "solid, verified information," literally none of it was true. Except perhaps the details about cheap mops and kidney beans.

Should I message Joey about it? But he'd been so adamant that everything was okay and he *was* the boss.

I turned to Ike. "Who else will be here tonight?"

"Mmmm. Let's see. Mary and Thornton Heffer, husband-and-wife writing team? Big hit with *The Darkest Crime* a few years back."

It rang a vague bell.

"They're part of the festival committee. Ziryan Barzani, he works in the hardware store in town."

"I know Ziryan! He's a dote."

"He is. He's also on the festival committee. Can charm the birds from the trees. Sara Dineen, the ceramicist, and her wife Trayna. Then there's Simarjit Kaur, the Indian playwright? Just won an award. Vivian said Ben has three friends from LA staying with him, guess they'll be there. Here we are."

We were turning off the road.

Now, *this* was unexpected: Ben's house wouldn't be troubling *Architectural Digest* any time soon. A solid old foursquare, it could have once been the residence of the parish priest.

The front door was invitingly open. Ike led me through the entrance hall, towards the back of the house, down a few steps and—hold on! Suddenly we were in a sleek extension which stretched towards the sea.

The inviting space offered what interior magazines might call "indefinable, relaxed ease." Deep rugs, attractive sofas and pools of flattering lighting.

Dotted about were discreet tables, which would materialize at the precise moment you needed to put a drink down. The artwork was unflashy and there was a welcome absence of talking-point *objets*, such as, "This cat-o'-nine-tails was a favorite of the Marquis de Sade's."

At an art deco cocktail cabinet, Ben was dragging a glass through a bucket of ice. "Anna! Ike! You made it." He was a smiley delight, kissing me on the cheek and hugging Ike.

I passed over the orchid I'd panic-bought from Farrelly the Flowers. (Who had greeted me with almost-outrage. "Haven't you enough flowers!" When I'd admitted my purchase wasn't for me, he pinched his lips and said, "Let me guess. Ben Mendoza's do? So that's how it is. All I've left after the go-boy's spree is orchids in pots. I've already sold two white ones for tonight. We'll give you purple. Help you to stand out.")

"Vivian's upstairs, doing her thing," Ben said. And I did *not* imagine the surge of strong emotion which emanated from Ike.

"She should be down soon," Ben added.

"And maybe not." Ike straightened his shoulders. "Vivian's her own woman."

Well, well, *well*. So that's how things were around here? Should I have been stomping off, furious with Ike? I mean, maaaybe . . . ? But all I was, was entertained. My only regret was that I had to leave on Monday—Vivian and her shenanigans were inspirational. I wouldn't mind a couple of months living here, having commitment-free fun.

"Anna? To drink?" Ben asked.

I had an atypical craving for Sprite. "Although I might move to wine in a while."

"Sure." Then to Ike, "I've got that Jamaican porter you like."

"You have not!" Ike brightened. "And I've a promising lead on Nigerian Guinness for you."

Lord, that pair had *so much* in common.

A slight woman wearing a sober pinafore dress approached me with a smile. "I'm Mary Heffer."

Aha! One half of the crime-writing spouses! "Lovely to meet you. I'm Anna Walsh—"

"Oh!" Mary stepped back.

Startled, I wondered what I'd done wrong.

"Excuse me, I just need to—" Hurrying away, she almost bumped into Ben who was back with my drink and a bowl of wasabi nuts. "So you've met Mary," he said. "Let me introduce you to everyone else."

I spotted Ziryan. He and I hugged like long-lost friends.

"This is Simarjit Kaur, Vasyl Shevshenko . . ." Ben introduced me to probably twelve people in total, everyone friendly. Except . . . "Where's Thornton got to?" Ben wondered, looking around. "Mary's husband? Maybe he's outside having a smoke." He went to check.

The adrenaline of being in Ben Mendoza's house made me a little shaky. Nauseous, actually. There was a pain low down in my stomach.

My attention was caught by a collection of small, strange paintings, all of birds, each with a distinct personality.

"Ben? These paintings. I *love* them."

"Oh. Okay. Why is that?"

"I feel I know what they're thinking. Like this one, she's all, 'Can you believe those assholes clamped my car'! And this one is, 'That fiiiirst Martini goes down like nectaaaar.'"

"Wow." He seemed surprised. "So, your work on Kearney's Farm? Is that what you do?"

"I did PR back in New York. But right now, I'm . . . taking time out." It was almost true.

"Waiting for the well to fill up again. I get it."

"To be honest," I admitted. "I might need a new well."

He laughed. Now *that* felt good.

"I've spent the last, oh, coupla weeks just bird-watching," he said. "Sometimes it's good to take the foot off the gas."

If you were an Oscar-winning director, that was a luxury you could enjoy. But a lowly PR burnout? Not so much.

"I hang a feeder out there." He nodded towards the darkness. "They come in the morning. Chaffinches, robins, wrens. Word has gotten round. More have been coming every day. But yesterday a kestrel showed up. Wasn't pretty."

A kestrel? A bird of prey? "You mean?"

"Yeah." He drew a line across his neck. "Nature. Keeping it real."

For the hundredth time that day, I felt *watery*. And hungry, actually. When were we getting fed? These wasabi things weren't cutting it, I wanted chocolate.

What was wrong with me?

Hold on—teariness, cravings, that pain in my abdomen. It couldn't be . . . Surely not?

"Ben, which way is the bathroom? Thank you."

I locked the door and took a look. Blood. Plenty of it. I was having a period.

I'd expected to never get one again and I was in shock. Even before I'd begun HRT, they'd been erratic, but once I'd started the meds, they'd stopped entirely. Tonight's visitation must be because my body had finally run out of medical progesterone.

Well, *thank* you, Dr Lowry Riordan, you judgemental arse. Because of your "good conscience" I wouldn't get to sleep with Ike Blakely tonight. I had no issue with period sex, but not with him. Not for our first time.

As soon as I knew they were real, the cramps felt worse. No way could I sit through this dinner. I needed to go to bed with a hot-water bottle and a card of Solpadeine.

I made my apologies to Ben Mendoza—and to Vivian *in absentia*—gave Ike a brief but factual explanation, and suddenly I was back in the pickup, being returned to town.

We didn't speak until Ike parked outside the Broderick. "You need painkillers?" he asked. "Sweets?"

I was touched and surprised. "I'll be okay." I was sure I had some sort of tablets and Emilien would give me ice cream.

"You're here until Monday?" Ike said. "Can I see you?"

"Tell me why you want to. Is it because of your conspiracy theories? Or . . ."

Silently, he unclipped his seatbelt, shifted his big body towards me, placed his thumb on the red catch of my seatbelt, looked me straight in the eye and slowly, deliberately, set me free. The belt slid its way up my body, then one giant hand was around my waist, while the other clasped the back of my head. Without hesitation, Ike moved his mouth to mine. It was a kiss. A proper one, full of heat and promise. Too soon he pulled away. "Conspiracy theories? No."

Stretching across my body, he opened the truck door and said, "You'd better go. I'll text."

38

After taking two Panadol, I got into bed with my iPad. Buoyed by the sudden retreat of pain, it suddenly seemed possible to face my emails. They tended to be grim, financial things, nothing at all to bring cheer, so why would I bother? My bank statement had arrived a couple of days ago and I'd done an excellent job of ignoring it. Now, though, I took a look. My mortgage had gone out but a payment from the letting agent had come in. Breaking even, you could say. If only I wasn't buying ridiculous fluorescent boleros.

Who knew how the next part of my life would unfold, but holy moly, the security of "owning" a place was priceless. Margaret was the person who deserved my gratitude. Back in the day, it was she who'd identified my apartment as The One, then pestered me relentlessly until I went to see it.

A gorgeous, affordable little one-bed in Two Bridges, a neighborhood right at the bottom of Manhattan, it had lots of light and a beautiful bedroom, overlooking a small garden. The only negative was that, just one floor off the ground, I could be vulnerable to break-ins.

It was the first apartment I'd viewed that I could imagine myself living in. But this hopeful realization was wiped out by the grief that Aidan wouldn't be with me. I felt as broken as I had in the very early days. But when I woke up the next morning, I was ready.

Without even noticing, I'd been changing. Healing, really. Glimmers of a possible future had been making occasional appearances. Always followed, though, by corrosive guilt—which felt like it might not leave for a long long time. Maybe never.

But I was still alive. It was time to stop acting as if I'd died with him.

On my second viewing, I felt certain that this was the place. As if to copper-fasten the deal, a butterfly showed up, fluttering about, coming with me from room to room. Aidan was giving his blessing. *Thank you.*

Walking to get the subway home, I was already making plans. I'd have to see some expert about security, oh Lord, the *tedium* of it all, that stuff had been Aidan's remit and, honestly, it was quite high on the list of the things I missed about him. Jolting me from my introspection, my phone rang. As always, it was Jacqui. My heart as heavy as a rock, I said, "I'm on my way."

Far from Joey, Jacqui and Trea becoming a happy family, things were really toxic. Jacqui had broken up with Handsome Karl and was having friends-with-benefits sex with Joey. Except friends was exactly what they weren't.

Their whole thing was so messy. Months earlier Joey had told me that Jacqui kept setting him up for failure. I'd scoffed at him—but he'd been right. She asked for things he couldn't give, always to do with Trea: he was to see her on specific days at specific times. Even when he protested that he couldn't, she stuck to her guns, then raged when he let her down.

She couldn't stop herself and I understood why. With every fuck-up, Joey felt guilty. This gave Jacqui a small amount of power over him. But it was false power—and unsustainable. The game-playing, the rage, the longing, all of it was eating her up to the point where I was worried.

And I despaired of him. He wasn't stupid: he must know she couldn't have emotion-free sex with him.

At her apartment, she was in tears. "Anna, I fancy him so much and have to keep seeing him. I wish I could just cut off all contact."

"Stop sleeping with him," I said. "It's making you feel worse. You can't go on in this state."

"I don't believe he's 'working.'"

"Jacqui, he is."

Her anger flared. "Why are you taking his side?"

This was so tiring. Joey had pulled off the first deal, the one with the cargo ship. But he was working harder than before, to capitalize on the momentum. "Jacqui, I know you're not keen but I think you should see a therapist."

Instantly, her tears dried. "You're saying I'm mental. Nice, Anna, very nice."

"That's not what I meant. Jacqui, no!" I was babbling in panic. "I want to help, but forget I said anything."

She was the person I loved most in the whole world. Having lost Aidan, I couldn't run the risk of losing her. I wasn't sure I'd survive.

A couple of hours later, Joey turned up. "Sorry," he said. "I told her I couldn't get here at the time she wanted."

I nodded, too worn out to engage. I just wanted to escape.

"Was she pissed?" he asked.

"She's a wreck, Joey. I'm worried about her. She's not able for . . ." Despairingly, I spread my arms to encompass him. ". . . this. You've got to be kinder to her."

"How? What should I do?"

He needed to either stop sleeping with her or fully commit, but it wasn't my place to say it. I was worried I'd already said too much.

"Jacqui needs certainty. And remember, there's a little girl in the middle of this. She's got to be your priority."

"Certainty?" He knew what I meant. "Noted."

I began to gather my stuff.

"So . . . ah?" He was obviously looking for a neutral subject. "How's the apartment-hunting going?"

Unexpected pleasure sparked. "You know what? I think I've found a place."

"Oh, wow, congratulations. That's big, right? You know, with Aidan . . . ?"

His sensitivity surprised me. "I felt so guilty," I admitted. "But I'm still alive . . ."

"Yep. So you gotta keep living. Doing it for him as much as for you."

"That's it, that's how I feel. Take a look at the brochure. Cute, right?" I couldn't hide my fondness. "But there's this little garden. Am I paranoid or would it be easy to break in through the back of the building? I'd only be one floor off the ground."

He studied the photo. "Yeah. But. Get an alarm. Proper doors and windows."

"I'm clueless about that stuff. The guy would tell me I needed the God-tier version and I wouldn't know if I did or didn't. Maybe I'll ask Luke to come with me."

"D'you want me to take a look? I know about home security."

"You? How?"

"From another life. I'm literally an expert. Saturday do you?"

". . . Aaaah. I'll need to check with the realtor. I'll text."

I had to call Luke, though. "You know I'm looking at apartments?" I explained my situation. "Joey said he's an expert on home security."

"He said that? Yeah. It's . . ." Luke hesitated over the word. ". . . true."

Next, I sought Jacqui's approval.

"What would that tool know about home security?"

"Luke says he does."

"He's so compartmentalized . . . His left bollock doesn't know what his right bollock is doing. Well, go on ahead. Although he'll probably be eight hours late, if he shows at all." Then, "Why don't you just move in with us? If he ever buys us that apartment he keeps talking about, you, me and Trea can live together."

I didn't want to, not anymore. The realization shocked me. Women were always there for other women—that was one of life's immutable truths. But the nonstop drama was exhausting. Jacqui needed more emotional support than I could give. Over two and a half years on from Aidan's death, I was still depleted of everything: compassion, joy, the energy to wade into Jacqui's life and try to fix it. The basics were all I could manage—washing myself, showing up at work, paying bills—and viewing the occasional apartment. But there was nothing extra, nothing left over.

I'd even gently extricated myself from the dismal weekends in Boston with Aidan's family. They had, just as gently, let me go. They were lovely people but the weekends felt more like vigils. Returning to New York on a Sunday evening, I always felt worse than I had on Friday. Perhaps they did too?

For the longest time, having given up on a meaningful life, I'd been totally available to Jacqui. She was my only truly intimate relationship. While I'd been going to the psychics, I'd made a circle of "recently bereaved" friends, but they'd drifted away. My older friendships had lapsed because people thought I should be back to normal by now. Occasionally I could show up and put on an act but for days afterwards I felt destroyed.

Nevertheless, fresh shoots were stirring. I hadn't seen Angelo since that afternoon at the exhibition, but I'd have liked to.

How was poor Jacqui to know I was different, if I didn't tell her? But she was too strung out and I was too tired.

When I arrived at "my" apartment, Joey was already there, charming the realtor (a woman). She seemed reluctant to leave us.

Silently Joey moved through the empty rooms, shaking window frames, removing and replacing a ventilation grille, examining the lock on the front door. We finished our short tour in the bathroom.

"You need a whole new front door," he said. "Something much stronger, with deadlocks. You're right about the garden. The windows are your most vulnerable points. They need locks and alarms, all of them."

"Even that tiny one?" I pointed at a window, maybe eighteen inches square, high up in the bathroom wall.

"It's big enough. A kid could get through there, no bother. Once they're in, they open the door from the inside, let the big guys in. Happens all the time."

"No, it doesn't." He was *so* cynical.

"Anna. It does."

I frowned at his conviction. "How do you know?"

"How do you think?"

"*You* were burgled?"

His expression was strange. Urgent. "Try again."

"I don't know." I was baffled. "What am I missing?" Then I went cold. "Joey, *you* were the kid?"

He was completely still, his eyes on mine.

"Joey?" My voice was a husk. "You broke into houses?"

Silently, he inclined his head.

A thousand words rushed into my mouth. All I could manage was, "When?"

"From age ten, until I got too big."

". . . What age was that?"

"Thirteen."

"Who did you . . . who made you do it?"

"My dad and Keith, my brother."

Nothing in my life had prepared me for this conversation. "And then . . . what? You were set free? That must have been a relief."

Joey shrugged.

"It *wasn't?*"

"They didn't want me anymore. I'd been part of something," he said. "I belonged. I mattered. If it wasn't for me, they wouldn't have gotten in."

"But . . ." I hardly knew where to start: what they had done to Joey was criminal.

"Overnight, I was nothing. I'd no mates anyway, I'd pretty much stopped going to school . . ."

"What about your mum?"

"What could she do?"

"Protect you! Make them stop."

"She had to do what she was told." His eyes were suspiciously bright. "Until I met Luke, then Gaz, I was . . ." He cleared his throat. "I was all on my own."

I was stunned into silence.

I'd known none of this. But Joey didn't exactly invite heart-to-hearts.

"Luke and the guys are my real family, have been since I was fifteen, sixteen."

I stopped breathing—was he still operating on the wrong side of the law? And if so, what did it mean for Jacqui and Trea?

"You have the worst poker face." He managed a twisted smile. "All above board now. Has been for a long time. But I don't talk about it. Jacqui doesn't know."

"Joey." I was insistent. "If she knew, she'd understand you better and—"

"Never going to happen." Suddenly we were back to defiant Joey. "And you are *not* to tell her."

"But . . . I have to!"

"No. It was, like, decades ago, no longer relevant. So, you want a list of what you need done here?"

". . . I think I've got it."

Out on the street, still dazed, I said, "Thanks for doing this."

"Anytime." He was staring over my head.

"Joey?" I needed some sort of acknowledgement. "Are you okay?"

"Me? Never better. Gotta go." Already he was hailing a cab.

I watched him slide in, disappearing into the stream of traffic even before his door was closed.

Disturbed and weepy, I went home and hid out for the rest of the weekend. There was no way I could see Jacqui. How would I explain my broken state?

But I needed someone to talk to and Luke was the only candidate.

"Do you know why I'm calling?" I asked him. "Have you been speaking to Joey?"

"Um, yeah. But not about anything major. What's up, Anna?"

"He viewed that apartment with me. He told me about when he was a kid, breaking into homes—"

"He told you?" Luke was astonished.

"Does Rachel know?" I asked. "She does? Can I come by?"

In their living room, I sobbed my way through handfuls of tissues. "The saddest part isn't even being made to break into houses. But being abandoned when he outgrew it. Just, cast aside, like he was nothing. And he was only . . . *thirteen*." I howled with grief.

"Anna." Rachel picked her words carefully. "Maybe this isn't really about Joey."

"It is, though. I keep feeling the way Joey felt. When he said he was 'all on his own.'" Another storm of tears shook me. "I felt it, Rachel, I *felt* his aloneness. I still feel it."

"In February it'll be three years since you lost Aidan." Her tone was careful. "It could be your own aloneness you're feeling?"

"It's not." My voice was thick. "I'm telling you, it's *his*. What can I do? Should I try talking to him? But that would be weird, because of Jacqui . . ."

"Do nothing." Rachel was adamant. "This will pass. Listen to me, Anna, it's *important*, your feelings will settle. Jacqui is your friend, Joey isn't, this is all messed up. Don't make it worse."

I took a long, shuddery breath. "Okay." If I called Joey, I'd be crossing a line. If Jacqui found out, the consequences could be catastrophic.

Early the following week, all hell broke loose when Joey told Jacqui they shouldn't sleep together any longer, that it was confusing for both of them.

Maybe it had nothing to do with the scolding I'd given him, what now felt like a lifetime ago. Probably not, I told myself, remembering a great saying: You're not the bride at every wedding or the corpse at every funeral.

But let's face it, you have to be the corpse at one funeral.

I had thought certainty would be the best thing for Jacqui. But now I wished I'd kept my mouth shut. Seeing her so upset was horrible. Worse still, if she found out I'd suggested it, she'd blame me and I was so scared of losing her.

"There are other men out there," I promised her. "Great ones. But you'll never meet them if you stay hung up on this commitment-phobe."

"I want this one."

"He's never going to be the man you want him to be."

"He already is."

My fervent wish was an unlikely one: the chance to rewrite history, even by just a couple of weeks. Failing that, to never see Joey again.

The second option was actually a possibility. Joey probably wanted to avoid me as much as I did him: from his behavior that day after we'd left the apartment, it was obvious he'd regretted opening his mouth.

Barely a week later, I got a last-minute call from Jacqui—Joey had once again let her down and my presence was required. There was no way I could refuse.

The evening ticked by with agonizing slowness, but once we got to 11 p.m., I thought I was in the clear. Then he arrived.

"Trea asleep?"

I nodded.

"I'm here now." His tone was polite. "You can go." He sat on the far end of Jacqui's couch and looked at his phone as he spoke. "The usual apologies and thanks. You've heard it all before, you can write the script."

I got my stuff together, threw on my jacket and went to the door. "Okay. Bye."

"Yeah." He didn't turn his head. "Bye."

But something resuscitated my sorrow. Turning back into the room, I slid onto the couch. "Joey. Are you . . . okay?"

"Totally." His face was blank.

"Joey." I tried to swallow away the lump in my throat. "What you told me . . . that day in the—"

His eyes flashed bright with anger. "I shouldn't have said anything. Now you think I'm some tragic case—"

"You were a child." I couldn't hold back my tears.

He looked appalled.

"You were a child." Now I was full-on sobbing. "And you were . . . *all alone.*"

"Aw, Anna, *no.*" He was so uncomfortable. "Please stop."

I couldn't. I sat and sobbed, then he was at my side. I reached for him, crying into his neck.

"Sssh, Anna, sssh." He spoke into my hair. "There's no need for this."

It was wild that *he* was comforting *me*, a woman weeping over a tragic past he no longer cared about. "Stop crying. Please stop."

"I can't," I choked. "I honestly can't."

"It's okay, Anna." His voice was the same low caress he used for speaking to Trea. "That was the past. Look at me now, it's all okay. I'm good."

I lifted my head and said, with teary defiance, "You're not. But you did nothing wrong."

"I know—"

"You *don't.* You're angry, you push everyone away, it's like you hate the people who love you."

His face, so close to mine, registered shock.

"Joey, you've got to let somebody love you."

He looked almost puzzled, then his lips touched the skin beneath my eye, a tiny flutter as he kissed away one of my tears. Then another. *What the hell?* I'd already begun struggling out of his hold when he murmured, "Anna." My eyes met his and my body froze. *Oh God, no.*

His hands were in my hair and his mouth was on mine. I was trapped in a bad dream: Jacqui's Joey was kissing me. This was every sort of wrong.

Abruptly, he reared back from me. "Anna, we can't do it like this—"

On my feet, I said, "What are you talking about? We're not going to do anything." I gestured around the apartment. "Jacqui's my best friend!"

He looked very young. "Anna, I'm sorry, I thought . . ."

"I didn't mean me!" I was panicking. "You should let people love you but I didn't mean me. Listen, Joey, this didn't happen. It will never happen."

"Okay." But his hands hung loose. He seemed puzzled and sad.

"It can never happen," I stressed. "And Jacqui can never find out. *Ever.*"

He took a breath. "It didn't happen. It will never happen. And Jacqui can never find out."

39

Check-in at the Broderick was at three o'clock. My family's conviction that they were exempt from rules combined with their fondness for a bargain meant I was braced for Mum and Helen's arrival from twelve thirty onwards.

My day had already been lively. As soon as Gannon's had opened, I was in there, buying tampons, strong painkillers and my progesterone. (From Aoife Gallowglass, Emilien's wife!) Back in bed, on a codeine high after two fizzy Solpadeine, I saw that Ike had texted, then *Ben* had texted, each asking if I was "doing okay." Pleasantly dizzy, I imagined living here and having things with both men simultaneously. Not literally simultaneously . . . no, wait! *Yes*, literally simultaneously. The idea of the two of them tending to me in bed made me shiver. I hadn't yet had a threesome and at my age, it was well overdue. It must crop up on those appalling lifestyle lists: By age forty-eight, you should have . . .

A)   Bought your own home
B)   Skied a black diamond at Val d'Isère
C)   Piloted your personal helicopter
D)   Been bitten by a dog
E)   Had a threesome

But leaving Vivian out? No, she wouldn't stand for it. So it wouldn't be a threesome, but a foursome. Not a love triangle but a love square. Ah, what the hell. Why not?

A life of commitment-free sex with men I fancied seemed *glorious*. After a while I might start yearning for something deeper but in the short term, it would be so much fun.

Unfortunately, though, I was leaving on Monday. In an ideal world, Joey would pay me to stay here indefinitely, keeping a light eye on things. But the world was not ideal. Still, the few days here had done wonders for my confidence: I was hopeful that some decent work would come my way when I returned to Dublin.

I messaged Ike, told him I was slightly off my head from codeine, reminded him that my sister and mum were arriving soon but that generally *I was available*. While I waited to see what he'd suggest, I texted Ben, the tone markedly different. After all, he hadn't snogged me in the cab of a pickup truck. But he *had* given me a glass of Sprite and a handful of wasabi nuts, so I went the "Beautiful home, generous hospitality, my appalling manners" route, finishing up with a warm reference to his bird feeder. I might have been slightly high but it was clear I'd composed a *beauty* of a text.

Still nothing from Vivian, though! I'd sent three messages now. She must be busy, probably in bed with someone. Ike perhaps? Or Ben? But it hadn't stopped *them* from checking in on me.

Interesting that I wasn't remotely jealous about Ike perhaps being with another woman. How evolved I was! Could this be adulthood? Or was M'town one big polygamous community, where everyone slept with everyone else and I had gone native?

No. That was just the Solpadeine talking. Any polygamous capers seemed to center on Vivian. The rest of the town was likely as monogamous as all other places (which is to say, never quite as monogamous as it appeared on the surface).

My phone pinged and my heart soared. A photo! From Ben! Of his bird feeder. Titled *The Killing Fields*. Then a voice-note. "Anna, heyyy." His voice was *delicious*: deep with undertones of humor. "Hope you're doing better today. Too bad about last night. But we've got to get you out here again. Aaaand, yeah, maybe see you in town over the weekend? Yeah . . . okay. Hopefully. Bye."

Ooooooh! I hugged myself with delight—but had the good sense to hold off on an immediate reply. Between the excitement and the blood loss, I couldn't trust myself.

While I thought of it, I googled Mary and Thornton Heffer. The internet told me that seven years ago, their first book had been a worldwide success, the second not so much and the third not at all. It was more than three years since they'd had anything published, which sounded tough. Not just the fall from being feted by the great and the good, but financially. Mary had probably had a lot on her mind last night. Thornton too, although I hadn't met him before my abrupt departure.

I did another search and discovered that apparently their net worth was "> $50,000." But that same site called Mary "he" and said "he" was 173 cm tall (she was shorter than me and I was 159 cm).

What about those paintings I'd seen at Ben's? I must get the artist's name. Not that I could spend money on anything right now. But perhaps they'd been done by a M'town amateur and cost almost nothing? But they *should* be expensive, I decided. They were special. Maybe Angelo could represent the artist, earning them a fortune and as a thank you, I'd be given a freebie. What a lovely thought!

I listened to Ben's message again, then looked at the photo of the bird feeder—and the penny dropped: Ben Mendoza was the artist. How could I have been so stupid? He'd practically *told* me.

Ben? You're the artist of the beautiful bird paintings? I'm such a thicko.

Hey, don't talk about my friend Anna like that! I just mess around with paint, to try to relax.

There was so much I wanted to ask: Were they for sale? Would he sell one to me? Did he have a dealer? Would he like me to put in a good word with a moderately successful one in New York? Because I could . . .

But at least I *knew* I was in the grip of strong emotions, ranging from embarrassment to the need to impress a famous person to greed (for a bird painting). Not to mention the codeine. I was not reliable. So I sent a reply full of praise and didn't *ask for anything.*

Still in top form from the drugs, I found myself very proud of how Angelo and I had transitioned to friends. It was mostly down to him. He was a rare person, who loved deeply but with a light touch. In our early days, still torn up with guilt about Aidan, the space Angelo had given me was what made it all work.

It was only towards the end that I'd realized there was a detachment to him. And *I* had also changed, that was obvious now: I no longer wanted a relationship where I had limitless freedom. If I ever became serious about another man—and I wasn't sure I was even bothered—I wanted to love and be loved in a different way.

Right then! Time to go downstairs to await the premature arrival of Mum and Helen. At ten to one, barely two hours early, in they came. Despite my misgivings, happiness surged at the sight of Mum with her cauliflower perm and "good" coat and Helen in her habitual black Lycra, looking like a Special Forces operative.

Then I noticed Regan, a solemn-eyed, dark-haired girl pulling a black Trunki. This was unexpected but fine; not only did I adore her but she was a tiny little thing. She could sleep in a drawer.

But, wait a minute, Margaret was bringing up the rear. Two seconds later, Claire strode through the doors, a fabulous figure, shoulder-robing a white coat. And she was flanked by her youngest daughter Francesca.

Suddenly Mum was right in my face. "I know what you're thinking!" She held my arm too tightly. "But we're here out of concern. All of your sisters, your nieces and of course myself and your poor frail father have been *sick* with worry about you. Staying in bed all day, not even *wearing foundation*! Then you high-tail off to the wilds of County Galway with Narky Joey to 'flush out' vandals. You think we wanted to come down here? On a bank holiday?"

"You said you did. You went on about the ceili and the funfair."

"We were trying not to embarrass you."

"Is that right?" I glared.

"Yes, missy, it *is* right."

But there was no point. I'd only been her daughter for forty-eight years but I knew she'd *never* admit to being in the wrong.

Sure enough, two seconds later, she dropped her bags and declared, "C'mon! Let's go down the town and laugh at the crappy shops! Then we'll tie Margaret to a pole and cover her in candy floss! We'll get chips! And win a fortune on the Penny Falls. I know a 'hack' to make all the money fall out. After that, we'll go for cocktails and . . ."

"Let's check in first," Margaret said, nodding at an unreadable Courtney.

I was terrified they'd booked one room between all six of them. They weren't short of money, especially Mum and Claire, but they liked living on top of each other. Poor Courtney would have to put order on them. Already I was dreading the outraged hubbub, as they exclaimed, wheedled and generally made an absolute show of us all in the lobby while normal families came and went.

Another concern was that Mum had got wind of Joey's magic credit card. Because she lacked boundaries, she could easily tell Courtney that Joey was "practically my son" and to charge any rooms to him.

My worst fear—and the most likely outcome—was that they'd all be in with me. But in a stroke of clemency, only Mum, Margaret, Helen and Regan proposed to share my quarters.

Thanks to a last-minute cancellation, Claire had managed to book herself and Francesca into the Fassbender Suite. That was the thing about Claire, she was comfortable slumming it if she thought it would be a laugh but she was *never* afraid to spend money.

"Photo!" Mum said.

"I'll take it," I said quickly. They couldn't keep disrupting Courtney or Lyudmila.

Bringing the glitz were Claire and Francesca: Claire in the magnificent coat, magnificent boots and magnificent hair which fell in a laminated sheet past her shoulders; dark Francesca in a lot of luxe metal—ear-cuffs, piercings and a series of silver zigzags on the fingers of her right hand which gave me geometry-class flashbacks.

Moving along, we had Margaret, keeping it real. Then Helen, Regan and Mum, keeping it unsettling.

40

"Let's have a look at this Fassbender Suite," Mum said.

On the first floor, it was an attractive, light-filled bedroom.

"Very nice." Claire scanned the four walls. "But where's Fassbender?"

"You thought he'd be sitting here in a glass cube?" Helen asked.

"A girl can hope. Not technically a *suite* either, is it?"

"What's the difference?" Mum asked.

Margaret had her phone out. "A suite is 'a *set* of rooms,'" she read. "Emphasis mine. I must admit I'm only seeing the one room."

"There's a sofa bed!" I was afraid they'd go back to reception and complain. "As well as a normal bed."

"Still doesn't make it a suite," Claire said. "But what the hell, who cares!"

"I need feeding," Mum announced. "Where'll we go?"

Everyone looked at me.

"I've only eaten here in the hotel."

"No." Wherever Claire traveled, she was all about "The locals love it." According to her, only basics scuttled back to the safety of their hotel to eat. "I haven't come all this way for an anonymous club sandwich in a bland hotel."

"You'd be lucky to get a club sandwich, anonymous or otherwise, here."

"I'm too weak with hunger to walk another step," Mum said.

"Just this once," Claire conceded, so the seven of us descended on Emilien. Where we all had toasted sandwiches because "I couldn't recommend anything else," he said. "It would be irresponsible."

Margaret exclaimed, "Isn't it great we're all here together?"

In dolorous tones, Mum said, "It's only four of my daughters. Wouldn't you miss Rachel?"

"You saw her last night," Claire said, the M'town newsletter open before her. "Okay! There's a lot on this weekend." Suddenly her laptop was out.

"We need a schedule. Who wants to go to *The Playboy of the Western World* in a tent tonight? Nobody? Good. Karaoke!" She was delighted. "In the parish hall this evening. Tenner in, for charity."

"It'll be crap," Helen said.

"That's the whole point! We're going." Her fingers were a blur on her keyboard. "The parade tomorrow morning?"

"The one in Dublin is a joke of a thing," Mum said. "Imagine how bad it'll be down here."

"You haven't been in five hundred years. It's good these days. We're going." More clicking from Claire. "A ceili tomorrow night here in the hotel. Yes! Attendance is mandatory. A long word, Mum, which means you can't opt out."

"Who says I can't opt out?"

"Me. Sunday morning, a scavenger hunt. No idea what it is, but also mandatory. All weekend, around the town they'll be serving Irish stew, boxty, rainbow doughnuts, green tea . . ."

"Free?" Mum asked.

"*Not* free, you old fool. Nothing is free in Ireland—"

"—except verbal abuse from your daughters."

"Okay!" Claire announced. "Schedule WhatsApp'd to you all." Obediently all our phones began binging and beeping. "Today, we go down the town to laugh at the shops, then an early dinner, karaoke and maybe late drinks."

"Anna!" Margaret had just remembered. "I brought you clothes. Dressy stuff. You won't want to look 'relatable' in your downtime."

She was the most thoughtful person I'd ever met. Always anticipating the needs of others. Speaking of which, she asked, "Should we make a reservation for dinner?"

"On it," Claire said. "There's a place—"

Helen groaned. "Not 'a small gem off the beaten track' where we'll have to sit in a weirdo's front room."

"Better than some poxy pizza place on Main Street."

"What time's the booking?" Helen asked.

"They don't take bookings. We'll just wander in."

"This weekend will be *busy*." I was anxious. "It might not be that easy."

"Wouldja *relax*. They're off the beaten track. Nobody knows about them, we'll be grand."

But at 6 p.m., after we'd walked almost a kilometer out of town, we discovered that "The small gem off the beaten track" had closed during the pandemic and never reopened.

"The fact they didn't answer their emails wasn't a clue?" Francesca asked as we tramped back to civilization.

"'Off the beaten track' means you can't expect a thirst-trap with hourly TikToks."

"*Hourly TikToks*," Francesca murmured. "If you could *hear* yourself . . ."

Poor Francesca. She had only come because she'd had "Three messy break-ups' and was afraid of being alone.

"What's that up there?" Helen was squinting at the cliff.

"The Big Blue. A bar."

"No. Further up, in the trees, are they . . . turrets?"

"It's her ladyship's house."

Breathlessly, Helen asked, "Have you been up there? Could we get an invite?" Helen had what she insisted on calling "The horn" for gloomy, Victorian houses.

"Ask her yourself. She works at the hotel," I said. "So what now? The poxy pizza place on Main Street?"

We picked up our pace . . . and just a moment! That cool woman sauntering up the street looked just like Rachel . . . because it *was* Rachel! And . . . Luke? Yes, definitely Luke, all tight-jeaned and ride-y. Who had they in tow? It was young Lenehan!

And bringing up the rear . . . was that—holy mackerel—*Joey*?

"It's RachelandLuke!" Claire had taken off at a sprint. Followed by the rest of us, lunging like lemmings, in her slipstream. Flinging ourselves at the new arrivals, you'd have thought we'd been sundered for several years.

"How come you're *here*?" we demanded in delight.

"Bank holiday weekend," Luke said. "Nothing planned. Yous are here, a no-brainer, we threw our stuff in the car, swung by to pick up Joey, then Lenehan and, yeah."

"Why didn't you text?"

"We did!"

On cue, our phones began to ping as we moved into coverage.

After I'd hugged Lenehan, I focused on Joey. "Hey!" I cried, my heart happy, my arms wide for a hug.

"Yeah, hey." Barely making eye contact, he slid away from me.

"You're back?" His reticence was confusing.

"Looks like it."

He seemed different, as if he'd been gone for a lot more than a day. No longer in the bad jeans I'd made him buy but in black, slouchy things, covered by a dark overcoat which looked both anonymous and expensive.

"His boys are away," Luke said. "Couldn't have him on his own on a bank holiday weekend."

I managed to say, "The more the merrier." But I was upset.

"How many?" asked the friendly young woman as we crowded into the pizza place on Main Street.

"Aaaah." Mum scanned our group. "Seven."

"There's maybe a few more than seven."

"Well, Regan can sit on Helen's lap—"

"—and Helen can sit on mine," Claire said.

"And you can sit on mine," Francesca called from the back.

"We've no tables for seven available at all tonight."

Back on the street, we eyed each other, wondering who to turn on.

"Tripadvisor says—" Margaret said.

"I'd rather die of hunger!" from Claire.

"We'll have to break up into smaller groups," I said.

A barrack of dissent rose but after we'd been turned away from two more restaurants, Claire faced facts: we'd have to throw ourselves on Emilien's mercy. However, a further rejection awaited—the lounge at the Broderick was *packed*.

"The prodigal go-boy!" Emilien declared. "Seeing as it's yourselves, we'll make a stab at room service. Go on up. We'll attempt a selection of toasted sandwiches. Are you drinking red or white?"

"Red," Claire said.

"White!" Mum said.

"We'll take four bottles of red," Claire said. "One of white. Tap water for Rachel."

"What about me?" Regan asked.

Emilien leant over the bar. "Hello. I didn't see you there. Thought I was hearing things. There's Sprite in the minibar above. That do you?"

"Sure will." Claire answered for her. "We'll take the wine now." She flapped her hands at him to get going. "Quick. Good man. I haven't had a drink in four hours. Thanks."

41

We tumbled into the bridal suite. At speed, everyone fanned out, bagsying the sofas and grabbing the armchairs, as if we were playing musical chairs. Even Lenehan was shoving and laughing with the best of us. Those who didn't bag upholstery colonized choice spots on the floor, resting their backs against the wall.

Only Joey perched on a windowsill, away from the fray; a wild haroo went up, "Armstrong! Get in here on the couch. Shove up there, Mum, and make room for Joey! C'mon, Joey! Loads of space!"

There was no easy way to say this: his presence was generating unease. He'd been on the fringes of our lives, even Lenehan's, for a long time, but other than Rachel and Luke, nobody really knew him. Not even those he'd slept with. His recent, tragic history—the divorce, the kids going away without him—had been met with sympathy. But his older history—Narky Joey, Joey the Heartbreaker—cast a shadow. Acknowledging these contradictory identities was impossible so the blunt instrument of overenthusiastic friendliness was deployed in an attempt to suppress all confusion.

"Climb in here on the couch, good man!"

Joey let himself be coaxed between Mum and Margaret. Shoulder to shoulder, the trio looked dreadfully ill at ease. "This is great!" Margaret declared, her face gray.

"Fecking great!" Mum agreed, miserably. Then, *most* anxiously, "Any chance of that wine?"

"Breathe, Mum." Claire was pouring wine into coffee mugs. (In her panic to start drinking she'd neglected to get glasses.)

"That's some arrangement!" Mum had noticed the biggest bunch of Joey's flowers.

"God, yes, they're gorgeous!" Margaret said. "Who gave you them?"

"Ah. Joey. As thanks for the work I did."

"Nice one, Joey," Claire said.

Joey nodded and didn't meet my eye.

"How did you get a place to stay at such short notice?" I asked Rachel.

"We didn't. But we brought a tent."

"It's March," Helen said. "You'll *die*. We'll fit you in here."

"Sweet Jesus, no." Mum sounded faint. "Luke can't share with us."

"What about Brigit's Airbnb?" I asked. "Gone? How about I go downstairs and plead with Courtney?"

"They've already done a big reshuffle and given the last room to Joey."

"Somehow, on a bank holiday weekend, they found a vacant room for Mr Joseph Armstrong," I said. "The go-boy strikes again!"

Joey's head lifted; he gave me a blank stare, then shifted his gaze away.

Panic began racing in my chest. It was obvious I'd been joking. Why was he so unfriendly? During our heart-to-heart on Wednesday night, we'd been so close. Now, less than two days later, you'd think he barely knew me.

"The solution," Mum declared, "is Claire and Francesca will give their suite to Rachel and Luke."

"Wait, what?" Claire asked. "Am I still paying for it?"

"We'll pay," Rachel clamored. "We will!"

"Come on," Mum coaxed Claire. "It'll be much more fun with all of us in here together."

"Fair." Claire raised her eyebrows at Francesca. "Fair?"

"Okay."

"What's this 'go-boy' business?" Helen asked.

Too shaky to explain, I left it to Lenehan. It was seized upon with glee. The Walshes always loved a nickname. Maybe this would mark the end of the lengthy reign of "Narky Joey" and see the dawn of the "go-boy" era?

A quick rummage through the bag Margaret had packed for me revealed it was full of my favorite things. During that unallocated window of time in New York when I knew I was leaving but hadn't yet departed, I'd gone wild, buying fun, impractical clothes that my previous life had had no space for. Because if not now, then when? If I was too old today to wear a tulle skirt with trainers and a plaid shirt, I'd definitely be too old tomorrow. (In my first job with Ariella, my look was HR-mandated "eye-wateringly kooky." As soon as possible I'd embraced a life of tailored suits—only to eventually find them too constricting. Clearly, with the tulle skirt, etc., I'd overcorrected.)

Back in the sitting room, talk had moved to karaoke choices.

"Bitta Britney," Claire said. "Or Beyoncé. Rachel?"

"Luke and I might do—" Rachel stopped.

"'Stairway to Heaven'? 'Black Dog'? 'Smoke on the Water'?"

"You'll just have to wait and see." Rachel smiled mysteriously. "Mum?"

"'Don't Forget Your Shovel.' That's a song and a half."

"They won't have it," Helen said. "Thank Christ. Anna?"

I wasn't sure I could. I felt too upset by the atmosphere with Joey.

"What's the go-boy's karaoke song?"

Joey shook his head. "I'll sit this out."

"Ah, *Joey*!" they cried, overdoing the disappointment.

"'mon, man," Luke coaxed, lounging back in his seat. "You can do your Agnus Dei song. By—who is it again? Mozart?"

"Bach." Joey was calm.

"Oh yeah." Luke smirked. "Bach."

"Yeah." Joey smirked back. "Bach."

They flat-eyed each other.

"From his Mass in B Minor?" Luke said. "What's that again? Oh yeah! 'Only the most perfect piece of music of all time,' amirite?" After an odd pause, they both dissolved into convulsions of laughter.

"What?" Helen demanded. "Private jokes? Oh no, not around us!"

"It's just . . ." Luke was still laughing. "Joey's cultured now."

"I like a bitta Bach, man, is all!"

"And the rest! Brahms. Mendelssohn." Narrowing his eyes dramatically, Luke said, "You've changed, man. I don't know you anymore."

More laughter followed but consternation was afoot among the rest of the group. "The go-boy likes classical music? The stuck-up fucker!"

"*We* like classical music," Mum insisted. "Making us sound like peasants! We love the football song, the Italia 90 thing."

"I've an even better idea for you." Luke shook his phone at Joey.

"Whatever it is, it's not gonna happen."

"Imma do 'Firestarter,'" Helen declared. "Margaret?"

"Oh no." Margaret was adamant. "Karaoke's not for me."

"Same," said Francesca. "I'd prefer to shoot myself in the ears."

"And me," Lenehan said.

"More wine!" Claire insisted, refilling mugs.

Over the din, we barely heard the knock at the door. "The toasted sandwiches!" Margaret said, her face very pink. "About time. I'm half-jarred already. We started drinking too early."

"No such thing," Claire said.

"But on an empty stomach . . . ?"

"All the better to feel the effects."

Teagan was our server. Holding a heaped tray, she surveyed the crowded room with dismay. "Where'll I put this? Oh my God, the go-boy is back!" Then, in a completely different tone. "Hiiiii, Lenehan."

"Let me take that for you." Luke slid her a tenner and had barely relieved her of the tray before hordes of hungry Walshes lunged at the food.

42

"Everyone out. Please! The karaoke will be finished if we don't hurry." When the last straggler had *finally* vacated the bridal suite, I locked the door, slung the key in my bag and turned around—to find Joey.

"Anna?" He spoke quickly. "Sorry. For being weird. The other night, I talked too much. Told you stuff . . . I guess I thought it would be a long time before I saw you again. Coming back here so soon, I feel . . ."

"Please don't." I was keen to make him feel comfortable. "Joey. It's all good."

His eyes slid away. "Just . . ." He looked at me. "I'm sorry."

"Really, Joey, please let it go. But I appreciate you telling me." Relief made me chatty. Almost exhilarated. "Can I tell you something? I missed you."

"I missed you too. Why d'you think I came back?"

"Oh." I blushed with pleasure. "Silly, isn't it?"

"Totally. Come on, we'd better get going."

"Thank you for the flowers!" I said as we went down the stairs. "So many! Weren't they gorgeous?"

"Least I could do," he murmured.

"I was so touched. Seriously. And that you told him to leave out the lilies. Joey, I *mean*."

"It was no trouble." He slid me a bashful smile. "I'm embarrassed now."

"Don't be! So you're really not doing a choon tonight?" I asked as we hit the lobby.

"I'm really not. What's yours?"

"It used to be 'Raspberry Beret.' Until I heard it was used in Guantanamo Bay. I'll never think of it the same way again."

Out on the street, where the Walshes were milling, a breakaway group had formed: Regan had decided, probably correctly, that she was too young for karaoke. Francesca and Lenehan had elected to join her.

"The Joe-boy?" Regan called up to Joey. "You can come with us. We're gonna do coloring and watch *Masha and the Bear*."

Instantly Joey brought himself down to Regan level. "Thank you, Regan, that's very kind."

What'd she call him? someone asked. *The Joe-boy? She's hilarious.*

"But someone needs to look after these guys," Joey told Regan.

Regan's nod was impassive as she watched Mum force a fluff-covered sweet, excavated from the depths of her pocket, into Francesca's mouth, both of them choking with laughter and reeling about the pavement. "You'd like *Masha and the Bear*."

"I love *Masha and the Bear*. I have three little boys—they love it too."

Regan cast eager glances around Joey's head. "Are they here?"

"No, honey, they're not." He got up. "But you have a super-great time with your cousin."

Startling me, my phone rang. It was Ike. I turned my back on the throng, hoping for privacy. "Hi. Hello."

"What are you up to?" His voice was low.

"Going to the karaoke with my visitors."

Silence followed. "I've to sort out Vivian's hot water. If I get it done in time, I'll come to the parish hall."

"Okay."

"But if I don't . . ." Another pause. Then, speaking faster, "Anna. I live just outside town. A house down near the shore. I'm sending you the coordinates." My phone pinged as the message arrived. "You're busy. You're only here until Monday. I'd like to see you. If you get a break in your schedule, you know where I am."

"Aaaah. Okay."

"Okay." And he was gone.

43

The parish hall had had a major glow-up: green bunting, green balloons and psychedelic lighting moving over the walls. Throngs of festive people were gathered around trestle tables. On the stage, a girl was doing a whispery, angsty song about déjà vu. Her eyes closed, she swung her hair very slowly and . . . oh? Was that . . . "Dr *Olive?*"

"It is, Anna," said the man at the ticket table. "How many of you are there?"

I counted us: me, Mum, Claire, Margaret, Rachel, Luke, Helen and Joey. "Eight, ah . . ." What was this nice man's name? Custard creams, that was all that came to mind. An image of him ducking to avoid getting one square in the face.

Inside, the place was really hopping. We looked on helplessly, regretting the dithering we'd done, ordering cheesecake after the toasted sandwiches. Had we left it too late to get a table?

"Anna," a woman called. "We heard you were coming with a crowd. We kept you a spot."

Now this person I did know! Her name was Pamela. She was another of the custard cream pensioners. In fact, I suspected she was an item with the man on the door, who might be called . . . I had it! Glen!

"This way," Pamela commanded.

As we fought our way through the forest of folding chairs, it gave me a small thrill whenever a local waved at me.

"They know you." Mum seemed confused. "They like you."

"Oh yes! I'm popular in this town. I could be happy here." God, I'd had too much wine too early. Drunken arrogance was already peaking and I was about to topple over into sentimentality. Time to move to water.

"Anna!" A tableful of Beardy Glarers, clustered around bottles of ale, greeted me with enthusiasm. "We're looking for a girl singer to do 'Where Is the Love.' Vivian's let us down."

"Ah shur, lookit, lads!" Every meaningless placeholder word I could dredge up, I threw at the men (who, I realized, were Peadar Brady and his tilers). "That'd be some craic!" No *way* would I be singing with them. And especially not filling in for Vivian, who was probably more talented than the real Fergie. "But the mum's down for the weekend, haha! Need to stop her from dancing on the bar, haha!"

No sooner had I escaped than I met Tipper Mahon, carrying a tray of drinks. His sharp eyes shone, he jerked his black beard upwards by way of hello and he had every appearance of a man about to embark on an anecdote. Very quickly I fixed my eyes on the far wall and kept going. When we reached our table, we had another game of musical chairs: no one wanted to sit beside Joey. So I put him between Luke and me.

"We're very handy for the bar," Claire observed, conjuring up a trayload of drinks in double-quick time and promptly disappearing again. The glass of wine she'd got me, I passed along to Mum—my stomach wasn't able—and bought myself a 7-Up.

On the stage, Dr Olive departed, to desultory applause; Ralph from the hardware shop took her place. To my astonishment, his "Suspicious Minds' was *exceptional*.

"Who's that, in the long dress, beside the stage, introducing the singers?" Mum pointed at a bouffy-haired woman in a column dress made from shiny bronze fabric.

"Is it Ferne?" Joey asked me. "Who gave me the discount on the haddock sweater?"

It *was*. Bringing unapologetic retro style.

"She's wasted here," Joey decided. "Give her the job announcing Ireland's votes in the Eurovision."

"Right!" Claire was back. "Apart from Margaret and Mum, I've signed us all up with your woman over there at the table. Her name is Muireann. Tell her whatever you're singing. Each of you owe me twenty euro." Over Helen's complaints she said, "It's for charity!"

"I'll Revolut it over," Mum said.

"You haven't got Revolut."

"And the joke's on you because I don't owe you money!" Loud laughter followed. Some private joke, I suspected. Another one.

"Claire." Joey passed her a twenty-euro note. "Happy to give to charity but I'm gonna pass on this."

"Ah, you're not!"

"I actually am." His smile was fixed.

"So tell Muireann. Otherwise your woman beside the stage will call your name."

"C'mon." Luke stood up and took Joey with him. Helen and I followed. Karaoke was fun, if done in a contained space, with friends. But this whole public performance was a different thing entirely.

My main issue was Ike. He could show up. *If* this was really happening with him, I needed a song I could perform with both dignity and allure.

"'Firestarter,'" Helen told Muireann.

"The Prodigy?" Muireann asked sharply. "Sorry. No. There are elderly people here. It might upset them."

"Oof." Helen had a think, then offered, "'Psycho Killer'?"

"Not that either."

"I don't want to do anything else. Can I have my twenty euro back?"

"You can, of course."

"'Heroes,'" I said. I'd realized Muireann was probably *Dr* Muireann. I'd do well to befriend her.

"David Bowie? Fair play. I thought we might get yet another Dua Lipa."

Right on cue, the next person on stage started singing 'Don't Start Now' and Muireann made a small, weary noise.

I had an intense longing to go for drinks with Muireann and have enthusiastic chats about how awful everything was. Suggested topics: the cheek of twenty-year-olds thinking they knew everything and that I was a halfwit; how my fear of casual incontinence was made worse by the very ads insisting that sufferers could live a fulfilled life; how the loudness of young men's grunting in the gym should be made a literal crime.

"Anna!"

I turned. It was Hal Mahon.

"Hi!" I was happy to see him. "Hold on, let me just . . ." I grabbed Joey. "C'mere. Meet Hal Mahon, Tipper's brother. One of the crew."

"The go-boy himself!" Hal extended a hand. "D'you know something? You're fierce handsome close up."

A shout of surprised laughter escaped Joey.

"Jeepers, I didn't mean to embarrass you." Hal was suddenly shamefaced. "I've no filter, so I'm told. And to be honest, it's Anna I've my eye on."

"You've great taste there." Holy smoke, Joey was *charmed*. "Thanks for your hard work on Kearney's Farm."

"Nothing to thank me for." Hal looked embarrassed. "All I do is donkey work. No skill to it."

"Hard work is hard work," Joey said.

Hal shook his head. "I was always told I'd amount to nothing. I'm only thirty-four but so far they're right."

"So?" I asked. "What're you singing tonight?"

"Nothing." He was oddly keen to tell us. "I'm barred from it. About five years ago I got carried away. Broke the mic and fell off the stage. I'm a liability. Muireann says it's for my own good and she's a doctor."

44

Back at the table, I said to Joey, "He's a dote, isn't he?"

Joey smiled. "Yep . . . Oh, here we go, an Ed Sheeran, what took them so long?"

Next was a girl singing something that the younger audience were loving but I had *never before heard.*

Quietly, Joey asked, "Do you know this?"

"Oh thank God," I exclaimed. "I don't. Joey, we've crossed that line. We're old. It's awful."

"It's not great," he said. "But being young is marginally worse."

Was it? Maybe. Here came Tipper Mahon, doing "Born to Run." Bellowing, throwing shapes, kicking invisible things . . .

Helen stretched towards me. "Can I boo him?"

"No! Helen, you can't boo anyone. Not here."

"Calm down, I won't. Although I don't like that man."

"You don't like anyone," Mum called.

"But I especially don't like him."

"Why not?" I was curious to hear her answer: Helen could be very astute.

"His beard is . . ." Helen said. "His eyes are . . . Look, I just don't like him." She added, "Maybe because he's only pretending to like you."

That gave me an unpleasant little jolt. "Why do you say that?"

"Dunno. But it's obvious. The way he looked at you earlier."

I believed Helen entirely: as soon as she'd said it, something inside me had clicked in agreement.

Did it matter that Tipper Mahon wasn't a fan? Probably not. But my head played a quick round of *What did I ever do to him?* Had I not haha'd enthusiastically enough at his relentless stories?

"Hey, Anna." A warm voice spoke into my ear.

It was Ben Mendoza! I jumped up, turned around, hugged him and exclaimed, "What are you doing here?"

"Night out. Same as you." Then, "Hey." He nodded at Mum, Rachel, the whole group.

"This is my friend Ben Mendoza." I was embarrassingly excited. "And this is my sister Claire, another sister Rachel . . ."

Politely, Ben greeted them all. When he got to Joey, he became more focused. "Back in town? Great to meet you. Thanks for what you've done for Brigit and Colm."

"So?" I forced Ben's attention back to me. "Will you be treading the boards tonight?" You see, this was how out of control I was. "Treading the boards," I ask you! Good job I'd stopped drinking.

"Naw. Gotta get back."

"Conference call with the Dallas office?"

"You know it!"

I didn't. But whatever.

"Nice to meet you all." Ben slipped away.

Joey leaned towards me. "I only left yesterday," he said. "What the hell have you been up to?"

In the aftermath of Ben, my stomach began churning and the low-down draggy pain had started up again. It was shocking to think I'd endured this every month for thirty years. It really was no fun at all.

"Anna, it's your pals!" Mum said as Peadar Brady and the tilers appeared on stage to deliver a high-pitched, melodramatic "Bohemian Rhapsody."

It was well-nigh impossible to not laugh. When it ended, the stunned silence was broken only by spots of muffled choking.

"They enjoyed themselves." Margaret eventually spoke. "And that's the main thing."

"Next," Ferne called, "we have Claire Walsh."

Her chin held high, Claire smiled her way to the stage. Where she *killed* "Oops, I Did It Again." A natural performer, she moved with sinuous confidence, involved the audience in steamy eye contact and generally brought the house down.

Through the clapping and cheering, I heard Mum say, her voice warm with pride, "She was always a show-off."

God, I really didn't feel well.

Luke and Joey were having another terse exchange, whatever it was about. "I said okay," I heard Joey say. "You don't have to—yeah, I said okay!"

"Next to sing for us," Ferne announced, "is Joey Armstrong."

"No, he's not," we protested.

But Luke, his hand on Joey's back, pushed him towards the stage and called, "He's on his way."

"He's doing it? Okay! G'wan, Joey! G'wan, the go-boy!"

"What song's he doing?" Mum asked.

"Gotta be some sort of 'rawk,'" Helen said.

We were all in agreement on that.

Waiting for the music, Joey seemed self-conscious. Nervously, he moved from one side of the small stage to the other, the savagely bright spotlights bleaching his hair to a pale blond.

Then the unmistakeable opener of "The Real Slim Shady" filled the hall.

Joey? *Rapping?* Oh my God, no, this would be horrible. I wanted to climb under the table.

Luke had his phone up, filming it. To blackmail him at a later date? That could be the only reason.

. . . But wait a minute, Joey actually wasn't bad. Looking *not entirely mortified* and he was all *over* the rapid-fire lyrics. *How? When?*

Rapt with anxiety, I couldn't take my eyes from him. Was it just me or was he picking up confidence . . . ?

"That escalated fast," I heard Mum say.

"That's not what that means, you old fool," Helen said.

The crowd seemed to be on Joey's side, singing along, shouting encouragement. He was definitely getting into it. Had I ever before seen him dancing? Not that this was actual *dancing* but his body was loose and fluid and, in some invisible way, very much on the beat.

"Holy fuck," Helen yelled, above the furor. "He's *grooving*. In a good way."

And he knew it. All at once, he owned it, smirking, prowling, making us scream—but also with a twinkle at his own ridiculousness.

By the time the song ended, we were on our feet, clapping and yelling. He was applauded all the way back to the table where, with weird intensity, he and Luke hugged, as if he'd just returned from war.

"How did we not know you could do this?" Rachel yelled.

He shook his head; his smile was shy. "Don't."

"Why Eminem?" Rachel asked.

"Trea."

"TikTok!" Rachel exclaimed.

"What?" I was *bewildered.*

"The TikTokkers have revived Eminem," Rachel said.

"Trea and I listen to a lot of nineties stuff."

Splitting my attention, Ferne summoned Rachel and Luke to the stage. Luke was the kind of man who caused a stir wherever he went—the hair, the height, the tight jeans—and the parish hall in M'town was no exception.

The audience stilled expectantly. But I'd say no one had anticipated that Rachel and Luke would do "You're the One That I Want." In the words of the song, it was *electrifying*.

If you had to be picky, neither Rachel nor Luke were great singers. But their connection was undeniable and it was such fun. From a PR perspective, my sisters were doing me proud. Thank the *Lord* that Muireann had shut down Helen.

But, courtesy of my prodigal period, I wouldn't be singing tonight. Lying in bed, a hot-water bottle on my stomach, was all I felt able for. Which meant that going to Ike's was also off tonight's agenda. I really fancied him but felt too unwell to navigate sex with someone new.

Not to mention the furor it would cause among my sisters if I disappeared. They'd be *delighted* for me, a lot of whooping and "You go, girl's." It would be horrific.

At the side of the stage I told Ferne I was out.

"That's a pity," she said. "But every cloud. You're the last person on the list, which means I can go home and take off this effing dress."

"You're stunning, though."

"I haven't been able to breathe for three long hours."

In a burst of solidarity I exclaimed, "Isn't it terrible how women aren't allowed to have visible stomachs!"

That made her laugh. "I hear you're off home on Monday? Come in to me before you go."

"To Fine Irish Knits?" I didn't want a cut-price fine Irish knit but how could I refuse?

"I'll let you into a little secret." Ferne's eyes sparkled. "If you promise to not tell a *soul*. I own Heather & Mist as well."

I gasped at the memory of feather-light mohair cardigans flowing through my fingers like whispering air.

Ferne was delighted. "A fan of the high-end stuff? So you won't be wanting anything from Janette's Jumpers."

"*That's* yours?"

"You're thinking cheap, acrylic rubbish? But I've lovely boleros in bright colors, the Gen Zs love th—" Whatever she saw on my face brought her to an abrupt halt. "Mother of God, Anna!" She looked as if I'd had a death in the family. "You bought one, didn't you? Go straight into Valerie. She'll give you your money back. Tell her I said it was okay."

We'd see. Dealing with Valerie took a lot of energy. "What else do you own?"

"Quality Yarnworks. The dullest of the lot. But does a very steady trade. They all do."

"Why—"

"—so many different shops? Because people like choice, even if it's only the appearance of it. Each place has its own personality. My bestie Rionna Breen has the same business model, but for home stuff—bed linen, rugs, throws . . . Oh cripes, I'm up." She grabbed her microphone and suddenly it was thank you and goodnight and if everyone could vacate the premises as quickly as possible because the hall needed to be cleaned for "Tomorrow's events."

Out on the street, plans for more drinks were abandoned because, according to Claire, "It's going to be a long and lively weekend. We cannot peak too soon."

I texted Ike, to tell him I still wasn't feeling great.

Tomorrow night? he asked.

Tomorrow night, I replied.

I hurried to catch up with Luke and Joey, on their way back to the hotel. "What was going on with you two?"

"Trea challenged me to do a song," Joey said. "And I was nervous af."

"He did it, though." Luke patted his phone. "I have proof."

"She sounds so grown-up." I'd still been thinking of her as a toddler.

"Nearly fifteen, so smart, so funny," Joey said. "She's great."

By dint of seniority, Mum got my bed; she elected to share with Margaret. Helen, Regan and I were on one pull-out sofa, Claire and Francesca on the other. Between skincare and dental regimes, it was a long time before we were settled.

As she pulled on her nightie, Mum remarked, "Could you imagine if we'd had to share with Luke Costello?"

"I wouldn't mind," Claire said.

"I wouldn't sleep a wink," Mum countered.

Finally, Claire turned out the lights and silence fell. One of us, probably Margaret, had begun to snore softly when Mum's voice asked, "Do you think he sleeps in his jocks?"

Helen said, "I know for a fact that he doesn't."

Mum gasped, "Have you seen him? *It*, like?"

"Haha, no, you pervert."

"You can't shame me! It's not..." Mum hesitated over the word. "...'cool.' As an older woman I can fancy whoever I want."

"We meant *us*," Helen said. "Me, Anna, *us*. We're the older women who can fancy whoever we like. Not you, you ancient pervert."

Claire interrupted, "Helen, how do you know about the no jocks?"

"Rachel said one night she was chilly so she put on a T-shirt. He put the foot down. No clothes in bed. Ever. He said he'd get her more blankets. He'd put the heat back on. But no clothes."

"I find that..." Claire's voice was strangled. "...extremely hot. The nudiness. The foot being put down."

"Go to sleep," Regan commanded. And we were so startled that we did.

45

I made an offer on the apartment in Two Bridges.

Jacqui was stunned. "You're *serious* about this? I thought you were just looking at places to get Margaret off your back."

"At the start, maybe. But now . . ."

"Anna, Two Bridges is miles away, it'll take you ages to get up town to me. What if I need you at the last minute?"

"I don't know."

I should have found a gentle way to admit that I no longer wanted to be on permanent call, but my lifelong fear of confrontation stymied me. And how could I hurt her when she was already so fragile?

"What's up, Anna?" Her voice was hard.

"I might be getting better. After Aidan. Ready to find a new home."

That wasn't what she'd meant and we both knew it. "Won't you miss us?"

"Jacks, I'll see you all the time. I'll still take care of Trea."

"By, like, appointment. But from now on, every time that prick bails, I'll be fucked."

"I'm sorry."

She turned away from me.

"Could one of your neighbors help?" I tried.

"In Manhattan? Axe-murderer central?"

But they couldn't all be axe-murderers. I didn't deserve Jacqui's resentment but I lacked the courage to tell her. I just wanted our boundaries to magically reestablish themselves in a happier, more harmonious way.

Angelo and I had had no contact since the evening, several months ago, when I'd flaked on him to watch Trea. Later that night he'd texted, telling me that all of the Finnish glassworker's pieces had sold. I'd thanked him for trying. Nothing since.

I'd thought about him but I was too enmeshed in *The Jacqui-and-Joey Show* to have the bandwidth. All at once, I was able. In fact, it felt urgent, so I called him.

We met for coffee (he had an infused water).

"Sorry for going dark on you." I was embarrassed.

"You were doing what was right for you. Never apologize for that."

"You're . . ." There was no other word for it. ". . . amazing."

He laughed and waved it away. "Totally not amazing. So what's going on with you?"

I told him about my new apartment. "I should get possession in maybe a month."

"That's quite a step," he said. "So. How's the guilt?"

"Oh my God." I was astonished at how astute he was. "Bad. Always. All the time."

"Survivor's guilt."

You see, nobody else ever spoke to me like this.

"How bad did you feel about meeting me today?" he asked. "Out of ten?"

"Seven?" I shrugged. "Eight?"

"But you still came. That's what's meant by 'learn to live with it,'" he said.

I was so grateful for Angelo acknowledging that, three years on, I was a long way from normal. And maybe would never be again. Not the way I used to be, at least.

"'Feel the guilt and do it anyway,'" I said. "That's going to be my new motto."

"You're already living it."

"And what's going on with you? I know it's going to be interesting."

"Is a gong bath interesting?"

"Yes!" I'd heard about them. "So you lie down? Someone plays giant metal gongs?"

"A type of meditation," he said. "You 'bathe' in the vibrations."

Apparently, it "helped to calm the soul." The part of me that was keen on silver bullets, magic solutions and easy answers to life's pain perked up. "Could you let me know the next time you're going?"

"They're held every new moon. Easy to figure out the dates."

Was it? I knew nothing about new moons; the only moon that got my attention was a full one, because I was usually awake half the night.

"Call me," he said, "if ever you want to give it a go."

The implication was clear: if I wanted to see him, I'd have to make it happen.

There was a resistance in him, a strength of will. It excited me.

As soon as the next gong session was listed, I booked two tickets and texted him the details.

On the night in question we met at the park, in the dark, carrying our mats and duvets.

Is this a date? I wondered.

Because I wanted it to be a date.

What did Angelo think? I could have asked but it was a novelty to just float. Whatever was going to happen would happen. Surrendering to the benign indifference of the universe was a glorious relief.

When he invited me to the Catskills for some comet-watching I said yes. I said yes to everything involving him, because he made me happy. *And* full of guilt. One feeling couldn't exist without the other and maybe it would always be this way.

But sleeping with him wasn't the major upheaval I'd expected. In bed, he was very present. It wasn't sex—he made love and he did it with every part of him: heart, soul and body.

"You fucked a Feathery Stroker?" Jacqui exclaimed when she extracted the details from me. "I don't know you anymore."

She was aiming for funny but there was too much truth for either of us to laugh. And I was ashamed of turning something so beautiful into a cheap gift to curry favor with her.

"How are you and Joey?" I asked tentatively. Because I hadn't been called on in the past few weeks for any last-minute Trea-watching. "Has he got more reliable?"

"That shithead? No! But instead of leaving me hanging, he sends along one of his buddies—Shake, Luke, that cretin Gaz."

Relief washed through me.

"Your sister's been here a couple of times. With Luke, like. She has the cop-on to know he's not safe with me." She forced a laugh and, a second too late, so did I.

"I'm going to Boston on Friday to tell Aidan's mom and dad about Angelo," I said. "I'm dreading it."

"Oh my God, you're serious about him!"

46

I woke early and starving. Breakfast wouldn't have started yet but if I went down, maybe the muffins would be out.

"Morning, Anna." It was Hari, one of the new waiters. "Regan and the go-boy are here already."

From the chaos of coloring pencils and drawings strewn across the table, it looked as if they'd been there for ages.

"Look, Anna! Joe-boy is super-good at drawing." A sheet of paper was rustled under my nose. "This is me! And a pet mouse."

The illustration was excellent. Regan was recognizable and the mouse was very cute. "Joey, this is great."

"Gold star, Joe-boy." Carefully Regan unpeeled a small shiny star and stuck it on the top of the page.

"You're awake early," Joey said to me.

"So are you."

"I'm always up early. I told Helen if she wanted a lie-in, Regan could give me a shout when she woke—Hey, thanks, Regan." She was sticking a gold star on Joey's jumper. He pressed his palm to his chest to secure it.

"You're a gold-star boy," Regan decreed.

"He sure is—oh thank God!" The baked goods had arrived.

"You okay?" Joey asked.

"I'm hungry and a little pukey."

"But you weren't drinking much last night."

"Not a hangover. It's my period." Because why should I be coy? It was a natural event half the planet endured every month.

All credit to Joey, he didn't flame with embarrassment, simply asked, "You need anything?"

"Just sugary carbs. Oh, here's Francesca."

"I've been sent to get croissants and stuff," she told Hari. "For my granny and aunts. Is that okay?"

"Is Mama awake?" Regan asked. "Can I come with you?"

"Abso-fricken! You can help carry these."

They left and it was just Joey and me.

Infused with strange clarity, I knew exactly what was about to happen. I cleared my throat. "Joey?"

He looked up, instinctively alert.

"Joey. I'm sorry."

His face drained of color. For several seconds he remained mute. "It's okay." He sounded breathless. "Water under the bridge now."

"It was the worst. *I* was the worst."

"I'm still standing. I mean it. I'm okay."

"Thank you for letting me say it in person."

His finger skated back and forth in a patch of spilt sugar. "I'm sorry too, Anna. About Jacqui. I didn't understand that it would get so . . . I was selfish, hurt, stupid. I'm so sorry."

"It wasn't just you. Things were already messy with me and her."

"But I should never have . . ." For a long stretch of silence, he stared at the table. Then, "Anna, I loved you."

I might as well admit it because it was true. "And I loved you."

His head shot up; his eyes blazed color. "You were so . . ." He moved his hand near his mouth. ". . . sweet to me."

"Oh, Joey," I gulped. Even now, my impulse was to protect him. Back then, I had seen the hurt child inside the man and it had broken my heart.

Then he hurt me terribly.

And I, in turn, was horribly cruel to him.

Yet the world had kept turning and life happened, happened, happened. And now, all these years later, we'd once again washed up on the same piece of shore. Maybe it could finally be put to rest.

"That night," he said. "It was one of the worst of my life—"

"Sorry, Joey, I'm so sorry—"

"—but it was the making of me. You showed me who I was and I wanted to do better, be a better man. Now I live in a different way." He shrugged. "I guess I should thank you?"

Doubtfully, I watched him. What on earth could I say? A breezy *You're welcome*? Out of the question.

"Hey." He reached across the table, squeezing my hand. "Don't look so sad. It's okay. I mean it. I'm good. It's all good."

47

"Who's still missing?" Outside the Broderick, Claire corralled those of us going to the parade.

"Helen, Rachel and Luke," Francesca said. "They've all gone back to bed."

Claire cast her eye over me, Mum, Margaret, Francesca, Regan and Joey. "Okay. Let's go. We want a good spot."

"If you have to make fun," I begged, "please do it quietly."

"What, *us*?" Their indignation was shrill. "We'd never do that! We're nice people."

Well, they weren't *bad* people but they couldn't seem to help themselves.

The crowds were already out in force but Claire commanded a path, leading us to the bandstand by the memorial, from where the parade would set off. Metal barriers separated us, the great unwashed, from the paraders. On the far side of the divide, about thirty children, dressed as snakes, moved in an unruly throng.

Claire squealed, as if she'd just spotted Harry Styles. "It's St Patrick!"

So it was. Or at least, a local in a long beard, wig and green floor-length caftan, an embroidered miter perched on his head. In one hand was a heavy wooden staff, in the other a reusable coffee mug. Doing plenty of pointing, Ferne and Rionna were issuing him with detailed instructions.

"He'll have to smite those snakes." Francesca nodded at the pack of cacophonous kids. "Not gonna lie, I'm excited for it."

"St Patrick didn't smite the snakes," Margaret corrected. "He banished them."

"What's the difference?"

"None," Claire threw in. "Because none of it happened. Opium of the people, PEOPLE!"

"'To smite.'" Margaret had her phone out. "'Strike with a firm blow.' 'To banish: Get rid of.'"

"Yeah, but you could banish them *by* smiting," Joey said.

"I'll smite the lot of ye if ye don't shut up," Mum said.

"And a happy St Patrick's Day to you too," Joey said.

Mum twisted her neck at an unnatural angle to stare at him. She was so startled she began to laugh.

"I think I fancy St Patrick." Claire's voice was low.

"You fancy everyone," Mum said.

"The way he's holding that thick, hard stick of his . . ."

"Waaaidaminute!" Francesca asked. "Why's St Patrick staring at Anna?"

What on earth? . . . St Patrick *was* looking in my direction, but only those with a filthy mind could say that the way his hand was wrapped around his rigid staff was suggestive.

Who was he? I tried to see past the long wig and beard . . . oh my God, it was Ike!

"You know him?" Claire demanded.

"Is it the goon?" Joey asked.

"Uh-uh." My face was annoyingly hot. "Yes."

"He spent the whole week trying to put the moves on Anna," Joey informed everyone.

"Oh Christ," Claire raged. "I wish I was single."

"So does your husband," Mum said. Both she and Claire dissolved into convulsions.

"Something's happening!"

With surprising speed, the little snakes had organized themselves into four rows of seven. Behind them, a band of drummers began to clatter. St Patrick strode to the very front, handed his coffee cup to Rionna as if he were Mariah Carey, gave me a smile-free stare and the parade began.

It was short but charming. A troupe of Irish dancers skipped along followed by the M'town Hurlers, looking frozen in their shorts. At least it wasn't raining. After them, a flatbed truck, peopled with clowns and blasting BTS, trundled past slowly.

Next came a thirty-strong group of Ukrainians in what must be their national dress—Claire studied their embroidered smocks with keen interest. "They've them on Matches for eight hundred euro. Or very similar anyway."

"Have a word with Lyudmila," I said.

A second flatbed truck appeared, hosting a quartet of traditional musicians, followed by a van of old people singing "Lily the Pink." The Living Well with Dementia group, I guessed. Mrs Skerett could very well be on board.

A cavalcade of tractors, if five could be considered a cavalcade, rolled by. *Two* of the drivers waved to me. "Anna?" Joey was at my shoulder. "What *have* you been up to?"

"Seriously. I haven't a clue who either of them are."

A few more vans and trucks, advertising Gannon's Pharmacy, Mike's Bikes and Kavanagh's Farm Supplies drove past. I might suggest that Brigit do one next year. Bringing the event to a close was a scattering of young kids, aged six according to Joey. Dressed in karate outfits, they threw enthusiastic kicks and punches. Very cute.

"That's it?" I asked.

"Looks like it," Joey said.

It had been nice but cold. "Let's go somewhere warm," I said. "For rainbow doughnuts. Or soup—"

"Whose phone is ringing?" Joey asked. "Anna. It's you."

I took a look. "Oh, that'd just be Ben Mendoza, Oscar-winning director, calling me." Then, stepping away, "Hey, Ben."

"Hey! So. Last-minute hang at mine tonight. Just drinks. Very relaxed. Any time from seven. Bring your mom and sisters, the whole gang."

We were meant to be going to the ceili but I was making an executive decision here. "Are you sure? There's a lot of us."

"Everyone's welcome," Ben said. "It'll be fun."

"Everyone's welcome?" I repeated.

"Everyone."

Oh-kay. He'd said the word "Everyone." Immediately I rang the hotel. Courtney answered.

"I don't know how you're going to swing it"—I was urgent—"maybe fake a burst appendix, but you need to take tonight off."

"I need to take tonight off anyway. I've worked sixty-three hours this week, I'm blind with exhaustion."

"You're coming to a relaxed hang at Ben Mendoza's."

"Anna! I can see again! It's a miracle. Wait, though. I'd better run out and buy a new bra. Bye."

My phone beeped: a text from Ike. **You going to Ben's tonight?**

Quickly, I typed, **Indeed I am.**

And then come back to mine?

I considered how to reply. The answer was obviously yes, but should I be coy? Ah, what the hell! I hit twelve smiley faces in quick succession, then slid my phone back into my pocket.

"Your attention, please, for a moment?" I got our group in a cluster and told them about the invitation. The response was—mostly—jubilant. Muttering stuff about, "Some old guy . . ." Francesca was out.

"'Everyone Loves Anna.'" Joey's smile went right to his eyes. "They'll be talking about it for decades, the Year Sweet-face Walsh Came to Town. Like something from a Márquez novel." He caught my look. "Yeah, Joey Armstrong reads Márquez novels." Then he corrected himself, "Well, Márquez nov*el*. Just the one. *Love in the Time of Cholera.* 'Fifty-one years, nine months and four days.' That poor man."

For the first time in a week, my lunch didn't consist of stuff stolen from the buffet. We found a pub where the man in charge let us all squash in. He brought us soup and soda bread.

Claire took a cautious nibble from the bread—she almost never ate carbs—then raved about it to the man.

"Lidl's finest," he said. "Or was it Aldi? One of them anyway."

Helen, who had joined us by then, said to Claire, "You thought he got up at four a.m. to bake it himself with his humble, culchie paws."

And all credit to Claire, she said, "I did, ya."

"So what's the plan for the afternoon?" Margaret asked.

"At leisure, according to Claire's itinerary." I planned to return to bed. I needed to be in tip-top condition for my shenanigans with Ike. This would be, at best, a two-night thing; there was no room for "Just not feeling it right now, sorry, babes."

"In that case . . ." Margaret lobbied hard for a walk on the beach. "The Atlantic waves," she said. "The ozone! The clean white sand."

She was met with a great deal of resistance: we were not an outdoorsy family.

"I need a run," Joey said. "Then Rachel, Luke and I are going out to see Colm."

"*Darby O'Gill and the Little People* is starting at the parish hall in half an hour," Claire announced. "Fiver in. For charity. It'll be a laugh!"

"'It'll be a laugh' will be the inscription on your headstone," Helen said. "First, Regan and I are going out for a quick gawk at her ladyship's manor. I looked it up—it was built in 1860!"

"Can I come?" Mum asked.

"Only if you ask me properly."

"Can I come too? Because . . . I have 'the horn' for other people's houses."

"Good woman. You're in."

48

"Can you invite Joey up to your room?" Rachel was calling from the Fassbender Not-Suite. "We don't want him left on his own. Luke and I will be with you all . . . in a while."

"What's keeping you and Luke?" I could hazard a guess. And good on them! I was in excellent form, having slept away the whole afternoon. I'd probably have slept for longer except Mum and the rest arrived back, bearing bags of chips and a dozen rainbow doughnuts, keen to tell me how wonderfully atrocious *Darby O'Gill and the Little People* had been.

To the room at large I called, "Can Joey be here while we get ready?"

"Will he be spying on me in my slip?" Mum asked.

"If you want." I rang his room. "Come up here. We've rainbow doughnuts and coffee. Mum says you're to spy on her in her slip."

"I did not!"

"Nah, you'll all be getting changed," he said. "I'll sit this one out."

"We'll do it in the bedroom. 'mon, Joey, don't be on your own."

Moments later, he was at the door, looking indecently handsome. "What the hell?" I cried. "What have you done?"

"What do you mean? Where can I put these?" A slab of green macaroons was in his hands.

"Is it your hair? What's different?"

"Nothing. Why?"

"You look . . ." in no way like a man who'd sworn off sex. Had he had his teeth whitened? Done a sheet-mask?

"Joe-boy!" Regan summoned him.

"Regan!" Joey pawned the macaroons off on me.

"Eye-drops," I called after him. "To whiten your eyes? You put some in. Yes?"

"No," he said. "Okay, yeah, sure. Anything to make you happy." He sat next to Regan.

"Are you going to Ben's birthday party?" Regan asked him.

"Ah, yeah, I am. Are you?"

"I'm too young. Francesca and Lenehan are 'hanging out' with me."

Lenehan? And Francesca? Well, well, well.

"But that just means they're babysitting me," Regan said.

"Aw, Regan. But it's not a birthday party." Joey was earnest. "Just an adults' party. I think you might be bored."

"No balloons? Or cake?"

"Nope. Seriously, you'll have a better time here. So what we gonna read?"

"*Where the Wild Things Are.*"

"Never gets old! Let's go."

In the overcrowded bedroom, I discovered that Margaret, star that she was, had brought along a bag of my going-out makeup—primers, smokey shadows, vampy lipsticks, contouring tools, the works.

With Mum, Claire and Helen also doing their faces, I had to kneel at the window, peering into the tiny mirror in one of the palettes. But I went for it, totally larding it on.

Margaret had also packed my favorite outfit: a leather midi-skirt and an off-the-shoulder top. When I finally managed to get near the full-length mirror, I looked good, at least from the front. From the side, I could have been thirteen weeks pregnant. Did I care? No. This was the age I was. This was the body I had. I wasn't going to deny myself a night with a sexy man just because my stomach stuck out.

I said a quick prayer that my period would continue to taper off and not make a dazzling comeback in a few hours. The thought gave me a brief wobble, reminding me that I knew almost nothing about Ike Blakely. What if we had no chemistry? What if we discovered we didn't even like each other? Well, only one way to find out.

Margaret's bag of goodies included my black boots, their height made manageable by a platform sole. The thing was, I hadn't worn them since a bunion had appeared from *nowhere* on my left foot during lockdown; forty minutes was all I could take before the agony got too bad. But maybe the bunion had shrunk? Maybe I felt like living dangerously? Maybe the period cramps would cancel out the torture?

Courtesy of my age, I needed to sit down to put them on. "Excuse me," I said to Joey and Regan, taking the only spare chair left, pulling on a sock and sliding my misshapen foot into the boot. Okay. No pain so far. Whipping the zip to my knee, I put on the other one and stood up, declaring, "I haven't been this tall in a year!"

Joey widened his eyes.

"Quite the transformation, right?" I couldn't stop smiling.

"You're cute," he stated, very matter-of-fact.

"Thank you." Look at how comfortable we'd become with each other! Was that a knock at the door? For a split second I didn't know the stunningly attractive woman, in a bandage dress and high shoes, standing outside.

"Let me in." She was impatient.

"Courtney!" For it was she. "You look *sensational.*"

"Teagan did me," she said. "She doesn't know when to stop. I'm wiping half of it off."

"No!!!!" I drank in her glossy pout, long lashes and cropped hair, slicked sideways and secured with a diamanté barrette that read SO BORED.

"*Courtney?*" Joey asked. "You look—"

"Different. Ya, I know."

"Not the word. You look great."

The excitement had brought the others tumbling out from the bedroom and bathroom.

"We'd better up our game." Claire stared in astonishment. "Courtney has just shifted the paradigm."

"I hear I missed some show at the karaoke last night!" Courtney pointed at Joey. "D'you know who told me they'd give him a bed for the night if he was stuck? Dr Muireann! And her the most sensible woman I've ever met."

"You should 'hook up' with her," Mum said. "Always handy to have a doctor in the family."

"Are you . . . blushing?" Courtney frowned at Joey. "Is the go-boy blushing?"

"Leave him alone," I said. "Can I do a quick survey on my hair?" Using a chignon pin, I piled it on my head, aiming for a "sexy" falling-down up-do. "Up? Or down?"

"Up!" The room was in agreement.

Except for Joey. "Down," he said. "Definitely down."

"Up it is." Ike could remove the clips later. That might be . . . nice.

"Good to know you respect my opinion so much," Joey murmured.

"Always." I smirked at him.

Rachel and Luke arrived and fell on the macaroons. "Where did these come from?" Rachel was full of wonder.

"Rose made them," Joey said.

"Rose?" I'd just remembered Helen's jaunt up to her ladyship's manor and was torn between two separate streams of information. "Where did you meet her?"

"Tinder." At my shock, Joey laughed. "The poor woman cleans my room. How else? We've been having the chats. She does the macaroons every year. So I ordered a batch."

I couldn't imagine "having the chats' with Rose, but sure, okay. "Helen, Mum, did you go to her ladyship's house? What was it like?"

"Anna." Helen pretended to swoon. "Regan, tell them about the big house."

"The witch's castle?" Regan looked up from her book. "It was like a witch's castle."

"Scary?" Joey asked her.

Thoughtfully, she said, ". . . Nice scary."

"It was the worst house I ever saw," Mum squawked.

Ignoring her, Helen said, "The gate was locked but we got into the grounds where the wall had collapsed. There was a swimming pool!"

"You mean a cesspit!" This from Mum. "Filthy green water . . . and *frog-spawn*."

"Such beautiful *tiles*. Fleur-de-lis pattern. Formal gardens—"

"You'd need a chain-saw to get through the weeds—"

"As for the house itself." Helen groaned. "Huge, gray, high, pointy, *gorgeous*."

"But." Regan was suddenly solemn. "If they don't fix it quickly, it will *fall down on all our heads*."

"Right, as always," Helen said. "If they took away that scaffolding, the whole thing would collapse."

"It's awful." Mum looked distressed. "Definitely haunted. The windows! Long, gloomy oul' yokes watching us. I never thought I'd say this about a house but it's far too big."

"I've literally just bought a Lotto ticket," Helen said. "That's how much I want it."

"She'd sell it to you for a fiver," Courtney said.

"Nah, I need, like, forty million euro."

"A fiver," Courtney repeated.

"Yeah, but . . ." Helen paused, then began to speak very quickly. "Imma tell yous my vision and you're not to laugh: a haunted hotel. Permanent Hallowe'en." Her face was aglow. "We could make a show called *Goth Island* there. Like *Love Island* but with pale emos roaming around in black overcoats, reading Emily Dickinson, catching pleurisy, swapping vials of their own blood."

"Applying right now," Francesca said.

"It wouldn't be an actual island, though," Margaret said.

"Love Island isn't an island either!" Helen was irritated. "It's just a house. You . . . parade-rainer!"

"I want no part of it," Mum said.

But the rest of us, including Courtney, were in.

"So all we need is forty million euro," Helen said.

"Job for Joey Armstrong." Luke laughed. "He knows people with money."

"Raising forty million for *Goth Island*?" Joey said. "Should be a breeze."

Quietly, Regan asked, "Joe-boy, was that a joke?"

Joey nodded and she seemed relieved.

49

"Courtney, have you a number for local taxis?"

"No taxis tonight. Her ladyship is otherwise engaged."

"How will we get to Ben's?" Claire was woebegone. "I don't want to drive."

"I'm working in the morning, I don't mind not drinking," Courtney said. "Four can fit in my Ka, but it'd be tight. You're a tall family."

"And I can get four in my old yoke," Rachel said.

But there were nine of us: Mum, Claire, Margaret, Rachel, Luke, Helen, Joey, me and Courtney herself.

I had a car: Mum's Multipla was sitting right outside the hotel, gathering moss. But my plans for tonight did not include hanging around, waiting to drive people home. It was imperative that I could skip away with Ike any time I liked.

"This is what we do," Helen said. "Yous go on. Imma stay with Regan, give her a bath. I'll come later in the Death Star."

Helen's Death Star was her black Fiat 500.

"Okay. Great. Thanks."

"Ben, you know my friend, Courtney Burke." There was a slight anxiety he might be cross that I'd pulled a fast one by bringing her along.

He frowned. Then, "Courtney! You look, wow . . . So sorry, took a moment to recognize you."

"No bother at all." Courtney was grinning.

"So let me fix you guys some drinks," Ben said.

"I'll help," Courtney said.

"Nope. You take care of a lot of folks," Ben said. "Let me get *you* a drink."

He disappeared. The large room was filling up fast—I spotted Ziryan, Valerie, the terrifying woman from Janette's Jumpers, and Karina the hairdresser, bang on trend in her oversized jeans, her red-blonde hair falling almost to her elbows. The night was shaping up to be a big one. There was her ladyship. Tonight, clad in a severe dress and what looked like an Hermès twilly around her neck, she had a cool, almost daunting appeal.

"Sexy Man!" Vivian, in a tiny dress, her red lipstick appealingly smeared, advanced on Joey. "You're back! I knew you couldn't stay away from me."

Joey's smile was small but entertained.

"You missed so much while you were gone," Vivian declared. "Did you hear about this little *amuse-bouche* here? On Thursday night?"

Who? *Me?* Oh GOD, NO.

"So hot for Ike Blakely that they both disappeared before we'd even had dinner."

"That wasn't why—" I protested. And Vivian knew it, the troublemaker! I'd texted five apologies to her.

Who's Ike Blakely? A rumble of talk had begun. *St Patrick? Does she mean St Patrick?*

"That's right," Vivian told Mum. "St Patrick in today's parade."

"I mean, *wow.*" Claire widened her eyes. "The way he held that staff of his."

"I can guess." Vivian was in full agreement. "Come and get it!"

"Abso-fricken!"

Kindred spirits, the pair of them. Embarrassment covered me like a fur. "Vivian." I was desperate to tell my truth. "You're completely misrepse—"

"Oh?" Her eyes sparkled with good-natured spite. "You're saying nothing happened?"

"No, but—"

I stole a glance at Joey. His face was shuttered.

"Ben needs help with the drinks." I escaped into the throng and found him in the kitchen.

"Ben, can I ask you a couple of questions," I said. "If I'm overstepping any mark, tell me to get lost."

"Sure." He gave me three glasses. "Put ice in those."

"Your paintings? Do you sell them?"

He laughed. "No. I do it just to stop me worrying about stuff."

"So you don't have a dealer? Have you any interest in a conversation with one? He's based in New York."

He wrinkled his nose. "Aw, come on, it's just amateur hour. Can you carry these drinks?"

Back at the cluster of Walshes, Joey was politely engaging with Rose. It looked like a meet-cute in an opposites-attract romcom for the over-forties . . .

called *Not Dead Yet?* Cosmopolitan Joey has decided to book his funeral? Extremely proper Rose is the funeral director? Joey is just a man with a very efficient approach to life—and of course, death—but Rose thinks he's dying?

. . . Here came Ike, making straight for me. He said a reluctant hello to everyone then quickly hived me off from the group. Suddenly we were alone and he was gleaming at me, watchful and silent.

"So, ahhh. Did you fix Vivian's hot water?" I asked, because one of us had to say something.

"Vivian's . . . ? Oh yeah, I did. I like the hair." He lifted one of the loose tendrils and bunched it in his hand.

"Thanks." Involuntarily, I glanced at Joey. Rose was gone, replaced by Karina, the hairdresser. She said something to make Joey laugh and I wondered how, in that moment, Karina felt? How would any woman feel if they met Joey and discovered he was single? Fluttery? Excite—Ike gave my lock of hair the gentlest of tugs, then opened his fist, letting it tumble down against the bare skin of my shoulder.

I smiled from under my lashes.

He stared in silence.

". . . Was it fun being St Patrick?"

He made an unimpressed face. "I do it every year."

"Oh." This was unexpectedly awkward. Now we weren't trading cryptic sentences about the trouble at Kearney's Farm, we didn't seem to know what to say.

After another uncomfortable patch, Ike said, "How's it been? With your mum and that?"

"Nice. Ya, great." The sooner we got out of here and down to his sexy-sounding house on the shore, the better.

But *would* the house be sexy? Would *he* even be sexy? Or had I constructed an entire imaginary scenario in my head? Holy Maloney, that was an unwelcome thought.

"So the go-boy is back in town," Ike said.

"Ah. Yes." I gathered myself. "Wasn't expecting that!"

"Weren't you, though?"

"Not at all, because the work had finished and . . ."

. . . I'd lost him. Ike was no longer listening. I followed his gaze: Helen had just arrived. Wearing tight black jeans, a zipped black jacket and black trainers, she looked as if she'd come to burgle Ben's house.

"Anna!" She'd seen me.

Ike looked wonderstruck. I could only imagine the great roaring sounding in his head, the dazzlement of stars exploding before his eyes . . .

"I'm Helen," she told Ike. "Anna's—"

"Sister? That's obvious. I'm Ike."

"Where's the Ben lad?" Helen looked around the busy room. "I'd better say hello. Anyone want a drink?"

"You can get me another of these." Ike indicated his bottle of IPA. "That way you have to come back."

. . . Aaaaaand all the shine drained from my night. I'd never hold Helen responsible for how the world responded to her. But Ike Blakely behaving like a besotted fool with me right next to him? I'm afraid that was a hard no.

This was never going to be anything other than a casual hookup but basic manners still applied. The outrageous nerve of him, openly preferring Helen to me. Not even trying to pretend. No *way* was I hanging around, playing second best, with this chump. His love-googly eyes were still following Helen around the room as I walked away.

No sign of any of my lot. Mum had probably led an undercover maneuver upstairs, to sneakily see the bedrooms; she was *obsessed* with other people's houses.

Waiting to figure out my next move, I lurked by a wall and carried out surveillance. Helen returned to Ike—without his drink, I was cheered to notice; she'd done it deliberately, I was sure. She scanned the room for me, asked him a question, he looked surprised, gave a cursory glance around, then lowered his head, giving her his full attention.

All his appeal was gone, snuffed out like a candle flame. He wasn't the sexy, noble, tough man I'd wanted him to be. He was just a bloke, who'd been distracted by the latest shiny thing. I'd projected an entire personality onto Ike Blakely based on a tool-belt and a reluctance to speak.

It wasn't even him I was upset about—an old injury had been pressed on, that was all—but launching myself back into the throng was beyond me. I was unsettled and sad and just wanted to sneak back to the hotel. Nobody would even notice I was gone.

In a split second my decision was made. "Excuse me, I just need to . . ." I slid through the clusters of people into the entrance hall. With a surprising absence of farce, I located my marshmallow coat. The way the night was going, it would have been no surprise if the search had me stumbling over Joey and Karina going at it like rabbits in a spare bedroom.

The idea made me feel sick until I remembered that Joey had renounced all of that.

Had he really, though? It was so . . . unlikely.

Quietly I slid out into the night. I was so keen to escape that walking two kilometers in these boots didn't seem like the ordeal it ordinarily would.

As I started off, a voice in the darkness asked, "Anna? Is that you?"

50

It was Joey. What was *he* doing, lurking out here alone in the gloom? I couldn't stop to talk because as much distance as possible needed to be put between me and the house.

I strode down the drive towards the road, Joey following. "Anna, slow down, could you?" Casting a look over his shoulder, he asked, "What went on in there?"

I was embarrassed. "Nothing."

"Nothing. Okay."

We walked on. When the drive met the road, I said, "I'm going home. Go back to the party."

"I want to go home too. But I don't want to intrude."

"You're not."

"So what happened?"

My face fixed firmly towards the direction of the town, I set off. "Ike. The goon. And me. There's been, I don't know, a flirtation."

"So I heard."

"You heard wrong."

". . . I'm confused."

There were no street lamps out here, just light from a slender moon, which made it easier to be honest. "Look. He's . . . I've . . . I was supposed to spend the night with him. At his place. But Helen. You know she arrived late? And"—my throat was tight—"The thing happened. It's been a long time, but—"

"What thing?"

"When he saw Helen. He looked at me. Compared us. Saw we were similar." I swallowed hard. "But she was better."

"No. Aw, no, Anna. You imagined it."

"You weren't there."

"Why would he prefer her?"

"Well, you did!"

Why had I said it? It was a lifetime ago! I was forty-eight years of age, I should have long matured past this petty snub.

"Wait now, what are you talking about?"

"Joey." I took a breath. "I'm emotional. Too emotional. Spending time with all of them." I waved a hand back towards the house. "My sisters, my mum. I've reverted to being about fifteen years old."

"What do you mean I did it too?"

"Joey. If you ever had any affection for me, any regard, I'm pleading with you to forget I said that stupid thing."

"Firstly, why are you speaking like a lady from a costume drama? Secondly, I have affection and regard for you in bucketloads, but I've upset you and that's not good. Wouldja tell me?"

This was the real reason I was upset; nothing to do with Ike. "It was twenty years ago. You won't remember."

"Try me."

"This is lamentable." But it wouldn't kill me to tell him. "The very first night you and I met—"

"In that sketchy bar in Midtown? Can't *believe* you brought your parents."

"You remember?"

"Oh my God, *yeah*, of course."

"Seriously? Why?"

"Anna." With a breathless laugh, he said, "I was *so* hot for you."

My skin fizzed. Did I believe him? Hard to know, but the skin-fizzing felt good. So much better than the memories of his rejection. "Then you met Helen," I said. "Suddenly I was invisible."

"Not true. You ran off. I let you go, too scared of looking weak. Helen stayed. Because I was an immature dick I slept with her. I shouldn't have inflicted myself on her. I regret almost everything I did in those years. I'm sorry I hurt you that night. But it was about me, not you."

My phone beeped. **Where are you?**

A second text followed immediately. **Have you left? Anna, please come back x**

"That him?"

"He's wondering where I am. If I'm coming back."

"Are you?"

"No. What he did was *rude*."

A mustard-colored glow appeared further down the road. "Stand in," Joey said as a car came round a bend, and sped past us.

When we set off again, Joey asked, "What if the goon came roaring down the road in his pickup? If he jumped out and ordered you to get in." In the faint light, I saw Joey standing on the white road markings, his arm outstretched, pointing at an invisible truck. "'Get in, Anna.'" He was enjoying himself. "'Get *in* my truck, then get in my bed.'"

"Say more!"

"Aaah, let's see. 'I've got a rock-hard love truncheon in my—'" He subsided into laughter. "Yeah, not going there. At his house, he'd scoop you up in his big, goon-y arms. Kick open his door! Fling you on his bed! And—well, how about it, Anna? Would you go?"

"No." I began walking again. After a long period of silence, I said, "It's not like we were twin flames or anything. I just wanted a night of grown-up fun—"

"Anna. Can you please not?"

"What? You've given all that up."

"But I'm still alive. It's a decision I made for my own good, but it's not always easy."

"Sorry. I find—*found*—it difficult to think of you as this no-sex man. I'll do better."

"Thanks." Then, Joey asked, "What happened with you and Torres? Did he cheat on you?"

"It's not why we ended."

"Did he ever?"

"I don't think so. But . . . if he had I might have got past it."

"Wow, Anna. You're very . . ." He considered the word. ". . . open-minded."

"That's how I felt about Angelo. But I wouldn't feel that way about everyone."

"Like who?"

I'd said more than I'd meant to.

"Anna? Who?"

My pace slowed. Coming to a stop, I stood before him.

"Well." My recklessness came from nowhere. I hadn't planned this, but it was the truth. "Well, like you, Joey."

"You'd mind?"

"I'd want to"—I swallowed—"kill you."

Our faces were almost touching. I was close enough to see the fair-colored stubble around that indecently sexy mouth. So near that I swear I felt the sweep of his eyelashes on my skin. "Anna?"

"Sorry." I stepped back. "I'm over-emotional, hormonal, I shouldn't have said any of that."

He nodded and as I turned to continue towards the town, he caught my elbow and swung me back to him, "Fyi, I would never cheat on you."

Some huge emotion flared in me. Then, "But how could you, Joey? When you don't sleep with anyone."

51

I kept moving, my eyes trained on our destination, until the ambient glow of Maumtully began to dilute the darkness.

"Joey, why were you outside alone in the dark up there?"

"It was hard." He cleared his throat. "Seeing you with Ike. I was jealous."

My heart seized. Between his departure on Thursday morning and his return last night, a lot had changed. Our cautious fondness had collapsed, liberating emotions which were older, deeper and far more dangerous.

Earlier tonight, getting ready, I was happy at how comfortable we had become. But we weren't comfortable: we were flirting.

Now that he'd articulated what was actually going on, I let myself fully feel the rush of longing.

"Yeah." He sounded rueful. "When Vivian said you'd slept with him—"

"I didn't, though."

"You can do what you like, Anna. I've no right to—"

"We kissed. Once. That's all."

"Still jealous." He shot me a smile.

". . . Is it because you miss sex? Or—"

"It's specific to you."

Fuuuuuuuuuuck.

"Joey?"

"Yeah?"

"If you wanted to kiss me, I'd be on for it." I stopped, appalled. The dark, the displacement, was affecting my judgement. Had I read this wrong? "Sorry!"

"Changed your mind already? This feels familiar."

"No." Turning my body towards his, I clutched the lapels of his beautiful coat. "Joey, I haven't."

Time was speeding up and collapsing down, everything happening too fast. We should hit the brakes. But my hands found his face, pulling him closer. "Please."

He studied me, his expression troubled. "You'd better come here then." A hand curved around my back, compressing the soft padding of my coat, pulling me against his long, lean body.

The other hand he slid to the nape of my neck, his thumb tracing a path along my jaw. Afraid it might not happen, I stretched up to meet him. Cautiously, he lowered his face to mine. You'd swear he'd never before kissed anyone.

Chastely, his lips met mine . . . and that was all. Nothing else. Initially confused, I got it—he'd meant it about swearing off sex. The disappointment was devastating.

But, with a whispered *fuck*, his lips parted, his tongue was in my mouth and, oh my God, *this* was a kiss. This was spectacular. Hot and sweet and swooningly intimate, it was made of twenty years of longing.

The ghost of every near miss we'd had was in the ether; it had all been leading to this.

Intensely present, our connection tangible, I wanted to stay on this country road, on this cold night, kissing him forever.

Even through my marshmallow coat, his ironhard readiness was impossible to ignore. Would he sleep with me? Or would he refuse? Shocking though the thought was, he actually might.

As if he'd seen into my brain, he pulled away. "Anna? What the hell is this?"

My head felt strange, as if I'd stood up too quickly. "You know what this is."

Silently, he considered me. "It's cold. We need to get back." Taking my hand, he tucked it into the warmth of his coat pocket and led me towards the town.

52

Everything I'd ever felt for him was back and magnified—huge tenderness, a protective instinct and an undeniable physical longing. Had our stars finally aligned? Or was this just one more in our long list of false starts and deliberate woundings?

As soon as we reached the town, he removed my hand from his pocket. "We need to talk."

Oh God, no.

My heart beating too fast, I tried to keep up as he strode towards the hotel. The roar of the Broderick's full lounge was audible from the street. "We can't talk there," he said. "My room."

On the first floor and very cramped, there wasn't even an armchair. The only place to sit was on the end of the bed. The moment my feet were off the ground, the agony kicked in. "Joey, my foot's killing me, can I take off my boots?"

He was shrugging off his coat. "Uh. Sure. Is it your bunion?"

Despite everything, I smiled. "You and your sexy talk."

Unzipping both boots, I shoved them to the floor and cradled my swollen foot, still in its sock, trying to rock away the pain. "Right," I said. "Talk."

Keeping his distance, he joined me at the end of the bed. Before I could protest, he'd unpeeled the sock and taken my distended foot in his hands. "Ouch. That looks sore."

"The state of my feet!" I protested, but his cold hands on the throbbing joint gave immediate relief. "Joey, that feels . . ." Light-headed, I tumbled back on the bed, glorying in the retreat of the pain. "It's just . . . Thank you."

My dread was deferred by a rush of natural painkillers. For some time, probably several minutes, I lay there, my eyes closed, listening to him breathe.

Then it came. "Anna, can you sit up, please?"

This would be some variant of how he shouldn't have kissed me and how I shouldn't have asked. And he was right, I shouldn't have.

Instead, visibly changing course, he asked, "Can you take your hair down? Is that difficult or . . . ?"

"Not difficult at all." Deeply grateful that he wanted something from me, I slid out the chignon pin. The weight of my hair tumbled and spilled past my shoulders. "Anna." His voice was low. "You're dangerous."

"I can do it again." Already I was scooping my hair onto my head, holding it in place with my hands. "Ready?"

Barely moving, he nodded.

After a breath, I opened my hands. His expression, as my hair cascaded down, gave me hope. "Good?" I asked.

"Yeah." With a breathless laugh, he said, "Better not do it a third time."

Once again I braced myself for "The talk." Instead, he reached for me, tangling his fingers in my hair. Our mouths met. Together, we toppled slowly to the bed where, for what felt like hours, we exchanged kisses so slow and intimate, I felt drugged.

I could have been twenty-eight again. I felt exactly the way I'd felt back then, that no one else would do.

Burying his face in the curve of my neck, he murmured, "What do you smell of? Something fresh. And something mysterious. And something . . . wild."

The kissing began again, even hotter than before. I was on fire with longing. So was he, if his deliberately measured breath was any indication. But he was serious about abstaining from sex.

His right hand was on my face, his left on my back; there wasn't even a hint that his fingers might brush off my nipples or slide up my thighs. I'd been playing dumb, not pushing things yet hoping to God his control would snap. But that wasn't right.

He was conflicted: his erection spoke for itself. As did his refusal to shut this down. If I tried to change his mind, he might go for it but afterwards he wouldn't forgive me.

During our frustrated shifting about, one side of his jeans had slid low. Lightly, I ran my thumb along the softness of his skin over the rigid curve of bone.

Sooner or later, we'd have to stop, but not just yet. A few more minutes, that was all I wanted. Well, not *all* I wanted . . .

During another repositioning, my fingers shifted a centimeter or two lower, touching a tantalizing edge of pubic hair. Palpable heat emanated from his rock hard—then my wrist was grasped, too tightly. "Anna, no. This is not going to happen."

My devastation was tempered with acceptance, even relief—at least the agony of longing could stop.

He rolled away from me. "I shouldn't have kissed you."

"I made you do it."

"I didn't take much persuading." He was standing now. "Anna, obviously I want to . . ." He gestured to his body. "But I can't. I shouldn't have let it get this far. That's on me. I'm sorry."

We needed to talk about this. "Joey, what's going through your mind?"

"I told you—I'm trying to change. To have relationships in a different way, to slow down, let things take time. But with you, Anna, I always want you. It's instant and . . ." He searched for the right word. ". . . merciless."

"What do you mean?"

"It means I can't let my dick make yet another mistake."

"Is that what I'd be?" I was appalled. "A mistake?"

He took a moment. "Anna." His voice had changed. "This is not to hurt you but two hours ago, you wanted to spend the night with Ike Blakely."

"I never took Ike seriously. He felt the same about me."

"You don't take me seriously either."

"I *do*." Joey was and always had been different.

"How can I tell? We've been here before." And with that, he won.

"You said you forgive me," I said.

"I do." He took a breath. "But I don't trust you."

If he had punched me in the stomach, he couldn't have hurt me more.

"Anna, this isn't—it's not me taking revenge." He looked distressed. "But I need time. That night changed me. I don't screw around anymore. It just messes me up. And you're buffering. Right now you don't know what you want. In a month or three or six, your life will look different. Any decision you make now is suspect. You haven't sold your apartment."

No, but—

"You might get back with Torres."

"No." I was on much more solid ground. "That's not going to happen."

"It did before. The last time."

"But it's different now."

"It's too soon. Think about it." He sounded exasperated. "I fuck you. We have a good time. Then you leave or *some*thing goes wrong and it all goes super-weird again. You want that? Because I sure as hell don't. We've hurt each other so much but it's finally coming good, healthy . . ."

I'd done this, I understood. I broke him and this was my punishment.

"I should leave."

"Don't."

"Joey, I *can't* stay. Not while I'm . . ." Full of love and lust and thwarted longing.

His eyes roamed my face. "I'm sorry, Anna."

53

The kicker was that back in the day, I'd had my chance with Joey—several chances, in fact. Like Trea's second birthday party.

Poor Jacqui had put insane amounts of work into the celebration, curating the guest list as if her life depended on it.

The core invitees were eleven kids from Trea's daycare and, by extension, their rich daddies and yoga-bunny mommies. (Or the nannies if the mommies and daddies were busy.)

A select number of Jacqui's and Joey's friends were also in the mix. Jacqui had several impressive, famous mates. Alas, Joey didn't.

I remember her saying, "Gaz is obviously the worst. But Shake and Johnno are nearly as bad. Why doesn't Joey have any unembarrassing friends? Apart from Luke, like?"

". . . I don't know, really."

"*Why* is he so loyal to those fools?" She despaired.

That *I* knew why and Jacqui didn't made me feel sick. If only he'd tell her.

"It'll be a great party," I said. "This is where you shine. Pulling off celebrations which are really fun but always special."

"Thanks, babe!" She seemed surprised. "It's been a while since I got praise. I feel like I fail all the time."

"You're amazing at everything."

"Joey doesn't think so."

"Never mind him. You're a *queen*, you deserve a man who treats you like one."

"Anyway." She sighed. "The menu. I'm thinking fennel and orange bites, micro arancini and caponata thimbles on arrival." The celebration was to be held in a private room in a "neighborhood Sicilian." But a "neighborhood Sicilian" on the Upper West Side. Which meant we were looking more at palatable luxury than earthy authenticity.

"I'm no expert," I said, "but are the kids likely to eat fennel and whatnot?"

"Jesus, yes, these ones probably would. Either that or nothing at all, because they're everything-intolerant. Even so, I'll have to do a full menu for the *bam*-fecken-*bini*. Spelt macaroni with vegan pecorino, base-free pizza with sauce made from tomatoes still on the vine. Ice cream made from sugar-free air." She paused. "At times like this I wonder if Trea and I should live in Ireland, so her childhood could be half normal."

"Do you mean that?"

"I dunno, Anna. It might be better for her, easier for me. But she'd be so far from her father, useless fucker though he is."

"But your parents would be there. Your brothers. They'd all help."

She trained a cool look on me. "Not sure I could cope with Ireland. It's somewhat lacking compared to New York. So. Is the Feathery Stroker your plus-one? You soft-launching at the party?"

We could, I guessed. Other than Aidan's family, only Rachel, Luke and Jacqui knew about Angelo. I didn't want him to be a secret—but I *was* grateful it wasn't out there in the world. No matter how much I got told it was okay to start living again, there were bound to be raised eyebrows and mutterings of *That's a bit soon, poor Aidan's only dead three years.*

Joey added another complication. Our paths hadn't crossed in several weeks, not since the night he'd tried to kiss me. I'd told nobody about it, not even Rachel. Some sort of protective instinct on my part: Joey would probably have been seen as an opportunist, a chancer always on the lookout for sex. But I felt he'd simply been confused.

Angelo and I linked hands and stepped inside the restaurant. Noisy and crowded, the speed at which the Whispering Angel was being poured down yoga-toned gullets told me that most of the nannies were on their day off.

Joey, as one of the hosts, was the first person we met.

"Joey, hey. Hi!" In theory I'd done nothing wrong with him, but guilt swept over me.

"Anna." His nod was polite. "Torres. Good to see you, man." He extended his arm to shake hands, then saw that Angelo's fingers were intertwined with mine. Quickly he looked at my face. He seemed surprised, upset even.

Stealing any response from me, a beguiling young man had descended, plucking Trea's gift from under my arm. "Let me place this on the gift stand." Even before he'd ferried away the elaborate, beribboned box to a table bristling with more of the same, Angelo and I were mobbed by a second delightful young man, who charmingly divested us of our jackets, even though my blazer had been part of my look.

By the time the drama settled Joey had gone.

"There's Rachel," Angelo said.

Oh, thank God. Rachel and Luke, my safe people. They joined us, along with Gaz who had Trea in his arms. A short while later, Shake and Johnno showed up and the afternoon, though never in danger of being full-blown fun, was fine. Children wailed, moms coaxed, men boomed and boasted, food was ignored. Everyone helped Trea to blow out the candles on a cake which wouldn't have been out of place at a modest wedding. After this, the departures were speedy.

"That's it?" Rachel blinked. "All a little abrupt. Okay, see you guys soon."

"I'll go get our jackets," Angelo said. As soon as he was gone, Joey stepped up. "Anna? You and . . . him? You're dating?"

I felt accused, judged, on *fire* with guilt. "Um. Yes."

"When did it start?"

"Not so long ago . . ." I trailed off.

"Can anyone apply?" he asked.

"Apply?" I spoke so quietly, I was almost inaudible. Jacqui was only a few yards away, stacking the gifts into piles.

"To date you?"

"Joey, please stop." I was keeping half an eye on Jacqui, hoping to God she didn't pick up on the tension.

"What," he asked, "if *I* wanted to date you?"

Over at the table, Jacqui's head shot up. I said, "You don't want to, Joey."

"But I do."

My heart thumping like a jackhammer, I watched Jacqui move closer.

"Joey . . ." Over his shoulder, I made eye contact with Jacqui.

Flicking a quick glance, Joey saw her, then refocused on me. "I do, Anna."

As dry as the Sahara, my mouth clicked out the words, "Stop. Please."

"What's going on?" Jacqui asked, her voice shrill with alarm.

Ignoring her completely, Joey said, "He's a lucky man." For once, there was no hint of sarcasm. His head low, he jostled past Jacqui, muttering, "Excuse me."

"What the fuck?" Jacqui was all disbelief and confusion. "Anna? Are you and Joey . . . ?"

"Nothing. Nothing is going on." But that was bullshit. I had to tell her the whole story: there was no way out of this. It would devastate her, I'd get the blame and maybe I deserved it.

"Can we talk?" I asked. "Someplace private?"

"Are you and Joey fucking?" She was wild-eyed with shock.

"No, Jacqui, I swear to you. Nothing like that." Terrified words tumbled from my parched mouth. "Absolutely nothing like that."

"Where is he?" She scanned the room. "Joey! Joey!" She went to the door, looking onto the sidewalk.

People seemed to be coming in and leaving at speed. Luke reappeared, carrying Trea. I thought he'd left. "Joey and Jacqui have got into a thing out in the street. Rachel and I are taking Trea back to ours."

"Should I——?" I didn't know how much Luke knew. Had Joey said anything?

"Stay out of it," Luke said. "For now. Let them have their——"

Angelo had returned with our jackets. One glance was enough. "What just happened?"

Angelo and I went to his place, where I told him everything—about how I'd once been mad about Joey, about the growing tension with Jacqui and the mortifying attempt at a kiss from Joey.

Being Angelo, he managed to have my back without judging Jacqui or Joey. In his world, there were no goodies or baddies, just imperfect humans who made mistakes.

When I finished the epic tale, he asked, "What do you need?"

"For Jacqui and me to be okay."

"And with Joey?"

"Nothing. I'd be happy if I never saw him again."

The look on Angelo's face told me it wouldn't be that simple. "But you are gonna see him, and, Anna, I can't be part of this drama."

"What do you mean?" Was he breaking up with me?

"You're attracted to Joey—"

"Not that way!" I was in a panic. Was everything good about to fall apart today?

"You have to be sure," he said. "Take time to think about it. Be honest. Ask yourself if it's loyalty to Jacqui that's holding you back."

"It's *not.*"

"How can you know when you've been too scared to ask yourself the question?"

"Angelo, are you . . . are we, like, *done*?"

"I don't know." He wasn't being mean; he genuinely didn't know. "But you're freaking out so much about Jacqui, you've got no space to consider if you want something with Joey. You need to go there. Ask those hard questions."

I stared at him, feeling terrified.

"If Joey is the one you want," he said. "You have to go for it."

Not long afterwards, Jacqui phoned me. "Get over here," she ordered.

My heart pounding, I left Angelo's and caught a cab. Arriving at Jacqui's block, Joey was waiting at the building entrance.

He stepped out to meet me. Rapidly, he said, "I told her I tried to kiss you. That you stopped me."

"And?"

"She asked if I wanted more. With you."

Oh *no*.

"And I said yes." His voice shook. "Because why would I lie?"

"You could have lied, Joey!"

"I don't lie."

"Joey, I love Jacqui as much as I loved Aidan." I was so distraught I felt sick. "Did you tell her about what happened when you were a kid?"

"No."

"She needs to know. I can't know while she doesn't."

"He kissed you and you didn't tell me!" Jacqui was so angry and I was so scared.

"Because it would upset you. And it has."

"Do you fancy him? You fucking do!"

"He's sexy. That's a fact, I guess. But even if I wasn't your best friend, I wouldn't go near him. He's not able for—"

"You're not my friend. A friend would have told me. No fucking wonder you warned me off him, Anna. You wanted him for yourself."

"I really, honestly didn't." I felt as if I was fighting for my life.

"You want me to move back to Ireland."

"But only"—I spluttered—"only to make your life less stressful. Jacqui, there's something you should know."

The blood drained from her face. "What?"

"No. Nothing like that. But when he was a kid, aged ten to thirteen, his dad and big brother used him—"

"He *confided* in you!" Her face was stricken. "Used him for what?"

"To break into houses."

"And?" She was nonplussed. "I thought you were going to say he was abused."

"He *was* abused, Jacqui."

"I meant sexual abuse."

"But . . . there are other kinds of abuse. When he got too big, at thirteen, they just abandoned him. It must have had an effect on him. He's so . . . afraid to trust."

"Why did he tell you and not me?"

"Because, just, circumstances. Remember he came to check security on my new apartment? It came up then."

"Sounds more like something he invented on the spot so you'd feel sorry for him."

". . . Luke said it's true."

In a small voice, Jacqui said, "You knew and I didn't."

I wanted to die.

"He's got a thing for you." Her voice was too loud. "You'll see. He'll make his moves and you'll let him because he is un-fucking-resistible and—"

"No, Jacqui, *no*. I'd never do that to you and anyway I'm with Angelo."

"Wow, Anna. Beating them off with sticks."

"I'm not. He's the first man in three years. Since Aidan."

"Oh, here we go. You lost your husband. We know."

Suddenly I felt small and scared. Had I gone on about it too much? Hogged the sympathy? Been a bad friend?

"I was there for you a million percent after he passed."

I wished she hadn't said *passed*. She knew it drove me mad. "Passed" sounded peaceful but Aidan's death had been an ugly, violent event.

But getting angry now would be dangerous. "You were and I'm so grateful, Jacqui. I'd have given up and died myself if it hadn't been for you."

"You're not getting it! I'm saying you're not the only person who lost the love of their life."

I couldn't help it: my frustration spilled over. "If Joey Armstrong is the love of your life, it doesn't say much for your life."

Unable to believe what I'd just said, I closed down with shock.

"Fuck you, Anna," Jacqui said. "Fuck you."

It was cold and calm and a long time coming.

Through countless small missteps, Jacqui and I had arrived here, a place where we were no longer friends.

All those unuttered grievances, festering resentments and swallowed irritations had been pushed down and down. But what goes down must come up. And up it had all come.

This was a dirty little secret which was rarely spoken about: intense friendships end.

For as long as I could remember, I'd been told that men will come and men will go but your girlfriends will be there forever. It took me several more years before I understood that the bond with your best friend is like every other relationship—sometimes it goes weird and you can't stop it.

"Give me back my keys," she said.

As I handed them over, I was stupid enough to think that there was still hope.

I did what Angelo suggested and tried being honest with myself. What I learnt was a shocker: if Joey had never been with Jacqui I'd have kissed him back, that night in Jacqui's apartment.

Unwrapping my memories of that almost-kiss revealed a cache of emotions I'd been in deep denial of. Remembering the touch of his mouth on my skin, as he kissed away my tears, made me light-headed and full of longing. I'd wanted him so badly I'd ached. But the wrongness of the situation had numbed me to the responses of my traitorous body.

Interred with this was an idealized version of Joey, a man who could be relied on to be faithful and endlessly loving. Fantasy Joey was *mad* about me—he and I could definitely go the distance. Only one thing needed to change: Joey would be an entirely different person.

As it was, by telling me about his childhood, he'd made me feel special. The only woman he trusted? Of course it had gone to my head.

A hard reality check was needed.

The healthy part of me wanted Angelo, who was kind, calm, a grown-up; my shadow self was drawn to Joey. But *if* anything ever began, as soon as I'd fallen for Joey his interest would die a sudden death. He couldn't help despising the women who loved him. Until he found a way to fix himself he'd always be that man.

If I'd been feeling self-destructive, I might have picked up the phone, invited him to my apartment, lit candles, put on beautiful underwear just so he could take it off me . . . And how long before I ended up in exactly the same condition as Jacqui? Suspicious, jealous and maddened with longing for his attention, his time, his want.

The huge complication was that I actually cared about him—and that meant staying out of his life. Hard to know how to manage it while being so close to Jacqui, but we'd have to figure something out.

The only thing was, Jacqui wouldn't speak to me. Four days after Trea's party she blocked my number, my email, everything. In desperation I went to her apartment block and stood in the street, pressing her buzzer over and over, praying she'd relent. I showed up at the hotel where she worked and as soon as I'd said my name, two security guards materialized—they'd clearly been warned in advance, which was deeply humiliating—and escorted me to the exit.

I called all our mutual friends and not one would get involved. In the end I had to ring Joey.

We met in the park, where we sat at opposite ends of a bench.

"This Angelo guy?" Joey asked. "Is he good to you?"

"He's lovely."

"Anna, I'd be lovely to you too. I know my reputation—it's deserved. But I'd be different with you."

"You just think that. You might for a while and then you'd get bored and—"

"No. I've never felt this way about anyone else. *Please*, Anna. Don't freak out but I'm in lo—"

"Joey, *stop*." I leant right into his space. "You don't get it. I need Jacqui to forgive me. It's literally all I want. Even sitting here with you I'm so scared that someone will see us and report back. Why did you have to tell her? By 'being honest' you destroyed the most important relationship I have."

That familiar confusion was in his eyes. "But, Anna, there's something special between us—"

"You only want me because I'm off limits—because I'm Jacqui's friend. You've got this crazy idea that you and me could . . . I don't know . . . try being a couple? But if you truly cared, you'd never have damaged me in Jacqui's eyes. You'd have kept your mouth shut and sucked it up."

"S-sorry."

My voice shook with emotion. "Being an adult means you swallow back something you're dying to say because it'll upset someone else. You don't ride into a situation thinking you're a hero when no one asks for it. Especially when the only outcome you care about is your own."

His skin was waxy from my onslaught. "God, Anna, I hadn't realized. Fuck, I was so selfish." He was tripping over his words. "I'm sorry, I'm so sorry. How can I make it right?"

"Talk to Jacqui. *Please*. She won't speak to me. Please, Joey, tell her it was nothing."

"I already did but I'll do it again, I'll do everything possible to make this right. Anna, I'm so sorry."

But whatever he said to Jacqui didn't work: my number stayed blocked. Unable to sleep properly or eat or do my job, I lurked outside her apartment one morning, hoping that a face-to-face meeting would change her mind.

When she emerged, with Trea in her buggy, and saw me, her face flashed with hate. Pushing the buggy, she belted up the street, putting distance between us.

"Jacqui, please!" I ran after her.

She whirled around. "Anna. I do not want to see you ever again for as long as I live. Stay away from me."

Distraught, I went to Rachel; her advice was to give Jacqui space. "No contact for six months."

"That's *far* too long."

"It needs to be several months. Whenever you show up now, you're wounding her again. It's keeping her pain fresh. Let her process this. It'll give you time to do the same."

I didn't need to process anything; I just wanted her to love me again.

"My" butterfly showed up, fluttering around like a worried friend, reminding me that I'd already survived a terrible loss.

Helen had a theory about emotional pain: what doesn't kill us makes us weaker. I didn't agree. I didn't think it necessarily made us stronger, but it had taught me how to survive. It wasn't easy, but it was doable.

But I dreamed about Jacqui, the way I dreamed about Aidan. It was a strange time because on the one hand I missed Jacqui all day every day, but on the other I'd fallen in love with Angelo. Both states—love and its absence—occupied me in equal and opposite ways. I was devastated and loved-up and joyous and heartsick.

Bits and pieces of information about her filtered back through mutual friends. But big news arrived five months into my six-month purdah: Jacqui and Trea were leaving to live in Ireland.

In one way Rachel had been right. Time apart from Jacqui had given me perspective: I knew I couldn't stop this. Admittedly, on the morning of their departure, a surge of adrenaline made me want to run through the streets and beg them to stay. But life wasn't a romcom, so I went to work, much shakier than usual, and got through the day.

Meanwhile, I'd been avoiding all events where Joey might appear, mostly in the hope that word would get back to Jacqui. Surely then she'd believe I had no interest in him?

It was months before he and I came face to face again, at a funeral, one we were both obliged to attend: Rachel and Luke's baby had died at thirty-seven weeks. Shell-shocked, Joey and I nodded at each other, exchanged helpless remarks about the appalling tragedy, then moved on.

Afterwards, my resolve to avoid him crumbled. What difference did it make? Jacqui was living a new life, thousands of miles away, what did she care?

As for Joey, I'd always been more exasperated than angry. There hadn't been a cold-blooded master plan to break up me and Jacqui. That was just an accidental side effect of being too self-absorbed to think beyond what he'd wanted.

And credit where it was due: he'd gone out there, defending my name and blackening his own. Mutual friends of Jacqui and mine welcomed me back into the fold. Jacqui was the only holdout.

I began showing up at nights out I'd previously avoided. Not often, maybe every couple of months. Joey and I were polite but distant. I never asked about Jacqui and he never offered any information. We both behaved as if all that bad stuff just hadn't happened.

54

"Courtney hasn't come in." Shrill with stress, Emilien was balancing four fried breakfasts on his arms. "She's not at home and she's not answering her mobile."

"But . . ." Courtney hadn't even been drinking last night at Ben's. Unless she had abandoned that plan and was currently sleeping off a hangover in a bed other than her own? And that was the least-worst scenario.

"Let me see what I can find out." I grabbed three muffins and hurried upstairs to the bridal suite.

Last night after I'd slunk, devastated, out of Joey's room, clutching my boots and socks, I'd gone to Rachel's room, praying that she and Luke were home from the party.

She opened the door, taking in my bare feet and smeared makeup. ". . . Are you okay?"

"Fine. But I'm leaving. Going back to Dublin."

"Now?" Luke had materialized at her shoulder.

"Yep."

Rachel and Luke exchanged a look.

"Why don't we get a drink?" Luke suggested, pointing towards the stairs down to the lounge.

"No." I felt humiliated, rejected, angry with myself, angry with Joey, ashamed of being angry with him . . . "Can I come in? Thanks." When I was installed on their couch, drinking their Sprite, I said, "I'm not staying long because I need to be awake for the drive."

"What'll you do when you get to Dublin?" Rachel asked, the way you'd humor a lunatic.

"Pick up my passport, go to the airport and catch a flight to . . . Kampala. Or Samoa." Any location very far away, where I could hopefully escape my shame and rule out the chance of ever meeting Joey again.

"Is this something to do with Joey?" Luke asked.

I blurted, "He wouldn't sleep with me."

"Yeah." Luke's voice was soothing. "He's doing his best to be a good guy."

"I *know*." I didn't want to hear about how great Joey was, how hard he was trying.

"He's had such a bad attitude towards women," Luke said. "And he wants to do better."

Yes, I *knew*. I effing *knew*. But there was no point being upset with Joey. The only person to blame was me.

"We can never get it right," I said.

The very first night we'd seen each other, wild sexual chemistry had sparked. But over the years, it developed into something more, a strong emotional connection.

"You're the expert," I told Rachel. "But this is what I think. We all have wounds, yes? Joey has his. I have mine. Any relationship has to incorporate the . . . whatever you want to call them—all our scared parts and the mad longings, you know, the *wounds*. Something about the way Joey and my wounded parts rubbed off each other just seemed to make more wounds. Does that make sense?"

Sounding *very* like a therapist, Rachel asked, "Would you like to be more specific?"

No. I totally wouldn't. Not yet. Maybe never.

"We're just one long string of Almosts."

A wave of tiredness made me woozy. "I'm going downstairs for a flask of coffee for the drive."

"Why don't you wait till daylight?" Rachel did more of her humoring-the-mad-person routine. "You can sleep in with me."

"And I can share Joey's bed," Luke said.

"Lucky you." My tone was so bitter that all three of us dissolved into convulsions. "Okay. Thanks. But I'm leaving first thing."

"After breakfast," Rachel said. "Then there's the scavenger hunt. And the funfair and—"

"First thing." My tone was clipped. "That's when I'm off."

But after twisting and turning half the night, when I finally fell asleep I didn't wake until nine thirty with such a roaring hunger I had to nip to the breakfast room in the hoodie and leggings Rachel had lent me—where the news that Courtney was MIA sent me hot-footing right back upstairs to the bridal suite, to discover a nest of bodies, all heavily asleep. I launched myself at the nearest one, who happened to be Helen, and shook her awake.

"Where's Courtney? Did she drive you home last night?"

Helen opened her eyes. All her makeup was still on. "Courts?" Helen's voice was hoarse. "No. She and your man—"

"The guard?"

"Who? No, the Hollywood lad." Finally she hit upon his name. "*Ben*. Pair of them disappeared. *Up*stairs. The Vivian pick-me was *so* pissed off. This town is hilarious. Let's live here forever."

"Did you drive home?" She couldn't have. I'd never seen a more hungover human.

"Are you joking? The Death Star is still up there. People made calls and someone called Farrelly the Flowers came in his van and took the lot of us. He says 'Hello, Sweet-face' to you. He wouldn't take any money because the go-boy bought so many flowers the other day."

Suddenly alert, I asked, "Where's Regan?"

"Gone to the beach with Joey."

I flinched at his name. When the shockwave passed, I got out my phone to call Ben about Courtney.

"Anna," Helen growled, summoning me back to her bedside, her eyes closed. "I need to ask you something. It's about Joey."

Oh, here we go. "Nothing happened."

Helen jerked upright in the bed, as if she'd been electric-shocked back from the dead. "I was only going to ask if it's 'Joe-boy' or 'the go-boy'!" She clutched my hoodie, her eyes wide. "But *nothing happened*! Which means . . . What's going on, Anna?"

I found Ben's number and pressed it. "*Nothing.*"

"It's the absolute opposite of nothing! Jesus, I sat up too fast, I might puke. Bring us a towel."

Whipping a towel from a rail in the bathroom, I tossed it to her, just as Ben answered his phone.

"Sorry, Ben," I said. "But would you know where Courtney is?"

"Ah, yeah. Yeah." He sounded half-asleep. "She's right here."

"All good. Sorry again." I rang off. Fair *play* to Courtney.

Everyone in the bridal suite was now coming to.

"Where did you spend the night?" Claire frowned.

"In Rachel's room."

"What was it like?" Mum asked. "Sharing the room with Luke? Had he his jocks on? Or was he, you know . . . ?"

"I don't know, he stayed with Joey."

"In the same bed?" Claire was suddenly flushed. "Joey and Luke? I wouldn't mind being the meat in that sandwich." Then, "Sorry, sorry! It's the testosterone. I can't help it!"

"It's nearly ten o'clock!" Margaret had just realized. "We'll miss the breakfast!"

"It's on till eleven today."

"Still! Everyone up!"

While they dragged themselves, complaining, out of bed, I ate two of my three muffins. Eventually they all left, leaving me free to pack up and do my furtive flit. But that wasn't going to happen, was it? If I hightailed it out of here, I'd be doing what Joey and I had always done—a big, dramatic something followed by a long silence.

During my terrible night's sleep, clarity had arrived. I'd long felt a rare tenderness towards Joey, something I was certain he needed and never really got.

What he gave me was harder to pin down—the closest word was probably respect.

But we could never make it happen. Messy circumstances, bad timing, whatever it was, it always blew up on us.

And here we were again. These days he was a principled adult, striving to do better. It was painful that we'd intersected at this part of his journey but perhaps he was right about me? How could I know what I wanted when nothing in my life was stable? In six months or a year who knew what would be going on? Unlikely as it seemed, I *might* go back to New York.

Right now, I was devastated. Maybe he was too? Or proud of himself for sticking to his plan? Either way, he and I were not going to happen.

I had to let him go. Again.

This was a chance to tell a different Anna-and-Joey story—or at least to change the ending. We could be civil, friendly, *kind* to each other.

There was less than a day to get through before he and I departed for Dublin and went our separate ways. Surely I could manage it?

A commotion at the door, accompanied by a clamor of complaints about their hang-xiety, the glare of the sun and the noisy bastards at the next table, announced the return of my roommates.

"Courtney's in," Helen said. "We couldn't ask her about last night because she was—"

"—a blur of productivity—"

"—serving everyone—"

"—giving second breakfasts to people who'd already eaten—"

"She gave me eight slices of toast," Francesca said.

"Get up," Claire ordered me. "We're doing the scavenger hunt."

"Even though we don't know what it is," Mum said.

"Like a treasure hunt but shit is my guess," Helen said. Widespread agreement greeted this. Even so, they remained enthusiastic.

"C'mon." Claire eyed me impatiently. "Put some blusher on. It starts at twelve and we want a good spot."

"I'm dying," I said.

"We're *all* dying. But we're still showing up."

"I've my period."

"At your age?" Mum squawked.

"I'm only in my *forties*. And I'm in *agony*." I wasn't in any agony but I needed more thinking time. After casting one or two more ageist slurs my way (plus a packet of unwanted Solpadeine, courtesy of Claire, who was like a mobile pharmacy), they eventually left me in peace.

Shortly after, my phone beeped. A message from Joey. **Hey x**

My heart clenched. But I'd survived all the other emotional upheavals Joey had been responsible for; I'd survive this. I should actually be getting good at it. Like whenever an airline lost my luggage. The first time I'd been en route to a week-long conference in Bologna. With only the clothes I stood up in, I'd felt naked and terrified. The second occasion (another work thing) also had me gasping and floundering. The third go-round was still pretty rough—but I'd developed a few basic survival techniques from my first and second experiences.

I knew I'd be okay, even if I didn't feel it right now.

Forcing myself to set aside my humiliation and think "friendly but loving thoughts," I composed a cheery reply. **Hey! ☺ What you up to?**

Scavenger hunt. You coming?

What the hell, I decided. Why not?

55

Before I could reply, a soft knock sounded at the door—a sheepish-looking Courtney. "I've been sent home."

"In disgrace?" I shepherded her towards an armchair.

"Hard to know." She was subdued but not noticeably in the horrors. "I let my team down and I *feel* disgraced. But Hari and Yelena came in to help, so now they're overstaffed below. And God forbid Kilcroney would pay me for standing around doing nothing."

"So tell me." I was *dying* to hear last night's details but also concerned for her. "Are you okay?"

"I was three hours late for work—that's never happened before, I'm an *exemplary* employee—"

"Ben," I prompted.

"You know," she said. "I'm not bad, considering that last night I blew up my life."

"Ben," I repeated. "Did you . . ."

". . . sleep with him? Well, yes. And no. We slept in the same bed. I've been working such long hours, his bed was so comfortable and it was late and I was . . . happy? Would that be the word?"

"It could be."

"There was a lot of kissing and staring into each other's eyes. But, Anna, wait till you hear, like *wait*. He *listened* to me. He wanted to know everything about me. We discovered we both can't stick cinnamon and that we love Coldplay—I've never admitted that to anyone ever before. They're my guilty pleasure even though I hate the phrase and so does Ben. I can't remember the last time anyone displayed that much interest in me. Probably when I got asymptomatic Covid and accidentally infected half the town. I was asked a *lot* of personal questions that day. Even though I was treated like a criminal, the attention was nice."

I could only stare, appalled that this amazing woman had been given so little in life.

"I fell asleep on his chest," she said. "I was so tired—too tired to pretend I wasn't."

"Were you dressed . . . ? Or not dressed?"

"Dressed, of course." She was impatient. "I'd spent thirty-eight euro on a new bra, I wasn't just taking it off."

"Did you want to?"

"For sure. But I fell asleep. Missed my chance."

"You'll get another one. What about your husband? Does he know you weren't home?"

"He'll know by now. Someone—several of his many enemies—will have told on me. No secrets here, Anna."

"Will it be . . . awkward for you?"

"Arra. It's awkward anyway. Maybe now it'll be a different awkwardness. A change can be good. Right." She stood up. "I'll go home and face the music. See you in the morning before you go."

"I'll miss you," I said.

"I'll miss you too. But you'll be back, surely? When the place below opens? Givvus an oul' hug anyway."

Like everything else she did, Courtney was great at hugs. We said our goodbyes, then I set off to find the scavengers.

Within moments, I'd met Hardware Ralph. "*Bualadh bos*," he said, "for sorting out the business at Kearney's Farm. It'll be a great asset to the town."

"And *bualadh bos* to you too for your excellent singing on Friday night. Listen, I'm looking for the scavenger hunt. Any idea where I might find it?"

"It's finished. The Hogmanay team won. They win every year. It's a racket. Your crowd are in the Boot talking about scones."

"I'll go there then." On a whim, I said, "Ralph. When I arrived in town, you and I had that chat—which rest assured I will *take to my grave*—why did you suggest I talk to Ike Blakely?"

"Aaaaah . . ." Ralph had a ponderous think. "He cares about the environment. It was him who led the objections to the Big Blue a few years back. For all the good it did. He's well respected. People might go to him for advice or . . . or . . . Lookit, you asked me who you should talk to. He was the only one who came to mind. I was trying to help. I've to go now."

Ralph hurried away. So had I thought Ike was more important than he actually was? Not that it mattered now.

The Boot was the same pub we'd been in yesterday. Mum, Claire, Margaret, Rachel, Helen, Francesca, Regan and Luke were crowded around a long table. Involuntarily, I scanned the room. *Where's Joey?* There he was, lounging against a pillar, talking to Rose. *Wow. Rose in a pub.* Then, *Double wow, Rose in jeans!* Although they were immaculately tailored and worn with a blazer. Stylish. *Ish.* I'd have loved to loosen up her look. Less hairspray. *Faaaar* less scarf action. More floaty Isabel Marant-inspired dresses. But maybe the dithery old intellectuals liked her formality.

Joey might have sensed my focus because he glanced up, saw me and smiled. Lord. He was so handsome I wanted to cry. I also wanted to rip open his shirt, tear off his jeans and— "Sorry!" I bumped into someone. Who happened to be lovely, *lovely* Aber Skerett, selling raffle tickets.

"Come over and meet my family." I dragged him towards the Walshes, many of whom were drinking pints of Lucozade, clinking with ice. "Everyone," I announced. "This lovely man is Aber Skerett. Buy his raffle tickets, they're for charity."

"Which charity?" Margaret asked.

"Rehabilitation of traumatized sheep," Aber said, with a twinkle.

"*What?*"

"No!" Much more soberly, Aber said, "Sorry. I thought you'd know I was joking. It's for the Living Well with Dementia group. We're trying to buy them a minibus."

"Fair enough so."

Mum summoned me and hissed, "Who's that posh yoke Narky Joey is talking to?"

"Rose Tolliver. She owns the tumbledown house you visited yesterday."

"*Does* she, now?" This pleased Mum. "You'd think she'd tidy it up a bit. It's an absolute *pig*sty."

Customers continued to flood into the pub, locals and tourists alike. The atmosphere was festive. I had several enjoyable chats—with Aber, Ziryan, Karina the hairdresser—but I always knew exactly where Joey was. If the hairs at the nape of my neck lifted, he was within touching distance. At some stage, a sudden drop in my adrenaline let me know he'd left—he must have gone out to see Colm.

Meanwhile, no one else seemed in any hurry to leave. The atmosphere wasn't unlike that of a house party. Bowls of chips appeared on the table;

Mum fished a deck of cards from her bag. Somehow I got embroiled in a long-running game of Uno with Francesca, Luke, Aber and Peadar Brady, which Aber ultimately won.

It was only when Margaret declared, "It's ten to five!" that we noticed the afternoon had disappeared on us.

"Luke and I haven't gone to the fairground yet," Rachel said. Hurriedly we were gathering our stuff and saying our goodbyes.

"I'll text Armstrong, see if he wants to come?" Luke said. Less than a minute later, his phone beeped. "Nope. Not back yet. He'll message when he is."

After a couple of hours messing around on bumper cars and losing about fifty euro on the money falls, despite Mum's foolproof method, it was time for dinner. Claire gave in and let us go to the not-poxy pizza place on Main Street.

By then it was twenty to nine. "I can't believe I'm saying this," Claire said, "but I need an early night." This was met with widespread agreement. We returned to the Broderick.

In the lobby, Luke said, "Hold up. Lemme just get Armstrong. We're leaving first thing, so we'll say our goodbyes now?" He pressed buttons on his phone.

A short time later, Joey jogged down the stairs, looking animated and agile. God, this was difficult. He moved among us, giving everyone an individual farewell, leaving me until last.

"I've something for you," he said.

"Joey." I was stern. "Haven't we spoken about this?"

He couldn't stop a smile. "I'm sending you a number."

"Whose?"

He got out his phone and pressed something. "Jacqui's."

I felt the blood drain from my head.

"We were talking earlier today," he said. "I mentioned that you and I were working together. She asked how you were. I said she should ask you herself. So she told me to send you her number. Said she'd 'love'—that's the word she used, Anna: 'love'—to hear from you."

"What else did she say?" My voice was faint.

"Just that really. But it sounds promising?"

Mute, I stared at him. *Does she still hate me? What if it's a disaster? But what if it's amazing?*

Watching my face, Joey said, "Just meet her. See how it goes."

Okay. "Thanks."

"It's the least I can do."

As consolation prizes go, this was a good one.

"Well," I said, "I guess *this* is goodbye. Again."

"It's not goodbye, you big eejit." He opened his arms. "Bring it in."

Seriously? Press myself against the hard length of his body? Smell the skin of his neck? Touch his silky hair with my fingertips. Not a *chance*.

Safely back in my room, before I lost my nerve I texted Jacqui.

Immediately she replied. **You want to meet? Where you based? I'm in Banagher, Offaly. You want to come to me? Or me to you?**

It was important to sustain momentum. My fingers trembling, I typed, **I'll come to you. I'm free from tomorrow. Indefinitely, like.**

Her reply came within seconds. **Wednesday. Come for lunch. I'll have house to myself.**

I swallowed hard. This was great. Absolutely amazing.

Except . . . lies of omission about Joey had caused our big bust-up back in the day. If we were going to rebuild our friendship, there could be no more secrets.

Much as I wanted to, I couldn't get round this—I'd have to tell her what I did to Joey.

56

A few months before my fortieth birthday, out of a clear blue sky, a craving for a baby took hold of me. Quickly, it became all-consuming.

Petrified, I went to Rachel, my go-to on matters of emotions, and asked, "How do I make it go away?"

"Are you sure it should? Why don't you listen to this?"

"Be my sister. Not a therapist."

"In that case, I haven't a clue. But you need to talk to Angelo. See if he'll change his mind about having kids."

Angelo was gentle, but adamant. It was a no.

"Wait, though—" There was every hope I could persuade him otherwise. After all, we loved each other. "What if you change your mind? In a few years' time? Because, Angelo, you *might*."

"Anna, no. Not now, not ever. I'm sorry."

He was too nice to remind me that being child-free was one of the central pillars of our relationship.

"You've a choice to make." His eyes were full of sorrow. "A tough one."

I waited a day. Then another, and another, until weeks had passed and the painful hunger was still there. When I told Angelo, he said, "Then we've come to the end of our time together."

I loved him deeply, but I was willing to give him up, to chase this other longing. We hugged, I cried, then I stepped away.

My options seemed very limited: I didn't have the heart to go on the prowl in New York. A sperm donor was the best route, but that also daunted me: how could I know what the best choice was?

All my free time became devoted to obsessive research, when a night happened, a party for Gaz's birthday. Although neither Rachel nor Luke lived in New York any longer, I'd stayed on friendly if distant terms with the rest of the Real Men.

The venue was only ten minutes from my apartment. I dropped in after a long day, still in my work clothes. And you know, it was *so* nice; I'd forgotten how fond of them I was. On my arrival, someone put a drink in my hand, then they formed a line to say hello. First came Gaz, who smothered me in a hug, and made much of my tailored skirt and pointy shoes. "Girlboss, bossing it!" He was followed by Johnno, who was visiting from Denver. Then came Shake who grasped my shoulders and talked earnestly of keratin hair treatments.

As Joey hove into view, I took a mouthful from my drink. Holy smoke, it was strong. I choked out, "Who made these? They're lethal."

"The birthday boy. Gaz's own recipe."

I looked around for a waiter. I shouldn't be drinking anyway, but this was strong enough to kill a horse.

Joey turned affectionate eyes towards Gaz, who was hugging a batch of new arrivals. "What's in the box you gave him?"

"Essential oils and a diffuser."

"He's gonna love that."

"Is he?" I'd thought he would, but was Joey being sarcastic?

"Oh yeah. Mad for a bit of wellness, our Gaz."

". . . So, ah, how's work?"

Joey lit up. "Good. Yeah. Thanks. Like, really good. I have an office and two assistants. Wait! Let me show you . . ." He rummaged in his wallet, producing a stiff, sharp-cornered business card bearing, in tasteful font, the words "Joseph Armstrong, Business Broker," followed by all the ways he could be contacted.

"Wow." I inspected it. "Well done. Congratulations."

I passed it back and he said, "No, no, keep it!"

His pride in his success made my heart clench.

"He's loaded," Shake said, passing by.

"Are you?" I asked Joey.

"I wish." He grinned, revealing his chipped tooth. "But, couple of years ago, I did get to buy Jacqui and Trea their own home."

My inhale was sharp. This was the first time in over three years he had uttered their names to me. "How are they?"

Joey shifted. "Good. Yeah. Living in Ireland now."

"That can't be easy for you and Trea?"

"It's not ideal." He was clearly uncomfortable. "But you know Jacqui got married? Had a little boy? So Trea has a kid brother, cousins, sees Jacqui's parents a lot. She's happy."

Dumbly I nodded. I'd been ambushed by an ember of an idea, so audacious it had shocked me into silence. Instead of abandoning my too-strong drink, I took another gulp.

"Obviously I wish she still lived here. But anything she wants or needs . . . Yeah." He smiled ruefully. "A pony. A trip to EuroDisney. I can deny her nothing."

The ember was expanding into a dazzling light: Joey would probably sleep with me.

Was this a good idea? A truly terrible one? Probably terrible, but I couldn't think about that, because what this was, was a rare opportunity. Joey was a known quantity: an unrepentant womanizer who avoided cozy domesticity. If I got pregnant I'd be on my own—which suited me.

In order to hold my nerve, I threw the last of my drink down my throat and reached for another from a passing tray.

Quietly, so Joey had to lean nearer, I said, "You don't have to justify anything to me."

"Uh. Yeah, thanks—" He'd noticed the change in me.

I took a breath. "Joey, are you seeing anyone right now?"

"No."

"Really? Why not?"

"I . . . don't know." His eyes flickered as he tried to figure out what was going on. "Are you . . . ah? How are you, Anna?"

"You know Angelo and I broke up?"

"What?"

"Done," I said. "Finished. I thought you would have heard."

"No." He looked like he was beginning to understand. "No one said. So . . . are you okay?"

My fix on his face didn't waver. "Life goes on."

A moment passed.

Then another.

Joey became very still. "Anna?" He coughed. "Could we maybe . . . get a drink sometime?"

"Sure. When?"

"When is good for you?"

"Now."

Shock showed in his eyes; then he said, "You wanna . . ." He hesitated. ". . . get out of here?"

Briefly I froze. "My place."

The bar was full of people we both knew. He got that he shouldn't touch me until we had total privacy.

I let us into my apartment and as soon as the door shut, sealing out the world, I slid my arms around his neck to kiss him.

I watched his mouth—*the* mouth—move towards mine. But he stopped, mistrustful. "We're really doing this?"

"We really are." I twisted away, leading him into my bedroom before I could change my mind.

As I pulled him towards the bed, he stopped again. "Anna, *why?*"

"Joey Armstrong, total ride. What woman would say no?"

Warily, he said, "You did once before."

Pity stabbed me at the memory of that night. "That was when Jacqui was my best friend."

After another doubtful pause, he asked, "You're *sure?*"

"So sure. Really, Joey, I want this, I want you."

"Okay." With a slow smile, he unpeeled his jacket, kicked off his boots and stretched himself the length of my bed. "C'mere," he summoned, with lazy confidence.

As I stepped from my shoes, I took a moment to catch up with this very strange reality. There was a time I'd have given *anything* to have Joey in my bed. And despite all our ups and downs, he was still so sexy . . .

Holding very spicy eye contact, he slowly unzipped his jeans and slid a hand in, boldly rearranging himself. Even through his clothes, the size was impressive.

I slid across the duvet, my head lowered submissively. "Hey." He frowned. "Why do you look so worried?"

"I'm nervous."

"You won't believe me." His voice was quiet. "But so am I."

He caught my skepticism. "With you I am."

I searched his face. Did he mean it? Probably not.

Surprisingly gently, his mouth touched mine. The pressure intensified, his tongue was in my mouth and sensation surged. Suddenly desperate for the taste and feel of him, my hands were in his silky hair then bumping down the knuckles of his vertebrae. Sliding my palms under his jeans and along the satin-smooth skin, I pulled his hips tighter against mine. His erection pressed down hard on my pubic bone, a muttered *Fuck* reached me and I was turned on, *really* turned on.

. . . I couldn't do this. Maybe the alcohol had worn off, but my earlier conviction that this was a great idea was fast evaporating. Tricking him into being a baby-maker was bad. Terrible.

Or was it? He'd get to have sex, which was probably all he cared about.

His mouth moved to my neck, dropping a line of small, sharp bites, each nip triggering a throb between my legs. His breath warmed my skin and his mouth moved lower, towards my collarbone. I didn't want to stop.

Burnt sugar was what he smelt of. That and warm bread, with a darker, muskier undertone—surprisingly familiar. Probably from when we used to stay in the same bed, at different times, at Jacqui's.

Skimming a hand up my thigh, he was already trying to slide off my thong. My doubts were back. "Slow it down there, cowboy," I whispered.

"Impossible," he whispered back. "Anna, I have it so bad for you."

Maybe he used that line on everyone—but what if he didn't? A fresh rush of guilt convinced me to let him do exactly what he wanted. In no time my top was off, then my bra, and he was applying his mouth with such devotion to my nipples that the original reason for this hookup was almost forgotten.

Efficiently my skirt was unbuttoned, unzipped—then gone. All that remained was my thong. But apart from his unzipped jeans, and the straining presence of his erection, he was fully dressed. I denied myself the pleasure of peeling the clothes from his body, having decided that if I didn't enjoy myself too much, I wasn't a terrible person.

Hooking his fingers under the stretchy lace, my last piece of clothing was being coaxed agonizingly slowly down my legs. At my ankles, Joey slid it with expert ease over my feet.

Returning, he held my stare while sliding two fingers into the wet heat of my body. His eyes widened. "Jesus Christ," he said, his mouth hovering over mine. "*Anna.*"

Desperately, all guilt abandoned, I lunged at him. "Joey, that's enough. Everything off *now.*"

He grinned. Raising himself from the bed, he said, "Let me get something."

"No need."

"What?" He stopped mid-movement, balancing his weight on one arm.

"It's okay," I said.

I'd thought he'd be overjoyed. Wasn't it what every man wanted—condom-free sex? But his smile stalled.

"It's fine. I'm . . . healthy." No way was I going to say *STIs.* "Are you?"

"Actually, yeah." Unsettled, he asked, "But you're on the pill?"

"I . . . well. Like, I . . ."

I just needed to say one word: *yes.* Just one word.

The silence lasted too long.

I couldn't go through with the lie.

"Anna?" Already he was rearing away from me, moving back across the bed. "What the hell's going on?"

"I'd ask for nothing." The words tumbled from me. "I'd tell no one it was yours. I know it's not what you want and I'm good with it—"

"You want to get *pregnant?*"

I was crying now, all of the sad yearning pouring from me. "Angelo doesn't want kids."

He looked devastated. "I knew this was too good to be true." Already shouldering his way back into his jacket, he asked, "What do you mean, 'I know it's not what you want'?"

"Because . . ." Surely this was obvious? ". . . it's always just about sex for you?"

"That's what you think of me?" He was a picture of pale horror.

"But you don't want commitment, responsibility. Isn't that how it is with Trea?"

"When I got Jacqui pregnant, I didn't want to be a father—we've already had this conversation. I *told* you. But when she was born, it changed me."

"But she's in Ireland and you're here."

"And I fly to Dublin every month to see her."

"Sorry," I stuttered, suddenly appalled.

"I *could* have tried to stop Jacqui leaving but in what world would dragging her through the courts be a good idea? I've already hurt her enough."

"Joey . . . I'm so sorry. Please don't leave. Look, take your jacket off again—"

"I don't need a consolation fuck." He was ashen. "And maybe you should get yourself some help."

Even before the door had slammed shut behind him, I knew this was the worst thing I'd ever done to another human being.

I'd put the worst possible interpretation on Joey's past actions in order to justify what I'd wanted.

My shame was bottomless.

My mouth claggy with fear, I rang him; he didn't pick up. Immediately I called again. When that went to message I sent a text, then another, and another, a long stream of self-abasing remorse.

With trembling hands, I went through my bag looking for his business card and tried all the numbers without success.

The next morning, after a night of broken sleep and terrible dreams, I called his office landline, where a smooth young man purred, "Mr Armstrong is not available at this time." When I pleaded with him to ask Joey to ring me, the smooth young man said, with obvious double meaning, "Mr Armstrong certainly has your number."

After work I went to his apartment and leant on the buzzer for hours without an answer. Over the next few weeks I returned at all kinds of strange times, day and night, without ever getting a response.

In many ways it was reminiscent of Jacqui's ghosting three years earlier. I felt like I was going to lose my mind.

Luke would have been the obvious intermediary, but he'd broken up with Rachel and left town. I had no way to reach him, but even if I had, I was too ashamed to tell him.

When all else failed, I wrote Joey an old-fashioned letter; he didn't reply.

Surprisingly, he didn't block my number or email. It was as if I wasn't worth the bother.

Meanwhile, despite the hurt it had caused, my longing for a baby intensified. Pressing on, I found a clinic I liked and could afford, submitted to the tests and was eventually given the go-ahead. Right at the point of choosing a donor, the tight grip of the compulsion seemed to loosen.

Confused and doubtful, I was afraid to slow my momentum and just as afraid to move forward. Then, in the midst of my agonizing, a stiff, cream card came in the mail: an invitation in curlicued script to the engagement party of Elisabeth Boyd-Hamilton and Joseph Armstrong.

The shock was intense: it was only five months since that shameful night. Had he been seeing Elisabeth when I put the moves on him? Or was it a more recent thing?

I went to the party, desperate to make amends, but I might as well have been invisible. I'd been invited just so Joey could blank me.

I got it completely: being denied forgiveness was my punishment.

Overwhelmed with remorse, it took a while to notice that my baby hunger really was on the retreat. It continued to slacken until, very gently, it set me down: I was free.

Unable to trust this unexpected reprieve, I waited several more weeks before calling Angelo. The master of the light touch, he just said, "Come on over. Let me cook for you."

I stepped back into the circle of his love, of my love for him, and, unlikely as it seemed, we picked up where we'd left off.

He forgave me for breaking the code of our agreement. I forgave him for denying me a child.

Joey, though, was a different story. Whenever I thought of him, the rush of shame was devastating. Eventually, when I couldn't block the memories, I blocked his number instead.

57

I was in a deep sleep when my phone rang: Lenehan, 3.37 a.m. This could only be bad.

"Anna, there's a fire at the farm. I can see flames." He sounded panicked. "Fire brigade's coming from Spiddal. I'm on my way over there now."

I was up and out of the sofa bed and reaching for a light switch. "Be really careful. I'll be with you asap."

As the overhead bulb blazed, a clamor of complaint went up from my sisters and Mum. "What time is it? Twenty to four? In the *morning*? Can someone please explain . . . ?"

"A fire at Brigit's." I was throwing on clothes, then hurrying down the stairs to bang on Joey's bedroom door. "Joey, it's me. Wake up!"

"Anna?" A towel barely protecting his modesty, he looked sleepy. Another man from the Luke Costello School of Nudie Sleeping. "What's up?"

"A fire at Kearney's Farm. Get dressed."

"Fuck!" Instantly he was awake. "Done deliberately?" As he turned away, he was already whipping off the towel, treating me to a glimpse of his delicious flank.

"I don't know, but what are the chances? I'll be downstairs at your jeep . . ." I'd just remembered Joey had returned to M'town without his car. A question began to form, some sort of anxiety. "I forgot, you don't have it. We'll go in mine. Mum's. The Multipla."

Out in the street, it was pouring rain. It took a moment to notice I was crunching on broken glass: the Multipla's windscreen was shattered. In fact, all the windows were smashed and the roof had been bashed in: the car was undriveable. Adrenaline propelled me back up three flights of stairs for the keys to Helen's car, then down again to the street, meeting Joey on the way. "The Death Star's parked round the back of the hotel," I said.

"What's up with your ride?" By then we were outside and he saw for himself. "Holy fuck."

In the Fiat, Joey was full of questions. "What did Lenehan say? How bad is it?"

"I don't know," I kept saying. "I don't know. But the rain's a good thing?"

"We can only hope."

Before long, an orange glow appeared in the night sky.

"Is that . . . ?" Joey said. ". . . That's not the sunrise?"

"Don't think so." I felt sick. Then came the faint sound of sirens.

The farm gates were open. We bumped down the track, the sirens gaining on us. The old Kearney farmstead looked unharmed but just beyond it, lit by demonic orange light, people were hurrying with buckets of water: Colm, Lenehan, his brother Ree and men who must be nearby neighbors.

Emerging from the car, the noise was as shocking as the heat—a crackling sound of burning wood, wires, whatever it was. Dotted about the land, four—no five—of the newly built cottages were ablaze. My heart sank to my boots. This was no accident, a one-off calamity.

Joey caught Lenehan and yelled, "What can we do?"

"Find something to carry water, fill it from the tap in the yard, don't get too close to the flames."

A burning roar sounded, followed by splintering and snapping as part of a building collapsed. Shreds of blackened plastic floated in the wet air. None of this felt real. Adding to the dreamscape, the fire truck hurtled up the track, still blasting its siren. Stopping close to the nearest fire, the noise shut off abruptly. Several men and women leapt out, fanning across the grounds, towards the burning buildings.

"What're they doing?" someone yelled.

"Checking for inhabitants!"

"They're empty," Colm hollered, running after a firefighter. "All the buildings are empty!"

"Get *back*. All of you get *back*. You're making our job harder."

That the firefighters had arrived was something. But it was hard to watch the flames continue to burn high and loud. *Come on, come on, come on.* Then a hose was unrolled, a thick rope of water was trained on one of the burning cottages and the tightness in my chest loosened a little. Joey and I exchanged a look of bleak relief.

"So what happened?" I was finally able to ask Lenehan.

"Dad was awake. He doesn't sleep much. He saw the flames."

More neighbors had begun to show up but the firefighters made them leave, taking Ree with them. Only Lenehan, Colm, Joey and I remained, the flames scorching our faces.

"In one of the emails"—I'd reached for my phone—"They said if we didn't leave, their next step would be to burn the place. Something like that, anyway. Let me find it . . . here it is, Joey."

From: ProudIrishPatriot1916@hotmail.ie

Next time we'll burn the houses won't be just paint

"My God," he said. "But ProudIrishPatriot1916 can be traced, right?"

"I think you'd need a warrant. Helen would know. But the police could easily do it?"

"Would someone be that stupid? To make a threat then carry it out?"

I didn't know. "There's something else, Joey. Misinformation has been posted on Facebook since January. An account called Local Hero. That's where all the rumors about four-story buildings and poisoning the dolphins originated."

"No idea who it is?"

I shook my head.

"You told me this wasn't over. I should have listened."

More townsfolk came, with umbrellas and flasks of coffee. A nimble, mustachioed man darted at me, placing a basket of still-warm muffins into my hands. It was only days later that I realized it had been Steve, the "mad" chef.

They were all sent away.

Suddenly things began to speed up when two fire trucks arrived from Galway city, carrying chemical extinguishers and extra hoses. Finally, one fire was out, revealing a charred, smoking ruin. Then a second inferno was quenched.

"Here we go," Joey muttered—Sergeant Burke had arrived.

First he exchanged words with Colm, then he came to Joey and me.

"I hope you're both happy," he said. "Bringing this palaver here."

"How can we help?" Joey was weary but polite.

"Need a chat with both of you. Come to the station nice and early in the morning."

"Certainly."

Burke gave us another glare then strode away.

I don't know how long we stood in the rain, silently urging the fires to cease. But by the time the last one was out, morning had broken. The world was no longer satanic but postapocalyptic: charred ground, blackened stumps of wall, the baleful sun presiding over a gray-white smoking hell.

I looked at Joey: my hopelessness was mirrored in his eyes.

"We'll head back, get some sleep," he said. "Eat something. Reconvene later."

As I drove back to town, I didn't think I'd ever felt so defeated. "How bad is this?"

He shook his head. "Maybe it's over."

58

"What time is it?" My voice was croaky.

I'd woken up in the bed in the bridal suite. Mum and Helen were at my side.

"About eleven."

When Joey and I had got back to the hotel it had been 7 a.m. I'd thought I'd smell nothing but burning forever more. I'd shampooed my hair three times; Mum had dried it. They'd all clucked around me, guiding me into the bed.

"Is Joey awake?" I asked now.

"About an hour ago. He said to let you sleep."

"Mum, I'm sorry about your car."

"Not at all! Mr Kilcroney says the insurance will cover it."

What insurance?

I had a shower, yet another one, and washed my hair again. When I left the bathroom, the bridal suite was busy, my sisters coming, going and packing up to go home.

"Food?" Francesca asked me. "Coffee?"

The idea made me queasy but I'd better have something before going to the police station.

"Regan and I can stick around for a few more days, Mum too," Helen said. "We'll get Artie to come down."

Discommoding people would make me feel even lower, if such a thing was possible. "Thanks, but Joey and I will figure it out."

Suddenly Courtney was there, a bundle of Easter eggs in her arms. Now I really *was* convinced I was trapped in an alternative universe.

"Anna, *a stór*. I'd hug you but for . . ." She indicated her bounty. "These are for you. From . . ." She consulted a list. "Pamela, Glen and family. Peadar Brady and the lads. Hardware Ralph. And Tipper Mahon and the crew."

Caught between her fingers were three envelopes. "Mass cards. From Moyna and Proinnsias O'Hehir, Gannon's the pharmacist and Augustina Mahon, she's Tipper's mother."

Oh my God. The lovely people in this town—welcoming, warm and fun. It made no sense but I felt responsible for bringing this horror to their doorstep.

. . . And why Easter eggs?

"Because there's no flowers. Some flash piece bought up the town's supply last Thursday. That was a joke, just in case it wasn't clear. As for the Easter eggs, the minute Paddy's Day is out of the way, the Easter eggs are on the shelves. I suppose people got excited."

"But what about Joey? He's just as upset as me."

"Joey got stuff too!" Claire had appeared. "A bottle of Jameson! A pair of thick socks! It's okay, Anna, dispiritingly gendered but okay!"

A kerfuffle at the door made me look up—it was the arrival of my breakfast, the tray carried by none other than Brogue-face Kilcroney himself.

The man looked very shook. "I want to offer my condolences for what you and Mr Armstrong went through last night. As a goodwill gesture I'm comping the entire stay for you, your family and Mr Armstrong."

"There's no need for—"

"What happened out there"—he jerked his head—"was all wrong. That's not who we are. As for your mother's car—a downright disgrace. Our insurance will look after it."

His unexpected kindness broke my heart. "Sorry for being so emotional," I gulped. "But poor Colm and Brigit. And not just them, what about Tipper, Hal, Declan Erskine, all the crew? They'd worked so hard and it was shaping up to be beautiful and it's . . ."

Kilcroney was stricken with discomfort: not a man who did emotions. "We'll organize a car to get yourself and Mr Armstrong back to Dublin."

"We've to have a chat with the police, I don't know how long they'll want us to stay in town."

"Not long, I'd say. They won't want to drag out your ordeal anymore than they have to." Quickly he left, passing Joey who was leaning against the doorway, looking desolate.

I got to my feet, he held out his arms and I rested my forehead on his shirt front.

"It's shit," he murmured. "I know."

"Have you been talking with Colm?"

"Yeah." He sighed. "I hate to ask, but can you stick around a few more days? A lot going on. Colm and the family are my priority. But the insurance company will be sending loss adjusters, they'll arrive later in the week. And I want to be sure the police are taking this seriously."

Wheeling cases and hoisting backpacks, the Walshes left as they had arrived— by attracting attention. Down in the lobby, the farewells were loud and lengthy.

As Mum hugged me, she hissed, "Do we really not have to pay?" She adored a bargain but would be appalled to be considered a grifter.

"You really don't have to. But you can if you want."

That did the trick. Like a trap snapping, her elbow clamped her handbag to her side, just in case her credit card made a bid for freedom.

Rachel grabbed me. "If it's any help, the people here in the town are *lovely*. They're very worried about the Kearneys obvs but they like you too, Anna. *And* Joey."

Regan and Joey were the last people to bid each other farewell. Joey got down to her level and she said, "Joe-boy, let's stay in touch."

He almost smiled. "Let's do that, Regan. It's been fun hanging with you."

"Sames."

Then they were all gone, leaving just me and Joey.

"Cop shop?" he invited, extending his elbow.

"Why not?" I replied.

Mum's broken car had disappeared from the curb but cubes of glass still crunched underfoot.

I had to ask. "What kind of fool wants you to leave town then trashes your car?"

Joey shook his head.

On the short walk, we were stopped probably ten times, each person insistent that the retreat would be a good thing for the town. "Whoever did that terrible thing last night, they weren't speaking for me."

"I believe them," I told Joey. "Whoever did this, it's just one or two people, with a specific agenda."

At the police station, I'd expected to find a consignment of detectives dispatched from Clifden, even Galway, trying to find a space to work from. For phones to be hopping off tables as the public rang with information tips. For it to feel important and *urgent*.

But the only person on duty was an unsmiling Burke. "I told you to get down here nice and early."

He pointed a pen at Joey, then at three orange chairs in the corridor. "Wait there." The same pen was pointed at me, then at a small, bare room. "In there."

My phone vibrated: a text from Ike. I need to see you.

A second text arrived immediately. It's about the fire.

Was there any point? The plug was probably going to be pulled on the whole venture. And he'd never given me any actual information, had he? Just winked and hinted and wasted my time.

Burke sat at the far end of the table. "Well?" he asked, as if I'd been called into the headmaster's office to explain away some transgression.

"Well!" I replied. "On Thursday I got an email that literally threatened to burn the cottages at Kearney's Farm. Here." I slid my iPad down the table, the email from ProudIrishPatriot1916@hotmail.ie highlighted.

He gave it a cursory glance. "ProudIrishPatriot1916? Oh, I know him well. I'll just go below and bring him in for questioning, will I?"

Sarcastic prick. "But you can get their IP address and—"

"Hold your horses! You'd need a warrant for that."

". . . But. You're the police. Warrants are your thing—"

"Just because someone threatens something doesn't mean they're the ones who did it. It could have been any keyboard eejit acting tough. Only one thing is clear, M'town doesn't want this hotel going ahead."

"That's not true, I've met so many—"

"You come down here from Dublin, thinking you know everything. But I'm the sergeant here. I know my community, they trust me."

What could I say to that? "So what happens now?"

With contempt, he shook his head. "You want some big investigation? With arson specialists arriving from Galway city? You want local people to lose their liberty because of a hotel catering for a crowd of moneybags bastards who could go anywhere in the world?"

"No, but—"

"Myself and the other officers here will get to the bottom of whatever went on. Some bored young fellas, probably. They'll be set on the right track and we'll all get back to normal."

"Do you *know* who did—?"

"People could have *died* last night!" he thundered. "Died! Next time you mightn't be so lucky."

With that warning, he said, "Off you go. Send in Armstrong."

"You mean we're finished?"

"Send in Armstrong, I said."

Reeling from the speed of the dismissal, I left the room and came face to face with Tipper Mahon, Declan Erskine and another crew member, whose name I thought might be Vazey.

"Tipper!" It didn't matter that he didn't like me; we were long past that. I clasped his hand, tears pouring down my face. "Sorry for crying, but all your hard work! You made it so beautiful and for it to be ruined, your heart must be broken."

Tipper seemed stunned. "Ah, shur," he stuttered.

"And Declan!" I moved to embrace him. "You too. And all for nothing."

Withholding eye contact, Declan mumbled, "No one died, I suppose."

Moving on. "Vazey? It is Vazey? I'm sorry we're meeting in these circumstances. My heart breaks for you all." I looked around. "Where's Hal?"

"Above home," Tipper said at the same time as Vazey said, "In Athlone."

"He's back," Tipper said. "He was away for the weekend, but he's back. I think."

"I nearly forgot to say, thank you for the Easter egg. And Tipper, your mum sent me a mass card. Can you thank her from me?"

"I can of course." He wouldn't look at me.

"Armstrong!" Sergeant Burke was out of the interview room. I'd forgotten about Joey, who was still on the orange chair.

"I'll be in the coffee shop across the road," I told him.

Café Grumpy, it was called. "I'm Glen and Pamela's daughter, Catreen," said the young woman behind the counter. "We're all mortified by what happened. What can I get you? On the house, like."

While I nursed a mint tea, I rang Helen. "If I gave you an email could you find the IP address and tell me who owns it?"

"No. But I know people who could. They'll need to be paid, though." Then, "Ah, lookit, it can be your birthday present from me."

"My birthday's four months away."

"Okay, it can be my 'sorry for sleeping with Joey back when dinosaurs roamed the earth.' How was I to know yous were in love with each other—"

"No, we weren—"

"Gimme the deets."

I took a breath. "Seriously? You can literally tell me the name of a person who sent an email?"

"I can get a physical address the bill payer is registered at. Probably even the device the email was sent from. But if they've a sophisticated cyber set-up—although how likely is that in Maumtully?—it'd be harder. Or if someone was using another person's computer, you couldn't prove it. And *none* of it could be used in court. Ping me what you've got."

"Thank you!"

"Slow your roll, I haven't done it yet. And listen, sorry for saying 'ping.' And 'deets.' I was feeling dynamic, got carried away. Give me a few days, I'll do what I can."

I sent ProudIrishPatriot's email to Helen. At the last minute, I also added ConcernedCitizen's details; there had been so much hostility in that message, about fucking me if I had a bag on my head, that it seemed sensible to check it out. Then—why not?—I rang Ike.

"Where are you?" he asked. "Café Grumpy? I'll be there in five."

A man of his word, he barreled in, big and busy. "The truck's on double yellows, I can't stay." He pulled up a chair. "What I'm hearing is whoever did it was told to burn one house but the fire didn't catch, not immediately, so he tried another. Then the rain started. He thought nothing would take. He panicked. Overdid it."

"Ike, why can't you just tell me straight out what you know?"

"I live here." His eyes darkened with exasperation. "This is my home. And it's a small place."

Finally, I really got it: he hadn't withheld information just to toy with me. It was because he had conflicting loyalties.

"*And*," he said, "I don't know anything for certain. Finding out was meant to be your job. I told you what I could without riling up more people than I already have. But ask yourself the question: who has the most to lose by a fancy resort setting up in the area?"

"I . . ." Hadn't a clue. The Broderick was a hotel but a totally different thing. There would be no overlap.

"Nicolas Burke will try to stop an investigation. But the insurance company will insist on a proper forensic examination. The individual who set the fires is just a misfortunate fall guy, a clueless man who's not well equipped for life. Probably got paid something like a hundred euro. He'll end up in prison but the people who're actually behind it will be grand."

Ike cast a glance at the truck outside. "Gotta go. One last thing. I'm sorry about Saturday. Putting my eye on your sister."

What did it matter now? "It's fine. I'm used to it."

"Once the go-boy came back, I knew I'd no chance."

"Joey?"

"You and him. Unfinished business."

He was gone.

After a while Joey emerged from the police station. I watched him cross the road, rangy in his dark coat, the breeze whipping his hair around his angular face. God, he was gorgeous.

I met him outside. "How'd you get on?"

He rolled his eyes. "The deluded gobshite thinks he can avoid an investigation. Listen, I've hired a car. It was driven in from Galway. I've to go to the Broderick to pick up the keys."

"How's the driver getting back to Galway?"

"He'll walk in his wooden shoes. Gonna take him three days because he has rickets." Then, "God's sake, Anna, I may be flash but I'm not a monster. Two cars came. Two drivers. Ours will go back with the other."

"'Kay." A question was sending signals from a worried part of me, something to do with Joey and his car, but trying to clarify it just made it dissolve.

As we walked, Joey said, "Officer Dibble was all about 'community policing' and 'we deal with our own.' But the insurance forensics will be savage. Criminal charges will happen for certain. I bet that Dibble is on the blower right now to Kilcroney. When we get back to the hotel, Kilcroney will offer us something—compensation. Help in rebuilding. A lifetime's supply of crimped crisps—*any*thing to keep the insurance company out of this."

"Why would he do that?"

"To avoid bad publicity for the town? The local economy depends on tourism. Then there are the festivals."

Reluctantly, I said, "I think I know who set the fires."

Heavily, Joey said, "Yeah."

"Hal Mahon? Yes? Why do you think so?"

"That pantomime in the cop-shop about him being 'above home' and also 'in Athlone.' Tipper and his mates . . . they're freaked *out*. What's your theory?"

"Ike Blakely texted, came to the coffee shop. Said a few things about 'the perpetrator' being 'clueless and not really able for life.' The type of stuff other people have said about Hal. Someone else got him to do it. He was only supposed to do one house but didn't know how to set fires, then it started raining, so he panicked."

"Hardly the work of a master criminal—" Abruptly Joey changed to Mr Smooth as a smiling man advanced on him with a car fob. "Ah, hello!"

"I'll wait in the lounge." Nothing bored me more than having the insides of a car explained, *nothing*. Except perhaps for the slow perimeter creep around a hire car, seeking out tiny imperfections for which I'd be charged a year's salary if I didn't point them out before I drove away.

Courtney was at reception. A thought popped into my head. "Courts? Do you know who's the administrator on Maum Marketplace? Or Maum Chats?"

"God, there's a few. What do you want to know?"

"Who Local Hero really is."

"I'll see what I can find . . . Wait now. Colm Kearney has done stints on Maum Chats. Have a word. He'll find the email address, no bother."

I wasn't sure poor Colm would be finding anything "no bother" ever again, but I rang him anyway.

"I haven't looked at Facebook in months," he said. "Let me see if I can find . . ."

After a tortuous wait while he clicked and sighed, he said, "LocalHero888@ gmail.com. All I can tell you."

"Thanks, Colm." Immediately I messaged Helen asking her to trace it.

In the lounge, Teagan, with her swingy ponytail and long lashes, was on duty. Unexpectedly, she hugged me. "I'm sorry," she said. "It's desperate. What can I get you? Kilcroney says you can have anything."

"Cake?"

"Sure! And brandy? For the shock?"

I was about to refuse, then said, "Okay."

"I'll give you the really dear stuff. A pint of it."

She'd made me smile. "And have one yourself for your trouble, miss."

"Kilcroney's the stingiest man on earth. He must be mortified about the whole business to be giving ye free rein. Here's the go-boy. What're you having?"

Joey grabbed a chair. "Ice cream? Three scoops. One of each."

"Sprinkles? Of caviar? Feck, we're out of caviar. Mini-marshmallows do you?"

"And smarties?"

Teagan bounced her pen against her teeth. "Give him an inch . . ."

"Since when did you like ice cream?" I asked Joey.

"I always liked it. But I pretended I didn't because I was afraid of seeming . . ."

I patted his arm.

"Would you mind if I joined you?" Dan Kilcroney, abject and ashen, stood before us.

"Please." Joey was icily polite. "Take a seat."

"Thanks. Thanks." His head lowered, he pulled up a stool. "There've been a few developments . . . of a financial nature." Kilcroney's eyes flickered meaningfully from Joey to me.

Beneath the table, Joey squeezed my hand. *Told you*. "Anything you want to say can be said in front of Anna."

"Fine, so." Nervously, Kilcroney licked his lower lip. "A group of traders here in the town, we want to cover the damage and the cost of rebuilding. I'll call in all the workmen I know. We'll get this fixed in double-quick time."

A second elapsed. Then another. In cool tones, Joey said, "A generous gesture. But unnecessary. That's what insurance is for."

"We'd like to keep the insurance company out of this."

"You mean keep the police out of it?"

"But . . . local lads up to high jinks." Kilcroney's swallow was audible. "We can't ruin their lives over a drunken mistake on a Paddy's Day weekend. They won't do it again. I can assure you of that."

"So you know who did it?"

"I . . . ah . . . I've my suspicions. Harmless young fellas."

"You should take that information to the police," Joey said. "Quite apart from the damage at Kearney's Farm, you can't have pyromaniacs stalking the same streets graced by the great and the good from the world of literature."

"They're *harmless*, I assure yo—"

"There's been a deliberate campaign of misinformation for weeks," Joey said. "The 'harmless young fellas' weren't behind that."

"That'll stop too. The rumors. Everything. You have my word."

This was a confession, wasn't it? Before I spoke, Joey's hand touched mine again: *Not yet*.

"Mr Kilcroney," he said. "You appear to have plenty of influence in the town. I'm thinking further down the road: what if we manage to finish the retreat, but mysteriously none of the locals will work for us? Or the farmers won't sell to us?"

"They will work for you. They will sell to you."

Joey was gentle. "You're overestimating my authority. I'm just a hired hand, answerable to a consortium of high-net-worth individuals. My brief here was to sound out the objections and fix them. Which I haven't managed to do. All I have to offer my employers is your word."

"Which can be relied on."

"Unless I come by new information whereby we discover what's really going on and who ordered the damage, I can't give them that assurance. We have no option but a full police investigation, with a detailed forensic examination of the site. There will be prosecutions, Mr Kilcroney, and convictions. Definitely jail time. And now, if you don't mind, I'd like to enjoy my ice cream."

59

Shakily, Dan Kilcroney stood. "I'll, ah . . . of course. We'll speak later on?"

As soon as he was gone, I said, "He's part of this."

"But there's no proof. Anna, can we go and see Hal?"

I was surprised, but, "Okay, sure. I've his address."

As we drove, I said, "It's hard to think of Hal doing those things for, like, a hundred euro. He seems so *nice*."

"Whatever about setting those fires," Joey said, "I can't see him wrecking your mum's car for money."

"You think someone made him?"

"Yep."

It was suddenly obvious. "Burke."

"That's who my money's on," Joey said.

Hal lived in a small house in a terraced row on the Clifden road. His mother Augustina, a woman perhaps in her seventies, answered the door. "He's in the kitchen."

When he saw us, Hal scrambled to his feet. "Anna. Mr Armstrong. I'm very sorry for all the damage. I'm sick about it. Anna, your mother's car, that was the worst of it. But Burke said if I didn't, he'd arrest me for the paint-flinging I did last Friday week."

Joey and I exchanged a look.

"Why did I fling the paint, sez you? He had me for possession of hash. Said he wouldn't press charges if I did the job."

"And the fires?" Joey asked.

"Same thing, the hash."

Joey frowned. "How much hash?"

"I dunno, a couple of grams. Maybe four."

"My drug days are long behind me," Joey said. "But I know that's a tiny amount."

Hal twitched a bony shoulder. "I still broke the law. He had me."

"Why did Burke want the cottages burnt?" Joey asked.

"To stop the resort from going ahead."

"But why?"

"I haven't a notion and I'm sorry for that too."

"That's okay. Tell us about setting the fires."

Hal rubbed his hand across his face. "He said to just do one but I hadn't a clue how. YouTube said to use fabric softener, the strips. Could you credit that?"

"Seriously?" Joey asked. "That's an actual thing?"

"It actually is. 'Highly flammable,' it said." Briefly Hal was animated, then shame regained its hold. "None of them would stay lit, just smoldered away. Then it started pelting rain. I got one fire going then came home. But the smoldering ones must have caught because they all went up.

"I didn't want to do any of it," he said. "I'm sick with myself for the trouble I've caused you. If I could I'd spend the rest of my life working to pay you back, but I'll be in prison. This lad on YouTube says I'll get ten years."

"But you were coerced," I said.

He shook his head. "Burke will stick it all on me and, to be fair, I'm the eejit who did it."

"But Burke—"

"Nothing will happen to Burke. I'm going to jail. He isn't. I'm no good at standing up for myself. I never was. Worse than stupid, that's what Tipper says."

"Tipper knew about it . . . ?"

Hal ducked his head. "I couldn't say."

"That's okay." Joey was gentle. "Hal, I don't know how everything will end up but you deserve better than this."

"I don't. And I'm properly sorry. I liked meeting the two of you, regardless. Anna, you're lovely. And you're . . ." He studied Joey. "You're lovely too."

Out in the parked car, Joey said, "He won't implicate anyone else because, I'm guessing, if he says nothing, Kilcroney or whoever will look after his mother. Financially, I mean. People like Hal always end up with a prison sentence, while the smarter, better-spoken ones thrive. It's soul-destroying."

"Joey, thanks for being kind to him. If you'd gone in hot and heavy, I'd feel even worse."

After a silence, Joey said, "In a different life, I could have been him. If I hadn't met Luke, if we hadn't left Ireland . . . There but for the grace of God. Or the grace of something."

"I'm still trying to figure it all out," I said. "So Burke is involved. Looks like Kilcroney is too. But why? What's in it for them? There's no way Brigit's place would steal customers from the Broderick. Ike said we should ask ourselves who has the most to lose by a high-end hotel opening up around here . . ." All of a sudden the penny dropped. Well, *a* penny. "Oh God."

"What?" Perplexed, Joey focused on my face.

"Ike kept trying to take me to the top of the cliffs. He hinted heavily that there was something to see."

Joey became very still; then, as understanding dawned, his mouth formed a silent *Oh*. "You mean . . . Rose?" His voice was faint. "You think?"

"I mean, maybe? No one else comes to mind. Should we ask her? She might be at The Broderick, working."

"She's not in today."

"We could drive up and take a look? Helen mentioned 'scaffolding.'"

"But that was to stop the house from falling down." Joey was insistent. Then, "Wasn't it?"

He didn't want it to be Rose. And maybe it wasn't. "It can't hurt to take a look."

The route was complicated: we went north out of town, skirting the cliff, then looped sharply back on ourselves to climb it from the far side. We drove up a long, lonely track which had probably once been a fine carriageway but was now crumbling to pieces. Neither of us spoke. My stomach buzzed with emotion that might have been anticipation but felt more like anxiety. When my phone rang, I jumped.

It was Helen. "Where are you?"

"In a car with Joey."

"Put me on speaker. I've news. So I went with the really expensive option. Turns out that the emails from ProudIrishPatriot1916 were sent from the home computer at Sunnyside, Clover's Lane, Maumtully, Co. Galway. The electoral register shows that to be the home of . . . would this name mean anything at all to you?" She took a breath. "Danaher Kilcroney?" She let a second elapse. Then she exclaimed, "It's Brogue-face! There he was this morning giving it Appalled of Maumtully. When he was the one who did it!"

Joey and I shared a subdued look. Now we had some sort of proof. A connection, at least.

"I've another one," Helen said. "ConcernedCitizen@eircom.net? The one who offered to fuck you, Anna, if you had a bag on your head? Yes? Sent from 12 Chestnut Crescent. That's the address of the Burke family."

"Burke?" Joey asked. "That absolute prick."

"I'll keep at it with the Local Hero address but I thought you'd want to know."

"Helen." Joey was croaky. "Quick question: in your opinion, who in M'town has the most to lose if a high-end retreat opens up?"

". . . Ah. Haven't a baldy."

"Don't overthink it. The first name that comes into your head."

"I know nothing about the town but from what I saw, it'd be her lady-ship, Rose."

"Why?"

"That house is amazing. All those trees . . . There's even an old funicu-lar track down to the beach. I mean, the place is a total shithole now and you'd need, like, ninety billion punders to fix it but it could be a totally cool as fuck hotel."

"Thanks, Helen." Joey wouldn't look at me, just stared straight ahead and kept driving. Dread settled on me, like a shroud.

Suddenly the road widened and improved, with a fresh-looking layer of tarmac. We had almost arrived. From this vantage, the house and grounds looked much bigger than from sea level.

Joey stopped the car in front of shiny new gates, which were secured with a padlock. I got out and stared through the gaps. In the front yard was a massive bin, a forklift truck, stacks of shiny, new-looking pipes and palettes of plastic-wrapped timber. Helen's scaffolding was in evidence, ladders link-ing each level, with a wheelbarrow parked at the top.

I noticed something. "Joey! That digger? The orange one. I think that's Tipper Mahon's. Which had sand put in the petrol tank. Allegedly."

"But a digger is a digger. Don't they all look the same?"

"See the sticker? 'Diggers do it standing up'? Tipper's has one. Maybe it comes with all orange diggers? Like the can of Monster Energy in the cup-holder." I got out my phone, but Joey was ahead of me, scrolling through the report of the damage done in the first attack on Kearney's Farm.

"Same number plate." His voice was tight. "Let me check the forklift . . . yeah, same number plate too."

"I've a feeling those pipes and timber might be the ones 'stolen' from Kearney's. We need to talk to her."

"Wait now." For the first time in ages he met my eyes.

"You have her number?" It both was and wasn't a question. "Ring her."

When he produced his phone and pressed some digits, my chest tightened. But it didn't have to mean anything, him having her number?

He took a breath and turned his back on me. "I'm here." He was so quiet. "Outside."

In the house a curtain was yanked to one side and there was Rose's face gazing in dismay. The curtain fell back and moments later, she was crossing the front yard. Briskly, she twisted a key in the padlock, opened the gate just wide enough to admit us, then locked it again.

"Come inside." Her face set, she walked ahead of us.

In a dark, old-fashioned kitchen, she said, "No coffee, Joseph, my apologies, but I can offer you tea."

"Just tell me what's really going on," Joey said.

"Joseph, I'm sorry." Rose was quiet and ladylike.

I went hot and cold as I understood that my dread was justified, that something really was in play here.

". . . Would you like me to step outside?" I asked. "Give you some privacy?" Was I being sarcastic or sincere? Perhaps both.

"Stay where you are," Joey said, but all his attention was on Rose. "So you, Burke and Kilcroney?"

"I had nothing to do with Burke." She sounded disgusted. "Dan brought me a proposal: restoring this . . ." She waved a hand. "Creating an opulent hotel. The ambition of Kearney's Farm had inspired him."

"Where was he getting finance?" Joey asked.

"He has remortgaged the Broderick."

"That would raise only a tiny percentage. Five million, if he was lucky. To do a decent job here you'd need ten times that amount."

"So it would appear . . . He grossly underestimated the sums needed."

"Is that where I came in?"

"I won't deny I know how you make your living," she said. "But I have genuinely enjoyed your company, Joseph, and—"

"I checked, you know," Joey cut in. "You don't have planning permission."

"No."

"No . . . ? Or do you mean, 'Not yet'?"

"Dan wanted to wait until the situation at Kearney's Farm was resolved before applying."

"'Resolved'?" I asked. Both Joey and Rose seemed surprised to find me still there.

Quietly, Rose said, "My concern was that two upscale hotels in such close proximity couldn't survive. Dan said he would take care of it."

"'Take care of it'?" I said. "By getting someone to burn down Kearney's Farm?"

"I knew nothing about that. I give you my word." She was dry-eyed but obviously upset. "The fire, the damage to Mrs Walsh's car, I would never have endorsed it."

"But you'd be okay with getting our investors to pull out, leaving Brigit and Colm destitute," Joey said.

"They won't be destitute. They just won't have a hotel."

"They *will* be destitute. They no longer own the land. They won't get it back. They remortgaged their house to raise enough money for their stake. They won't get that back either. So, destitute *and* homeless. And their little girl has cancer."

"I'm truly sorry about Queenie. But I was aware of none of the rest."

"The forklift truck?" I gestured towards the yard. "The timber, the digger? They're from Kearney's? Tipper and his lads were working here all week, but getting paid by Joey?"

"Yes."

"Talk to me about the planning permission," Joey said. "How do you know you'll even get it? A house this old must be listed—oh God . . ." He stopped. "You know someone in the planning office?"

With some reluctance, Rose said, "It's no secret that Dan's ex-wife Olivia is a county councillor."

"Olivia? You mean, the woman at the public meeting?" Joey asked. "The county councillor? She was married to Kilcroney?"

Hold on, *who*? Mrs Lopsided Wig? She was "The lovely Olivia" Courtney had spoken of?

"However" —Rose spoke quickly and anxiously— "There's no suggestion of—"

"Bribery?" I provided. "Corruption?"

"Absolutely none."

"Anna?" Joey said. "Let's go."

Rose reached for a book and extended it to Joey. "The biography of Alexander Scriabin I mentioned."

Joey took a moment. Then, "No, thanks."

60

Joey and I returned to the car and, without consultation, drove back to town. The faint question that had been tap-tap-tapping in my head was finally audible: how had Joey got out to see Colm yesterday? Without a car? Without Rachel and Luke driving him?

Because he hadn't been with Colm. That was how.

He had never actually said he was; I'd just assumed it because who else would he have been with?

Rose. It had been Rose. In the last week, something had sparked between them. Meanwhile I'd tried to hustle him into bed on Saturday night.

Had he rejected me because he had something going on with her? It had never occurred to me that she might be his type. But I was the one who wasn't his type. The humiliation was scalding. Even more painful was the sense of loss.

But Joey owed me nothing. He could do whatever he liked with whoever he wanted. With or without Rose, he still didn't want me.

And excruciating though this was, I couldn't think about it now; more important things needed my attention.

I tried to focus. It seemed that whatever was going on with Burke and Kilcroney, the original idea had been Kilcroney's. Between Rose's account of events and Helen having traced that IP address, there was probably enough evidence to arrest him. Maybe even convict him?

But arresting him would implicate Hal Mahon. Plus, Kilcroney was the biggest employer in town. Everyone might not like the man but without him jobs would be lost. Even if he wasn't convicted, the whole ugly mess would damage tourism and the festivals. Then the place really *would* turn against Brigit and Colm.

Each new realization felt like a slap in the face. I wasn't built for this. Out of nowhere, beauty PR seemed heart-stoppingly appealing. The worst that could happen in that world was a bad reaction where a customer's face started peeling off or perhaps stockholders might lose some money. But this sad, grubby business had life-changing, reputation-destroying, liberty-curtailing consequences.

Give me sparkles, all things pink and fluffy and a page of bullshit about ceramides. *Please.*

Back at the Broderick, Joey parked the car. "We go in and see Kilcroney?"

"Wait. I need to ask you something."

"It was just a friendship. Well, the beginnings of one, so I thou—"

"Stop. Stay focused: what long-term outcome do you want here? Considering Brigit and Colm are depending on the goodwill of the town for their retreat to be a success? That's what I wanted to ask."

"Oh, I thought—"

I outlined my concerns about Kilcroney. "If he goes on trial, I'm guessing that Brigit and Colm will be blamed. Your consortium will get the very result I was hired to prevent."

"By then the consortium won't even exist. As soon as they discover the details of the fire, they're gone. Not pouring anymore money into a problematic venture."

"So Colm and Brigit are already done for?"

He paused. "There's another option. But if I cut a deal with Kilcroney, am I 'perverting the course of justice'?"

I did a quick google. "'Fabricating or destroying evidence, intimidating a juror or witness, intimidating a judge.' That's how you pervert the course of justice in Ireland. You're in the clear."

Joey's eyes flickered as he thought this through. "How do we know that Kilcroney won't do it again?"

"His remorse earlier looked genuine."

After more silent contemplation, Joey said, "We'll go in, have a chat, see what he offers. But we agree to nothing. Insist on a day or so to think about it. How does that sound?"

Courtney looked up from the reception desk, very alert. "He's in the back office." She beckoned us behind the counter.

"Courts." I stopped and held her shoulders, then indicated to Joey that he should wait. "Are you okay? Did—"

"—he find out? Yep. Told me to get out. So myself and Teagan are staying with Grinner for a few days. The two little fuckers stayed with Burke."

"And Ben?"

"Is 'giving me space.'"

This wasn't ideal. But maybe the sleepover with Ben had been the necessary catalyst to eject Courtney from her marriage?

"At the moment, though, there's more important stuff going on." Courtney nodded at Kilcroney's door.

In his office, Kilcroney was alone, at a desk, looking broken. "Rose called me," he blurted. "Lookit, here's the whole story." Tripping over his words, he said, "When the building began below at Kearney's, I saw an opportunity with Rose's place. If it looked like there was local opposition to Kearney's, the money men would pull out, so my project wouldn't have competition." Then he stopped. After several breaths, he said, his voice low, "I didn't know the Kearneys would be financially ruined. I'm deeply ashamed and that's the God's honest."

"But you don't have enough money to do the job," Joey said.

"I was hoping maybe the investors might switch to me and Rose when Kearney's Farm went wallop."

"*Jesus Christ.*" Joey's scorn could have burnt holes in metal.

"I've digital evidence to link you to the fire," I said to Kilcroney. "A private detective has found that the email threatening to burn the farm was sent from your home."

"S-sorry." He looked green.

My phone started ringing. Speak of the devil—it was Helen.

"I've more news," she said.

"I'm putting you on speaker."

"'Local Hero'? The IP address is registered to the home of Mary and Thornton Heffer, Shore Road, Maumtully."

The crime-writing couple. Mary's discomfort around me at Ben's dinner party suddenly made sense.

"Thanks, Helen. I know them."

After she'd hung up, I asked Kilcroney, "Do I need to talk to Mary and Thornton?"

Miserably he shook his head. "I paid them to post those things. I take full responsibility for every part of this."

"*Every* part of it?" Joey asked. "So you actually set the cottages on fire? And wrecked Mammy Walsh's car?"

"I did." Steadily he met Joey's gaze.

No one had seen this coming.

". . . Many locals think it was another individual," Joey said.

"It was me. Only me. Nobody else."

"Arson is a serious crime," Joey pressed. "Carries a lengthy prison sentence."

"I know. I'm guilty."

Well, that had thrown me. "What's the story with you and Nicolas Burke?" I asked.

"Twenty years ago I gave him a loan to buy his house."

"Which he repaid?"

Kilcroney shook his head.

"Okay, so a charge of bribery is added to the list." Although I wasn't sure if it counted as bribery if the money had been given so long ago. "Handy to have a local guard in your pocket, to do your dirty work and look the other way when you break the law. Who else knew what you were up to?"

"They're in no way to blame but I got Tipper, Declan Erskine and Vazey to steal the stuff, move their machinery and start work on Rose's place last Monday. They only did it because I promised them the contract. The responsibility is mine and mine alone."

Joey took a breath. "We're not committing to anything. But what's your offer?"

Kilcroney's eyes sparked with desperate hope. "Immediately making good all the damage out at Kearney's." He stumbled over his words. "Paying compensation to them. Bringing in extra men to make up for the time lost. Replacing Mrs Walsh's car."

"How would you get funds?"

"That second mortgage I took out on this place? I don't need the money now my mad skite with Rose isn't happening. Or I could sell the Big Blue—people are always wanting to buy it."

"Obviously we can go straight to the law with our evidence," Joey said. "And that's game over for you. If—and it's an if—we decided to give you a chance, what's the guarantee you won't do it again?"

"I've nothing like enough money to do it properly," he stammered. "I was in way over my head. It's all over, the whole project, such as it was. I swear to you. You can trust me."

"I don't trust anyone," Joey said.

I flinched.

"Tell me about Rose. Whose idea was it?"

"Was what?"

"Her giving me her sad story—how hard she worked, what a struggle it all was."

". . . We knew you had connections," Kilcroney blustered. "With investors and that. But there was no plan to . . . I don't know what you're getting at. It's true what Rose said: it *is* a struggle for her. She was just being friendly, is my guess."

Joey stood up. "We'll be in touch tomorrow."

Back in the lobby, he said to me, "We need to talk to Colm."

"And we should check out of here. I'll be down with my stuff in ten minutes."

61

In the car, on the way to Kearney's Farm, Joey said, "Anna, can we—"

"Just a moment. I need to make a call." I found the number. "Ike? Got a minute? How are people feeling? Generally?"

"Everyone knows what happened."

"How?"

"Because," he bit out, "They do. Small place, I keep telling you. Maybe Declan Erskine told his brother, who told twelve other people, you know how it is."

"How's the town taking it?"

"No one blames Hal. If anything happened to him, you'd get blowback. No one really blames anyone. It was just a clash between two businesses, that's how people are seeing it, nothing to do with them. No one—except maybe Burke—likes what was done to the Kearneys. But because Kilcroney was behind it, they're fine to turn a blind eye."

"You mean everyone would be glad if the whole mess could be just magicked away?"

"That."

Could it be that easy? But for good or for ill, it was clear the town's delicate ecosystem would be damaged badly by a criminal investigation. Maybe pretending everything was fine was the fastest way to ensure it *became* fine?

"Thanks, Ike." Another call was beeping: Tipper Mahon.

"Anna." His voice was heavy. "I'm sorry. With every ounce of my heart."

"For what exactly?"

"I knew what was going on. I kept my mouth shut. Myself and the boys started work at her ladyship's while ye were paying us."

"Why, Tipper?"

"Dan Kilcroney's been good to me down through the years. Given me a lot of work. But I didn't know the Kearneys would be wiped out. I thought they were on easy street with their Airbnb and barn and that."

Scolding him wouldn't help.

"There's no excuse for what I did," Tipper said. "Declan and Vazey are mortified too, but I'm the gaffer, I made the decisions. We'll give back the double pay to the go-bo—to Mr Armstrong."

"I'll tell him. Okay, Tipper." I hung up and said to Joey, "Keep the insurance company out of this. Tell Colm to take Kilcroney's offer. That's the only way forward."

"I agree."

"What about Burke?"

"Nothing we can do. We touch him and the whole thing unravels. Not everything can be tied up neatly."

He was right, but briefly my impotence made me furious.

"But his wife did sleep with an Oscar-winning director," Joey said. "Maybe it all shakes down in the end."

At the beautiful stone and glass house, Brigit was back from Dublin. "Just for tonight." She looked heartsick. "I had to come."

Holding her tight, I said, "I think all the stuff here is going to be okay."

In the kitchen, Colm was plucking socks from a clothes horse and lobbing them into an overnight bag. He seemed more alert than previously.

"Queenie herself decided," he greeted us with. "She's having surgery on Wednesday morning. I'm heading up to Dublin tomorrow with Brigit."

"Wow," Joey said. "Are you okay?"

"Haven't a clue. But a decision had to be made. Only time will tell if it was the right one. So what's the latest? Out there?" He nodded towards the town.

"How much do you know?"

"Kilcroney, Rose Tolliver, Nicolas Burke, Hal Mahon. Hash, rain, fabric softener, remortgaging the Broderick. How'm I doing?"

"Bang up to date. Can we speak with all of you?"

"Brigit!" Colm called. "Lenehan. Come here!"

We gathered at the kitchen table.

"Okay," I began. "The bottom line is that Kilcroney's offered to fix everything, super-quickly. He swears it won't happen again. He says he's the one who did the fires, not Hal. Insisted, like."

"That's . . . noble?" Lenehan said.

"Also," I added, "on Thursday, he sent an 'anonymous' email, threatening to set the place on fire. Helen got proof it came from him. So, we've evidence, in case he thinks about starting any new nonsense."

"But how's everyone taking it?" Brigit asked. "You know, all of it."

"Ike says that people want everything to settle. Obviously they won't forget what went on, there's a lot of sympathy for you but—"

"—no investigation?" Colm said. "What do you think?" He and Brigit exchanged a long look.

"Best way forward, I think," Brigit said.

"Aren't you angry with Kilcroney?" I looked from Colm to Brigit to Lenehan.

"I would be if it wasn't for Queenie," Brigit said. "But she simplifies everything."

"Yeah," Colm agreed. "I just don't have the bandwidth to hate him. He had his reasons. Money. It wasn't personal."

"If the retreat can still go ahead without anymore hate, we can keep our energy for Queenie," Brigit said. "I'll take that. With pleasure."

"Okay. Sorted," Lenehan said. "I'll start dinner."

"Did you two check out of the Broderick?" Brigit asked Joey and me. "Anna, you can have Queenie's room. Joey, we'll put you in Sully's."

I helped Lenehan make dinner, did a load of washing and scrubbed the kitchen. Joey went around the house, changing light bulbs and remote-control batteries, then ironed freshly laundered clothes for Brigit and Colm to pack.

Around 10 p.m., the five of us took a break and Brigit opened a bottle of wine. Halfway through my first glass, I had to go to bed, where I plunged into sleep, like a stone tumbling off a cliff. Most nights, my aging bladder woke me a couple of times but nine hours later, when I woke, I hadn't moved an inch.

Queenie's room was washed with shy, buttery light. Unmoving, I lay in the yellow glow, while chunks of information assembled themselves for me.

It was time to put on my big girl's pants. Even though I wasn't at all keen on the expression—did they mean my big girl underwear? Or my big girl's trousers? I preferred to put the situation another way: it was time to be painfully brave.

These were the facts: Joey and I had an undeniable connection but we were never going to work. One of us always ended up devastated and this time it was me. But I'd got over him in the past: I'd get over him again.

Joey and Rose? I had no idea what it was—a friendship, a flirtation—but it was definitely something. Joey liked Rose; at least he had until he suspected she'd been using him. And it was that—Joey's mistrust of everyone—which was the most important thing, because it was partly my fault.

I wanted him to be happy.

Downstairs, no one was up. I took a coffee and sat outside. Droplets of dew still clung to the grass.

"Hey." Joey was at my side. "Can I join you?"

"Sure."

"So beautiful here," he said. "Especially at this time of day. Anna, can we talk?"

Our eyes met. "Joey, you owe me nothing."

"Rose and I went to a classical concert in Galway on Sunday. That's all."

"Joey." I had to swallow. "Yesterday, watching you implode when you thought Rose had only pretended to like you, it was . . ."

He paled. "Okay. Right . . . I thought she and I had a connection."

This wasn't news. Painful as it was to hear, it was healthy he'd admitted it.

"You'd checked if she had planning permission because you thought she had another motive for being friendly? Do you do that with everyone who's nice to you? Because that's a hard way to live."

He took a big breath. "Anna, you might not get this because people tend to like you. Me, I just make them uncomfortable. First I was Narky Joey, now I'm that flash fuck from Dublin, the go-boy." He looked pained. "Remember, on Friday evening in your room in the Broderick? Margaret and your mum were mortified sitting next to me. Same at the karaoke. Apart from Luke and Rachel, everyone scattered, getting as far away as possible.

"But Rose seemed interested in *me*. We liked some of the same things, especially music. We had good chats, it felt . . . yeah . . . *good*. Then to discover it was only because she was scouting out a finance stream? That hurt. I felt . . . so stupid."

"You're wrong though," I said. "She knew what your job was, but she enjoyed being with you. She *said*."

"It wasn't anything romantic."

I wasn't sure that was true. "You've had trust issues for a long time. You said it yesterday to Kilcroney: you don't trust anyone."

"It's just how I am."

"It's not, though. Stuff has made you that way. Joey, staying away from love, sex, whatever you want to call it, I get what you said about it making you feel bad. But you're lonely." Carefully, I ventured, "The therapy you did with Elisabeth was helpful? Maybe you could try it again?"

302

I expected he'd scoff at the suggestion. But he surprised me by saying, "I mean, *maybe*. The man, Trevor's his name, said I could come back if I ever needed to. So, maybe."

"*Yes*-ee. Joey, you've checked out of an important part of life. You should be going on dates—"

"Wait. Stop. So what was Saturday night about for you?"

"It's obvious how I felt. But I'll survive."

He nodded and, even though I'd forced this, a part of me died.

"Do you think we could be friends?" he asked.

I shook my head. "At least one of us always ends up in bits. We need to give up on it. Us. Trying to make it happen."

"You know I really care about you?"

"Oh Joey, I really care about you too. But we're not good for each other."

"I'm sorry." He sounded choked.

"Please, Joey, just be happy. Promise you'll try."

"I promise I'll think about going back to Trevor. I 'heard' what you said. I respect it. I'll do what I can. Okay?"

"Sure." But it was no longer my concern. "So will we drive into town now and tell Kilcroney he's in the clear?"

"Let's go."

62

Kilcroney was pathetically grateful there would be no investigation. He made promise after promise that the repair work would begin this very morning, that it would be even better than before and that a "brand-new Honda Civic" would be with Mum early the following week.

Back at Kearney's, Brigit was cooking breakfast. "How did it go? All okay? Thank God." She sagged with relief. "Jesus, this has been horrific."

"I think it's over now," I said. "I mean, the stuff with the retreat."

"And as long as Queenie gets through this, we'll manage?"

"Of *course.*"

"Colm and I are heading off after breakfast. You want a lift to Dublin? Seeing as you're without a car?"

"Brand-new Honda Civic coming soon. But a lift would be great." I turned to Joey. "That okay? You don't need me here any longer?"

"No. I guess not . . ."

"Call Colm and Lenehan there, would you?" Brigit was sliding rashers and sausages onto plates.

God almighty, it was fried things, lots of them. "Just toast for me," I said quickly.

We all sat. The others began horsing into their disgusting breakfasts, then *talking* about them. We got chapter and verse on where the sausages hailed from, then a long story about the Dutchman who sold the eggs.

I tried to zone out and keep down my toast.

"Anna," Brigit said. "Whatever happens tomorrow, Queenie's recovery will take a while. Colm and I need to focus on that. So would you work for us?"

"Oh!" This was unexpected. "Doing what?"

"Two main things," Brigit said. "One, keeping an eye on the mood of the town, seeing if it all quietens down. Dealing with any new quibbles that might come up."

I'd be glad to do that, I realized. Leaving before seeing proof that there was no lingering rancor was making me anxious.

"Second part would be working with Lenehan on the Airbnb and barn hire. We've five yoga retreats in the next couple of months, plus a wedding coming up after Easter, and my head has never been less in the game."

"I've no experience of yoga retreats or weddings."

"You could do it in your sleep. You're an organizer, Anna."

"I might look like I'm twelve"—Lenehan flashed a smile—"but I'm all over it. Just, it's too much for one person."

"How would two days a week sound?" Brigit interjected. "Your current rate, plus accommodation. Not the Broderick, but one of the beautiful cottages on Shore Road. Nothing to stop you doing interviews or other work on your free days. Rachel and the rest can visit or you can be in Dublin four or five days out of every seven?"

This wasn't a no-brainer. What if Joey got over his mistrust of Rose and they began swanking around town, a loving couple? Or what if I got too used to life here and could never hack it again in a big city?

But Brigit and Colm were in circumstances too awful to imagine and I could, in a small way, help. And like they said, it was only two days a week, I could still keep looking for a job in Dublin. As for Joey? Once again I silently repeated my mantra: *I've survived Joey Armstrong in the past, I'll survive him again.*

"Okay, thank you. Yes. That would be lovely," I said.

They were delighted.

"You won't regret it," Colm said. "From Easter on, the place gets busy. A million things to do. Great people come to stay."

"You've already made friends," Brigit reminded me. "Courtney, Ben, Vivian—"

"Steve?" Colm asked.

"The mad chef?"

Colm rolled his eyes. "He's not mad, just massively overworked. It gets easier in June because Kilcroney hires a couple more people in the kitchen."

"Wait now . . ." I remembered the nimble, mustachioed man who'd given me a basket of warm muffins. "Was he there the night of the fire?"

"That's him!" Colm enthused. "He's the best."

"After the surgery tomorrow"—Brigit crossed her fingers and muttered an incantation—"we'll have a better idea of how long we'd need you for. But look up the holiday homes on Shore Road on your phone there. They're gorgeous."

Six of them, set in a loose semicircle, looked like an old-fashioned village of whitewashed cottages.

"Only built two years ago," Brigit said. "Everything works! And the *view*. Looking straight out to sea."

The front door and window frames were painted a cheery red. Inside, slate tiles lined the floors of a large living room and kitchen. Upstairs in the eaves were two bedrooms, small and cozy.

"Wi-Fi?" I asked.

"*Excellent* Wi-Fi," Brigit said. "No one can understand why. Some sort of phenomenon."

"Ree did a school project on it," Lenehan said.

"Who owns them?" I didn't want it to be Dan Kilcroney or Nicolas Burke.

"Various people, all locals—Ferne O'dowd, Rionna Breen, Mr and Mrs Barzani, Ziryan's parents. Rionna Breen's is the one to aim for, because interiors are her business. High thread-count sheets, mattresses that won't trigger scoliosis . . . What do you say?"

"No scoliosis?" I managed to laugh. "How could I resist?"

63

Jacqui's house was unexpected. Detached and double-fronted, with a leafy garden and a shiny SUV on the gravel drive, I was *not* prepared for this level of solid respectability.

As I lingered outside, trying to find the courage to press the doorbell, it felt as if my actual blood was trembling. What if she still hated me? What if we were just too different now? While we'd been estranged there was always hope. But that could dissolve right here, in the unforgiving light of reality.

Before I'd even touched the bell, the smartly painted front door was opening—and there was Jacqui, reconfigured as a sexy yoga mom: glowing skin, shiny, swingy hair and long, toned legs in sleek leggings.

Color flooded her face, our eyes met and my heart hopped into my throat. The eye contact lasted too long to be comfortable. "I saw you coming." She sounded flustered. "I was waiting by the . . . So, ah, come on in."

As I followed her down the hall, she said, over her shoulder, "You look great."

"So do you."

"What have you had? Botox?"

"Oh my God, *yes*." Suddenly I was on more solid ground. "And fillers, Profhilo, whatever is going."

"Have you had the Morpheus facial?" she asked. "Sweet Jesus, the *agony*. Even though they gave me Oxy."

"You got *Oxy*? How'd you manage that!" We were in a beautiful, light-filled kitchen-living space, painted in Instagram gray.

"I know the right doctors." She threw me a wink, suddenly behaving like her old self. She pointed at a long table in pale wood. "Sit down. Will we chance a wine or stick to tea?"

I wasn't sure. Maybe some lubrication would help. But too much and things might get messy.

"Fuck it," she said. "I need the wine. Red, white, pink or orange?"

"Pink. But just half a glass, I'm driving. That's Claire's car." I nodded towards the front. "It's too sensitive and too fast. If I as much as take a deep breath, it accelerates like a rocket."

We hahaha'd weakly.

Busying herself with glasses and a corkscrew, Jacqui asked, "Have you had a thread lift?"

"No. I don't know why but the thought gives me the shudders."

"Yeah, me *too*. There's this woman I know, well, a friend of a friend, actually I've never met her but she was out having dinner with Paul Mescal's mother, or maybe it was his auntie? Anyway, one of the threads snapped and half her chin toppled into her dinner. Could you *imagine*?"

"Holy *smoke*."

As soon as Jacqui sat—close to me, at an angle—all the breezy chat about injectables dried up.

"Cheers." She touched her glass off mine. "I think?" Then, "Holy fuck, this is wild."

"Thanks for seeing me."

"Oh. Well. When Joey told me . . . It seemed like a good idea, you know?"

Right. Here we go. "So. Tell me how you've been."

"Good. Grand. We left New York, Trea and me, I don't know, twelve, thirteen years ago? I have a little boy, Ollie, he's nine. I got married to Ollie's dad, Griff. He's great. Really great. And Trea loves him. I work in guest relations in Arcadia—"

"That's—"

"—'the most expensive hotel in Ireland'?" She rolled her eyes. "It used to be, when it opened, was it five years ago? I don't know now. My hours are regular, which is what I care about. I have no idea how I did it in New York, all that late-night stuff. So what's going on with you?"

"I left New York in October. Angelo and I broke up. Officially, about a year ago, but much longer, really. Mutual. Amicable. As good as a break-up can be."

"Aaaand . . . ?" Out of nowhere, tension flared. "What's the story with you and Joey?"

"We were working together."

"Something to do with Brigit's spa, he said." Her face had colored up again. Oh my God, she was starting to cry.

"Sorry, I didn't think I was going to . . ." Fat tears landed on her hands. She jumped up, grabbed a roll of kitchen paper and sat again, a sheet of it pressed to her face. "Anna, you and I, we were so close. To me, we were nearly the same person. And you did the one thing friends aren't ever supposed to do."

Desperately, I said, "I didn't, though."

"He kissed you. You didn't tell me. There was an emotional affair. Whatever you did, Joey thought he was in love with you."

"There was no emotional—"

"You should have told me." She was crying hard now. She waved her sheet of paper. "I'm not crying because of him, but because of you. It would have been hard finding out about him with anyone. But that it was you was absolute agony."

"Oh, Jacqui . . ." Tentatively, I put my hand on her back.

"It reminded me of when we were in school, teenagers. The ones I liked always wanted you."

What?

"Remember Rozzer? He was one of the few tall ones. My choices were so limited. You came up to his knee and he still fancied you."

I had only the vaguest memory of a Rozzer.

"I'm sorry I didn't tell you about the kiss, Jacqui. I didn't want to hurt you. I was afraid you'd blame me. But those things happened anyway." As the memories of that time came back, I was also crying. "I was terrified of losing you. You were the only person I felt safe with."

"I know." She sobbed. "That's what's so bad. After Aidan died, I carried you, Anna. You relied on me totally. Then you stabbed me in the back—"

"I didn't—"

"—and you were not easy to be with, Anna. I don't know if you know that. You had this . . . face, like you were made of concrete. Gray, flat, you never smiled. You were zero craic. I started to think you were enjoying it, like, 'poor, tragic Anna'? Joey used to tell me that I was taking advantage of you and that pissed me off so much because, literally, I was the only person in your life. You didn't want to see anyone else, remember? Said you'd be no craic—that was for fucking sure! I thought it would be like that forever, taking care of Trea and taking care of you." She took a mouthful of wine, then stared sullenly at nothing.

After a long, loaded silence, I dared to ask, "Is there more?"

"Yes! Yes, there is. Anna, I thought you were happy to mind Trea, that it gave you a sense of purpose. Then, out of the blue, you're buying an apartment at the bottom of Manhattan, you might as well have moved to Pennsyl-fucking-*vania*! I'm wondering what's up, you start giving me pass-agg vibes and next thing, you're hanging out with Angelo—a Feathery *Stroker*! Anna! Then *you* start showing Feathery Stroker tendencies, like going to energy vortexes and other mad stuff. I mean, seriously. You go from being a craic-less slab to being a Feathery Stroker's moll!"

Painful as it was to hear, this was her side of a story which had several versions. *And* I'd forgotten what a great turn of phrase she had.

"I was like, Where's Anna? I want my Anna back!" She inhaled sharply. "Then! After the shit-show at Trea's birthday party, Joey fucking tells me he's in love with you. It's obvious now he hasn't a clue what love is but at the time all I could think was, There's poor tragic Anna effortlessly stealing this man I'm *insane* about. Insane being the accurate word." Tearful and red-faced, she stared at the table, breathing heavily.

In the silence that followed, I felt her every feeling. She'd wanted tenderness from Joey. Not only had he withheld it from her, the mother of his child, he'd given it to me, one of the two millstones around her neck. No wonder she'd been so angry. The mix of jealousy, betrayal and exhaustion would have had me lashing out too.

"I get it." I put my arms around her and squeezed her tight.

"Thanks." She snuffled into my shoulder.

Eventually, I found the courage to ask, "How do you feel about him now?"

She cry-laughed. "Last-man-on-earth stuff. Wouldn't touch it. Look, I wasn't doing so well back then. Having a baby is the biggest, maddest thing. My entire world had changed and I was wrecked *always*. Being a single mother, which I mostly was, was hard. I couldn't go out and have fun and you were, like I said, no craic. I thought if I could make Joey love me, everything would be okay.

"When I'd been back in Ireland a few months, I stopped being so mental. Me trying to 'tame Joey.' Doomed! Would I have even wanted him if he was tamed? Then I met Griff and he's funny and sexy, but not a sociopath."

". . . You mean Joey's a sociopath?"

"Yeah." Then, "Look, I don't know exactly what a sociopath is—"

"They can't feel empathy. According to Rachel."

"Oh, really? Maybe he's a narcissist, so. Or just a gaslighter. Whatever it is, it's not good." After more thought, she said, "Ah, look, what do I know? He'll never be my favorite person but . . . I suppose he does his best. Himself and Trea are thick as thieves. Full credit, he always tried with her. Maybe I was too hard on him in New York but I was sleep-deprived and craic-deprived and all I could see were the ways everyone was fucking me over."

"He always tried with Trea?"

"Well, yeah. Decent with money and she spent every second weekend with him and Gaz. Even when we moved back here, he flew over once a month and stayed for three or four days."

"You kept saying he was the worst dad in the world." And at the time, I'd believed it.

"But I was angry, heartbroken, off my rocker . . . To be fair, when I got pregnant, he told me upfront he didn't want to be a dad. I was *so* jealous of his other girls. Handsome Karl wanted to bone me day and night and I hated him because he wasn't Joey. And I was always so tired and you—"

"—were a craic-less slab and a millstone around your neck."

Jacqui paused, unsettled. "I shouldn't have said that. Oh, Anna, I'm sorry. Thing is, back then I didn't understand how it was for you. But my dad died six years ago—"

"I heard. I'm sorry. I wanted to send a card but—"

"—and I get it now, how it is when a person dies, it's not like it looks in the movies. You've no choice about what feelings come for you. You can't just decide to stop being mental."

Then she said, "Go on. Your go now. I'm having another wine. You sure you don't want one?"

"Certain." This was potentially volatile. A quick getaway could become necessary.

Nervously, I began giving my side. "I became . . . resentful that you thought I was always on call for Trea—"

"—I was giving you something to do!" Then, "Sorry. I'll keep my mouth shut. Keep going."

"But you're right, for a long time, I *was* glad to have something to do. When I started to change, I was too scared to tell you. Too tired, too full of grief and guilt, too lots of things. I wish I could have been different." Then I blurted, "Jacqui, I'm so sorry about Joey. Hand on heart, at the time, I swear I had no interest in him."

"But you were mad about him when we first went to New York."

"That didn't last. And after Aidan died . . ." I shook my head. "It was years before I could think about another man and when I was able, it had to be Angelo, because he was such a . . ."

"Feathery Stroker?"

I actually laughed. "Exactly. Honest to God, he was exactly what I needed. But the thing is, I *did* care about Joey. I felt . . . so sad for the younger him. And kind of buried in me was this idea that if he could be a perfect version of himself—you know, not terrified of commitment—then I'd let myself fancy him. But he couldn't, so I didn't."

She studied me. "Did you know he fancied you? How could you not? He told me he was in love with you."

"And you said he doesn't know what love is."

"Ah, maybe he does," she conceded. "He loves his many, *many* children."

For no reason, I found that extremely funny.

"Speaking of which, have you met Elisabeth? Oh, Anna! She's so jolly hockey sticks. You think you were no fun after Aidan? Ha! You could have taken lessons from Elisabeth. First time I met her, I wanted to have Joey sectioned for his own good."

I snorted with laughter. No one was as funny as Jacqui. *No* one.

"I will *never* understand what he saw in her. She's got the longest face on Planet Earth, her chin is down to her actual belly button. And her clothes! Anna, it's a literal crime. All that money and she dresses like a Quaker from the 1700s. Only thing she's missing is one of those giant buckled hats."

It was so mean but I couldn't stop laughing.

"She's so *prissy*. And she tried her best to make him prissy too." In strangled, polite tones, Jacqui said, "'Och, Joseph, sit up straight.' 'Och, Joseph, will you say grace'?"

I was almost crying with laughter—a release of tension as much as amusement.

"By Christ, she took no shite from him, though!" Jacqui said. "I think that's what he *really* liked. He likes them bossy." With a smirky side-eye, she said, "You were bossy with him, weren't you?"

"Not on purpose. Only trying to persuade him to do what you wanted."

"So what's going on with the two of you now?"

If my friendship with Jacqui were to resume, it had to be built on honesty. "I'm . . . ah . . . mad about him."

She swallowed hard and held up a finger. "Wait! Just checking my feelings. Small twinge but . . . looks like it's gone. If you're here looking for my blessing, go forth and let him rail you."

"He won't."

"What? Rail you?" She rolled her eyes. "Is he still at that no-hookups madness? He's over-correcting, that's his problem."

"Jacqui?" I took a breath. I'd never told another person what I'd done. Not Rachel, not Angelo, nobody. My own shame had kept me silent. But a strong urge to protect Joey had been in the mix: he'd been so humiliated. "I did something terrible to him about eight years ago."

"Tell me."

So I did.

"Was that such a bad thing to do?" Jacqui asked when I'd finished.

"Yes!"

"But . . . you know what he was like then. Shagger McShagger."

"I hurt him—"

"Good enough for him!"

"—now he doesn't trust me—"

"Taste of his own medicine!"

"—and he probably never will."

"Right. I get you. Oh, Anna, what a mess. And tell me about this woman in Maumtully. Rose?"

I pounced. "You know about her?"

"He mentioned they were at some classical thing together on Sunday. What's she like?"

"Two words: Hermès scarves."

Jacqui used her two index fingers to make a cross. "This is baaaaad."

"She's polished. Ladylike. Cultured. Posh."

"He loves those posh ones." Jacqui shook her head. "What a *weird* kink."

As I began to cry, it was Jacqui's turn to do the comforting. "Oh, I'm sorry, babe."

Through my tears, I said, "Did you ever think we'd see the day? You letting me cry on your shoulder about Joey Armstrong."

"Welcome to the club. What took you so long?" Then, "I really missed you, Anna. I missed you the way you used to be. But I even missed you being a concrete slab."

"I missed you too. To put it mildly."

"I have other friends now. But none of them are . . ." Her voice began to wobble again. ". . . you. I got over him. But I never got over you. I'm so happy you're here." She looked up, her red, tear-stained face unexpectedly jubilant. "You and Joey working together, maybe the purpose—cosmically, like—was to bring you and me back together."

"Actually, it coul—"

"Anna, stop, I'm pretending to be a Feathery Stroker."

"I know, I know." I was as gleeful as she was. "You're the absolute best. I fucking *love* you!"

After that, I didn't stay for much longer. "We need to manage our energy here," I told her.

"You're probably right. But you'll come back?"

"Of course."

On a total high, I drove to Margaret's, went straight to bed and slept for thirteen dreamless hours. The following day, I was woken by Jacqui ringing.

"Anna?" she croaked. "Are you destroyed?"

"Oh God," I whispered. "Completely. Every bit of me hurts."

"It was a lot," she said. "Yesterday. Wasn't it?"

"But a good 'a lot.'"

"Totally. *Any*way." She was suddenly cheerful. "You and me, we're back in business. When can you come again? You have to meet Trea, Ollie and Griff. And I'll come to M'town. I'm going to fix you up with some man—"

"Oh, Jacqui, noooo."

"Oh, Anna, yesss! Soon it'll be: Joey who? You'll see."

64

"There's movement in her legs and some sensation," Brigit said, over the phone. "Everyone's 'cautiously positive.'"

"This is good news," I said. "Really, really good news." Wasn't it?

"Time will tell." Brigit sounded so tired. "But listen, can you stick around in M'town until the end of June? We could really do with you."

Three months was longer than I'd expected but a combination of compassion and a swollen ego made me agree. Three days later Claire drove me back, with a carload of my possessions. It was only a week since the fire, the longest few days I'd ever lived through.

As promised, Rionna's cottage was a gem—the furnishings were beautiful, the Wi-Fi was indeed a wonder and the ever-changing view of the sea was mesmerizing.

But it was outside the town, a little further from the main drag than I'd realized. Which wouldn't matter if I had a car but Mum hadn't let me borrow her shiny new one because "look what happened the last time."

However, Rionna's cottage came with a bicycle. Four, in fact. "Mine" was yellow, had daisy stickers along the handlebars and a deep wicker basket on the front. The thought of cycling into town in the sunshine, my hair streaming behind me, to buy freshly baked bread and just-picked tomatoes, appealed greatly.

Claire had elected to stay for my first night. But when we cruised into Main Street looking for kicks, most of the restaurants, even some of the pubs, were dark and silent. The un-poxy pizza place had a sign saying it would reopen on Holy Thursday but several others gave no information at all.

"What the hell?" Claire said. "It was so fun last weekend! Is it not like that all the time?" Her tone implied that, as a native, I should have answers. "We'll have to go to the Broderick for toasted sandwiches."

"No, Claire, no, please. I don't want to see Kilcroney."

"Building bridges, babes. Got to be done."

Fuck it. She was right.

Lyudmila was at reception. "Where's Courtney?" Claire asked.

"Night off. Watching *Ireland's Fittest Family* with Teagan and Grinner. You want toasted sandwich? Go on inside. I will do."

Claire and I were literally the only people in the lounge. Then, holy smoke, here came Kilcroney, carrying a small table.

"Anna. Claire." He was neither friendly nor unfriendly, just business as usual. "Keeping well? Good."

It was done now, meeting him for the first time since all the drama, and it had been fine. Maybe we actually could all move on from this?

"Let's text Courtney!" Claire was looking for a night out. But Courtney had enough going on without Claire Walsh pouring drink down her throat then bundling her into a taxi to go dancing in Galway.

"No. Courtney's mid-crisis."

Claire was shocked. "So we just . . . go back to the *house*?"

"Yes. Sorry."

That night, between Rionna's quality sheets, I dreamed I was running through a deserted hotel, looking for Joey. Up and down stairs, along corridors, I was pushing open doors, searching rooms, all of them empty. He was gone and gone forever. I woke up, desolate.

I got back to sleep but woke again, to the sound of rain thundering onto the roof, loud enough to wake the dead. I wondered if Hal was up on the cliffs, dancing around in his pelt, drinking bottles of port, seeing as it was perfect weather for it?

It was a relief when it was finally time to get up.

Downstairs, Claire was situated at the window, watching askance as torrents continued to fall. "Now that's what I call rain!" Her tone was bright. Too bright. Then it all fell apart. "I didn't sleep a fucking wink. What's the story with the weather? Fuck's sake, should we start building an ark? So lookit, I'm going to head home."

"Already?"

"Yeah, you know . . . My hair doesn't thrive in this weather."

"Ooookay."

She grasped me by the shoulders and said, "You are a brave, amazing, resourceful woman and I have enormous faith in you."

. . . What does she mean?

She'd picked up her LV wheelie and when she opened my red front door the racket of the rain was remarkable. "*Every* faith!" She darted into the deluge, slung her case onto the back seat of her car, then got behind the wheel.

Rolling down the window, she did a U-turn that had the brakes squealing. Calling, "In awe of your courage, babes!" she was gone.

Oh. Well. Fine. I texted Courtney, Vivian, Ike and Lenehan that I was back, put on Talking Heads, then set about unpacking. *Home is where I want to be.* After hanging up my clothes, putting my books on the bookshelf and unfurling my rug onto my new bedroom floor, I dared to glance out of the window. Christ alive . . . *we're in for nasty weather . . .*

I replaced two of Rionna's prints with pictures of my own, immediately swapped them back to Rionna's because hers were nicer, then sat on the exceedingly comfortable couch, staring out at the sheets of rain, thinking, *This is* not *my beautiful life.*

Nobody had returned my texts. I'd ring Jacqui! The thrill of being able to just pick up the phone to her would take a long, long time—if *ever*—to feel unremarkable. Which was when I discovered I had no coverage. This was . . . inconvenient. Still, I had Wi-Fi, so I WhatsApp'd her. Then I did the M'town people, in the hope that their Wi-Fi would work long enough for them to read my messages. *Transmit the message to the receiver. Hope for an answer someday.*

Feck this, no more Talking Heads: they were narrating my life in a way I didn't like. Silence was safer.

. . . Why were no cars passing by? Where *was* everyone? I should go into town, see who I'd bump into?

. . . It was only then that I understood what "not having a car" meant, when the weather was this bad. *That's* what Claire had been telling me.

I was alone in this house, with no phone signal, unsure of how far I'd have to go before I found another living human. I was . . . trapped.

Trapped was a big word, though. *Histrionic.*

But also *apt.*

I could do nothing but dwell on things. Too much had taken place, too much loss and love, Joey and Jacqui, the Kearneys and Rose, Queenie, Hal . . . I hadn't landed yet on solid ground.

Thoughts of Joey just would not stop. Knowing that he and I would never work triggered spikes of panic—I'd have given ten years of my life for things to have played out differently.

Even at his most narky and me at my most cautious, we'd had something, even if it was just sexual chemistry. But for a long time I'd known there was more to him than just bad-tempered hotness. We'd brought out a tenderness in each other.

The scar tissue from old hurts had us stymied, though. And wishing wouldn't change anything.

My phone beeped and I threw myself at it. Jacqui! **At work, I'll call later.**

Good. Great. Thank God. Wait now . . . ? Far out to sea, the sky appeared to brighten. Astonishingly quickly, the rain stopped and the sun appeared, shining sheepishly. *You're forgiven, you're so forgiven!* Zipping myself into Margaret's anorak, snapping a bicycle clip onto my shin, I hit the road.

It had been a long time since I'd cycled a real bike but as they say . . . except it wasn't true: riding a bike is *not* like riding a bike. Balancing was much trickier than when I was fifteen. I was grateful I didn't have an audience.

Considering I used to be such a whiz on the Peloton, real cycling was surprisingly hard work. Huffing and puffing, my thigh muscles on fire, I made slow progress. But the Applegreen forecourt at the edge of town was in my eyeline when out of nowhere, a new deluge began, this one accompanied by a blustery wind. Trying to control my bike was like trying to persuade a skittish horse to attempt Becher's Brook. I literally could not move forward. The bike wobbled all over the road, only happy when I fell off.

Drenched, I had no choice but to return home. With the wind behind me, I got to the house in seconds, so there was that.

A couple of hours later, the steady downpour tapered off again, then stopped. The light cleared and the sun broke through, all smiles. There was every chance that nature was playing the same cruel trick as earlier, but, edgy with cabin fever, I stuck my bicycle clip back on and once more ventured forth. Just as I passed the halfway mark, the downpour began again, heavier, wilder and blowier than before.

Back indoors, having used the last of the towels, I knew that nothing, not even Saharan-style heat and aridity, could lure me from the house again today.

I'd give it another go tomorrow.

Seriously, though, you could go mad from this.

65

Another bad night followed, where the racket of the rain did battle with the howling wind. In the morning, the milk I'd taken from Margaret's fridge had gone sour. Now I really had to go to town. While Claire had been here with her car, I should have filled the house with supplies. But yesterday morning I'd been blissfully unaware that "just popping to the shops' would be a major undertaking.

As weather-proofed as possible, I stood at the window, braced for a gap between squalls. When one appeared, I was out there fast, pedaling for all I was worth. Getting as far as Applegreen would do, they'd have the basics—and there it was! Still a way off but visible. Picking up my pace, something drew my attention to the horizon. Above the surface of the sea was a shaft of dark color: rain. And it was moving nearer.

In a purple-gray column, it scudded across the waves, coming my way, like it was personal. In literal moments, it had arrived, wet, cold and blowing me around the road.

It was like a time the wind blew my umbrella inside out, except this time I was the umbrella. My bike fell over, throwing me hard against the tarmac, bruising my entire left side from my cheekbone to my ankle.

If a kindly neighbor came running, asking if I was okay, instead of hopping to my feet, mortified at falling, I might allow myself to say, "God, I don't know . . ." *That's* how shook I was.

But the few houses along this stretch of shore were set back from the road; no one had seen me. As I lay, my face on the wet ground, I was doing financial calculations. I couldn't live here without a car, but could I afford one?

Slowly, I stood and, wheeling the fucking bike, with its stupid fucking daisy stickers and its stupid fucking wicker basket, I limped home. Where I couldn't even make myself hot, sweet tea because there was no milk. Or sugar. Or teabags.

That was the final straw. There was no option but to go back to New York. I couldn't live like this: lonely, unrooted, scared about money, wet, without transport, without hot, sweet tea and once again in bits about Joey Armstrong.

Except I had Jacqui.

And there it was: life gives, life removes, life shifts things sideways. Life reshapes, repurposes, files things away. Life heals, reveals, uncovers, all in its own sweet time. If I could just lean into the journey, I'd be okay.

For a moment, I knew it with such certainty that I looked around, expecting a butterfly. Nothing to see. Perhaps one had been on their way but had been blown off course and was now in Tierra del Fuego?

Or maybe I had become my own butterfly?

. . . Nobody in town had got back to me. The only conclusion was that the entire population had been killed off by a poisonous gas cloud. Not just all of M'town but the whole country.

In fact, I could be the last person alive on *earth*.

I actually scared myself so I called Courtney on WhatsApp. But her phone rang and rang. Courtney was dead. That was the only possible conclusion. Courtney *always* picked up.

Shite.

My phone beeped. Courtney had replied. **All going on here. The 2 sons kicking off. I'll give you a shout asap xxx Welcome back.**

Okay, Courtney wasn't dead. Vivian had never replied to *any* message from me. Ike no longer wanted to ride me so why would *he* bother? Lenehan, though? I was here to work! I emailed him, saying he should come over and get me.

Then he messaged—he and Ree were in Dublin visiting Queenie. He wouldn't be back until Friday.

Friday! Three days away! Could I last until then?

Sometime in the afternoon I had to go upstairs because the sea was getting on my nerves. Then I heard something . . . was that a car? Parking outside my house? I had a visitor!

A woman was at the front door. I knew her. She was . . .

"Augustina Mahon. You came to see Hal—"

"Yes! Hello, come in." A rush of joy almost toppled me. "Yes. Come in, Mrs Mahon. Sit down. I've nothing to offer you. Would you like tap water? Is Hal okay?"

"He's in bed. This weather would depress a saint."

"It absolutely would, Mrs Mahon! Isn't it awful?"

"*Awful.*"

"But is everything okay?" Why was she here?

"Ralph McIntyre drove past. Saw there was no car. Between that and the weather, I'd thought I'd come and check. Hal is too down in himself to text you."

Again I asked, "How is he?"

"He gets like this sometimes. The business last week with your mother's car and all, he was very upset. He's very sorry—"

"I know. No one blames him."

"He'll be grand in a while. It comes and goes. You never know when it's going to happen. Not like me. Every year as soon as the clocks go back, I'm bad. November is a wipe-out. But by February, I'm on the up again." She passed me a tin of biscuits. "Thanks for what you did for Hal, yourself and the go-boy."

"Oh, not at all. I'm just glad it worked out."

"Except Burke is still above." In the Garda station, in his job, she meant.

"But what can we do, Mrs Mahon? Some things we just have to suck up." I looked at the tin of biscuits. "Thank you, but there was no need. I really am sorry I've nothing to offer you."

"Will I drive you into the shops?"

"Would you? I'll pay for your gas—"

"Stop that nonsense."

"Where is everyone?" Aldi's car park was almost empty.

"Hiding out till Easter," Augustina said.

I got myself a trolley and roamed through the deserted aisles, throwing in anything I might ever want. Especially wine. In the crisps aisle, I saw one of Peadar Brady's boys—Jimbo? "Hi!" I exclaimed, delighted. "How's things?"

Jimbo nodded. "Anna. Mrs Mahon." Then kept going.

That was odd.

And when we finally got to the checkout, the lone woman on duty—Orla, if her name badge was to be believed—beeped my stuff through without comment. No assessing looks, no enquiries as to whether I was "The woman down from Dublin."

"Stocking up," I said, giving it some fake cheer.

Orla, giving the impression of a woman suffering from moderate depression, didn't engage. Unlike my first few days in town, then again after the fire, when I'd been regarded as a minor celebrity, no one was interested. I wasn't looking for special treatment but I craved *some* social interaction.

"Nothing personal," Mrs Mahon said, passing me her Bags for Life. "We're all in the doldrums."

Back in the cottage she helped me unpack, stayed for a cup of tea, then another. When she showed signs of leaving, panic nearly choked me. "Would you like a slice of toast?"

"I've to make Hal his dinner."

"Have some toast. I've Nutella! Or we could open the biscuits."

"You need a hobby," she said. "Do you knit?"

"I don't need a hobby, Mrs Mahon, I need a car. And for the rain to stop. And—"

"I do embroidery. It's a help, especially in the bad weather."

My mouth stayed closed.

"I'll pop by again soon," she said. "We'll see about getting you some transport."

"That's very good of you."

But maybe it would be easier to just go back to New York.

66

"You're not going back to New York, you headcase!" Jacqui said. "I'll come over on Sunday, it's barely an hour's drive and we'll—"

"—brainstorm?"

"Brainstorm? Are you mad? We'll get langeroo! I'll stay the night, drive back for work in the morning."

Jacqui and I seemed to have picked up the best parts of our old dynamic, as if we'd never fallen out. Only a fool would think we wouldn't hit *some* pockets of turbulence but hopefully we'd handle them better now.

I still got her, she still got me and, the best bit of all, she lived "nearby." (My perspective of distance had changed dramatically.)

"How can you even *think* of leaving now we're friends again?" she demanded. "You have a great life!"

I guess I did.

Even so, it was twenty-four more long, wet hours before I saw another human being. When Courtney arrived on my sodden doorstep, I almost cried with happiness.

"Oh my God, *come in*. What a surprise!"

"I messaged. You didn't get it? This effing place! Has the magic Wi-Fi upped and gone? No, no wine, Anna. All I have is thirty minutes."

"We'll talk fast. So tell me everything."

"Everything? You mean Ben? I haven't seen him. He said he was giving me space I didn't ask for. That was the last I heard."

This was disappointing, on many levels. Mostly the "revenge on Sergeant Burke" one.

"We can't keep living with Dad, his flat is too small and too hot. But Kilcroney's given me and Teagan a free room in the hotel, even though we're coming up to Easter."

"When's that?"

"Tomorrow week is Holy Thursday. Busier than Paddy's weekend. The rain might have stopped by then. Now, c'mere to me, did something happen with her ladyship and the go-boy?"

I felt myself go pale. "Why?"

"They were spotted in Galway Cathedral at some Mozart thing the day before the fire."

"They're just friends, apparently." My tone was impressively calm. "Although it's nothing to do with me."

"That right? The pair of you seemed . . ." Courtney thought about it. ". . . fond of each other. *More* than fond."

"But we've never been able to get it right."

"Oh, Lord." Now she understood.

"It's a long story, Courts. I'll tell you sometime. Right now though, I'm doing my best to not think about him, not talk about him . . ."

"I get you. I do. And I'm sorry—"

We were surprised by a rap on the door. We exchanged a look and went out to discover a small truck reversing in: it was Mrs Mahon and Hardware Ralph.

"I don't know if it's much better than a bike," Mrs Mahon said. "But while Hal is laid up, you can have his moped." Then, "Ralph! Can you get it out of the truck without having a heart attack? Good man."

As early as the following day, there was a change in the air. A lifting, a lightening. I began puttering about on the moped, cautiously at first, then with a little more verve. Passing through Main Street, townspeople raised their hand when they realized it was me. I bought myself an Americano from Catreen in Café Grumpy. The next day, when I crossed the threshold, she called, "Your usual, Anna?"

Work had resumed on Kearney's Farm; the progress was heartening. Hal was still out of commission but Tipper and his crew were hard at it, along with several other construction workers.

Initially Tipper and the lads were sheepish, but it passed. Rose or Burke hadn't been spotted around town but in general there didn't seem to be any lingering upset after the fires. Could it really be this easy?

I popped into Ferne in Fine Irish Knits, hoping the offer of a discount on something beautiful from Heather & Mist still stood, but she just wanted to discuss Joey and Rose's outing to Galway Cathedral.

"She's some operator," Ferne chuckled, with admiration. "It'd be no big surprise if she persuaded the go-boy to invest a ton of money in the Shithole on the Hill."

My stomach plunged. "He'd never do that. He's totally committed to Kearney's Farm."

"Who says you can't have both?"

"Because there wouldn't be enough demand for both places to survive."

"Look at me with my four not-very-different knitwear outlets," Ferne said. "And I'm thriving."

There was an unimaginable difference between jumper shops and luxury hotels but I decided to keep that to myself; my focus was firmly on a discount.

"Anyway, go on up to Heather & Mist and pick out something nice for yourself."

Hurray!

Lenehan came home on Friday and I insisted on starting work on Saturday.

"You're keen," he said.

It was more that I needed the distraction. While I was trying to get the hang of my new job, there was no room in my head for Joey. But it was a different matter once I was in bed, asleep. Last night, I'd dreamed that he'd taken off his T-shirt. Inked in enormous letters across his chest were the words I LOVE DULCIE. Who *on earth* was Dulcie? In the dream, I'd literally howled.

As promised, Jacqui visited on Sunday and inspected Maumtully with suspicion. "Nice enough," she sniffed. "But we've a marina in Banagher. And Banagher, of course, is on the Shannon, which is the longest river in—"

"—the world!" we said together, harking back to a time when some idiot frat boy insisted that Ireland was pathetically small, then Jacqui and I promptly wiped the floor with him.

News of more visitors arrived; Mum and Dad were coming for Easter. Very quickly, Helen, Artie, Regan and Helen's Best Friend Bella Devlin were also on board.

Bella Devlin was an issue: Artie's twenty-year-old daughter, she inspired so much awe, Anna Wintour herself would have second-guessed her choice of footwear. Bella Devlin's taste was impeccable. Every stitch she wore was designer vintage, courtesy of her mum Vonnie. But at least she was nice.

Absolutely lovely, in fact. Well aware of her privilege, she was deeply kind to the lumpen peasants. (By which I meant me.)

Next to throw their hat into the ring were Margaret and her family. Then Rachel and Luke.

No word from Claire, though. I sensed it would be a long time before she returned.

Margaret, Rachel and Helen all rented holiday homes near mine. Mum, though, wanted to stay in the Broderick. "I've no 'beef' with the man."

"You just want a freebie."

"How *dare* you?" Then, "Do you think he would?"

They could sort it out themselves, I decided. They were all adults.

On Good Friday morning, the sun glinting off the blue sea, Claire rang, greeting me with, "What the hell! Francesca and *Lenehan?*"

I almost choked. "What? Seriously?"

"They're a thing! She's on her way down in the car with Mum and Dad. Anna, it has to stop. I can't go back to . . . that . . . hole. My most stylish child can't possibly live there. She's even given up on the polyamory. Everyone else, their children are productive little dullards. But Francesca had so much promise. She was about to move to Berlin!"

"Lenehan's going there at the end of the year. An internship in some hospitality 'disruptor.'"

"What now?"

"Claire, come on. Lenehan is his parents' son, he's going to travel and live a full, fabulous life. M'town was never going to hold him."

". . . I thought he was just this small-town boy—"

Man! I heard someone—probably Francesca—shriek. *He's a man!*

"A small-town man, then!" Claire yelled back at her. The line went dead.

The weekend was a riot. The place was thronged, the rain gave us a break and the sun shone often. Easter-themed fun abounded. Ike, dressed as the Easter Bunny, led the Sunday-morning egg hunt with the same ill-will he'd channelled for the role of St Patrick.

I was *so* glad nothing had happened between him and me. At the time I'd been bouncing around like a sugar-starved child who'd been given free rein at a pick n' mix counter. One or two nights might have been fun but that's all I'd have wanted—and now that I was living here, it could have been awkward.

The subject was broached late that evening, in the Spanish, when we'd both had a couple of drinks. "I wouldn't have minded," he said, with a sidelong smile.

"Neither would I," I said. "But we'll just, aah, park it."

The very moment the last tourist departed on Easter Monday, a black cloud settled over the town. In a panic, I wanted to leave too.

Things got worse when Hal recovered from his bout of depression and needed his moped back. Dark, dark days.

Trying to lift my spirits, Augustina Mahon gave me an embroidery beginners' kit and an invitation to her monthly Sewing Circle. "Nice bunch. Lyudmila and Yelana, they put us to shame with their needlework. Young Ziryan comes. And Tipper's wife, Sinéad, but only to stay on the right side of me, because I'm her mother-in-law. Her heart isn't in it. Tell me, Anna, do I seem like a woman with a 'wrong' side?"

"In all honesty, Mrs Mahon, you don't."

"So we'll see you on Wednesday week."

"Yes, but—" No!

Being car-free would be my get-out, I decided. Then Pamela and Glen Custard Cream went to visit their son and grandchildren in Adelaide and loaned me their car for the month they were gone.

This meant I was able to whiz over to Jacqui, see this much-vaunted marina, meet Griff, Ollie and Trea, stay the night, get "langeroo" and drive back for work in the morning. It was wonderful. Griff was very easy, one of those level, steady people. Funny but mercifully not in a life-and-soul way.

Ollie, a walking encyclopedia, was sweet as could be but *terrifyingly* boring. It was his age, Jacqui said.

Trea was also afflicted with age-related personality issues. Tall, blonde and standoffish, she wore a disdainful smile as Jacqui and I reminisced about the days I was her babysitter. Jacqui said she'd be nice again by the time she was twenty.

The May bank holiday was the next high spot in M'town. Immediately afterwards came the plunge into depression. By now I was getting used to the rhythms of the place.

I'd only seen Burke once since the fire; he hadn't even looked at me. As for Rose, our paths had yet to cross. But they were bound to and it was important I behaved myself. Honestly, though, it was difficult to even look in the direction of her house. Which was insane. It didn't matter what Joey did or didn't get up to with Rose—or anyone. All that mattered was that he didn't want to get up to it with me.

But even in the troughs, good things happened. The Living Well with Dementia group finally got their minibus. The inaugural outing was to the cinema in Galway city, accompanied by Aber, Ziryan, Pamela and Glen Custard Cream and me.

Karina in Crowning Glory cut and colored my hair for a shockingly reasonable price. As thanks, I took her and the other hairdresser Gráinne for drinks in the Spanish, then the Boot, then McMunn's. ("I *miss* Grinner," I remember telling them. "Let's visit him.") Perhaps it was the alcohol or the company or my beautiful new hair, but it was the best fun. The following day I had a pleasingly excellent hangover. Now and again we all need a night where we wake up in flitters the next day.

One Friday, I messaged all my favorite M'town people, suggesting a post-work pizza. Ben, Ziryan, Aber, Vivian, Hal, Karina, Dr Muireann and Farrelly the Flowers showed up and we had such a good time we did it again the following Friday, then the next.

When the inevitable WhatsApp group was set up, Aber named it "Anna's Gang."

"It's not *my* gang," I said, but Aber insisted. "Before you came along, Ziryan and I hadn't exchanged more than two words. That first night we all went out, some mysterious disagreement between Karina and Farrelly got squared. Poor Muireann never came for a drink because of everyone looking for free, on-the-spot consultations. Now she has us for protection. You've brought us together."

Anna's Gang was undoubtedly a mixed bag, Farrelly the Flowers probably the most mixed of all. Unshameably nosy, he extracted the nitty-gritty of our lives while divulging nothing of his. All I'd established was that he lived alone, being "Too young" to settle down. All details of his actual age were under wraps; I'd have put him anywhere between forty-three and sixty-one.

And somehow embroidery had gotten a hold of me! One day I cared not a *jot* about needlework, the next I was clicking, clicking, clicking, obsessively scouring the internet for linen squares and silk thread. It did what weaving had once done for me: devoting two hours to sewing a leaf both calmed and uplifted me.

Augustina Mahon and I began to drop in on each other unannounced to shriek and coo over our latest thread delivery.

To my disappointment, nothing further transpired between Ben and Courtney. However, Courtney hadn't gone back to Burke; that everyone knew of his humiliation was genuine solace. When the IT company shut down their Galway office or the rainfall was once again torrential, the sad, head-shaking chats around town frequently ended with, "'Tisn't all bad. Didn't Ben Mendoza sleep with Sergeant Burke's wife. Shur, God is good."

67

Mourning Joey was a constant ache. But we all lose people we love.

Meanwhile, I was part of a community who cared about me, my family was just a drive away and—still mildly crazed with gratitude about this—Jacqui was my friend again.

Could I be blamed for an occasional bout of smugness about how well I was doing?

Then something happened.

A bright evening in late May, I'd just left my little house, heading into town, when out of nowhere, shock and sorrow winded me. I felt bereft, without knowing why. Patching thoughts together, it took several seconds to understand I'd seen a jeep like Joey's, driving in the direction of the Shithole on the Hill.

It might not have been Joey. But I had to go back inside and have two cups of sugary tea and a Caramel Galaxy.

For the next week I was haunted by now-familiar nightmares where, all night long, I searched for him in a deserted hotel, broken by my loss.

"Present for you." Jacqui dropped her weekend case on my hall floor, then passed me a small paper bag.

"You didn't have to bring anything," I said, obediently. "Your presence—"

"—is the present," she finished. "Yuck."

I foraged in the bag. "Condoms! How thoughtful. Thank you, Jacqui."

"By the time this Loaves and Fishes festival is over, I want the whole box emptied."

"I love your optimism but you haven't seen the state of the visitors."

The town was overrun with poets, "inaccessible" novelists and a certain type of actor, several staying in the five holiday homes around mine.

In fact . . . "Jacqui, *look*." Three men had just emerged from the house two doors along.

Her face, as she studied the men in their linen suits and striped waistcoats, was a mix of confusion and contempt. "What's with the straw boaters?"

"Some sort of crossover with Bloomsday? Haven't a notion, really."

Far was it from me to criticize Vivian but conceptually the Loaves and Fishes Feast was a mishmash. There were readings, fishing trips, bread-making and—God help us all— "feasting on the beach."

"Okay, forget them," Jacqui said. "What about mad Steve? Colm says you're compatible."

"He's confusing 'compatible' with 'short.' Two people being below average height isn't a good enough basis for a relationship."

"What about his mustache? Colm says it's magnificent. And you'd never go short of pains au chocolat."

"All true. Steve is nice, I like him." But I was off romantic entanglements.

"Hold on to the condoms anyway," Jacqui said. "Sooner or later Joey Armstrong's mickey will be released for good behavior. Think positive."

Now and again, she said this. Well intentioned, it was to reiterate that Joey would never come between us again.

"I do better when I don't think of him at all."

". . . God. Anna. Is it bad?"

"Yeah." I sighed. "Jacks, can we not talk about him?"

"Okay. Of course. Sorry. Right then! We're going down the town. One question: are we laughing *at* them or *with* them?"

"How about we mix it up?"

"Lovely stuff. Let's go!"

At the tiny dock, we watched barefoot, baggy-trousered thespians wobbling about in rowing boats as they scanned the waters for fish. When the "fleet" (all four boats of it) returned, Hal clambered out, red-faced from his exertions with his oars. We went for a toasted sandwich in the Boot, where we bumped into Aber, Karina and Farrelly the Flowers. This set the tone for an entire weekend of eating, day-drinking, reminiscing, staying out late, making new friends and laughing a lot, sometimes *at* the visitors and other times *with* them.

Rose was much in evidence this weekend, in the thick of the thesps. We treated each other to cool smiles, then looked away.

"That's her?" Jacqui hissed, staring openly. "Joey hasn't mentioned her. But I guess he wouldn't, not to me. They *could* be banging—"

"Oh, Jacqui!" I was in anguish.

"—but it's unlikely, is what I was going to say. Like, the *cut* of her. Literally poker-up-her-arse stuff? Sorry, Anna, I'll stop."

On Jacqui's last morning, I pleaded, "Don't go!"

"How about I come back in August with Griff and the babies *for a whole week*?"

"Yes!" I screamed. "Please!"

She opened my front door, about to stow her wheelie bag in the car. Outside the nearest cottage was a red-faced man in a linen suit; both were the worse for wear. When he spotted Jacqui, he boomed, "*Always in your mind keep Ithaca!*"

"Good spot, is it? Any designer outlets?" Jacqui let her case fall. Incapable with laughter, we clutched each other.

"*To arrive there is your destiny.*"

She stuck her head out. "He's still at it," she whispered. "Oh, Anna, best weekend ever."

I'm happy, I realized. *I'm really happy.*

Not long afterwards, when Brigit asked if I'd stay until the end of the summer, I, with a lightly tanned face and a heart overspilling with love for all of mankind, readily agreed.

Everything was delightful until I informed Courtney of my joyous state.

"Happy?" She sounded uncertain. "Well, enjoy it now, because we're all looking at a *long, cold, lonely winter.*"

68

Angelo was coming to M'town! With Ben's blessing, I'd shown his paintings to Angelo, who wanted to see them in real life. The week before his arrival was spent reassuring Ben that Angelo was almost irritatingly moral, that he would not offer representation just because he thought Ben's Oscar-winning name would flog the paintings. (Ben, like many creatives, once you'd scratched beneath the charming surface, was cripplingly insecure.)

On the night of Angelo's arrival, Ziryan, Karina, Ike, Aber, Hal, Vivian, Ben and I took our places in the Spanish. Right on time, in he came, triggering an epidemic of dropped jaws. I'd gotten too used to his look, but it really *was* quite the statement. As usual he was all in black: black shirt, black tie, straggly black hair and black suit, got up like a John Wick tribute act.

The Spanish boasted the coolest demographic in town—it was why I'd chosen it—but every single customer looked nailed to the spot. Even Dr Drew, who had spent eighteen months living in Medellín, was transfixed.

Angelo looked around with his mild smile and I was on my feet, swept towards him in a tsunami of fondness. The other customers clicked out of their trance and began to inch nearer, like a pint-holding zombie apocalypse. Just before they made contact, I plucked him to safety.

The familiar acquisitive light had appeared in Vivian's eyes: Angelo was in for some serious love-bombing. And if something happened with the two of them? Well, *fine*. If Angelo was happy, then so was I.

Vivian, however, was to be disappointed. Angelo spent three days walking the beach at Ben's side where, from what I gleaned, Angelo was his most wise, philosophical self. Eventually Ben was convinced and I got to see Angelo for his final night.

I picked him up from Ben's in Jimbo the tiler's truck. (Jimbo was in Morocco for a week.)

"You cause too much of a sensation in town," I told Angelo. "We wouldn't be able to talk there. We'll go to my house."

"Sure. All good. Hey! Why don't I cook for you?"

No! A flashback to the production he made of every home-cooked meal filled me with anticipatory tedium. Then I caught his eye. He knew and he found it funny.

"I'll make something," I said.

His look was meaningful and I cracked up. "It won't be just apples and protein bars. I've a toasted-sandwich maker now."

Over the months, the whitewashed cottage had become more me. "Nice." Angelo studied it. "Really nice. Cozy. And you look great." With his arms, he drew an arch around me. "Very—let me find the word—*unwound.*"

"That's just because I haven't brushed my hair in a week. Wait though, I do embroidery now! It's so relaxing. Let me show you! I'm doing these napkins and—"

I was halfway to my craft box before I saw the—yes!—anticipatory tedium zip across his face. Suddenly so much was clear. "I was really boring about my weaving?" I couldn't stop laughing.

"Passionate." He was very kind. "You were passionate."

"A monomaniacal looper, you mean?"

"Passionate." He was also laughing.

Abandoning my show-and-tell, I sat, facing him. "Tell me how you are," I said.

"I am . . . sad. And glad. Sad I'm not with you, glad that I am."

So far, so Angelo. I *loved* it. There was nobody like him, anywhere.

"Life without you has been . . ." He thought about it. ". . . interesting, I guess is the word."

"'Interesting' is what enlightened people say when the rest of us would say 'shite.'"

He laughed. "It hasn't been shite. Because it happened slowly, right? We grieved each other while we were still together, yeah? Well, hey, I did."

"Me too. Listen, Angelo, what exactly went wrong with us? Should we blame lockdown?"

"Is there any need to blame anything?"

"But we were so happy together and then . . ."

"Then? Go on," he twinkled. "Say what you want to say."

"It felt like you were always cross with me and always washing the bed sheets. Like, every time I saw you, you were marching past, a bundle of sheets in your arms."

"Yep. Fair."

Most people would go on the defensive. *No, I wasn't! Twice! I washed them twice.* But not Angelo.

"What was it about?" I asked.

He shook his head. "Nope. Nothing. Forget it."

"Tell me. I can take it."

"It was when we were pretending you weren't perimenopausal . . ."

Suddenly, I got it. "My night sweats?"

"You wouldn't see your gynecologist."

Now I remembered it all. My defiance, his concern and the many mornings I woke up, the sheets drenched.

"Important thing is," he said. "What happened happened, and we're still in that river, head above water, being carried forward."

"So wise, Angelo Torres! Tell me, are you happy?"

"Heeeey, you know my thoughts on happiness." Angelo insisted that every human remained forever incomplete. When we yearned for more status, money, love or stuff to make us feel happy, it was simply our empty place attaching itself to something tangible. Accumulating externals would never cure us. Instead, we should make peace with being unfillable.

"But my acceptance is pretty good right now. Tell me about you."

"I think I'm in the right place. I like this gentler life. Less money, less stuff. Good people around me. Especially Jacqui, she's only an hour's drive away. Well, an hour if you go in the middle of the night."

"Well, all right!"

I wondered if I should tell him about Joey. I settled for saying, "I've made so many mistakes in my life."

"Same—"

"There's plenty of regret and shame but none of it about you. But I feel sad that our part of my life is done. I'll never be that person again, the one I was when I was in love with you and you were in love with me."

"Yeah." He sighed. "But that's the curse of being human. To be moved forever forward, with no control over our direction. To rephrase Emily Dickinson: Because I could not stop for life, she kindly stopped for me."

"I don't know if I understand that." Quickly I held up a hand. "No need to explain!"

Another knowing smile passed between us. Angelo was a little *explain-y*. Or perhaps I wasn't curious enough.

It didn't matter though, because I loved him. For the briefest moment my body remembered the slow devotion he'd given me in bed, how he'd committed with every single part of himself.

But a time had come when I couldn't be bothered with the lengthy, intense production. When all I wanted was a quick in, out, lovely, job done, thank you.

"And the thing is, Angelo, I'm so grateful that we met when we did, that you—what would you say?—walked that part of my journey with me. You are the best, best, *best* man."

"Same. All of it. Back at you. Every single word."

69

Was that a car I heard? I stopped typing in order to listen.

"Finally!" Lenehan exhaled with relief.

Peering out of the office window, I saw the carload of four bump their way down the track, heading for the main road. "C'mon!"

Gathering our cleaning stuff, Lenehan and I hurried over to the Airbnb, where I speedily stripped the beds and he started on the kitchen. The countdown was on because another lot was due in three hours. Now we were into July, Brigit's Airbnb was booked back to back for eight weeks.

Flinging open windows, scrubbing the bath, mopping the tiles, it was fast, physically demanding work. After two hours of sweeping, polishing and emptying bins, then smoothing fresh towels, topping up coffee pods and placing a basket of Steve's scones on the kitchen table, the little house was finally ready.

Lenehan, his hair damp with sweat, took a moment to survey our achievements. "Legends, the pair of us. Onwards."

Back in the office I started again with my emails. I was variously: negotiating rates and quantities with a high-end wine company; trying to source well-seasoned logs for our wood-burning stoves; and wooing semi-celebrity yoga instructors. We were still about eight months out from the resort opening but every single one of these details, plus *countless* others, needed to be nailed down.

It was definitely work, but nothing like as stressful as my job with Ariella. And! I had a—*tiny*—side hustle. Teagan was creating her own skincare range. Its USP was seaweed, a "powerful humectant," she told me, with great earnestness.

The three prototypes—day cream, night cream and serum—weren't bad.

"Any notes?" she asked.

"The smell." It was ferocious. "The seaweed has to be dialed way down. Sorry."

"All right, back to the lab. By which I mean Grinner's kitchen . . . Would you like to help?"

Surprising myself, I said, "Why don't you come over to mine and we'll do it there?"

It was so much fun. Teagan would arrive with a box filled with oils, nut butters, artificial fragrances and steadily reducing amounts of seaweed and we'd play around with them.

"Sweet-face Walsh, happy birthday to you!" Farrelly the Flowers was at my door, two bouquets in his arms.

Without waiting for an invitation, he strode confidently into the kitchen. "These" —he set one bunch on the table— "are from the Mahon family, paid on Tipper's Mastercard, fyi. Just in case you were thinking it was only Hal and the mammy. These are courtesy of Gannon's Pharmacy. I hadn't heard you were a big spender in there?"

"I'm not. Just my HRT every month."

It was gratifying to see a whisper of mortification cross his face. The nosy article was usually unshameable. ". . . Ah, right! I've more stuff out in the van. But nothing at all from the go-boy."

I hadn't expected anything but, still, my stomach flopped.

"Had ye a falling-out?" he asked. "Lover's tiff, is it?"

"We were never lovers, so no."

"Weren't ye?" A pursed mouth, an assessing frown. "I had it wrong, so. *All* wrong. You know, you're looking great for a woman of forty-nine. Are you still getting the Botox?"

"Yep." I'd found a dentist's office in Galway where, once a month, a GP did cut-price jabs. I wasn't ready, not just yet, to let go of that.

Farrelly headed back to the van, reappearing with several orchids and other sundries, which he arrayed on the table. "The white orchid is from Ferne and Rionna," he said. "The yellow is from Pamela and Glen 'Custard Cream'—another of your private jokes, is it? The purple is courtesy of 'all' at the hardware place, I don't know why they say 'all,' it's only Ralph and young Ziryan, but I'm just the messenger boy. The pink prosecco is from Aber Skerett, the box of Lily O'Brien's comes with 'love and best wishes' from Peadar Brady and the boys. And this fine teddy bear is from . . . my good self! Many happy returns of the day, Sweet-face Walsh. Will we see you down the town later?"

"You will. With Jacqui and most of my sisters."

"'Most'? Who's snubbing you? The tall colleen with the coat? Lenehan Kearney's mother-in-law-to-be?"

"That's the one."

"Is young Helen expected?" Farrelly asked. "She's a funny character. And the babeen is coming too? Lovely hurling."

70

Early August brought two lots of glad tidings. Tiding one came via a phone call from Helen. "Great news! Mum's failed her eye test and been put off the road."

"What way is this news 'great'?" I asked.

"Her car! The Honda Civic that Brogue-face gave her? You can have it, she says. An advance on your inheritance. Like I said, *great news*."

Wait now . . . "Is she upset?"

"She's fucking furious! It's your doctor who's behind it, the prick who wouldn't give the HRT—"

"Lowry Riordan?"

"Him. She's writing to the medical council to get him struck off. Maybe Dr Propofol could give a second opinion?"

Dr Propofol was Dr Muireann. In April she'd given me a six-month script for HRT; as a result the extended Walsh family regarded her as a "Tame" doctor. Claire had wanted to ask her for Ozempic.

"Don't call her that," I pleaded. "She's incorruptible. I *deserve* that HRT."

"Calm the kaks, I'm only messing. The car is yours."

The second part of August's good news was that Queenie was coming home! Which meant that Brigit and Colm would also be back. I'd be surplus to requirements so decisions needed to be made. Try Dublin, to give the job search another go? Or . . . return to New York?

But within moments of Brigit tumbling from the car on her return, she'd grabbed me and muttered right into my ear, "Don't think you're going anywhere. We were always going to take on staff the nearer we got to the opening. Starting September, we'll be gearing up *fast*, we'll need you for three and a half days a week. Right up to the launch, which will be in March. Okay?"

Relief that those big, frightening decisions could be deferred, combined with the knowledge that my puny will was no match for Brigit's, had me nodding obediently. "Okay." Then. "Where's Queenie?"

"Here!" Taller than I remembered, her hair a mass of wild curls, she was hefting a big bag with ease. "Who's coming for a swim?"

"Everyone!" Colm declared, seemingly restored to the cool, confident man I'd known back in the day.

Beside the car, Brigit was crouched over a suitcase, unzipping it.

"Lenehan," Colm ordered, "Ree, Bridge, Anna, get your togs."

"But I haven't—" A swimsuit was flung at me.

"You do now," Brigit grinned.

The luggage abandoned in the front yard, we made our way down to the pebble beach, splashing and squealing in the cool, green water. Further out to sea, four dolphins were playing.

It was hard to believe this was real. Queenie was back. Queenie was *better*. Look at her there, drenching us all, laughing her head off.

Quietly, Lenehan asked me, "Are you crying?"

"Nope. Salt water in my eyes."

"Yep. Same here."

"Anna." Someone was at my front door, banging away like the house was on fire. "Basking sharks in the bay! D'you want to come out and see them?"

It was Hal. I tumbled off the couch I'd been sleeping on and opened the door. "Morning," I mumbled. "What time is it?"

"Nearly seven. Did I wake you?"

"Sharks?" Jacqui's son Ollie came thundering down the stairs in his PJs. "Can I see them?"

"No!" Jacqui yelled, from my bedroom. "He'll fall out of the boat and get eaten."

"I won't!"

Jacqui appeared in silky sleep shorts and a tiny top, her hair tumbling around her. "Morning, Hal."

"You're a fecken goddess," Hal said. "Telling you, you could start your own religion. Sign me up now!"

"Oh Jesus, don't encourage her." Griff came down the stairs after her.

"Lookit, they'll be gone," Hal said. "Who's coming?"

"Basking sharks don't eat humans," Ollie said.

We braced for a lecture on the natural world but Hal spoke first. "The lad is right. He'll be safe with me."

At that, Jacqui, Griff and I—even Hal—almost collapsed laughing. Nevertheless, Jacqui said, "Okay, he can go."

"Anna?" Hal asked. "You coming?"

"No." Three times in the past three weeks I'd been woken early to see the basking sharks. I wasn't exactly over them, but given the choice between marveling once more or another hour in bed, the bed won. Truly I had gone native!

"And Miss Trea?" Hal enquired.

More laughter. Trea never got up before mid-afternoon. M'town was overrun with teenagers who spent their evenings on the dunes, snogging, experiencing first love and getting langeroo on wine stolen from their parents' stash.

As promised, Jacqui and her family had come for a week, but because it was August, no holiday rentals were available. So Jacqui and Griff were staying in my room, Trea and Ollie in the small twin room and I was on the pull-out couch.

Despite us all being on top of each other, there was no snark, no pass-agg remarks about the last of the milk being drunk, etc. Jacqui was as fun and hilarious as she always was, Griff was no trouble, Ollie, though tedious if you got locked into a monologue on, for example, the mating habits of puffins, was a little dote. And I never saw Trea.

Except . . . that evening, just as we were about to go down the town for our dinner, she appeared, talking to someone on her laptop.

"You want to come for food?" Jacqui asked her.

"Nah. You do you." But her smile was nice.

I skirted behind Trea to get my phone off charge—to my shock the person on screen was Joey. I caught only a glimpse but it took a few days to feel normal again.

In general, I did a good job of remaining positive during my busy, *busy* days, but lying in bed at night, listening to the noise of the sea, I often fantasized that he was with me.

His absence was always there. I even missed the things we'd never get to do. One night, lots of us went into Galway (in the Dementia minibus) to go dancing. It was genuinely joyous—then my heart stabbed with pain that I'd never have a night like this with Joey.

But I was alive and life was long and new adventures would unfold.

71

At the end of August, the kids went back to school, Queenie repeating the year she'd had to abandon back in March. Seeing her mates move on without her, leaving her sharing a classroom with the "kids," made her cry.

There was a rush to reassure her that one day it would all even out, that she'd have friends of every age: information she refused to believe. I wished I could give her my rock-solid certainty but that's the thing about humans, we can't know until we know.

Moving into September, M'town had begun its post-summer slump into depression when news broke, so good it would have buoyed the *Titanic*—Courtney Burke had moved in with Ben Mendoza! It was official: they were in love and didn't care who knew.

Actually I'd known for ages but that fact I kept to myself because show-offs are never popular. Yes, it had been *me* who had counseled both Courtney and Ben through their doubts and fears. Courtney's biggest concerns were her two sons, who had allied themselves firmly with their dad. Ben's greatest fear was that Courtney would undermine any chance of her own happiness in order to placate the boys.

In the end Courtney had fixed on the position that life was always messy. "The lads want me to go back to their dad," she said. "Which, cold day in hell, like. So go big or go home, I'm committing to Ben."

Ben offered Teagan her own apartment within his house but she refused it, insisting loudly that Ben and Courtney deserved "a honeymoon period." Privately, however, she admitted she couldn't live under a roof where her mum was "getting drilled." Instead she moved in with Karina the hairdresser.

Meanwhile, Sergeant Burke quietly applied for a transfer.

Brigit hadn't been joking when she said they'd gear up fast, come September. A thousand different aspects of the resort suddenly became time-critical. Staffing was the highest priority but from the most luxurious facecloths to the perfect buckets for the Ayahuasca puking, there were countless decisions to be made daily.

I was working hard—we all were. By the end of the month, I realized I hadn't been to Dublin once. Was this . . . my life now? Six months in, was I a full-time resident of M'town?

One way or another, I knew I was done with New York. I made the momentous decision to give my tenants their one month's notice, then engage a realtor to sell my apartment. Next, I emailed my resignation to Ariella. Immediately I powered off my phone in case she rang and yelled at me.

When I felt brave enough to switch it on again, there were no furious voice-notes, no expletive-riddled texts or emails. Just . . . nothing. Which kind of said it all.

Well, excellent! I WhatsApp'd a general invitation for pints in the Spanish asap.

By the time I got there, Hal, Aber, Ziryan, Ike, Karina and Gráinne were already halfway through their first drink. Then in came Vivian, looking sultry, sexy and—hey, it can't be tiptoed around—a little grimy. The first night I'd ever met her I'd thought it was a consequence of her long journey home but it was just her look.

She pulled me aside. "Can we talk? About Rose Tolliver."

My stomach plunged. "What about her?"

"There's a rumor she's doing a solo run, still looking for investment for Tolliver Hall."

Alarmed, I thought through the implications. What would it mean for Brigit and Colm? Nothing good, surely?

". . . Aaaaaand." Her eyes twinkled. "If we put that together with the sightings of Sexy Man Armstrong up there a few times over the summer, what can we conclude?"

I felt as if I'd been punched.

Vivian meant no harm. To her, this was just a delicious piece of gossip. "What do you mean?"

The smile fell from her face. ". . . Hey, nothing, nothing. Just a stupid rumor, Anna, I'm an idiot, forget it."

She'd wanted me to conclude that Joey was putting a finance package together for Rose—oh, thank the Lord, Courtney had arrived.

"Just a sec." I abandoned Vivian.

"Anna." Courtney was concerned. "What's up?"

"Courts." In a low voice, I told her what Vivian had said.

"There's no rumor," she stated. "If there was, I'd know about it. No. Rumor. Put it from your mind."

But there was more. "Courtney?" My voice was hoarse. "Has he been spotted in town?"

"Few times." She kept her gaze steady but she was finding this hard. "Never for long. I didn't tell you because you didn't want to talk about him. Will we go someplace else, the two of us? We'll say you've your period. Again. It'll be your thing."

"I love you, Courtney."

"That's handy, because I love you too."

Back in my house, we drank tea and I talked myself back to baseline calm. "He can do what he wants, I'm nothing to him, he's nothing to me. But even if she was looking for investment, he wouldn't help her, he's far too loyal to Brigit and Colm. Isn't that right, Courtney?"

"Certainly is."

"And to be fair, he can do what he wants with her. He's welcome to come to M'town and I appreciate him keeping out of my way. Because I'm nothing to him, he's nothing to me." How many times had I said it already? "Nothing to me. Right, Courtney?"

"You're upset now." God love her, she was trying to wrap this up, she had Ben Mendoza to get home to. "But it'll pass."

"Of course it'll pass. Soon. Courts . . . how many times was he spotted?"

"Three, that I know of."

"And he never stayed overnight?"

"He'd be a bigger fool than I already think he is if he chanced a night under that roof. It's unstable," she added.

"You're the best. Sorry for keeping you so long. I'll be fine in the morning."

In the morning I wasn't fine. But I *would* be. A butterfly didn't have to put in an appearance for me to know that for certain.

Late September, Angelo broke the news that Ben Mendoza was to have his first exhibition on the last Saturday in November. The gallery chosen to host this cultural highlight wasn't a legendary New York hotspot but Brigit's Barn, Maumtully, Connemara.

I had concerns about holding a big event on the last weekend of November in a small town in Ireland. But Angelo said people would trample down the doors for an exhibition of Ben Mendoza's paintings, no matter where it was held. Not necessarily a good thing, he'd stressed. Most would be rubberneckers.

His plan was to invite art lovers who actually *bought* art: wealthy types who might consider this weekend the opening salvo in their holiday festivities, kicking off five weeks of vegan eggnog and keto mince pies. (Before the juice cleanses and face-lasering of January. Rich people had their own calendar.)

The exhibition would be opened by some Hollywood name. (Still to be decided on. Basically, whoever Ben could persuade to come.) The minute Vivian heard, she delayed her annual migration to Barbados by two months.

Angelo was across the list of international invitees but asked me to organize accommodation, transport, etc. The demands on my time were already brutal but, oddly, I felt that this extra work could be incorporated. All I had to do was *not stop*. Taking any break, even slowing down, would be fatal. But continuing to graft ten to twelve hours a day would keep all the balls in the air.

At the end of October, the clocks went back: it was as if a thick black blanket had been dropped on the town.

"I won't smile again until next Easter." Hardware Ralph trudged away, looking like a man about to take his shotgun down from above the mantelpiece.

The staff at Gannon's the pharmacy were run ragged, trying to keep up with demands for antidepressants. Even so, people just disappeared. Augustina Mahon was gone. Dr Olive too, although she'd be back in three weeks—that was her pattern, I was informed. Jimbo from Peadar Brady's tiling crew was another casualty.

Assembling the team to work on the exhibition, the last thing I wanted was to put vulnerable people under pressure. Luckily not everyone was prone to the seasonal low: Ziryan, Aber, Ike, Grinner, Ferne and Pamela and Glen Custard Cream were my excellent little squad.

Naturally, because we were working to a deadline, November sprinted by. Way too soon, the day of the exhibition was upon us.

72

"No more sparkle." I ducked Teagan's contour brush. "It's a daytime thing. I can't have a sparkly face."

"The sun sets at five p.m." Teagan was bouncing with frustration.

"So I might come back and you can sparkle me then."

"And do eyelashes? Okay. Stand up, gimme a look at you. Not *bad*." She hauled me to the full-length mirror.

I was wearing more makeup than I had in the whole of the previous year put together, my hair (courtesy of Karina) was in long, loose waves and I was very pleased with my dress, a low-cost purchase from Dunnes in Eyre Square. Teagan was right: I actually *was* "not bad"!

"Send Mum over," Teagan said. "She's in the barn."

To me, Kearney's Farm was always stunning. Even when it was stormy, I loved the soft greens and grays of the land and the wild churn of the sea. But on a calm bright day like today, the clear green water in the bay and the strange, wild landscape would lift the heaviest of hearts.

Brigit's barn was all action—Colm, Queenie, Ree and Courtney were flitting about, ferrying buckets of ice, uncorking wine, arranging water jugs. Ferne O'dowd had set up a discreet sales desk in a corner. Sully—recently returned from Bolivia—was sellotaping raffle tickets to hangers for the cloakroom.

We were doing well for time. It was only two forty and people were always late; the earliest arrival would probably be at three fifteen.

"Courts," I called. "You're up next."

"God, you look lovely," she said. "You should wear a metric ton of makeup more often."

"Haha. Right, lads, what can I do?"

"Tell me if Adam Driver really is coming," Queenie said.

A rumor was doing the rounds that he was launching the exhibition. To be fair, Ben *had* directed him in a movie about eight years ago.

"You know I can't tell you. I'm so sorry."

"Bad Anna," Queenie said. "Because you're so mean, your job is to check the bathrooms."

I turned to do it—and there was Ben. "You're not meant to be here yet!" I exclaimed.

His poor, doleful face made me smile.

"I couldn't stay away," he said. "I'm being held together by anxiety. Angelo here yet?"

Angelo was lost in transit. His plane had been redirected from Shannon to Cork, where no hire cars were available. He couldn't persuade any taxi driver to take him on what would have been an eight-hour round trip, so he was making his way via buses and trains. Brigit was aware of his progress but his phone was almost out of battery.

"Come on." I linked my arm through Ben's, leading him to the first painting. "Let's do a walk-through of your beautiful work."

"The press will savage me?"

We've already been through this several times. Se. Ve. Ral. Times. Then! Thank God, Angelo showed up.

"You're here!" I yelped.

Angelo gathered me into a hug, then moved on to Ben. "So sorry, man. What a journey."

"Was it horrific?" I asked.

"No way. Just unexpected. Got to see a lot of the beautiful Irish countryside. And those kids are great."

What kids?

"But I feel bad I wasn't here sooner for my boy Ben. Your first exhibition is a big deal."

"You're here now."

A ruckus at the door had me turning my head. Holy moly, Ike Blakely had arrived, along with his habitual mood. Which meant that so had the first lot of invitees; Ike had driven them from the Broderick in the Dementia minibus. They were ten minutes early.

Ike made an *eek* face in my direction.

"Boys." Urgently, I pawed Ben's arm. "Action stations. This thing is live." Then, summoning Ree, "The wine, good boy! Sully! The coat hangers!"

Where the hell was Brigit? We needed *all hands*.

Angelo and Ben descended on the eleven guests (the capacity of the bus). These, mostly New York collectors, had been a big presence around town for the past two days. A man called Merv was trying to give Ike a fifty-euro tip.

"No need for that." I smiled. "It was Ike's pleasure to drive you."

I pulled Ike away and hissed, "You're early."

"Why wouldn't you let me take your man's money?"

It was typical of Ike to go on the attack to avoid apologizing. "You're early," I repeated. "For the first time in your life, I'd guess."

"You think I don't know?" he said, hotly. "I got to the Broderick ten minutes ahead of time. I was afraid of being late because you'd eat the head off me. But Ziryan had them all lined up in their coats, ready to go." Ziryan and Aber were in charge of the "Town" end of things. "They're wild keen, probably for a bitta day-drinking." He looked around. "Vivian not here yet?"

Vivian, of course, was the minder of the "special guest." Who wasn't Adam Driver but a solid character actor called Gary Carradine. You'd know the face. He'd popped up in about a thousand movies, often playing a wise stoner. The response when I mentioned him had been, "Nope, never heard of the man." But as soon as they saw a photo, it was all, "Oh, *him*! From that thing, he was a pothead philosophy teacher. Funny fella."

God alone knew what they were up to right now.

"I'd better get back for the next lot," Ike said. "But Grinner McGee wasn't far behind me in the school bus."

Grinner had been an absolute star. It was obvious where Courtney got her work ethic from. As well as keeping McMunn's running seven days a week, he drove the yellow school bus, which brought the local kids into Oughterard. He'd volunteered his time and his bus for this weekend and had been back and forth to the private airstrip in Galway, as guests NetJetted in from around the world.

In view of what Ike had said about day-drinking, it was heartening that his busload had surged to inspect Ben's paintings. In no time, Merv was in conversation with Ferne O'dowd, who was in charge of sales. Next thing, a red dot was on one, two, no *three* of the works. That man was clearly bursting to offload money.

Lord above, Grinner was here already; it was barely 3 p.m.! His charges were "The Europeans": British, German, French, Belgian and Dutch art lovers, twenty-seven of them. Bearing trays of wine, Queenie, Ree and a couple of their mates were bobbing around them, like pilot boats around a ship.

What was keeping the food? Oh, thank *God*. Brigit and Steve had come in, which meant it was ready. Several of Ree's classmates shoaled away, then returned, bearing trays of miniature food; uptake was enthusiastic. Surprising—because rich people didn't tend to eat—but good.

"Courtney!" She had returned from the makeup station Teagan was running in the nearest cottage. "You look amazing."

"If raccoons are amazing." She assessed the action in the barn. "What the hell happened? They're here already?"

"Ziryan's fault, according to Ike."

"Everything is always someone else's fault, according to Ike." The cogs in her head were turning. She grabbed Teagan, who'd just come in. "Go over and help Sully with the coats. Wi-Fi password, madam? Of course, brigits-barn, all lower case. How can I help, sir? The restroom? Certainly." She scanned the people around her. Queenie was nearest. "Queenie here will escort you. Phone charger? Right this way . . ."

Several more red dots were scattered on the wall, looking like an outbreak of some benign pox.

Oh thank God, Ziryan and Aber had arrived. Ziryan could do eighty things at once. But if Ziryan was on site, so was Ike and his second vanload, which meant more people needing attention. Nearly all of the guests were present and correct—and Vivian had finally shown, Gary Carradine in tow. His impressively bushy beard sported a red streak that might be ketchup. Or could be Vivian's lipstick. Honestly.

Look at her, in spike-heeled shoes and an extremely short denim skirt, her long, pale legs bare. On top she wore a tweed hacking jacket over a beautiful lace blouse.

"Mr Carradine—" My hand was outstretched.

"Gary, Gary—"

"Gary, thanks. I'm Anna. Thank you so much for doing this. What can I get you to drink?"

"Ah, yeah . . . maybe a little . . ." He thought about it. ". . . sherry."

They can't help themselves, famous entertainers, they just can't. Even a B-lister like this man was so used to having his every whim indulged that they evolve past knowing how difficult they're being. In a blind panic, I was wondering who in town I could persuade to drive out here with a bottle of sherry. Nobody, that was who. Everyone useful had already been pressed into active service.

"Cool," I said. "Cool, cool, cool. Only thing is, we have none."

He laughed. "That's okay. How about a green tea?"

How about a glass of the red wine that's right there by your elbow?

"Gary!" Ben had popped up. "So good to see you, man."

"Benjamin!"

Even as we watched, Gary Carradine was finishing a glass of red wine, while reaching for another, then gracefully tipping that second glass down his throat and stretching to pluck a third from a passing tray. He was windmilling in slow motion and if I hadn't been worried that he'd be too drunk to do his speech, it would have been beautiful.

At three fifty, the Irish guests arrived. Unlike the rest of the invitees, they'd resisted every offer of assistance with transfers, accommodation, directions—anything that might have made it possible to keep tabs on them. They fell in the door, crowing mockingly at something one of them had said. Six people had been invited. Eleven had turned up.

Grabbing drinks, handing overcoats without bothering to get their ticket, they swarmed through the crowd, chatting, laughing, greeting old friends. At four thirty-five, when the rowdiness approached critical mass, I pushed through the bodies to reach Gary. "Time to start."

"Sure." He climbed the steps to the temporary stage, which had been constructed, free of charge, by Tipper Mahon.

"Courts," I hissed. "The wine."

"On it."

At speed, she insinuated through the guests, giving our wine servers a discreet shoulder tap: the signal we'd agreed upon to disappear the remaining wine. Ceasing serving felt disgracefully inhospitable but if our guests got messy drunk—and inevitably, with limitless alcohol, some would—they'd have a hangover tomorrow. Forever more they'd associate Ben and M'town with shame and nameless terror and we didn't want that.

On stage, Gary Carradine tapped the mike. In his gravelly, Hollywood voice, he said, "For those of you who don't know me, I'm Jeff Bridges."

We were treated to charming stories about how polite Ben was on set, how rare that was—what about that time Tarantino had threatened to kill him, haha—what a talented artist Ben was, no matter the medium. Proud to know him, proud to call him friend. Gary hit every mark.

Next up was Ben, who, despite his anxiety, was his usual charming self. Scanning the paintings, I couldn't see a single one which hadn't been sold. My shoulders were beginning to drop when I sensed a presence low down at my left side. It was a young boy.

Looking up, he said, "Hey, missus." Then grinned.

I know that smile. Hot-cold with shock, my head whipped around. Joey was at the back of the room, his gaze trained on me. Leaning against him was a boy, older than Hey, missus. In his arms was a younger child.

As soon as Joey's eyes met mine, he looked away.

73

I wanted to collapse onto a couch and gasp into a paper bag. I couldn't though; too many people were depending on me.

Ben's speech ended and the guests discovered there was no more wine. Naturally the eleven Irish people vamoosed "like shite out of a goose" as my dad would have said—the canny articles had their own transport arrangements.

Our overseas visitors weren't so lucky. Desperate to return to town to keep drinking, a free-for-all broke out.

"Hey! Can we go with Grinner?" Merv called, waving fifty-euro notes. "Sir, Mr McGee, can we get a ride to town with you?"

Ike had departed with one full busload of US people: somehow Merv had not been one of them, so he was trying to buy his way onto the "European" bus.

"Grinner!" I made *No, no, no* eyes at him. We had a *system. Go,* I messaged. *Go, go, go.*

Grinner fled. The only remaining guests were Merv and his crew.

"Merv." I intercepted him. "Ike will be back for you in five minutes tops."

"Five minutes?"

"Absolutely." It wasn't a *lie,* per se. I'd have bristled if I'd been called dishonest. But Irish people, we lapsed into our native tongue when we described units of time. "Five minutes' translated to "eighteen minutes." Possibly twenty.

I spoke soothingly but my thoughts were of Joey and his boys. There was no sign of them. Gone back to the town? It was the best thing because I was so shook. However, underneath that relief was a deep, dark disappointment.

Then Joey came out of the bathroom, trailing the three boys.

"—it's to dry your hands, not your butt," he was saying to Isaac, the mini-Joey. "If you sit on it, you could break it."

"He knows that," the eldest boy said. "He was just being disgusting."

"*You're* disgusting." Isaac launched into a series of running kicks, like a martial arts display.

"Dad." The youngest one pawed Joey. "I want a juice."

I watched Joey reach into the black satchel slung across his body. "Blackcurrant or pear?"

"Pear. No, apple."

"There's no apple, baby boy. Pear's nearly the same—oh." Joey saw me. He appeared shocked. God knows why, he *knew* I was there. Head down, he grabbed his sons and hustled them towards the exit.

Leaving without acknowledging me? Oh no, no, no. "Joey?" My tone was sharp.

"Uh, hey, Anna."

"Exactly, yes, *hey*." I felt sore. "What are you doing here?"

"I'm sorry. It was a long drive—by the time we got here, we all needed a runabout. We should have left immediately. I'm sorry."

What was he talking about?

"We wanted to see." The tall, dark-haired one was concerned. "It's our fault. Sorry."

"Sorry," Zeke whispered.

"Sorry." Isaac didn't sound it. But I had no idea what he was apologizing for, so did it matter?

Joey's sons seemed keen to shoulder the blame for some mystery transgression and that wasn't cool. They were only kids.

"Hi." I smiled at the eldest. "You must be Max."

Politely, he asked, "How do you know?"

"I can read minds."

His smile was withering. "Who are you?"

"Boys." Joey cleared his throat. "You know Regan? Anna is her auntie."

"I know Regan." Isaac was twirling in a circle.

"She knows you too, Isaac."

It was the maddest thing but after the Paddy's Day weekend, Joey and Regan had "stayed in touch." By which I mean, Regan had pestered Helen day and night to remind Joey she'd been invited to Zeke's birthday party. Joey made good on his promise so Regan—and Helen, of course—had gone.

On her return Regan was besotted with Isaac. "That boy is a disgrace," she told me. "His mama told him not to go in the garden and he went in the garden! His sneakers got muddy and he ruined her good, clean floor!"

Staring dewy-eyed into the middle distance, she repeated, her voice faint, "He's a disgrace."

I had sighed long and hard at having to witness a second generation of Walsh women falling for those Armstrong boys, then waited for Helen to describe Elisabeth's house.

"Anna, it was GOD AWFUL. Everything was a weird pink-beige color, what they used to call 'flesh-tone' before the people who make underwear realized not everyone is white. It was like being inside a giant plaster. The telly was kept in a cupboard. So was the toaster. Have you ever heard such *lunacy*?"

Helen stopped, then swallowed. "Anna, this is hard to say, but I . . . like her. She's nice. So good with all the children—cheerful, like a primary school teacher, bit loud but you can't have everything. And not above mopping her own muddy floor even though she was in a *viiiiiile* Oscar de la Renta frock. Nothing wrong with her, she's just different from us."

"How do you know our names?" All suspicion, Isaac squared up to me. "Did Regan tell you?"

"Nope."

The youngest boy, leaning against Joey's legs, raised his hand. Sounding doubtful, he asked, "Do you know who I am?"

Holy smoke, he was gorgeous.

"You're Zeke. And you're . . . six? Seven?"

He giggled. "Five."

"No! You look way older!"

Perhaps he did, but how would I know? The only small child I had dealings with was Regan. But the greatest compliment you could give four-year-old Regan was to pretend you thought she was five.

Isaac threw me a scornful look. "Regan's really small," he declared. "She's four, but she only looks three."

What? Negging *already*? He fancied her back, by the look of things.

"Dad?" Zeke whispered. "I'm hungry."

"Okay. Rice cakes? Or you want your dinner?"

"Dinner. Chips. I want to go to the place."

"Anna, we're going to head," Joey said. "These boys need feeding."

"Would you like to join us?" Max asked. "We're going to—what's it, Dad? The Broderick, for toasted sandwiches. You get crimped crisps."

Well, *he'd* changed his tune. "Thanks, Max, but I'm working right now."

"Ah, *come*," Isaac yelled, his smile impish.

"Come!" Zeke giggled, getting in on the act.

"There's ice cream," Max said. "Three flavors."

"We'd love you to join us." Joey was calm. His expression was sincere. "But if you're busy . . . ?"

The thing was, once I got Merv and his cohort onto the bus, my evening was mine.

But going for food with Joey and his kids would be an act of self-harm: I'd feel terrible later and tomorrow and the day after that. However, in the now—and we only have now, right?—I wanted it more than life. "Okay. As soon as I'm done here, I'll come over."

I heard Joey's exhale.

74

"Spaghetti bolognese," Zeke said to Emilien.

"No," Joey said. "Sorry, Emilien, he doesn't want it—"

"I *doooooo*."

"—he just likes saying it because they're big words. Pasta with butter will do him."

Beside me Max spoke quietly. "I need to tell you something."

"Lovely. Off you go."

"I know you can't read minds but I won't tell Isaac or Zeke. Why spoil the magic?"

It was so hard to muffle my explosion of laughter that my eyes watered. "That's kind, Max." When I could speak properly I said, "You seem very mature."

"I've had to grow up fast." He was solemn. "Because I've two younger brothers. But Dad gets to hang out with me. Recently . . ." He decided to try the word again. "Recently there, we went to *Wicked*, just the two of us. Zeke would have cried. He's afraid of witches."

"And Isaac?" I watched Isaac, who was halfway across the lounge, laughing scornfully at Merv.

"He acts like nothing scares him," Max said, "but Dad says he's just better at hiding it. Dad told you our names, didn't he?"

"Yep."

"We're sleeping here tonight even though we don't have pajamas! There's bunk beds. It was the only room left in the whole hotel, how lucky was that! We're getting ironing boards stuck to the ladders to stop Isaac and Zeke climbing up because they'd fall out."

"*And crack our skulls,*" Isaac called.

"Ironing boards?" I asked.

"Lyudmila's suggestion," Joey said. "Duct-taped to the ladders so the smallies can't climb up."

"I bet I could," Isaac said.

"I bet you could too," Joey replied. "But please don't."

"Okay, Dad."

Isaac took up residence at an empty table, where he sat smirking across at us. Joey met his cheeky challenge with a not-bothered face. Quietly, Max and Zeke slid from their seats and went to their brother.

Joey shifted his body towards me. "Anna, I'm sorry." He spoke very quickly. "We'd only got to Trea's when Brigit rang. We left straight away, but by the time we got here the boys had been in the car for five nearly unbroken hours. They needed to let off steam. I tried keeping them at the house but Isaac . . ." He sighed. "He ran off to the barn. I had to come after him."

"Joey. I have not one clue what you're talking about."

"Torres? Picking him up from Galway station?" He seemed to think I knew all about it.

"*You* got him here?"

"Yeah. Brigit was freaking out, wondering who she could send. Everyone here was needed, she said. But she knew I was due in Banagher today. It's only an hour from Galway station, so the boys and I set off on a rescue mission."

I was dumbfounded.

"We should have left as soon as we got here—"

But how could he, with three kids in tow?

"When the speeches ended I got hold of Isaac but Zeke needed the bathroom. So we, ah, hung out in there, playing with the hand dryer, until I thought you'd have left."

"You didn't have to hide."

"We agreed to be no-contact. I've tried to respect it."

An oppressive silence ensued. Then he blurted, "But . . . I think about you, Anna. A lot. I'm sorry. Thing is, even before today, I was wondering if I could message you? To see if we could talk?"

"Pasta with butter!" Emilien announced, bearing plates. "Two pepperoni pizzas!"

"Over here, garkon!" yelled Isaac from the other table.

Joey fixed Isaac with a look. "Absolutely. Not." Whatever they heard in his tone had all three of his sons suddenly very serious, returning to the table.

"Sorry for being cheeky," Isaac told Emilien.

"No bother." Emilien slung their meals in front of them.

Joey spoke quietly to Isaac. "Good boy."

"That's me!" Isaac threw him a smile.

As the kids settled themselves, Joey asked, "Everyone good?"

"Yep."

Isaac fed a triangle of pizza, pointed side first, into his tipped-back head. "I'm a sword-swallower," he gurgled.

"I want to do it," Zeke said.

Isaac gave him a slice, then they were both at it, while Max looked disdainful.

"Don't choke," Joey said. "That's all I ask."

Instantly Isaac grabbed his throat and began coughing dramatically. "I'm choking!"

"Me too," said Zeke.

"Queenie and Ree are coming into town to hang out with the boys for a while," Joey said to me. "Could we—you and I—get a drink? Have a catch-up?"

Oh no, I was losing control of the situation. Having pizza with his sons was foolhardy enough but just the two of us going for drinks?

"Please," he asked.

Briefly we were locked in a gaze, then I looked away.

But I hadn't said no.

After the three flavors of ice cream, the boys insisted on showing me their room, which had a double bed and two sets of bunk beds shoehorned in. There really were ironing boards duct-taped to the ladders.

"It's cozy." Max nodded. "Like in Granny Linda's. We sleep in Dad and Uncle Keith's old room. I go in the same bed as Zeke, but I'm upside down. Dad does the same with Isaac. No one wants to share with Isaac because he sticks his smelly feet in your face." Extravagantly, he tutted.

So Joey's mum was in his life again? That had to be good.

Joey's phone beeped. "Queenie and Ree are in the lobby. Let's go."

Downstairs, from the detailed instructions Joey gave the two teenagers, I realized they weren't "hanging out" with the boys but babysitting them.

"I'll be up in an hour or so," Joey told the trio.

"Nice to have met you," Max told me. "I've heard so much about you."

"Really?" That sounded unlikely.

"No. But it's polite?"

"Of course." I couldn't help smiling.

"I'm an old head on young shoulders, Mum says."

"Tomorrow"—Isaac pointed a finger my way—"we want to see where *you* live."

"Isaac!" Joey was mortified.

"Sorry," I said, "I start work very early tomorrow." Checking all the guests out of the Broderick, making sure their transportation had arrived, etc.

"That's okay." Isaac flashed a grin. "I wake up super-early. Then I wake everyone else."

"Isaac!" Once again, Joey was embarrassed. "You can't invite yourself to a person's house. You must wait to be asked."

Isaac fixed me with such an over-sweet expression that I said, "If you're still here when I finish, you can come over."

"Whoop!" He punched the air and leapt several inches.

Impossible to know if he really was delighted or just being a little brat but my money was on the latter.

75

We went to the Snug, a tiny, dark pub where I was unlikely to meet anyone I knew. I wanted Joey all to myself, even if it was only for fifty-three minutes.

"Tell me how you are," he said.

"I sold my apartment in New York. Just went through last week."

"Wow. And you feel . . . ?"

"Good. A little sad sometimes but nothing major."

"And work?"

"Doing three and a half days a week for Brigit and Colm, plus other bits and pieces. Having fun with Teagan's skincare brand—I know, right?"

"Are you going to stay in M'town?"

"I don't know. It's so easy here. But I worry if I don't get back on the ambition treadmill soon, then I'm donzo forever. I just can't decide."

"Anna. Sometimes not making a decision is making a decision."

"Listen to you! You sound like Angelo!"

"Jesus H!" he groaned, then smiled. "You've friends here?"

I laughed. "Now you sound like my dad! But yes! I love Courtney with my whole heart. And Teagan. And Karina the hair. Aber, Hal, Ben, Mrs Mahon, Pamela, Glen . . . There are lots of great people here—and some absolute doses, just like anywhere. And thank you for Jacqui. She's made a huge difference."

"It's good? You're close? She's forgiven you for . . . everything?"

"'Everything'? You mean *you*? Oh, she's so over you."

He seemed amused. "Good to hear. And, aaah . . ." He swallowed. "Did anything come of it, with you and the goon?"

"Ike? No."

The ensuing silence felt oppressive. "You were right," I said. "I didn't know what was going on for me back when . . . you know, you were here."

"Can I ask you something? Tell me to sling it if I'm overstepping but . . . is there somebody? For you? That you're seeing now?"

"No."

Again, I heard his quiet exhale.

"What happened with you and Rose?"

"We've gone to a few concerts together."

And . . . ? What else?

"Anna, it wasn't a thing. A relationship. I told you it was never about that. You suggested I try trusting her. So . . . I tried."

Right. "There were rumors she was still looking for investment for the Shithole on the Hill. Wouldn't that be disastrous for Brigit and Colm?" I watched his face.

There was a shift, a tiny one, into business mode. "Are you asking me a question, Anna?"

"Okay. Is Rose still looking for investment?"

There was something there, a flicker, a reluctance. When he spoke, he sounded formal. "*If* I knew, I'd be bound by confidentiality." Then, "Anna, Rose isn't a threat."

When I stayed silent, he repeated, with emphasis, "Rose is not a threat. You can trust me on that. I swear. I haven't seen her since, I think, July."

Several seconds elapsed, then because the relief was so lovely, I decided to believe him. "I'm a little messed up about her."

"Same as I'm a little messed up about the goon. And Torres."

"And you still drove across the country to pick him up from the station." I smiled. "Joey Armstrong, being the bigger man."

"Yep. That's me." Then he said, "I've been seeing, I don't know if you remember, I told you about Trevor? The therapist?"

"I remember. How's that working out?"

He seemed conflicted. "Okay, I'll tell you and if you feel ambushed, I'll shut up. The thing is, you've come up a lot in the sessions."

"Because of that night in New York?"

"Not really." After a pause he said, "In other ways. I think about you a lot. I miss you—"

"Stop."

"Anna. I'm in a different place to where I was, when we . . . the last time we met. Could we—"

"No."

"No, what?"

"I don't know," I realized. "But whatever it was, it's no. Because you'll hurt me. I'm doing fine, Joey, but it took a while."

Sad and serious, he said, "I hate that I did that to you."

"Like I said, one of us always ends up in bits."

"But we're really good at having fun with each other. That week in March, before . . . we had a great time. At least that's how I remember it. Am I wrong?"

He wasn't.

"I've been thinking about how kind you were when I told you about Dad and Keith."

"How could anyone else be kind when they didn't know?"

"Exactly—why didn't I tell them? Why were you the only one?"

"Jacqui's theory back then was you were trying to manipulate me."

He looked stricken. "I wanted you to *know* me."

Then he said, "I need to apologize for how I behaved the night of Ben's party. Back in my room, I shouldn't have led you on, then abandoned you. Or I should have done what I really wanted to do. I was so selfish."

"Making you kiss me? I was the selfish one."

"Look, ahhh . . ." A light sheen of sweat was visible on his forehead. "Sorry to do this without any warning, but, Anna." He swallowed. "Look, I'm just going to say it. I've been mad about you since forever. It never really stopped."

And?

"It still hasn't."

I waited, my heart in my throat.

"This may not be of any interest to you . . . but I wondered . . ." He began again. "I would really like us to try. To have a relationship. Romantically, I mean."

His honesty knocked me sideways. It was obvious how difficult he found it, being this vulnerable.

"It might be a disaster," he said. "But we'd never know if we didn't try."

Is your dick still under lock and key? I was afraid the words would rush into my mouth and say themselves. "What about your . . . rule?"

"It was never intended to be forever," he said. "Don't you remember? That night, I said I needed time."

He *had* mentioned something but I'd thought I was just being fobbed off. "Is it still in force?"

Slowly, deliberately, he shook his head. A smile hid behind his face.

Jealousy scalded me. "Have you . . . seen active service?" Because if he had, the hot green ooze might destroy me.

"No."

"How do you know"—I glanced in the direction of his groin—"That it even works anymore?"

"It'll work." He flashed an unexpected grin. "With you, it'll definitely work."

Oh God, this was a lot.

"Can you think about it? What I've said? Please?"

"Joey, my life is good now."

"Anna, the greatest failure is not to try."

"Joey Armstrong quoting Insta platitudes at me?"

"Told you." There was a small smile. "I'm in a different place."

"You need to get back to your boys."

"Sure." We both stood up. "And remember, Anna." His tone was wry. "You miss one hundred percent of the shots you never take."

At home, in bed, I kept thinking of Joey's face and voice when he said, across the lounge, to Isaac, "Absolutely. Not."

Calm. Powerful. In control. A man who meant business. The hottest thing I'd ever witnessed and I wanted him to use that tone with me.

"Joey, it's too soon for us to sleep with each other."

"*Absolutely. Not.*"

"I'm keeping my clothes on, Joey."

"*Absolutely. Not.*"

"Just my underwear, then? Please."

"*Absolutely. Not.*"

If he and I ever actually happened I'd get him to act it out with me.

"A pleasure, Mr Huxham." I assisted Merv, the last guest to leave, up the steps into the coach, which was purring curbside outside the Broderick. "Do come again."

Not even 7 a.m. and I'd already got forty-six guests and their luggage onto the big bus bound for Galway Airport. In several last-minute rescue operations, I'd located forgotten laptops, found a mislaid passport and raced up the stairs of the Broderick twice to retrieve medication from drawers.

"Anna! Aren't you done yet?" Isaac had returned to pester me. "I've waited *ages.*"

I gave the nod to the driver that it was safe to leave. The doors swished closed, the coach moved off and Isaac grabbed my hand. "Come *on*."

"Waitttt." I was very stern. Instantly he was sheepish.

"Sorry."

The bus reached the end of Main Street and turned a corner.

"Isaac!" Joey ran out into the street. "You were told to let Anna do her job!" Turning to me, he said, "Anna, I'm so sorry, Zeke needed—"

"All grand. Just a few more minutes. To be sure they're really gone."

Max came out, holding Zeke's hand. "They're gone," Isaac announced. Right, they probably were.

"Can I go in your car?" Isaac asked me.

"Don't you need a car seat?"

"No! I'm nearly seven!"

"Anna?" Joey checked. "You're good with this?"

"I mean, sure. But my house really isn't exciting."

Minutes later, the three boys clustered on my front step as I pushed open the front door.

"Manners," Joey reminded them.

With a sigh, Isaac checked himself. "May I come in?"

I laughed. "Are you a vampire?"

"I don't know." He liked the idea. "Am I?"

"If you are, you need to ask permission to go into another person's house. If they say yes, you're good."

"Okay, may I come in?"

"Yes, Vampire Isaac, you may."

"I don't want to be a vampire," Zeke said.

"I know I'm not one." This from Max. "But I have good manners. May I come in?"

"Sure. You too Zeke. And Joey."

"Thanks, Anna," Joey said.

As the boys streaked through the house, Joey spoke quietly. "Anna."

"What?"

He laughed. "Nothing. I just want to keep saying your name. Any excuse. I like the feel of it in my mouth."

Startled, I stared at him. His eyes darkened.

"Your pupils just dilated." I was awestruck.

In a low voice, he said, "There's a reason for that."

The atmosphere was so thick I could barely breathe.

Stepping back, I asked, "What you said last night, Joey? How serious were you?"

He took a moment. "Yeah, more serious than I've ever been about anything."

Suddenly overwhelmed, I had no idea what to think.

76

As soon as they left I did two rounds of laundry, scrubbed the house and pelted into Aldi to stock up for the week, basically doing everything that had been neglected during the previous demanding days.

While it was still light, I walked to the beach, then had an early dinner at Ben's with Courtney and Angelo. Back at home, I watched an excessively poor movie, then went to bed.

The next time I woke up was Monday morning. I put on jeans, boots, three T-shirts and a hoodie—but *no bra*, a small reward to myself for the hard work on Ben's exhibition. I was swaddled in so many layers that no one would guess. Who knew, if it worked out, No Bra Monday could become a thing.

I opened the front door to check the weather—cold out there. But dry and, crucially, *not windy*. It was safe to cycle to work. Stopping at Café Grumpy to pick up my Americano, Catreen called, "Anna! Have you heard the news?"

"What news?" Aber's sheep had escaped again and eaten eight winceyette nighties off Augustina Mahon's washing line?

"Rose Tolliver's shitheap on the hill is getting a major glow-up! It's gonna be a luxury hotel."

I froze.

"Investors, big money, all happening," she said. "Between Kearney's Farm and now this, M'town has hit the big time! Anna . . . ? You okay?"

All plans abandoned, I stepped into the street. My hands trembled as I rang Joey.

"Anna?"

Shaking with anger, I asked, "What the hell, Joey? Rose's shithole? When were you going to tell me?"

"I couldn't—"

"What will it do to Brigit and Colm's place? It'll steal all their business!"

"Anna, wait, take a breath. They're totally different. Kearney's Farm is a retreat, that's its identity. The Shithole on the Hill will be—what was Claire's phrase?—'death by upholstery'? But the two customer profiles will boost each other—"

"Well, congratulations!" My heart going like the clappers, I ended the call.

My phone lit up—Joey. I rejected it. He rang again. Same.

Two nights ago, he'd told me Rose wasn't a threat. He'd sworn I could trust him. But all along, all *fucking* along, he'd been in bed with Rose. Maybe not literally—although how did I know? *May*be literally!

I needed to call Brigit to see how they were doing. "Brigit! What the hell is Joey *at*—"

"Listen, don't freak out, it's all good."

"*How?* It'll take all your business!"

"There's market space for both places. Joey did tons of research. He did all the numbers backwards and forwards. It'll work, he says."

This was too much. Way too much. "Brigit, could you cope if I didn't come in today?"

I hadn't taken one sick day in the last eight months. I'd worked far more hours than I was paid for. If she refused, it would break my heart.

"Sure." Her voice was soft. "You've been working so hard. Take a duvet day. See you tomorrow."

My bike abandoned outside Café Grumpy, I made my way along Main Street, trying to walk off my shakes. Townspeople greeted me with their usual nosy warmth, keen to discuss the exciting developments. But I gave wobbly smiles and kept moving.

The Broderick was my destination; I needed Courtney. No way could she be blamed for missing the rumors—with Ben "drilling" her day and night, she'd had a lot going on.

It might be an idea to check she was actually at work but then I'd have to stop walking and I couldn't manage that.

Fucking asshole with his dilating pupils and "I've been mad about you since forever"! I'd been fine. Happy! Adjusting to this new chapter of my life, enjoying living here with my new friends, my bicycle clip, my unkempt hair. And once again Joey Armstrong had come along and fucked things up on me.

And you know what? It wasn't just him. *I'd* fucked things up on me by ever having anything to do with him. When someone shows you who they are, *believe* them! He'd shown me who he was the very first night I'd met him, when he'd gone home with my sister.

To my shock, Lyudmila was on reception. "No Courtney?" I asked.

"In Dublin with Ben, going on TV show."

I'd forgotten. And she couldn't be disturbed—Ben was too needy. But I was in trouble. There was a real danger of me going home for my car, then driving up the hill to Rose.

As if I'd manifested her, there she was, the Lady of the Shithole, carrying her bucket of cleaning materials.

"Congratulations, Rose," I called, my voice too loud.

"Thank you." She looked pink-cheeked and happy.

"Very noble of you to come in and work this morning."

"Poor form to let my colleagues down."

I moved closer. "All paid off in the end, didn't it?"

"Many times I'd given up hope but—"

"What was it this time?"

"I beg your pardon?"

"A Mozart recital? A sonata on his *flute*? Whatever you did, it worked."

"I have no idea what you're talking about."

"You and Joey."

She seemed concerned. "Joseph has nothing to do with my project."

"Ha. Ha. Ha."

"Some months ago, after the debacle with Dan, I offered the opportunity to Joseph. He turned me down."

"What?"

"He turned me down." Something in her tone was . . . generous?

"Why?"

"I'm not privy to Joseph's innermost thoughts." She looked concerned. Kind, even. "Perhaps *you* should ask him that question?"

Six missed calls from Joey and five unread texts were on my phone. So? He'd done nothing wrong? But my feelings hadn't yet caught up with the facts. I was too accustomed to being disappointed by him and too weary to think clearly.

I retrieved my bike, went home and called Jacqui. But she didn't pick up. Moments later a text arrived: **At work. Bizzy Bizzy. Will call asap.**

Unable to climb the stairs, I pulled off several of my layers and curled up on the couch, pulling the throw over myself. I shut my eyes.

77

The sound of a car outside woke me. Thick-headed, I reached for my phone. I'd been asleep for over three hours.

"Anna?"

What?

"Anna?"

The room darkened; my mystery visitor had pressed their face against the window, trying to see in. Oh God, no. It was Joey.

"Go away," I called.

"Can I come in?"

"No."

"Can you come out?"

"No."

I braced myself for another question so I could, once again, shout "No." But nothing.

He'd yell something else soon. But still nothing. I felt as if I were holding my breath, so sighing heavily, I flung off my blanket, got up and wrenched the door open. "What?"

Joey, in a dark coat, his collar up against the cold, leant against his car.

"Why are you here?" I asked.

"To tell you I've nothing to do with Rose's venture. You wouldn't take my calls so I came in person."

"There was no need. She told me herself."

"Wait, you already know? You believe it?"

"Yeah."

His eyes moved over me. I couldn't read his expression but he wasn't happy. Pushing himself from the car, he moved to the driver's door.

"Hey," I called. "She said she offered it to you first. Why'd you turn her down?"

He paused. "Would you believe me if I said it was because of you?"

"Nope. See ya."

"Okay. Bye, Anna." He opened the car door.

I turned back into the house, then asked, "Would you have made a lot of money?"

"Oh yeah," he said. "Tons."

"Seriously?" I was genuinely interested. "How much?"

"Enough to keep my four children in private schools for the next academic year."

"You shouldn't send them to private schools," I said. "They'll get the wrong values."

"Isn't it lucky then that I turned it down?"

"Yep, it all worked out."

"Except it didn't."

"How's that, then?"

"I thought it might convince you that I'm not a terrible man. But it hasn't. To you, I *am* a terrible man. I always will be."

I shrugged. His face changed. To my alarm, he seemed about to cry.

"Hey. Wait. Joey, wait."

Mutely, he shook his head and got into his car. I hurried out, catching the driver's door before it shut. "Come into the house, Joey. Please."

He looked at me, tears spilling from his eyes. I was appalled. Even Angelo didn't cry. But to see it from Joey, of all men, broke my heart.

"Come on." I took his hand, closing both of mine around it and led him into the house. "I'm sorry, Joey. I know you're not a terrible man. I'm the terrible one, punishing you for something you didn't do."

Looking hollowed out with exhaustion, he sank onto the couch.

"What can I get you? Coffee? Something to eat? A nap?"

"Nothing."

The room was cold. The fire needed to be lit. Making for the door, I said, "Two seconds."

"Where are you going?" He sounded alarmed.

"Out the back to get briquettes."

I was barely gone a minute but when I returned he'd fallen asleep, his head on a cushion, his beautiful coat abandoned on the armchair.

It gave me painful pleasure to drape the throw over his body and tuck it in around his chest, stroking it gently over his ribs. While he was oblivious in sleep, I could treat him with unending tenderness, stare at his beautiful face, at the scattering of little boy freckles across the bridge of his nose. As

I stroked his silky hair off his forehead his hand shot up and grabbed mine. "Please stay," he murmured, instantly disappearing back into sleep.

I sat on the floor, holding on to his hand, watching the lift and fall of his chest as he inhaled and exhaled. In and out, in and out, keeping himself alive—the miracle of it. Joey was breathing, Joey was alive. *I* was breathing, *I* was alive. We were both alive. That was no small thing.

With a sudden gasp, he jerked awake and sat up. "Oh, thank God." His breath was coming hard. "I was afraid I'd dreamed you."

"Are you okay?" I asked.

He studied me. "That depends on you. Am I?"

I nodded. "Sorry for being a bitch. A mad one."

"I'm sorry I couldn't tell you about the Shithole. After Rose offered me the chance, I knew she'd keep trying with other brokers. I was freaked. But the research told me not to be. I'd heard that maybe she'd pulled something together but the little I knew was embargoed. And deals fall apart all the time, right up to the last second—"

"It doesn't matter."

"Hey, come up off the floor, would you?"

As soon as I stood, his hands closed on my hips and tumbled me down, to lie beside him, under the throw. There wasn't really room for the two of us. His arm, tight around my waist, was all that kept me from falling off. My head had ended up in the crook of his elbow, so I shifted to see him properly. Suddenly our faces were almost touching, we were breathing each other's air and as I watched, his pupils went dark.

"It happened again," I said. "I saw your pupils dilate."

"As I said, there's a reason they do that."

I could ask him. It was safe. "Tell me."

"Because. Anna Walsh. I'm in love with you."

The words, their impact, made me choke. "Really, Joey?"

"Anna." He took a breath. "You haunt me."

All at once, I saw right into his soul and he into mine. I believed him. He trusted me. Our final few barriers had dissolved, replaced by a miraculous bond.

"And I'm in love with you, Joey." Such relief to finally say these words.

My mouth was on his, his was on mine and, oh my God, the taste of him, the touch of his tongue, the smell of his skin. He broke off and whispered, "Anna Imelda Walsh," moving his fingertips across my face, as if checking I was real. Then, "Anna." Kiss. "Imelda." Kiss. "Walsh." Kiss.

We gazed at each other. Cradling his perfect face in my hands, I moved my thumbs along his cheekbones and pulled them across his lips. I even traced the lids of his eyes. "You're so beautiful."

"You're more." Dropping a line of butterfly kisses along my scar, he murmured, "Sweet-face. Always."

Skimming the front of his trousers, his sharp inbreath thrilled me. My fingers traced the outline of his erection and it twitched, like a living thing. Under the throw, his free hand slipped beneath the hem of my T-shirt. When his fingertips reached my skin, I shuddered.

He tensed. "Is this okay?"

I managed a gasp-laugh. "Are you insane?"

Sliding his hand upwards he met my bare breast.

"It's No Bra Monday," I managed.

I felt him smile against my mouth.

Lightly, his thumb circled my nipple, moving close, but not close enough. Agonizingly slowly, another circuit began, this time getting nearer. Striving for his touch, I almost wrenched myself out of my own skin. Then his thumb glanced off the sensitized tip and a sharp squeak escaped me.

He took a quick look at the window, realizing that all of Maumtully could come along and spy on us.

"Unless you're into an audience . . . ?" he said.

"No."

"Me neither."

"Upstairs."

My heart pounded. What if, after all of this build-up, things went weird and sad?

"Hey." He held my face in his hands. "We've got a lot of past, you and me. Good chance we're gonna be reminded of it. But we don't freak out, okay? We talk about it, we don't give up and we practise until we get it right."

But what if I'd gotten too old and . . .

"We're both a bit older," he murmured. "None of that matters."

He'd read my mind. His fears were my fears. And we had a plan B.

78

"This is my bedroom." I swung the door open and crossed the threshold.

With a flash of a smile, he followed me in. Maintaining eye contact, he placed the palm of his hand on the door and shut it very deliberately. When the click sounded, he backed me against the wood and considered me in silence.

His physical presence was daunting: his height, the heat from his body, the hardness that strained towards me. He slid his index finger down my neck, lighting up all the pleasure points in my body, then kissed me, this time with more urgency.

My hands went to his waist, feeling the narrow tightness of his muscles beneath the cotton. I *loved* his body, I always had. My fingers fumbled, opening his shirt wherever they could locate a button. "Why you wearing a suit?" I could barely speak.

"On my way to work when you rang." In a deft motion, his hands slid under my thighs, lifting me so I could wrap my legs around him. "I came here instead."

Tightening my hold, I pulled his thick ridge against me, generating a strangled "Uhh" from him—and an almost identical sound from me.

It made us both smile.

His hands swept up the curve of my waist and ribs, taking my T-shirt off in one frictionless move. Suddenly bare, in the cool air of the bedroom, my skin tightened.

"*Anna.*" He took one nipple in his mouth, then moved to the other, while fireworks sparked inside me.

"Is this okay?" His voice was thick. "You'll tell me if anything isn't?" Walking me backwards to the bed, he lay me down, moving his mouth and hands over my body with reverent skill, paying attention to my breathing, as if I was an instrument he was tuning.

I wanted the pleasure of undressing him, but when I lunged his way, he held my wrists in one hand. "Not yet. Let me enjoy this."

Kissing my stomach, then moving lower, he smoothed away the rest of my clothes, then surveyed me, propped up on pillows. "Anna." It sounded like a prayer.

"Now you," I managed.

He stood to toe off his shoes.

"Seriously," I begged. "Hurry."

He shrugged away his tailored jacket, the silky lining sliding it off his back. Next he opened a button on the shirt I'd tried to ravage. Dear God. Joey Armstrong, the hottest man alive, was in my bedroom, removing his clothes. For me.

When he noticed just how rapt I was, he smirked, giving a glimpse of him at his most confident, and slowed everything down. With those long fingers, he took his time slipping open the buttons until his shirt was gone.

Bare-chested, his shoulders defined, his abs tight, ink of various colors on his arms, he took a moment. Then his hands went to his waistband. Lazily, he popped the button. At the rasp of his zip being lowered, a ball of heat ballooned in my stomach.

"Joe. Ee." My voice was low and urgent.

He peeled off his trousers, revealing the delicious jut of his hip bones, then long, defined runner's thighs.

Only one item of clothing remained . . . then he stopped. Idly, his hand snapped the elastic waistband as he shot me a look. I was in torment and he knew it.

"Come here!" I pulled him down, to lie beside me.

"Still okay?" He sounded breathless.

"No." I wanted him between my thighs.

"Anna." His voice was hoarse. "I don't have condoms."

"I do." Some other time I'd tell him they were a gift from Jacqui.

The box was in the drawer beside the bed. *Dying* from the feel of his velvet-soft skin over his ironhard girth, I slid the condom on. He gasped as if he was in pain.

"All good . . ." he managed. "Just. I've thought about this a lot, late at night . . ."

That made me smile. I'd had my own late-night thoughts.

Reaching for each other, he eased himself up into my body, stretching and filling me. The absolute bliss of it. Sliding down to meet him, we couldn't have gotten any closer. I contained him, held him, if I squeezed my muscles I could actually feel the shape of him and—

"Anna!" His voice was low and forbidding. "Gimme a chance here to last five minutes."

Stern Joey was so sexy. Something I'd revisit as soon as possible.

As we moved with each other, my eyes were on his face and his on mine. My hips tight in his grip, it was clear we weren't going to last long, either of us. I was *so* turned on; his breathing had become tight and careful, as he eked out his endurance.

Touching my most sensitive part, he said, "Show me how."

I couldn't. It was too intimate, too soon.

"Here?" He circled his thumb in a way that changed everything. "Like this?"

"Joey, yes, but—"

"Ssssh."

Within moments, all control was gone. Delicate and exquisite, the pleasure built and burst, until I hovered on the top note, almost unable to bear it. As the after-waves continued, I pressed into the heel of his hand. He pushed back, varying the pressure, until the spasms of ecstasy tapered away.

When, eventually, I opened my eyes, he was smiling. "Yeah?" His voice was soft.

"Yeah." I let out a shuddering breath. Then, "Still okay?"

"Totally." He flashed a grin. "I made you come."

"Not for the first time."

"What?" Confused, then he got it. "Seriously? Anna, you shouldn't have told me that, not now, I'm already in a bad way . . ."

I began to move again.

"Not yet." He sounded panicked. "You need more—"

"Shush!"

With purpose, I continued moving up and down.

"Anna." His breathing was harsh. "Oh my God, *Anna.*"

The gasps became sharper. I was turned on as much by my own power as his animal arousal. He made attempts to touch me again so I took his hands, put one under each of my knees, trapping them, then knelt down *hard.* "No. This is for you."

I licked my fingers and began to play with my nipples. He watched, riveted. Then I smiled. "Come for me, Joey."

His every muscle clenched. Helpless sounds came from his throat, becoming more urgent. With a hoarse cry, he was there, pulsing up into me.

Already I was wondering how soon we could do it again.

"C'mere." He pulled me close. "Jesus Christ," he murmured into my hair. "You nearly gave me a heart attack. I came too fast. But I can take care of you . . ."

"You already did. You can do it again soon."

"Promise?" Instantly he fell asleep and woke about twenty minutes later.

"*Anna.*" His voice was soft and his eyes shone. "You're still okay? Any regrets or . . . ?"

"No. Nothing. None."

"You're a right sexy little piece, d'you know that?"

"To be fair, you really have a knack for it yourself."

"Aaah." He shifted. "Can I say something? Do you remember when you kinda . . . told me you'd heard I was bad in bed?"

Even though it was forever ago, I did. "Sorry." What we'd *done* to each other.

"I needed to be told," he said. "I had no clue about anything. So I, ah . . . bought a book. On how to . . . be with someone. So they'd enjoy it."

"It worked."

He flashed a smug smirk. "Joey Armstrong: amazing in the sack. Lucky you, Anna."

79

"Joey, can I ask you . . . things?"

"Uh. *Sure*." He propped himself up on his elbow. "Anything."

"Right." I took a breath. "On and off, for a long time, you've liked me. But what if I was just an idea? What if you find your emptiness is still there? Because, Joey, I'm not sure another person can fill it. What if you blame me?"

"C'mere." He peppered my face with kisses. "So. I've gone to therapy, twice a week, for the past eight months. Before that, I did over a year in couples counselling, then individual sessions. I'm the only one who can, yeah, 'cure' me."

He was talking a good game . . .

"But I've actually done stuff, Anna. I've made up with my mum and my brother. I get how it was for them back then—they hadn't much choice. Even my dad. He's dead but it's not too late to forgive him. I'm trying. It's progress that I even want to."

Okay.

"The sense of being completely alone? If it comes back, it's mine to deal with. Anything else on your mind?"

"Why me, Joey? Is it just because you never 'did' me? Was I just another woman on your bingo card?"

He flinched. "I always had it bad for you, not gonna lie. But . . . Okay, I'll tell you what I like about you. You're independent. I mean, you come across as girl-next-door, but you're actually not, are you? I mean, you just walked away from that secure life in New York."

"A bout of insanity."

"Stop that. You're really fun to be around. You're genuinely kind." His tone became more somber. "After 'that night,' even though I was sore and, like, fucked up, I knew you were hurting too. All your apologizing . . . I knew you cared about me."

"I did."

"You know your own mind, not afraid to boss people around—"

"Jacqui said that. That you like them bossy."

"I don't like 'them' bossy. I like *you*. In good form, bad form, tearing me a new one . . . You've *great* taste in music. You can't cook and you don't pretend . . . Yeah, that's what I'm trying to say!" he declared. "You're *you*. You don't pretend to be anyone else."

"What don't you like about me?"

"Do I sense a camper van in my future?"

That made me laugh. "You'll grow to love it."

"In that case, I love everything about you. So, Anna, why me?"

"For the longest time I was confused. There was the whole Narky Joey thing. Then Jacqui was always so angry, but it seemed to me you were a good dad, even if it wasn't the way she wanted. When you told me about you as a kid, I saw how frightened you were. That you wanted to live differently. But you couldn't manage without your defenses." I stopped. "And even knowing that, I hurt you so badly—"

"Anna. Hey. Let's stay focused." He kissed me. "I couldn't manage without my defenses until . . . ?"

"Until you did a ton of therapy. And walked the talk. And grew up."

He beamed, delighted.

"I love you. I'm mad about you. Look, this is important: you know the worst of me—"

And he knew the worst of me.

"We're going into this with all the facts," he said. "Even so, things aren't simple. I've four kids. I live in Dublin, you live here. But could be worse, you could be in New York, right?"

I nodded.

"Do you want to be with me?" he asked.

Again, I nodded.

"Anna, more than life, I want to be with you. I want this to work. I'll do everything I can. If we don't do a runner at the first sign of trouble, if we show up for each other and talk, we can probably figure this out."

On the floor, in the pocket of my jeans, my phone rang.

"You need to get that?"

"No."

Eventually it stopped, then began again.

"Sorry." I picked it up. "It's Jacqui."

Quickly I clicked out **Sorry for ringing earlier. Can't talk now. Getting railed by Joey.**

I flashed the screen at Joey, who promptly began shaking with laughter, then I pressed send.

"What's so funny?"

"All of it. 'Railed.' That it's from you to Jacqui and that it's all good." Suddenly worried, he asked, "It is, isn't it? This won't mess things up?"

"I don't think so."

"'Railed,'" he repeated. "That's a new one for me. I'm going to rail you, Anna Walsh." He tilted his head at me. "Yeah. I like the sound of that. Or 'boned.'"

"I like that better. Maybe it's my age?"

He slid over me, propping himself up on his arms, his body close but not actually touching mine. Making intense eye contact, he said, "Anna Walsh, I'm gonna *bone* you."

I was entertained, but also . . . into this.

"Drill you?" he asked.

"Say it."

"Anna, I'm gonna *drill* you. No, wait. Anna, I'm gonna *pound* you."

"I like 'bone' the best."

"Okay, Anna, get ready, because I'm gonna *bone* you."

Something was moving about down there. I took a look. Yep, he was *definitely* going to bone me.

But what he actually did was make love. With slow, mindful thrusts, he eased himself in, right to the hilt, then all the way back out again, keeping me quivering on the edge for a long, long time.

"I love you," he breathed.

"Oh, Joey, I love you. But, Joey, I can't endure this much longer."

"Not just yet." His chest heaved. "Wait."

No, that was impossible. Sliding my own hand between us, I went straight for my—

"Anna, no." Laughing, he grasped me by the wrist. "Absolutely. Not."

That was all it took. Those two words in his stern tone triggered a detonation which left me speechless and incapable.

"What happened there?" he asked, his eyes narrowed with interest.

"Tell you later," I managed. "Don't stop."

Afterwards, when we could both speak again, I stumbled through an explanation. "In the Broderick, when you said . . . And your voice was . . . And I felt . . . So yeah, those two words, you sound 'hot and cross.'"

"But that time with Isaac, I wasn't cross. He knew that. I wasn't cross with you either."

"Okay, not cross. A little forbidding. Just the right amount." Dreamily, I said, "You and those boys, you're lovely together."

"You liked them?" His face lit up. "Because they like you. Zeke calls you 'the kind lady.' Max—what were his exact words? 'Capable of conversation,' that's it! So serious, my little man. And Isaac? I might have to fight him for you. Even Trea says you're 'not embarrassing,' which is high praise."

"Seriously? That's a relief." I touched the tip of my tongue to his chest— he tasted delicious—then traced my fingers along the section of sheet music inked on his bicep. "What's this?"

"First five notes of 'Since I've Been Loving You.' Led Zeppelin," he added.

"I know who it's by!" I was offended.

"Sorry. Of course you do." He laughed. "I'll always love them. But I love so many different kinds of music these days. You? Best song to make you happy?"

"So many . . . but I'll go wiiiith Madonna. 'Vogue.' You?"

"Patti Smith. Anything by her. Always. So, best song to be sad to?"

"Amy Winehouse. *Back to Black*. The whole album. You?"

"'White Wine in the Sun.' I cry every time. Or, 'If the World Was Ending.'"

"I know that one. But it's *such* a love song, Joey."

"And that's why it's sad."

"I guess. All right then, best song to have sex to?"

"I . . . don't . . . know," he said, thoughtfully. "I've never really . . ."

"Oh my God!" I was full of enthusiasm. "Start thinking. We need to audition *lots*. Gimme my phone." Ignoring the string of emoji-riddled, capital-letter filled texts from Jacqui—I was certain she'd understand—I went into Spotify. "I'll pick the first one. You can do the next. Amaze me, Joey."

I caught a flash of a smile. He looked so happy.

". . . This one is doing it for me . . ."

". . . Oh, Joey, this is sexxxxxxxxxxxxxxxy . . ."

". . . holy fuck . . ."

". . . oh my Godddd . . ."

". . . Yanno, Anna, I'm starting to think it isn't the music, it's just you."

We'd veered from Blackstreet to Dusty Springfield to My Chemical Romance to David Bowie, changing moods and tempo, getting excellent results from all of them. It had been the most fun I'd ever had in bed.

Late in the afternoon, the light fading from the sky, I said, "We should eat something. How are you with toast and Nutella?"

"Let me take you out. We could go into town? The Spanish? The Broderick? Wherever you like."

I hesitated. "Joey, if we did that, it'd be like beaming the news up into space for the whole world to see."

"Don't you want people to know?"

I did. But, "Just warning you. There would be no coming back from it."

"I don't want to come back from it." Then, "Do you?"

"I'll put some clothes on."

The Broderick was the only place serving food. When we walked in, it was tumbleweed city. Utterly deserted.

"Still in town?" Emilien asked Joey. Then he noticed me—and actually blushed. Quick on the uptake, round here.

"Sit down, sit down." Emilien appeared quite agitated. "Toasted sandwiches, gin? Ice cream after?"

"Lovely."

The gin took a while to arrive. "The sandwiches will be along in about half an hour, you know how it is around here." Emilien disappeared again.

Joey moved his thumb across my palm. "I can't believe I get to hold hands with you."

"You get to do a lot more than th—Oh, hi, Peadar." It was a surprise to see Peadar Brady here in the Broderick: he was a loyal customer of the Boot.

"Anna," he declared. "And the go-boy!"

Joey stood to shake Peadar's outstretched hand.

"What brings you to town?" Peadar asked Joey.

"Aaah, Anna does."

"Anna?"

"Yeah. I'm in love with her."

Peadar chortled. "Shur, that was obvious." He trained his gaze on me. "You were harder to read. But looks like it all worked out. I hope you'll both be very happy."

A few more customers had arrived. The place was really quite busy for a Monday night in late November.

"Anna. Mr Armstrong." Tipper Mahon appeared at the table. "Tiler Brady." He nodded at Peadar.

"Hi, Tipper," I said. Then, "Hi, Sinéad." Because Tipper was accompanied by his wife. And . . . "Vazey, good to see you. Declan. Hal! Hi. And Mrs Mahon, hello, you're over your Novemberitis? How come you're all out tonight?"

A stupid question: it was obvious that, instead of getting our drinks, Emilien had been making calls, because here came Ziryan and Aber. Wait a minute—Ziryan and Aber? Looking rumpled and very together. Well, how *lovely*.

Shortly afterwards, Karina and Gráinne tumbled in. "Ah no!" Karina declared when she saw us. "It's true!" Then, "Sorry, Anna. Delighted for you. Just a bit disappointed for myself."

The energy in the lounge tightened—Vivian had arrived. The crowd parted to admit her, to study Joey and me, her face a picture of confusion. "Seriously?" she asked. "Sexy Man Armstrong and Anna from Dublin? I'm just not seeing it."

"Get them eyes of yours tested!" Augustina Mahon was clearly no fan of Vivian's. "They're mad about each other!"

I spotted Ike, lurking nearby. He slid over and muttered, "Unfinished business, didn't I tell you?"

I laughed. "I should have believed you."

"Make way!" Emilien had brought our toasted sandwiches. "Let them eat their meal. Are any of you intending to buy a drink or are you just here to gawk at the pair of them?"

"Just here to gawk," Peadar said. Several others—Tipper, Vazey, Declan Erskine and a few more Beardy Glarers—joined in.

"I'll have a drink," Hal piped up. "If somebody else pays for it."

"And I'd like a drink," Sinéad Mahon echoed.

"But we're doing Dry November," Tipper told his wife.

"Fuck it, Tipper, it's December in four days, I'm dry enough. Emilien, a vodka and Coke, make it a large one, and whatever Hal and Mrs Mahon want."

"Arra. Might as well get me something too," Tipper said.

"Lookit, if Tipper's having a pint, I'm having a pint," a Beardy Glarer said, which kicked off a large-scale crumbling of resolve. Soon it was pints all round.

"As a wise man once said"—Farrelly the Flowers strode across the lounge—"'I'll have a Babycham.' Emilien, no, that's a joke, I'll have a pint." He turned his attention to me. "I knew it. I did. I said it to you. Didn't I?"

"You did, Farrelly, you did."

"I don't know how your mother will take the news but the babeen Regan will be delighted."

"My heart is broken," Hal said. "But who could resist Mr Joseph Armstrong?"

"Quite." Here came Dr Muireann. "Christ on a bike, the *day* I've had. Out the door with throat infections, suspected pleurisy, morbid thoughts—and now *this*. Emilien, bring me a large, strong something. Teagan! Where did you come from?"

Teagan stood before us, as if made of stone. Only her eyes moved, flicking from Joey to me, then back again. "It's true? I swear to God, I *can't*. Nothing but old people falling in love and having disgusting old-people sex. It should be illegal!"

"Teagan Burke!" Hal was horrified. "This is a love story for the ages."

"'Ages'? More like 'Ag*ed*.'"

"Is it time for your ice cream yet?" Emilien had returned.

Joey looked at me.

Take me home and bone me, I tried to convey.

"Yeah, yanno, Emilien"—Joey was standing up—"no ice cream tonight. I think we're just going to head."

"Grand." Emilien blushed again.

"We'll be off," Joey said to the crowd. "See you all soon."

A clamor of distressed voices broke out.

They're leaving!

Course they're leaving. Would you stay if you could be getting it from Sexy Man Armstrong?

Or Anna Walsh. She's just as sexy.

Did you know he calls her Sweet-face? A secret known only to a few.

"Enjoy yourselves," Dr Muireann called after us.

"Yes, enjoy yourselves, enjoy yourselves!"

And we did.

Epilogue

"Happy birthday." Farrelly stood on my doorstep, bristling with cellophane-wrapped arrangements of flowers. "I nearly had to buy a new van."

He strode down the hall towards the kitchen but I said, "Nope. Utility room, Farrelly."

"A *utility* room, is it? Well, well, well." He was sticking his head in and out of doorways, opening cupboards, generally taking stock of my light, bright new house. "This is some transformation. So you went with the reclaimed floorboards in the end? I'm a carpet man, myself. Can I see upstairs?"

"Off you go."

Abandoning the flowers on a draining board, he took the stairs two at a time and opened one of the bedroom doors. I followed him up.

"I'm guessing this is Max's bed? Very *orderly*. Wouldn't he remind you of a young novitiate in holy orders? And he's sharing with the child, Zeke?"

Farrelly nodded at the collection of teddies on Zeke's bed. Suddenly sotto voce and earnest, he said, "Mind that ye don't baby him too much. I see it too often with the youngest child."

"Okay." It was very hard to not snigger.

On the landing, Farrelly advanced upon, hesitated, then stepped back from a door emblazoned with a skull and crossbones. "Isaac's? Trea's?"

"Isaac's." I nodded at another room. "And that's Trea's."

"I won't go in. They're entitled to privacy." In other words, he was scared of them. He glanced around at the remaining doors. "That's the bathroom, which means *this* must be yours!"

His hand on the doorknob, he caught my look. "I'll, ah . . . give you privacy too." He dropped his voice to a whisper, "Is he *in* there? The go-boy?"

"Not yet. Coming later with the kids."

Clattering back down the stairs, Farrelly said, "You've worked miracles with this place. I thought you'd never get rid of the smell of Dr Muireann's poor mother, not that it was bad, she was a fastidious woman, never let the standards slip. But too much honeysuckle talc could choke a horse."

"I can't take any credit," I lied. I was so *proud* of my sweet little house. "Tipper and the lads did all the work."

"But you were the one giving the orders. It was your 'vision'—'Chic, cozy and coastal'? I hear Rionna Breen was a great help with the soft furnishings. What was it she said again? 'If I ever see another starfish cushion, I'll scream.'"

I had to laugh. "Is there nothing you don't know about me?"

Momentarily, he studied me. "Probably not. Come here." He went into the utility room. "One of the bouquets is from your ex-in-laws. From when you were married. When the order came through, I was stymied. Who's Dianne Maddox in Boston, sez I? Then I put two and two together. It's good ye're still in touch."

I nodded my agreement.

It was a long time since Aidan's family and I had gently slipped from regular contact. Although we'd all grieved Aidan, our pain had different shapes. Hardly surprising, as we had loved him in unique ways. At some stage it became apparent that far from being united by our mutual loss, we no longer had anything in common.

Nevertheless, an invisible thread connected us and social media kept us current.

"This one." Farrelly lifted a cluster of vibrant blooms from the draining board. "She said to go 'all out.'"

My heart swelled. Dianne was incredible: not only had she lost her eldest son far too young, she had the generosity to acknowledge his widow's fiftieth birthday.

"I'll go out to the van for the rest," Farrelly said.

"Okay." I'd got stuck on the impossible fact that I was alive and Aidan wasn't. The only "message" I could ever take from his death was that I shouldn't waste what I'd been given—something I forgot far too often. But today it was front and center.

I hope you approve of what I'm doing with my life, I told him.

Because, I realized, *I* did. I liked living and working in M'town. Being a four-hour drive from my parents and sisters wasn't perfect. Nor was being an hour away from Jacqui. And managing me, Joey and his children was so complicated that Elisabeth, Joey and I shared a detailed online calendar.

So far, though, it was working beautifully.

And I liked my job. Doing four days a week for Brigit and Colm suited me: I could take the pace and live on the money. Now and again I'd remember how hard I'd worked in New York—*how* had I managed such a stressful life?

Farrelly had returned with more flowers. "Do you really think he'll come?" he asked. "Horace Bland?"

Shocked, I asked, "How do *you* know about him?"

"Ah, Anna." My naivety entertained him. "No secrets round here."

Dolphin Cove had opened its doors in April. Business was definitely promising. But yesterday, a phone call from a woman with a loud, nasal voice had ramped things up several gears. After making Colm, Brigit and me sign non-disclosure agreements, she divulged she was the personal assistant of some high-status man who wanted to book three villas for a week. "ETA four days' time."

As the exact identity of the man was still a secret, Horace Bland became his working title. We had been excited, giddy, fearful—then payment in full arrived in the bank account and we crossed the "fearful" part of our feelings off the list.

"Who do you think he is?" Farrelly asked.

I shrugged.

"Ah, Anna! Make an effort."

"Timothée Chalamet," I rattled off, "President Zelensky, Elvis back from the dead. Look, I haven't a clue." All that really mattered was that Dolphin Cove was picking up momentum. "Gotta go. I'll be late for work."

"Happy birthday," Courtney called at me. "How you feeling?"

"In my prime, Courts, my *prime*." I followed her into the office for the daily update from each department. Less formal than it sounded. My title was Head of Communications, Brigit was Head of Human Resources but basically we all did everything. (Except for food and beverages, that was Steve's area.)

"Right," Courtney, Head of Reservations, said. "Nineteen new check-ins today."

"I apologize in advance," I muttered—because seventeen of the nineteen were my parents, sisters, their partners and children, in town to celebrate my birthday.

"The worse they are, the better," Colm said.

Dolphin Cove had been averaging about two-thirds occupancy, so he and Brigit had decided to offer my loved ones a cut-price stay, as an exercise in seeing how we'd cope closer to a full house.

"Seriously," I said. "Ziryan, you in particular—"

"I know. Be afraid of Helen."

Ziryan was Head of Guest Experiences, right across fitness, the spa and all things feathery-strokery.

"And you too, Steve," I said. "Warn your staff again: she'll order things that don't exist."

"Got it."

"Also, they'll be early."

The vanguard—Mum, Dad, Helen, Artie, Regan and Helen's Best Friend Bella Devlin—showed up at ten past two. Hot on their heels were Margaret and her lot, followed by Rachel and Luke. After a lull of an hour, Adam and Claire came, with three of their four children. The only one missing was Francesca, who was currently based in Berlin with Lenehan.

"Hi, hi, hi." Brightly but with zero interest, Claire flashed her teeth at my colleagues. "Can I borrow the birthday girl? Glam-squad time. See you all later."

At my house Jacqui jumped from her car. Triumphantly, she waved a huge ASOS bag at Claire. "Finally! With ten minutes to spare! I was FaceTiming the delivery guy, *crying*, telling him it was a matter of life and death."

"Thank *God*."

Bearing suit carriers and shoeboxes, talking nonstop, Claire and Jacqui thundered up to my bedroom.

"The Gucci tunic was a bust," Claire called. "Color was wrong, wrong, *wrong* for her."

"But, Claire"—Jacqui was all excitement—"The Miu Miu dupe! The *shape*. It could really work, if we get her shoes right."

I was the "her" they were talking about and I might as well not have been there.

For the next hour, I obediently put on and took off four different dresses, matched with a variety of shoes, as they scrutinized me with narrowed eyes and pursed mouths. Occasionally, apropos of nothing, Claire would yelp, "It's rented. They're all rented. I didn't *buy* any. I know I spend too much but I'm really trying."

Eventually they decided on a classic black fit-and-flare worn with my own shoes. "You've good kneecaps," Claire informed me. "That's why it works."

I liked the look. Which was just as well.

"Flirty," Claire and Jacqui told each other. "Fun. Flattering. All the 'F's."

No sooner had they left and I was back in regular clothes than the front door rattled, then Joey's boys swarmed into the hall, waving cards and gifts.

"Do mine first." Isaac flung himself at me.

"No, mine!" Max insisted.

"Mine! It's a fart cushion! We'll do it on Max, then Dad, then Wesley, then—"

"Calmly," Joey ordered. "We'll sit at the table and open the gifts *calmly*."

While the boys colonized the kitchen, Joey tightened his arms around me, placing his mouth on my neck where a pulse jumped. "Anna." He breathed. "The relief of you."

Unable to wait, I pulled him down to kiss me. It had been just two days since we'd seen each other but it felt more like months.

"We're waiting," Isaac yelled. "*Calmly*."

Joey leant his forehead against mine. "You've no idea," he said, "how much I love you."

Pulling his hips against me, feeling him harden at speed, I had to laugh. "I kinda do."

"I'll get you later." His voice was low.

I shivered, anticipating several rounds of *Absolutely. Not.*

Reluctantly we moved apart, until he was decent, then went to the kitchen.

"Reverse order," Max announced. "Do Zeke's gift now. He never gets to be first."

The beautifully wrapped box—I suspected Elisabeth's hand in this—revealed a bracelet woven from colored string. "I made it," Zeke said.

"I love it!" Immediately I put it on, then moved to admire the fart cushion from Isaac. "I love this too!"

Max's gift was a mug, which said *Anna's Tea*. "And I also love this!"

"I bought it by myself with my own money." He was trying hard to mask his pride; my heart crumpled.

Joey surprised me with one of Ben's bird paintings.

"I thought they were all sold!"

"He did one specially for you."

"Oh, Joey, thank you. I really *really* love it."

"You are so welcome." He was almost as proud as Max had been. "Okay, I'd better get started on dinner. Hey, was that the doorbell?"

"I'll get it!" Isaac raced to admit Teagan and Karina, then scampered back in. "I sent them upstairs."

While Joey cooked chips, Quorn nuggets and broccoli, Teagan and Karina set about transforming me—highlighter, contouring, eyelashes, general gleaminess, alarmingly big hair ("Don't worry, it'll drop")—until a scrap broke out on the stairs.

"I want to give it to her!" Isaac's voice was mutinous.

"No. You get to carry it!" That was Max. "I get to give it to her."

As if they were conjoined, they hobbled together into the bedroom, both clutching like grim death on to a plate of food.

"Your dinner, modom," Isaac announced, then smirked at Max. "Boom. *I* gave it to her."

Rolling his eyes at him, Max was suddenly very mature. "You know the rules, Anna. If you don't eat your broccoli, there'll be no birthday cake."

Zeke, bringing up the rear, pulled me down to whisper, "Just do your best. So long as Dad can see that you tried."

"It's like Christmas!" Zeke cried.

Courtesy of Claire—never a woman who did things by half—Brigit's barn twinkled with so many fairy lights, it was probably generating panicked communications from spy satellites. *Mayday, mayday. Weird illuminated, like . . . thing visible in the West of Ireland.*

As I stepped inside, Mum was the first to reach me, followed by Dad, Claire, Margaret, Rachel, Helen, Jacqui and their assorted menfolk, children, stepchildren, boyfriends-in-law, the lot. The stream of bodies overflowed and encircled me, forming layer upon layer of love, more people continuing to appear: Courtney, Colm, Queenie, Brigit, Ree, Ben, Hal, Karina, Aber, Ziryan, Vivian, Gráinne, Teagan, Steve, Augustina Mahon, Hardware Ralph, Ferne, Rionna, the Custard Creams, Ike Blakely and a whole throng of Beardy Glarers whom I now found it no bother to differentiate between. *How* had I ever found them a homogenous, beardy mass? Jimbo was *nothing* like Vazey. Who was *nothing* like Peadar Brady.

In the spirit of friendship, her ladyship had been invited but was "away on business." (And she genuinely was. Work on Tolliver Hall was well under way; she was a busy woman.)

"Your attention, please!" Claire called. A big screen began delivering video messages from Teenie, Angelo, Nell, Kamilah, Monifa, even Franklin, followed by a montage of images, starting with me as an infant, then an anxious-looking toddler, then a young child. Next came six different shots of me in the television room, crouched behind a pouffe, only the top of my head visible. "We used to call it Spot the Anna," Claire told the crowd. "She was always trying to disappear."

In a boxy, too-big uniform, here I was on my first day at school, then making my First Communion and my Confirmation and, of course, starting secondary school, all knobbly knees, crooked teeth and mild terror.

Holy smokes, *no!* One of my early teens, my fringe so long it covered my face: I looked like a gonk. A year later, here were me and Jacqui, gawky and grinning, sticky with lip gloss, she so tall and me so short, thinking we were the bomb, God love us. Another of us in low-rise combats, cut-off tops and—kill me now—bucket hats!

A wistful sigh moved through the room at a shot of Shane and me on a Greek ferry, sun-kissed, tangle-haired and shockingly young. Followed by us wearing hilariously woeful expressions, bundled up in hats and gloves in our freezing flat in Turin.

Picking up speed, we rattled through a few Walsh Christmases and birthdays, then came an artfully overexposed close-up of Aidan and me, laughing as we ran through a shower of white petals, on our wedding day. We looked as beautiful as movie stars.

In the next picture, pinched, pale and clutching a new-born Trea, I barely recognize myself, my face cut from eye to lip and—just like Jacqui said—as animated as a slab of concrete. I look deeply stunned, homeless in my new reality, unable to believe all I'd lost.

But moving along, I'm suddenly polished and svelte, my scar less livid, picking up an award for a skincare campaign. And here's another award photo, followed by a group shot of rowdy, drunk people at my house-warming in Two Bridges.

Angelo begins making appearances around now—on vacation in the red rocks of Sedona, then at a lunar eclipse in Baja California. Oh poor me, crying *hard* at Teenie's New York leaving party; I was heartbroken. But, wow, check me out, cling-wrapped in a Roland Mouret dress, winning another professional accolade.

Next is a lovely one with Dad, grinning goofily, looking like we're being devoured by poinsettias, the year I won four rounds of Christmas bingo at his golf club. Then a photo with Mum at her "surprise" eightieth birthday, followed by a wild-looking night out in Manhattan. Next up is a Walsh family pandemic Zoomshot with everyone yelling at Mum, "You're still on mute!"

Then! Me in M'town, at that first St Patrick's Day parade. This gets an enthusiastic cheer from the assembled crowd. Here's Lenehan and me at our desks, pretending to be calm and efficient; a selfie of Jacqui and me, laughing so much we're barely recognizable; Teagan and I pouring homemade serum into bottles; Courtney front and center, beaming as I plant a smacker on the side of her face; me in an orange hard hat and hi-vis jacket as Tipper and the lads commence work, after Dr Muireann's mother moved to residential care in Oranmore and I bought her house with the proceeds of my New York apartment. At the edge of the picture is a sidelong slice of Joey in motion. Even a sliver of him is enough to put the wanting on me.

Oh Lord—Jacqui, Karina, Gráinne and me, in drunken disarray, wearing matching "Langeroo" T-shirts at the Banagher marina. The next photo—Courtney, Dr Muireann, Karina, Gráinne, Lyudmila and me gathered at a table in the pizza place on Main Street, looking irritated, as if a very important discussion has been interrupted—makes me bark with laughter. We'd either been complaining about the stupidity of everyone or insisting we were still hot. That was all we did.

Oh, a lovely one of Joey, sharp and cool in a suit, and me in a swishy party dress, at Elisabeth's wedding to Wesley. Followed by a shot where I've obviously fallen asleep on my new couch, late one evening.

"Hey!" I twisted around to Joey, who was at my back, his hands light on my shoulders. "Did you take that?"

"Yep." He sighed. "You were so cute."

The funny thing was that I had an almost identical one of him, sweetly vulnerable, asleep on that same couch, after a tough week.

The next picture is a cluster of Joey, Trea, Jacqui, Max, Isaac, Zeke, Elisabeth, Wesley and me.

Jacqui speaks right into my ear. "He loves his many, *many* children." And I almost choke from shoving down the laughter.

Then comes one of Joey, Jacqui, Trea and me. *Yeah, no big deal. Just a casual hang. Massive falling out? Yah, no idea what you're talking about, babes.*

The last photo is of Max, Isaac and Zeke, surrounding me as I eat my broccoli, less than an hour earlier.

The lights go back up, claps and cheers rise to the roof, then Claire and Mum are coming my way, bearing a candlelit cake.

"Is it like being at your own funeral?" Claire asked, gleefully. "That's how I felt at my fiftieth!"

To quote the sexiest man I'd ever known: absolutely not. I felt *extremely* alive, caught in a burst of unalloyed joy, appreciating every grain of it.

Amplifying my gratitude was the bittersweet insight that time moves relentlessly on: it gives and takes, removes and replaces.

Beautiful as this night was, not everyone could keep me company to the end of my journey; some would peel away or fall behind or splinter off. Aidan had had to leave, while my path and Jacqui's had forked sharply before reconnecting. As for Joey, we'd spent over twenty years criss-crossing each other's routes and now our journeys had merged.

In decades to come, when the world has once more reshaped itself, when humans continue to be happy and unhappy and happy again, when tonight's children have had grandchildren of their own, someone might stumble across one of my birthday cards—perhaps lodged, long-forgotten, behind a plank of wood here in the barn. The old-fashioned communication might seem quaint—imagine *hand*writing something! Or perhaps they yearn for the glory days when messages were written in pen instead of, say, unwieldy charcoal?

Trying to decipher the out-of-date words, they might wonder, "Who was Anna? What was she like?"

And I'd tell them, if I could: I was an imperfect person who made mistakes, did strange, selfish things and at times just baffled myself. But I tried to do better and when it didn't come right the first time, I tried again.

Looking around Brigit's barn, at all the beloved people—Jacqui and Joey, Mum and Dad, Margaret, Helen, Claire, Rachel, Courtney, Hal, *all* of them—I think: This is my life. Everyone is here tonight because I love them and they love me.

How lucky am I? I love and am loved.

And that is all there is.

Acknowledgements

As they say, it takes a village: I absolutely loved writing *My Favorite Mistake* but I couldn't have done it without the help of an awful lot of other people.

I'm profoundly grateful to the entire team at Michael Joseph, for working so hard and so generously on this book: My visionary publisher Louise Moore and her gifted associate Grace Long; Liz Smith for bringing so many great marketing ideas to every publication. Working with her and her fabulously creative team, including Jen Breslin, Colin Brush and Ellie Morley, is always such fun; Akua Akowuah, Christina Ellicott, Laura Garrod, Kelly Mason, Sophie Marston and Hannah Padgham, in sales; Lee Motley for another great jacket; Emma Henderson for her meticulous proofing and Dan Prescott for copy-setting; Alice Mottram in production; Richenda Todd for the copy-editing; Stephen Ryan and Jill Cole for proofreading; James Keyte and Helena Sheffield in the audio team; Roy McMillan for his painstaking coaching and gentleness as I voiced the audiobook. And, of course, Gemma Correll for the cover illustration, I *love* it.

At PRH Ireland, Cliona Lewis, Sorcha Judge and Carrie Anderson have been incredible as always.

At Curtis Brown, my esteemed agent Jonathan Lloyd and his associates, particularly Olivia Edwards and Rachel Goldblatt, have always been hugely supportive. And thanks to Liz Dennis, Georgia Williams and the foreign rights and the TV and film departments for taking such great care of my books.

Enormous thanks to the fabulous Kealey Rigden for all the publicity and events work. As well as Fiona McMorrough and all at FMCM.

I'm so grateful to the people who read this book at different stages as I wrote it and who gave me all kinds of helpful feedback along the way: Jenny Boland, Tara Flynn, Róisín Ingle, Caitríona Keyes, Ljiljana Keyes, Mammy Keyes, Rita-Anne Keyes, Lynn McKee, Eileen Prendergast and Sophie White.

There are two friends who have gone above and beyond—Kate Beaufoy and Louise O'Neill. God knows how many versions they've read. (Sorry, lads.) They've both given great editorial advice, big and small, taken panicked late-night calls from me and offered ceaseless encouragement and love.

I'm very grateful to Sarah Moore Fitzgerald for her excellent editorial eye and heart-warming enthusiasm.

And for all kinds of love and support, I'd like to thank the angel-in-human-form that is Judy McLoughlin.

Since my first novel was published four thousand years ago (approx.), countless booksellers have supported my work. I'm extremely grateful. As I am to the many book bloggers and reviewers who have taken the time and trouble to report on them with such positivity.

Over the years countless other writers have recommended my books, given me cover quotes and provided a community that's supportive, funny and warm; I'm very grateful to them all.

There aren't enough adjectives to thank my beloved husband—positive, unflappable, interested and always on my side, none of this would be possible without him.

I can take no credit for the magnificent phrase, Feathery-Stroker™—this was the invention of Caitríona Keyes and Anne Marie Scanlon, and what a gift to the world!

"Simarjit Kaur" became a character in this book because of a donation made to Freedom from Torture. Kate Osborne paid for "Jacqui Staniforth" to be a character in a previous book, at a fund-raising auction for the Medical Foundation for the Care of Victims of Torture, and now she appears again.

This book is dedicated to Beth Nepomuceno, who for many years has provided help and support to the Keyes family in countless different ways. She is endlessly obliging, incredibly kind and loving, and behaves as if nothing is too much trouble.

Finally you, my beloved reader. I'm deeply grateful you've picked up this book and to each and every one of you who've read my books over the years. It's such a privilege to write the books I write, to be published, and none of it would happen without you.

This isn't strictly a sequel: you needn't have read any of my other books to enjoy this one. However, if you have, then you may know Anna from *Anybody Out There*, and you will recognize members of her family from the other Walsh novels.

Many of you have told me that Anna is their favorite Walsh and I'm very fond of her myself. She's kind and unconventional and probably never thought she'd wind up back in Ireland, living in a small place with zero privacy. But existence, as I've learnt myself, is full of unexpected plot twists; I really hope you're happy with the choices Anna has made and how she's living out her wild and precious life.

Thank you again xxx